First published in Great Britain in 1994
by Simon & Schuster Young Books
Campus 400
Maylands Avenue
Hemel Hempstead
Herts HP2 7EZ

Typeset in 14pt Meridien by Goodfellow & Egan Ltd, Cambridge
Printed and bound in Portugal by Edicoes ASA

British Library Cataloguing in Publication Data available.

ISBN: 0 7500 1663 9
ISBN: 0 7500 1664 7 (pb)

ROY APPS

The Twitches' Chrissy-Mess

Illustrated by Carla Daly

SIMON & SCHUSTER
YOUNG BOOKS

CHAPTER ONE

It was Christmas Eve.

Two shoppers made their way towards the twinkling light of Spamleys' toy shop. They were singing their favourite carol. The tune was *The Holly and The Ivy*, but the words were their own.

"The Gertie and the Lily
Now they are both old crones,
O-o-f all the Twitches in the wood
They have got the knobbliest bones."

. . . they wailed. They sounded like two cats
fighting over a fish head.

This was hardly surprising, because they were
twitches; that is, they were *twins* who were also
witches. Their names were Gert and Lil and the
song they sang was about themselves.

They walked into Spamleys' toy shop and made their way to Santa's Grotto, which was hung with gold angels and silver fairies.

"Urgh, yuk! They're *so* pretty!" declared Lil.

"Yes, where's the slime and the mould and the muck?" Gert asked Father Christmas. "Call this place a *Grotty*?"

"No, I call it a *Grotto*," corrected Father Christmas. "What present would you like?"

"I'd like something to go in my hat," said Gert.

"Like a nice pink ribbon, you mean?" asked Father Christmas.

"No, like a couple of big, black, hairy spiders," cackled Gert.

Father Christmas looked rather flustered. He
was used to dealing with noisy children; he was
used to dealing with their rude parents; but he was
not used to dealing with disgusting old twitches.
He quickly turned away from Gert to her sister.

This was his first mistake.

"Would you like me to fill up your stocking with
Christmas presents?" he asked Lil sweetly.

This was his second mistake.

"Would I? You just try me, mister," whooped Lil.

"No, Lil! He doesn't mean—" began Gert.

But too late.

Before you could say "big-fat-warty-toad", Lil had pulled off one of her stockings and was waving it in front of Father Christmas. Out of the stocking flew dust as dense as a desert storm and cobwebs as big as hair nets. And no wonder, for the last time Lil had washed her stocking had been thirty-seven years ago.

"Montgomery! Come back here!" cried Lil as a monster moth fluttered out of her stocking and into Father Christmas's woolly white beard.

Beating his beard frantically with his hands, Father Christmas jumped back against the wall of the grotto.

This was his third mistake.

The wall wobbled a little . . . then it wobbled some more . . . then with crash and a thud it tumbled down . . . along with the other three walls, the ceiling and all the gold angels and silver fairies.

Everyone in the toy shop turned to look at Gert,
Lil and Father Christmas as they dusted
themselves down.

Father Christmas stumbled to his feet. "Got
you!" he yelled, grabbing hold of a fluttering white
tuft just below his left ear.

He pulled hard.

Montgomery the moth flew off.

And so did Father Christmas's magnificent white beard.

All the shoppers in the toy shop gasped. They stared at Father Christmas's clean-shaven cheeks, which were as pink and as pimply as a grapefruit. The children began to cry and the parents began to shout.

Then Gert said, "If you're Father Christmas, I'm a fairy!"

"Of course I'm not Father Christmas!" said the pink and pimply man who wasn't Father Christmas.

"Then you are an imposter!" declared Gert. "My sister and I are twitches and unless you tell us where the *real* Father Christmas is, we will curse you until you turn into a cross-eyed toad!"

The man who wasn't Father Christmas stared at them blankly.

"We're waiting," croaked Gert.

CHAPTER TWO

"Snakes and snails and huge rats' tails,
Spiders and ants and lice . . ."

. . . Gert and Lil chanted, dancing around the man who wasn't Father Christmas. All the customers began to make for the door, terrified they would also be turned into cross-eyed toads.

AND SNAILS AND HUGE RA.... LICE... SPIDERS AND ANTS AND HUGE RATS TAILS

The Father Christmas impersonator looked nervously at Gert and Lil. "OK!" he said. "If you must know, the *real* Father Christmas is still in Lapland, busy sorting out last minute problems with his presents. He hasn't got time to sit around in a grotty Grotto like this all day."

"Who are you, then, if you're not Father Christmas?" asked Gert.

"I'm usually to be found on the second floor selling braces and suspenders," said the man who wasn't Father Christmas, "and my name is—"

17

"HAROLD PERKINS!!!" boomed a voice behind him. It belonged to Mr Sidney Spamley, owner of Spamleys' toy shop. In his left hand he held a lop-sided and rather battered gold angel. In his right hand he held a crumpled-up silver fairy. "How dare you make a complete laughing stock of me and my toy shop! I want every angel and every fairy replaced."

Harold Perkins' face dropped. "How can I do
that, Mr Spamley sir, on my wages?"

"Simple," snapped Mr Spamley. "Instead of
asking the real Father Christmas to leave you and
your children a stocking full of presents each
tonight, you can ask him to leave two dozen gold
angels and one dozen silver fairies. Understood?"

Harold Perkins nodded his head sadly and
Mr Spamley stormed off.

"You . . . you twitches!" fumed Harold Perkins. "Look at this mess!"

"Yes, it is rather splendid, isn't it?" cackled Gert.

"Splendid? Splendid?" said Harold Perkins through clenched teeth. His cheeks were as red as ripe tomatoes.

"Yes. You see it's not an ordinary mess," explained Lil. "It's a *Chrissy-mess*."

"Just you wait! I'll . . . I'll . . ." began Harold
Perkins. "I'll . . . *tee-hee-hee*!"

"You'll . . . tee-hee-hee?" inquired Gert.

"I'll . . . *tee-hee-hee* . . . *ha-ha-ha*!" giggled Harold
Perkins. He giggled so much he began to shake. He
began to shake so much he had to clutch himself
with both arms.

"Only one thing makes people giggle like that,"
snorted Lil. "Montgomery, the mighty moth! The
naughty thing must've flown back down Harold
Perkins' vest. I must rescue him, Gert."

"Don't be an *angel* all your life, Lil!" croaked
Gert sarcastically.

"Language, Gert, please!" squawked Lil in a very
strict tone of voice, because *angel* is a very rude
word indeed for a witch to use.

"Let's get out of here while we can! Harold
Perkins doesn't look at all happy."

Harold Perkins was snorting like a runaway
train.

"What about my moth!" squawked Lil.

"You've got hundreds more in your wardrobe at
home," Gert snapped back.

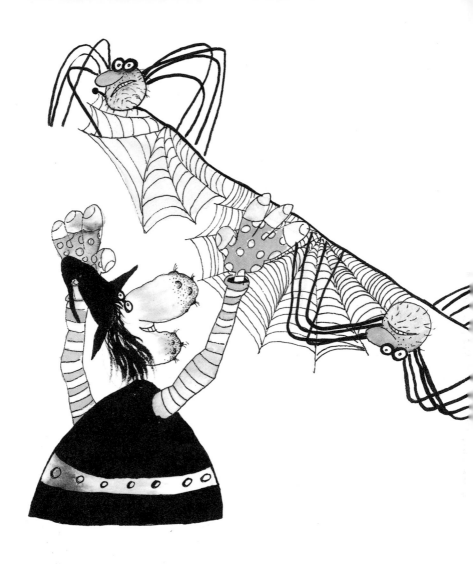

She grabbed hold of Lil's bony elbow and hauled
her out of the reach of Harold Perkins' shaking fist,
out of Spamleys' toy shop and all the way up the
street back to their hovel.

That night, Gert and Lil put up their Chrissy-Mess decorations. They hung spiders' webs across the ceiling, they knotted a rat's tail wreath for the front door and they smeared snail's slime all over the windows.

Next they hung their stockings up on the
mantlepiece and placed a plate of mice pies and a
glass of freshly-squeezed beetlejuice on the hearth,
ready for the real Father Christmas.

And then they went to bed.

As she snuggled down amongst the stale biscuit crumbs and toe-nail clippings, Lil said, "I wonder what it was that Harold Perkins was going to do to us?"

"I don't know," retorted Gert. "But it wouldn't have been very pleasant. Anyway, we've seen the last of him."

But that was where she was wrong.

CHAPTER THREE

Next morning, Gert and Lil tumbled down their
rickety old stairs to the sitting room.

"He's been!" croaked Lil. "And he's left a note!"

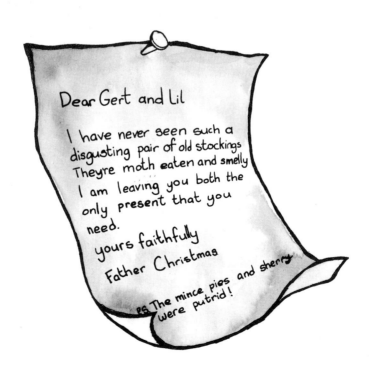

Dear Gert and Lil

I have never seen such a
disgusting pair of old stockings
They're moth eaten and smelly
I am leaving you both the
only present that you
need.

yours faithfully

Father Christmas

PS The mince pies and sherry
were putrid!

"Told you he'd like them," cackled Gert.

"What is *this*?" asked Lil, pulling a large,
lavender-coloured bar of soap out of her stocking.
Gert found exactly the same thing in hers.

"It says SOAP on it," said Gert. "Perhaps it's for
washing with."

"Urgh!" said Lil.

"I suppose we could give it a try," suggested Gert doubtfully. "It *is* from Father Christmas, after all."

So they slipped their bars of lavender soap into their pockets. Then they put on their tall black hats and set off for their favourite washing place: the mucky pond in the park.

"It's just so, so grungy for washing in," croaked
Lil merrily, as she dunked a crabby toe into the icy
water. "All this scummy foam will help keep my
skin as crinkly as a potato crisp."

"I bet I can guess what flavour crisps as well,"
cackled Gert with a twinkle in her eye. She looked
at her sister's scraggy foot. *"Cheese* and *bunion!"*
    Gert's jokes were like her teeth: very old and
very bad.

"Talking of bunions, a bit of that witch-hazel
will be just right for scratching them with,"
Lil grunted. And she stood up and leant
out over the pond to try and reach
a nice prickly piece of twig at
the end of a branch.

Suddenly, they heard a voice giggling behind
them, "Hey you twitches! *Tee-hee-hee!*"

Gert spun round. "Well I never! Harold Perkins,
the famous giggling Father-Christmas-
Impersonator!" she exclaimed.

Lil spun round too, which is not a wise thing to
do when you have hold of a slippery branch over
an icy pond.

"Aaaarghhhh!" she shrieked as she hit the water
with a gurgle and a splash.

"*Tee-hee-hee! Tee-hee-hee!*" chortled Harold Perkins.

"It's not funny!" spluttered Lil through a mouthful of soggy leaves as she staggered out of the pond.

"Oh, yes it is," cackled Gert.

"Serves you right *tee-hee* for cursing me *tee-hee!*" added Harold Perkins.

"We never cursed you!" snapped Gert.

"Of course you *tee-hee* cursed me *tee-hee!*" he giggled. "You cursed me with this giggle *tee-hee!*"

Lil shook with laughter till the slime all slithered off her dress.

"That wasn't a curse! That was a moth!" explained Gert.

"Can you get rid of it please *tee-hee?*" pleaded Harold Perkins.

"Easy," said Gert.

"Take off your vest," said Lil.

"What! Here in the park *tee-hee?*" trembled Harold Perkins.

"Why not?" asked Lil.

"Dorothy – that is, Mrs Perkins – is very particular about me taking my vest off in public *tee-hee*," explained Harold Perkins.

"Better go to your house, then," snapped Gert.

"Good idea," agreed Lil, with a shiver. "That way I can dry off a bit." She blew hard into her hankie and a newt popped out of her left nostril and back into the pond.

CHAPTER FOUR

Harold Perkins stood in his sitting room and took off his jacket, his jumper, his shirt and his vest. Mrs Perkins and the twins, Mark and Spencer Perkins, watched from the far side of the room.

"Reach for the skies!" instructed Lil.

Harold Perkins lifted his arms high above his head and Lil scooped out Montgomery the moth from inside his vest. Harold Perkins gave a sigh of relief.

"I see Father Christmas left you the angels and fairies," said Gert, pointing a craggy finger at two large boxes on the floor.

Mark Perkins looked at Gert glumly. "What I really wanted for Christmas was a cricket bat," he sighed.

Gert thrust a bony hand into her pocket. "Instead of a cricket bat, why not have a Bertie Bat instead!" she suggested, and pulled out a great, black flapping bat.

"Thanks!" said Mark admiringly.

It was Spencer's turn to look glum. "I really wanted a chemistry set," he sighed.

Lil thrust a bony hand into her pocket. Something in there rang hard on her knobbly knuckles. "Instead of a chemistry set, why not have a bottle of Limp Lizard Leg and Squashed Beetle Cocktail!" she suggested.

"Thanks," said Spencer. "What does it do?"

"Just try putting a bit on your teacher's chair," said Gert with a toothy grin. "You'll soon see."

"Aaargh!" screeched Lil suddenly. "I'm foaming at the wrists!"

And indeed she was. Frothy white bubbles were appearing from out of the sleeves of Lil's jumper.

"They're lavender soap bubbles," said Mrs Perkins. "And very sweet they smell too!"

"Then happy Christmas, Mrs Perkins!" yelled Lil, tossing her bar of lavender soap into Mrs Perkins' lap.

"Or rather, happy *Chrissy-mess*!" chortled Gert, tossing Mrs Perkins her soap, too.

"What about me?" moaned Harold Perkins.
"Don't I get a present?"

"You couldn't give him back that old moth,
could you?" asked Mrs Perkins. "It'd make such a
treat to hear him giggle once in a while instead of
moaning."

Gert held out Montgomery on the palm of her
hand. "There, just stuff the little fellow down the
front of your husband's shirt whenever he's
moaning," said Gert.

"Thank you," said Mrs Perkins. "I just wish we had something to give to you."

"You can have this after-shave Aunt Myrtle sent me," said Harold Perkins. "You'll love it. It smells like something you'd get out of a blocked drain."

Gert had a sniff. "Mmmm . . . really pongy," she cackled.

"And you can have these hand-knitted jumpers
Aunt Deirdre sent Mark and me," said Spencer.
"They're really *itchy*."

"So they are," cooed Lil, rubbing them with a
scrawny hand in a way that sent goose-pimples
shivering up Spencer's back. "It'll be just like
wearing a cheese-grater."

"How about you two Twitches staying for Christmas dinner?" suggested Mrs Perkins. "We've got a big turkey."

"Actually," said Gert, "my sister and I don't eat turkey."

"Why ever not?" asked Mrs Perkins.

"Because it's *fowl*!" cackled Gert, clutching her sides with laughter.

"I think it would be best if we brought round our own Christmas hamper," said Lil. "We got it from Horrid's, the Top Witches Store."

CHAPTER FIVE

"Was that a vegetarian dish?" asked Mrs Perkins nervously, when Gert and Lil had eaten the last scrap of their Christmas dinner.

"Er . . . not exactly," said Gert.

"It looked like ratatouille," said Spencer.

"It *was* ratatouille," said Lil. "But a special sort of ratatouille. It was from rats."

"Urgh!" said Mark.

"Yuk!" said Spencer.

"Yes, that's what we think," said Gert.

"You know," said Mrs Perkins, "what with everyone getting presents they like – eventually, this has been one of the best Christmases ever."

"Come on, Lil," said Gert. "Let's toast the Perkinses with a Chrissy-mess song."

"Only the first curse, then," said Lil.

"Right. You wail, Lil. And I'll screech . . ."

> *"We Witch you a Crabby Chrissy-Mess*
> *We Witch you a Crabby Chrissy-Mess*
> *We Witch you a Crabby Chrissy-Mess*
> *And a Hag-gy Newt Year.*
> *Grot-Toadings we bring*
> *And Frogs fat and thin*
> *We Witch you a Crabby Chrissy-Mess*
> *And a Hag-gy Newt Year."*

Look out for more gruesomely funny titles in the Red Storybooks series:

The Twitches by Roy Apps

Gert and Lil are fed up. Although they've been witching for 113 years, they've never made up a successful magic spell. Something drastic needs to be done . . .

The Twitches on Horriday by Roy Apps

"Witches don't have holidays", Gert explained. "They have *horridays!*" When Gert and Lil win a free trip to Spain, the posh hotel is a terrible disappointment – there are no cobwebs in sight, the restaurant won't serve warty toads, and the rooms smell as if they've been *cleaned* . . . urgh!

A Vampire in the Family by Roy Apps

Nearly everyone has a strange relative. But Bruce's grandad is weirder than most – he's a vampire!

Nigel the Pirate by Roy Apps

Nigel is in for the surprise of his life when he becomes an apprentice pirate to the notorious Cap'n Bonegrinder on *The Bloody Plunderer*.

Wonderwitch by Helen Muir

Wonderwitch has all a witch could want – a tall hat, a black cat and a broomstick. But she's bored with turning people into toads, and decides to try something different . . .

Storybooks are available from your local bookshop or can be ordered direct from the publishers. For more information about Storybooks, write to: *The Sales Department, Simon & Schuster Young Books, Maylands Avenue, Hemel Hempstead, Herts HP2 7EZ.*

PENGUIN BOOKS

THE END

...igson isn't only the writer of the critically acclaimed *The ...ies*, or the creator of Young Bond, which has been trans-... twenty-five languages. He's also an actor, scriptwriter, ... producer and former singer. He has written four crime ... adults, presented a film series for Channel 4 (*Kiss Kiss Bang ...* appeared as himself in many TV panel shows, including ... *I Got News for You* and *Never Mind the Buzzcocks*.

...aving university he formed an indie band, The Higsons, ...iving it up to become a painter and decorator (the pay was ...t was around this time that he started writing for television on *S... day Night Live*, and he went on to create the hugely success-ful co...edy series *The Fast Show*, in which he also appeared. Other TV ...ks include *Harry Enfield's Television Programme*, *Randall & Hopk... (Deceased)* and the sitcom *Swiss Toni*.

Hi... ork for radio includes the award-winning spoof phone-in prog... me *Down the Line* (BBC Radio 4), which became the televi-sion c...edy series *Bellamy's People* (BBC 2).

Ch... e doesn't do Facebook but you can tweet him @monstroso

Praise for Charlie Higson's writing:

'Ruthless' – *SFX*

'Entertainment of the highest calibre' – *Books Quarterly*

'adrenaline-inducing' – *S...*

'Ch... ...GQ

'Clever . . . fast-paced . . . inventive' – *Guardian*

'like a John Wyndham survival story . . .' – *The Times*

'Good, gritty and funny' – *Daily Mail*

'Double-oh so good' – *Sunday Times*

Books by Charlie Higson

The Young Bond series
SILVERFIN

BLOOD FEVER

DOUBLE OR DIE

HURRICANE GOLD

BY ROYAL COMMAND

DANGER SOCIETY: YOUNG BOND DOSSIER

SILVERFIN: THE GRAPHIC NOVEL

The Enemy series
THE ENEMY

THE DEAD

THE FEAR

THE SACRIFICE

THE FALLEN

THE HUNTED

THE END

MONSTROSO (POCKET MONEY PUFFINS)

CHARLIE HIGSON

THE END

PENGUIN BOOKS

PUFFIN BOOKS

UK | USA | Canada | Ireland | Australia
India | New Zealand | South Africa

Puffin Books is part of the Penguin Random House group of companies
whose addresses can be found at global.penguinrandomhouse.com.

puffinbooks.com

First published 2015
002

Text copyright © Charlie Higson, 2015
Map by Tony Fleetwood

The moral right of the author and the illustrator has been asserted

Set in 13/15.5pt Bembo Book MT
by Palimpsest Book Production Limited, Falkirk, Stirlingshire
Printed in Great Britain by Clays Ltd, St Ives plc

A CIP catalogue record for this book is available from the British Library

PAPERBACK
ISBN: 978–0–141–36214–4

For all of you . . .
Vicky, Frank, Jim and Sidney

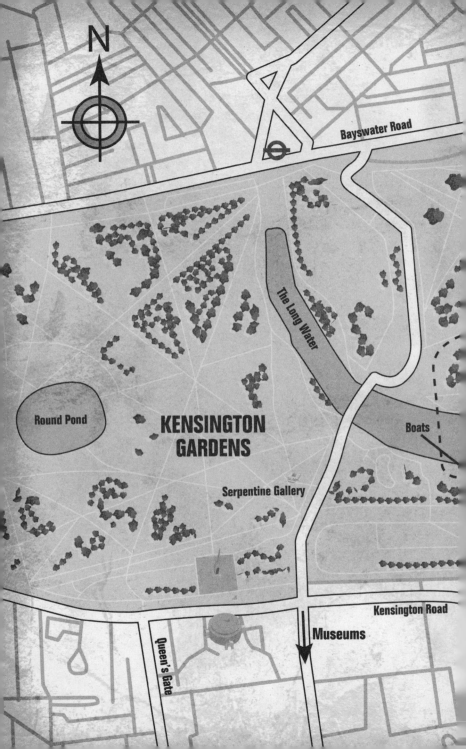

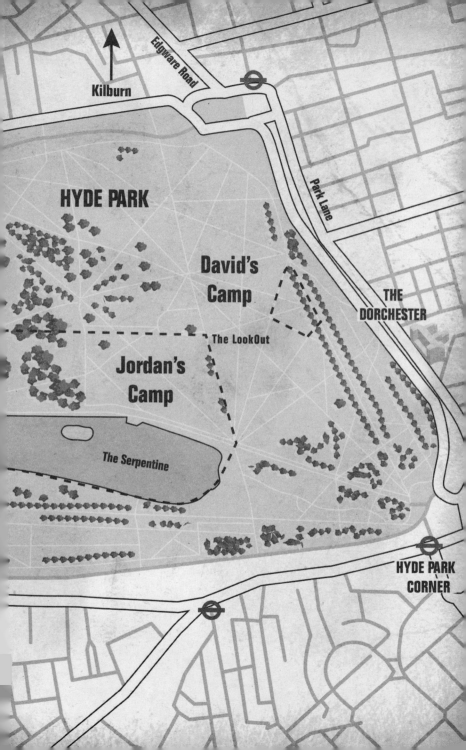

And War, which for a moment was no more,
Did glut himself again – a meal was bought
With blood, and each sate sullenly apart
Gorging himself in gloom: no love was left;
All earth was but one thought – and that was death,
Immediate and inglorious; and the pang
Of famine fed upon all entrails – men
Died, and their bones were tombless as their flesh;

From 'Darkness' by Lord Byron

THE EVENTS IN *THE END* RUN PARALLEL TO THE EVENTS IN *THE HUNTED*, UNTIL THE CLOSING CHAPTERS WHEN ALL SEVEN BOOKS COME TOGETHER.

1

They walked north up Exhibition Road, between the Victoria and Albert on their right and the Science Museum on their left. It was a wide road, wide enough for four lanes of traffic, with a weird grid pattern on it made of different coloured paving bricks. A line of tall poles, like flagpoles, ran down the middle.

Ryan's hunters stayed in a pack, marching in step, almost like a military unit. The hunters scared Paddy, with their huge dogs and their studs and their leather masks made out of the faces of dead grown-ups. They were filthy dirty and they smelt of blood and sweat and worse. They reminded Paddy of the wild kids he'd been living with in St James's Park before Achilleus and his friends had turned up. Ryan even had a string of human ears hanging from his belt.

At least Paddy felt safe with them, though. They were used to these streets. They owned them. He saw how easy they were, and on top of things at the same time. Listening, looking, aware of everything that was going on around them without making a big deal out of it. Five of their dogs trotted ahead, off their leashes. Sniffing everywhere, weeing everywhere, scouting around. The rest of the dogs, the biggest, meanest-looking ones, were kept on

short, heavy chains and walked obediently at the boys' sides.

Paddy liked dogs, wished he had one of his own. Not a big monster like Ryan's. He wanted a spaniel or a terrier of some sort. He'd had two Jack Russells before, had kept them with him right through the bad times when the disease hit. And a long time after. They'd been with him in the camp in St James's Park. The leader of the camp, John, had liked to play with them, making them chase rats. And then one night he'd killed them and eaten them.

Achilleus dropped back from his position at the front and joined Paddy.

'What you reckon, padawan?' he said. 'Think we should join this lot? Get out of the museum. Run the streets?'

'I don't know,' said Paddy, who hated the idea. Paddy liked having a regular place to sleep. Strong, thick walls around him. And there were other kids at the museum who relied on Achilleus.

'What about your friends?' he said and Achilleus huffed. 'What about them?'

'It's your job to be their champion. To be their best fighter. Their best killer. You couldn't let them down.'

'Most of them don't even like me,' said Achilleus.

'Does that bother you?'

'Nope. I know that in the end they need me, so they try to hide their feelings and keep me sweet. Just as long as they show me some respect I'm cool.'

Yeah. Akkie was the coolest person in the world. Paddy liked everything about him – his ugly, scarred face, the patterns carved in his hair with a razor blade, his mangled ear, the way he could be relaxed and not bothered one

4

moment and scary and tough the next. And when he fought there was no one better.

'One day they'll make the world right again,' Paddy said. 'We'll kill all the grown-ups, rebuild everything, and then they'll start making films again over in Hollywood, where that big sign is. They'll make a film about you, and you'll be the biggest hero, bigger than James Bond and Spiderman and the X-Men put together.'

'You're a dreamer, kid,' said Achilleus. 'It'll be a thousand years before it gets back to how things were. A thousand years before we can figure out how to do stuff like make films again, with CGI and green screen and all that crap you see on the DVD extras. First we got to figure out how to do something as basic as turning the juice back on. How do you make electricity? I got no idea. Don't even really know what electricity is. Might as well be magic. It powered my life before it got switched off — my TV, my phone, my console, my computer, the lights, the heating, the fridge . . . Without power, we're back in the olden days, Paddy, back in the Stone Age. That's why they call it "power", because electricity *is* power. It made us gods. Maybe Einstein and his science nerds back at the museum could figure it out. Ben and Bernie — they into all that type of thing. But, seriously, how long d'you think it's gonna be before we get a power station up and running again?'

'A long time,' said Paddy. 'A thousand years.'

'A thousand years is right. In the meantime there's just *this*. Hunting, killing, fighting to stay alive. Nothing's gonna get sorted until we've sorted the grown-ups. And that's something I *do* know about. That's what we doing now.'

Ryan and his hunters had come to the museum with a

car that they exchanged for some cases of beer. A few days ago a little girl called Ella had left with some other kids to go and live in the countryside, and then her brother, Sam, had turned up looking for her. So a scarred-faced guy called Ed had gone to bring her back. The car had been for him.

Achilleus had got talking to Ryan who'd told him they were going up to Hyde Park to check out a sighting of some grown-ups. They hadn't needed to persuade Achilleus to go with them. He was totally bored at the museum.

They came to the end of the street. Ahead of them was the park. In between was a big main road, with a pedestrian strip down the middle of it. In the past this would have been busy with traffic; now it was still and silent.

But the hunters weren't crossing. They were looking at something in the road off to their right.

A grown-up. A father. Standing with his arms held straight out in front of him, face turned up to the sky, like he was waiting for rain.

Paddy moved closer to Achilleus. Didn't say anything. Hoped no one noticed how nervous he was.

Hoped it wasn't all about to kick off.

'Should've spotted him before,' said Achilleus. 'But standing still like that . . .'

'They're all over,' said Ryan. 'We mostly ignore them.'

'Ed called them sentinels,' said Achilleus. 'Like they're sending signals to other grown-ups somehow.'

'What do you think they're saying?' Ryan asked.

'Maybe there's a special meal deal on at McDonald's,' said Achilleus.

A couple of hunters laughed. Paddy did too, but he wasn't laughing inside. The sentinels freaked him out. He

didn't like the idea of grown-ups communicating with each other. He didn't like the idea of grown-ups at all. Wished he could have stayed back at the museum. But he couldn't look moist in front of the others.

The father had a bloated purple face, like someone had tightened something round his throat, and his head was bulging out, ready to burst. His hands were puffy too, with fat, sausagey fingers. There was something ripe about him. Ripe and rotten.

Paddy told himself to man up.

'What do you reckon, Akkie?' he said. 'Can we take him?'

'Is up to you, caddie. You wanna whack him? Show off your skills?'

'Can I?'

'You asking if I'm giving you permission? Or you asking if I think you're up to it?'

'Both, I guess.'

'He's all yours. He ain't no threat to a warrior like you. What spear you gonna use?' Achilleus took the golf bag off Paddy.

Paddy carried Akkie's collection of spears in it. He was in charge of them. Cleaned them, sharpened them, suggested the best one to use in a fight.

'The *Gáe Bolg*,' said Paddy, hyped up and just a little bit terrified.

The *Gáe Bolg* was Achilleus's newest spear – the death spear, the belly spear – which Paddy had named after the legendary spear carried by the greatest Irish folk hero, Cúchulainn.

Although Akkie preferred to call it the Gay Bulge, which always made Paddy laugh.

It had a wide, leaf-shaped blade and it was a beauty. It was a perfect stomach ripper. It was the disemboweller.

'Nice choice, Champion,' said Achilleus and he pulled out the spear.

Paddy took it and weighed it in his hands, getting the feel of it, checking the balance. It was a bit too big for him – too long and heavy and awkward. He hoped the others wouldn't say anything.

'Where you aiming for?' Achilleus asked.

'The belly,' said Paddy, trying to sound all serious and expert and grown-up. 'I mean, this is the belly ripper, isn't it?'

'If you say so. Go in fast, like I showed you. Keep low, keep the spear out in front, come at him from off to one side, not straight on. Keep your arms strong. Swing hard and cut deep. Takes a lot to cut through clothes and skin.'

'Yeah.' Paddy was nodding, psyching himself up. Practising on a dummy in the yard back at the museum was one thing. Actually killing a person was something else entirely.

'Arms wide apart and well spaced,' said Achilleus. 'You'll get more power in your cut then. It'd be easier to spike him, but if you want to go for a slice that's up to you.'

'I think the slice is better,' said Paddy, still all serious. 'That's what this spear was made for.'

'Then what you waiting for? Go for it. Kill the puffy sod.'

Paddy hopped from foot to foot on the spot, like an athlete getting ready for his start. Jigging about, loosening up. And then he gave a shout and was off and running – remembering Achilleus's instructions – coming at the

father at an angle, not straight on, just as Achilleus had told him.

As he got closer, he gave a war cry, almost screaming, and he swiped the spear across the father's stomach. He could immediately see it wasn't deep enough or hard enough. It tore open the front of the father's filthy, greasy shirt, but did nothing worse.

The father barely flinched, just swayed slightly and carried on waiting for rain.

Ignoring Paddy.

The hunters cheered and laughed.

'Keep on it, soldier,' Achilleus shouted. 'Come back at him.'

So Paddy swung back the other way and this time the head of his spear dug deep. There was an audible pop, like a balloon bursting, and a spray of blood and brown liquid squirted all over Paddy who wasn't fast enough to get out of the way. After the liquid came the guts, spilling out and flopping to the ground, releasing a foul stink that made the hunters groan and cover their mouths and noses. The father rocked backwards and forwards and then toppled over on to his back and hit the road with a wet splat and a crack of skull on concrete.

Paddy knew he was going to puke.

'I'm covered in it,' he wailed. 'Bastard sprayed all over me.'

'Unclean, unclean! Keep away from me,' laughed one of the hunters and they all started moaning and making disgusted noises.

'Stupid idiot,' said Achilleus and he laughed too. 'You shoulda kept going, gone clear − you're gonna stink for days now.'

'Yeah – ha, ha! Ain't I? I got him, though, didn't I? I stuck him good.'

'You stuck him bare good, soldier.'

And Paddy puked.

Achilleus walked up to him. 'Bend over,' he said. 'Head down. Deep breaths.'

A thin stream of vomit spattered on to the road.

'It was the smell,' said Paddy. 'That's all.'

'Yeah.'

It wasn't the smell, though.

Paddy had never killed anyone before.

He straightened up, taking big gulps of air. 'I'm OK.'

'Good man.' Achilleus slapped him on the back and they followed the hunters over the road to where they were entering the park.

Paddy really hoped there wasn't anything much worse in there.

He really didn't think he could do that again.

The park was much bigger than Achilleus had imagined, with a road running through the middle of it, giving them a good view on either side. Off to the left was a mad statue of some dude in a giant chair set inside what looked like a steam-punk space rocket, all gold and shiny.

'That's the Albert Memorial,' said Ryan.

'Who's Albert?' Achilleus asked.

'No idea. Some dead guy.'

'Somebody obviously liked him. To build that thing.'

'He was Queen Victoria's husband,' said Paddy. 'I've come here once on a school trip.'

'You reckon someone will build a statue of me like that?' Achilleus asked.

'Yeah,' said Paddy. 'They should. All heroes should have a statue.'

They walked on. It seemed stupidly peaceful and safe. Birds flew everywhere, singing loudly. Squirrels ran and jumped between the huge trees that were laid out in straight lines going off in all directions. The grass had grown long between the trees.

'Why's it so quiet?' Paddy asked. 'It's weird.'

'Don't complain,' said Achilleus. 'If we get rid of the

grown-ups for all time it'll be like this every day. A walk in the park.'

'One day,' said Paddy. 'We can do it.'

But it *was* weird. Achilleus hadn't known it like this for a long time. He didn't want to show it to Paddy, didn't want to spook the boy, but he was staying extra alert.

They stopped by a group of red-brick buildings set back from the road. A sign outside said this was the Serpentine Gallery. Achilleus couldn't figure out why you'd have an art gallery in a park and he was even more confused by a tall, rusted iron tower that stood in front of the main building. It looked like a small Eiffel Tower gone wrong, all twisted and wonky.

'I think it's supposed to be art,' said Ryan, who'd noticed him looking. 'A sort of sculpture thing. You know, like that tower they put up at the Olympics?'

'Was that art?' said Achilleus. 'I thought it was a ride.'

'Well, whatever this thing is, it makes a good lookout tower,' said Ryan and he grinned. 'You wanna climb it?'

'Do I?' Achilleus asked back at him.

'Get the layout. See if we can spot anything.'

'Sure.'

Achilleus followed Ryan over to the tower. There had been a fence around it, but it was all broken down. Someone had hauled a ladder to the bottom of the tower, to make it easier to get up on to the first part. After that the struts and rungs of the sculpture were close enough together to make climbing pretty easy. Ryan hauled himself up on to it and Achilleus was right behind him. Slowly the ground dropped away and Achilleus was able to see more and more of the park.

The main impression he got was that there were lots of

trees, with big buildings beyond them. To the north, spreading right across the park, was a stretch of water that looked like a river or a lake. The road crossed over a bridge.

'That's the Serpentine,' Ryan explained. 'Is a good source of fresh water. That's why we regularly check out the park. Over on the other side is where they used to have big concerts and things. There's still a load of fences and stages and stands for food and that over there.'

Achilleus took it all in, getting a layout of the park in his head.

'You see anything shouldn't be here?' he said to Ryan. 'Any more grown-ups?'

Ryan shushed him. He had his head cocked to one side. Listening. Achilleus kept very still, trying to tune in to whatever it was Ryan had heard. All he could hear was the wind rustling the leaves of the trees, the iron sculpture creaking under their weight.

'What?' he said and Ryan shushed him again. He was scanning the area, his head moving like a radar – left to right, right to left.

Finally, from far away, Achilleus picked up something. It could have been a bark and, as he concentrated, he heard another. Then a third one, clearer and closer, more of a yelp than a bark. And behind it all a whining. Growing louder.

'Dogs,' said Ryan. 'Coming closer. They like it here. They chase the ducks. Sometimes they catch them. If there's any useful ones we'll take them.'

'I can't see them,' said Achilleus. He wasn't very good at this.

'There,' said Ryan, pointing over the top of the gallery, past a little sort of bell tower.

Achilleus spotted a movement at last. A pack of dogs, running through the trees. About ten of them. All shapes and sizes. Nothing too scary.

'Incoming!' Ryan shouted and started climbing down as fast as he could in his leathers and belts and buckles and chains. Achilleus beat him down and saw that the hunters had grouped up into a defensive formation, those with the biggest dogs at the front. Ryan took his own dog from a guy who'd been holding her for him and led the group round to the other side of the gallery.

The newcomers had scented Ryan and his dogs and were running around in circles in a state of manic excitement. Most had their hackles up, but some were wagging their tails; others were doing that belly-crawling, submissive crouching thing – whimpering. The bravest had their teeth bared ready to attack.

Achilleus quickly checked them out, deciding which were harmless and which were a threat. A big Rottweiler with a chunk of fur missing from his side looked to be the leader of the pack. He was coming closest and the smaller dogs kept running up to him, licking his face and rolling at his feet.

He had one damaged eye and was limping where it looked like he'd been in a recent fight and had his front leg gashed.

'He ain't no use to us,' Ryan said. 'Nothing but trouble. We take him out and the rest will back down.'

Achilleus looked to Paddy, but he could see he wasn't up for it. The little boy was weighed down by the golf bag and still clutching the *Gáe Bolg*. Achilleus guessed that killing dogs wasn't his thing. Wasn't sure that killing grown-ups was his thing either, to be honest.

14

'I'll do it,' he said and took out his trusted old spear, the one he'd made months ago from a sharpened steel pole. He'd added a leather grip and it had a pommel at the end that became a useful club in a close-up fight. Twirling it in one hand, he strode out past the hunters, keeping his eyes fixed on the Rottweiler. It made a lunge towards him, but was obviously wary of Ryan's bigger dogs that were setting up an unholy racket, yelping and howling, straining at their leads, up on their hind legs. It was all Ryan's hunters could do to hold them back. Achilleus needed to get this over quickly.

'Come on, you ugly bastard,' he said, walking steadily towards the Rottweiler. It held back, and held back, and held back, and then at last attacked. Achilleus was ready – legs firmly planted, eyes never leaving the dog's eyes – and as it leapt up at him he thrust forward with his spear and took it cleanly in the chest. Stepping aside so that the weight of the dog wouldn't hit him. He'd killed it instantly.

The fight went out of the other dogs. They calmed down and stopped running around and Achilleus was able to properly check them out. There were three yappy little things, nasty little bruisers, scarred from battle. Four larger mongrels with matted fur, smart-looking, but probably not much use to Ryan's guys. And then there was an Alsatian. Skinny, but in better shape than the others. That was the one he'd pick. The others could be left to run around harmlessly. They weren't going to be a threat to anyone.

'The Alsatian,' said Achilleus, pointing at the dog. 'Leave the rest.'

'You want it?' said Ryan.

Achilleus looked at Paddy who was grinning like a kid at Christmas.

'Don't need a dog,' he said, and Paddy groaned.

'Oh, go on, Akkie,' he whined. 'Let's keep him. I'll look after him. He'd be a good guard dog.'

No, he'd be another mouth to feed. Another living thing to be responsible for. And it would need to be trained. Made safe.

'Forget it.' He turned and walked away. 'He's all yours, Ryan.'

Ryan made a signal and two of his hunters went in quickly, managed to catch the dog and put a collar and lead on it. It thrashed about, snarling and snapping at them. One of them hit it with a stick and it quietened down.

There were tears in Paddy's eyes. He was trying not to let anyone see.

'We don't need no dog,' Achilleus repeated, and before Paddy could say anything there was a shout.

'Guys!' A hunter was over near the back of the gallery. Achilleus noticed that some of the dogs had also gone over and were snuffling around, tails wagging.

'They've found something,' said the hunter. 'A scent.'

'What do you reckon it is?' Ryan asked, joining the boy. 'An animal? Another dog?'

The hunter was sniffing the air. He wrinkled his nose.

'I reckon it's the bastards we're looking for,' he said. 'Must have got inside.'

'Bastards?' said Paddy, looking at Achilleus.

'Is what they call grown-ups,' Achilleus explained.

Ryan was walking round the building. 'Check and see if there's any openings,' he said.

'Here!' shouted another hunter. 'There's an open door. And I can smell them. There is definitely at least one bastard in there.'

3

It was dark inside the building. The open door they went through led to a narrow, dirty corridor. This was probably a service area, behind the main gallery. Paddy kept close to Achilleus. The smell of the stuff the grown-up had sprayed on him was much worse in here in these cramped conditions.

'Jesus, Paddywhack,' said Achilleus. 'Did you just open your lunch box?'

Paddy said nothing. He was gagging and struggling not to be sick again, his head spinning. Felt like he might actually pass out. This was the smell of death, he thought.

It really wouldn't be cool to throw up again. There was never enough food and to puke half of it up like he'd done, that was bad. He so wanted to hang on to the rest of what was inside him, even though it churned in his guts like acid. His dogs used to eat their own sick. Nothing went to waste. Paddy wondered how hungry he'd have to be to do something like that. He was shaking, his teeth rattling in his skull. He tried to tell himself that it was because he was cold. His clothes were damp from the spray and as it dried it cooled. It wasn't that, though. He knew it wasn't that.

Paddy was scared. No argument. He never used to get this freaked out, but lately it had got worse. He'd gone out

west with Achilleus and the Holloway kids. That had been a nasty experience. He knew how easy it was to get hurt, to get killed. Before joining up with Achilleus's crew he hadn't been that bothered about staying alive. His world had been sick and painful and friendless. Now he had good friends and a better life, he wanted to hold on to them.

Stupid to get killed now, here in this dumb building in the middle of the park. As long as he was with Akkie, though, he'd be OK. Everything would be all right . . .

The corridor passed by a kitchen. Nothing worth scavenging in there. It had been cleaned out months ago by the look of it, probably last year when everything started to go wrong. There was really nothing of any use. All there was, was grown-ups.

Ryan was leading the way, his big dog sniffing the air, tensed up. He held up his hand and they all stopped. Ryan had brought four of his hunters in with him and two of his dogs, the biggest two. The others had stayed outside with the rest of the pack.

Paddy still had the *Gáe Bolg*, its blade covered with dried blood, turning crusty. Stupid. He should have cleaned it. He wasn't doing his job. When this was over, he needed to clean all the weapons. He didn't want Achilleus to get mad at him.

Oh God, but he wanted to be sick. His skull was pounding and he had a headache coming on that you wouldn't believe. Was it too late to go back outside and join the others? Get some fresh air.

Which was scarier? Going back outside without Achilleus or staying in here with him . . . and the grown-ups.

Ryan beckoned them on and Paddy went with them. They rounded the end of the corridor and Paddy saw the

big open space of the gallery off to their left. Back here there were a number of smaller rooms, storerooms mostly by the look of them. The dogs were sniffing and whining at the closed door of one, the fur sticking up all along their backs.

'Hold!' said Ryan and his dog moved away, obeying him. The hunter with the other dog pulled him back on his chain. Ryan looked to his team. Someone was going to have to look in the room.

Achilleus stepped forward. 'I'll do it.'

Paddy tucked in behind him. 'You sure, Akkie?' he said.

'Relax, caddie, I got it covered.'

Achilleus moved towards the storeroom door. It was made of metal and there were dents around the handle where someone had attacked it. Probably whoever had first broken into the gallery rather than grown-ups. One of the hunters aimed a torch at the door. It was open a couple of centimetres.

'Shine it in there,' said Achilleus, and he turned to another hunter. 'When I say, pull it open wide and stay clear.'

The hunter nodded and gripped the door handle. Paddy could tell that he was nervous too. They all were. Except Achilleus, of course. He was cool. Always cool. Paddy watched as he took up position in front of the door, legs planted, hands wide apart on his spear, ready to stab. Paddy held the *Gáe Bolg* out in front of him. It would keep any grown-ups away. Ryan and the other guy had their dogs held tight, gripping the heavy chains. That left one hunter, who was armed with a big sharpened crowbar and standing just behind and to the right of Achilleus.

'You and me, soldier,' said Achilleus. 'If any of them try to get out we knock 'em down.'

'Safe.'

Achilleus called over to the guy holding the door handle. 'Open the box . . .'

And the hunter yanked the door back. The torch beam shone inside. There was a big square room, some old benches stacked on one side, chairs as well. Some sheets of wood against the wall. And at the back, coming awake, blinking in the light, stinking and filthy, what looked like about twenty grown-ups, all piled on top of each other, like a nest of rats. And something else. Something dark and inhuman.

Paddy strained to see what it was, the sick rising in his throat again.

'Close it,' Achilleus said, and the hunter didn't need to be told twice. He slammed the door and leant against it.

'Too many to take on in there,' said Achilleus. 'Not worth the risk. We should try to get them outside where there's more room and more of you lot to deal with them.'

'They ain't gonna want to go out in the sunlight,' said Ryan.

'We could try to burn them in there,' said a hunter.

'Except we got nothing to burn them with,' said Ryan.

'I got some smoke grenades left,' said the guy with the torch.

The grown-ups were starting to push against the other side of the door.

'OK,' said Ryan. 'Lob one in – it might help, but be careful. They seem pretty keen.'

The grown-ups were hammering now.

'They'll follow us, smoke or no smoke,' said Achilleus. 'If they don't all come out we can come back in and mop up the stragglers. But I ain't going in there with twenty of them.'

'I wanna use a smoke grenade,' said Torchboy. 'I never get the chance.'

'OK,' said Ryan.

'I can't hold them much longer,' said the hunter at the door. 'They really do wanna dance.'

'Let's do it.' Ryan nodded to his team. Torchboy took a smoke grenade out of his pack and got it ready. The guy with the other dog started to walk back the way they'd come. Ryan followed him. Their dogs would scare the grown-ups, maybe keep them from following. Achilleus slapped his hand on the shoulder of the kid with the crowbar.

'What's your name?'

'Zulficker.'

'Well, Zulficker, you and me and the caddie here are gonna have to make sure they follow us. OK?'

'OK.'

Achilleus looked at the guy holding the door.

'You can just leg it. OK?'

'OK.'

'You as well.' Achilleus was talking to Torchboy now. 'Get the smoke in there and get out of our way.'

'Sure.'

'Here we go then.'

Torchboy struck his smoke grenade, which sparked and then started to pump out thick white smoke. The other kid pulled the door open. The grenade went in, turning over and over. Already it was getting hard to see in the corridor.

The two guys set off fast, back towards the entrance, as the first of the grown-ups emerged, coughing and sneezing. A mother with red weepy eyes stumbled towards Achilleus. She had a bad case of the shakes. Others quickly

filled in around her. Paddy saw a horrible gallery of swollen, bloated, diseased faces, covered in boils and lumps and growths, awful festering gashes, down to the bone. Bits missing – eyes and ears and noses. Some were naked, their bodies even worse than their faces, with patches of mould, terrible purple bruising. And they stank. Stank so bad Paddy forgot his own smell. Soundlessly they fixed on Achilleus, Paddy and Zulficker and moved towards them.

'Slowly now,' said Achilleus backing away, but suddenly a smaller father, a teenager really, came darting forward, hands up, fingers clawed. Zulficker jabbed at him with the sharp end of his crowbar, getting him in the chest. He croaked and dropped. The others kept on moving. And Achilleus's group was forced to speed up.

'Are they all coming?' said Zulficker, peering into the smoke.

'Enough of them,' said Achilleus and he glanced back over his shoulder. Paddy did too. Ryan and the others were approaching the door they had come in by, Ryan calling to the guys outside that it was them coming out, not some crazed grown-ups. They moved out into the light and Paddy turned back. The grown-ups were nearer, coming faster than grown-ups usually did. Achilleus stabbed at the weepy mother as she got too close and took her neatly in one eye. It was like she'd been switched off. She flopped over and crashed into the wall and slithered down it, thin yellow drool leaking from her mouth. The other grown-ups trampled over her.

'They sure are keen,' said Achilleus. 'And hungry.'

Paddy saw something moving along behind them. Something low and dark. The thing he'd seen in the storeroom. What was it? There was a tall father behind it, arm

outstretched, head tilted up. The dark shape had to be an animal of some sort. What else?

And then the smoke thickened in the corridor and Paddy couldn't see anything any more.

'Come on, caddie, you're gonna be left behind.'

Paddy realized that they'd reached the doorway and they spilt out into the fresh air. He saw that Ryan's hunters were arranged on either side of the path, weapons ready, dogs trembling with excitement. He gulped in great lungfuls of air. So glad to be outside again. So glad they weren't alone.

A father came out first; he was bald and, even before the hunters fell on him, Paddy could see his skin erupting, lumps growing on his scalp, his face swelling. A hunter stepped forward and swung at his head with a machete. But there was no real need. The guy's face was already splitting open, grey jelly-like stuff oozing through the rips in his skin. He was bursting. Paddy had never seen a live burster before.

The father collapsed to the ground, his flesh boiling off his body, his insides spilling out. Paddy wondered if they'd all go the same way, but while the others clearly didn't like being out in the light none of them burst like the father.

The hunters were merciless, chopping at the grown-ups from both sides as one by one they came staggering out of the door. Achilleus was among them, darting in and stabbing with his spear. Paddy didn't join them. He made the faces. He yelled at the grown-ups. He took up a position with his spear, copying the little plastic action figures he loved to play with. But he couldn't do it. Couldn't go in and cut them with the *Gáe Bolg*. It was a mixture of fear and squeamishness. The memory of the sentinel. The press of Paddy's blade against his skin. The

way it pushed back and then gave, went soft, opened up. The memory of the sentinel's belly ripping open. His guts falling out. Spraying his filth over Paddy.

Paddy wasn't ready for that again.

Was it nearly over? Paddy stared at the door. Waiting. The animal hadn't come out. The dark shape he'd seen crawling down the corridor. He was trembling. No idea what to expect.

A black nose peeped out of the doorway, sniffing, a face – brown fur and bright eyes.

A hunter moved in, spear raised.

'No!' Paddy shouted. 'Don't. It's a dog. It's just a dog.'

The hunter held back.

It was a brown Labrador, and as it came fully out Paddy saw that it had a yellow hi-viz harness round its body. It was on a lead, bringing a father out into the light. Blind. Empty eye sockets. Flesh rotted away almost to nothing. Instead of a white stick, he was feeling his way with a long, thin child's arm clutched in his free hand.

The hunters looked at each other, then to Ryan for leadership. To Achilleus. What should they do?

Achilleus stepped up behind the father and struck him quickly and cleanly in the neck, cutting his spine. The father fell and the dog turned, whimpered once, sniffed at him, licked his face. Sat down next to him.

Paddy watched as the dog looked at Achilleus, then got up, its tail wagging, and went over to him. Sniffed his hand. Achilleus knelt down.

And Paddy saw him smile in a way he'd never seen before.

'He's a champion, Akkie. He's a prince.'

'He's a princess actually,' said Achilleus and he laughed.

'What do you mean?'

'She's a bitch.'

'Does that mean she won't fight?'

Achilleus laughed even louder. 'Girls can fight just as well as boys, caddie. You've seen it for yourself.'

'Sure. Yeah. Sure. She won't be a princess, though. She'll be a warrior queen!'

Achilleus wasn't sure why he'd changed his mind. Paddy had pleaded and pleaded and pleaded with him and in the end he'd given in. There was something about the dog. Something special. For a start she was well trained, not at all aggressive. She might be good for Paddy. The little boy didn't need another killer around; he needed a friend. She might settle him down and give him a sense of security. It was like she'd been given to them. A gift from the gods. And she was Achilleus's gift to Paddy.

Jesus, the boy was happy. He was marching along the road back to the museum, chattering away, praising the dog. The fear had lifted from him. Achilleus felt good that he'd done a good thing – something that hadn't involved extreme violence.

Before they'd left, Ryan and his hunters had cleared out the building and lugged the dead grown-ups out behind the gallery where they'd made a fire from broken chairs and wood. Set fire to the lot of them, filling the park with smoke and the smell of roasting meat.

'This is how we live,' said Ryan, joining them. 'We keep these places clear of any bastards. We keep the park safe so that kids can come get water. We collect useful stuff. We clean up. And to pay us the settlements give us food and drink and anything else we need.'

'Don't seem to be so many grown-ups around here,' said Achilleus.

'Not any more,' said Ryan. 'Not since the other day. There was, like, an army come through. God knows where they all went. Some days we still find some hiding out like today, but otherwise I don't know where they are, where they gone.'

'I don't like it,' said Paddy. 'It's spooky. They can't all just disappear.'

'Sometimes,' said Achilleus. 'Have you felt it? Before a big storm? There's a stillness. Like the day's become heavy.'

'The calm before the storm,' said Ryan, 'is what they call it.'

'Yeah,' said Paddy. 'The calm before the storm.'

'So you saying we about to be hit by a big storm?' said Ryan.

'A shit storm,' said Achilleus.

'A sick storm more like,' said Paddy.

'I sure would like to know where they all gone to, though,' said Ryan.

'*I* know,' said a voice and Achilleus looked round to see

26

someone standing by the fence at the edge of the road. None of them had spotted him before. It was like he'd appeared from nowhere. Must have been hiding in the bushes or behind a tree. He had on a grey cloak with a hood and was carrying a crossbow and a long staff that he was leaning on slightly as if he had a bad leg.

Ryan's lot all stopped and took up a defensive position, ready for anything, wary of this new kid.

'Do I know you?' Ryan asked, his voice cold and hard.

'Nope,' said the boy. 'But you've been enjoying my beer.'

'Your beer?'

'Yeah. Ed bartered it with me.'

'So those crossbow bolts we got were for you?'

'Yeah.'

Achilleus knew all about the arrangements Ed had made to get hold of the car. The series of exchanges that had meant Ed ended up driving off west in a big blue people carrier and Ryan and his hunters had got drunk on the steps of the museum. Ryan had given Ed crossbow bolts, Ed had given them to this guy, who'd given him the beer, and Ed had given the beer to Ryan.

'So, you got any more beer?' Ryan asked.

'Might do.'

'I've heard of you,' said Zulficker. 'You're the kid called Shadowman, innit?'

Achilleus sniggered. 'Dumb name,' he said.

'Yeah,' Paddy agreed. 'Dumb.'

'You really Shadowman?' asked Ryan.

'Yeah.'

'Respect.'

'You don't run with no crew, do you?' said Zulficker.

'Not if I can help it.'

'So you reckon you know where all the grown-ups have gone?' Achilleus asked.

'Yeah. I've seen them. To the north of here. An army of them. Moving slowly down from Kilburn. And any day now they're going to get here and that is gonna be one bad day, let me tell you.'

'So what is it you want, Shadowman?' Ryan asked.

'I want to stop them.'

'Yeah, fair enough, but what is it you want from us? Precisely?'

'Why do you assume I want anything?'

'You're human.'

'Guess so.'

'You've broken cover,' Ryan went on. 'You've worked up a sweat to track us down and follow us and pop out the bushes on us here in the park. And you ain't out walking your dog, because you ain't got a dog. What I know of you, you ain't gonna do none of that without a reason.'

'If you want more beer, I can trade with you.'

'We ain't got no more bolts, Shadow. You cleaned us out.'

'I've got enough bolts.'

'So what is it you need?'

'You know a guy called Jester?'

'At the palace? Yeah.'

'He there now? As far as you know?'

'Raggedy kid?' said Achilleus. 'Wears a patchwork coat? Some call him Jester, some call him Magic-Man, some call him Bell-end. Slippery? Don't trust the little rat?'

'That's him,' said Shadowman.

'He's there,' said Achilleus. 'I know, because we saved his raggedy arse and took him there.'

'You from the Holloway crew?' said Shadowman.

'Yeah.'

'What do you want with Jester?' Ryan asked Shadowman.

Shadowman smiled.

'All I need is for you to take him a message.'

Maxie was kneeling by one of the vegetable beds in front of the museum. Scrabbling in the dirt. She'd gone into a sort of trance, forgotten what she was supposed to be doing. She stared down at her hands. They were streaked with mud. It looked like blood. She closed her eyes. Wanted to sleep. All her energy was gone. She could hear birds singing in the trees. So many of them. She realized she was shaking.

Pull yourself together, girl.

She stood up. Took a deep breath. She knew that after an adrenalin rush, when the body had been fighting to keep you alive, there was always a massive comedown. Turned out that was harder than she'd imagined. When they were doing things – fighting, moving, hiding – there wasn't time to think. Now there was lots of time. Too much time. As the weight of danger was lifted, it allowed darkness and depression to seep in. Post-traumatic stress – that's what they called it. She'd seen a documentary about it once. Soldiers coming back from the Middle East.

For them war had been easier than peace.

She didn't want war again, though. She didn't want to be back in the world of danger among the blood and the warm stink of attacking grown-ups. She didn't want to be

fighting for her life again soon, or any time, thank you, God.

She looked over to where a bunch of little kids were playing. They were all clustered round Paddy's new dog, which sat there patiently, as the kids' puppy, Godzilla, barked at it and jumped up to bite its ear. It sounded like they were trying to think what to call the new dog, all shouting out names . . .

'Chocolate – Brown Eyes – Mulan – Rogue – Killer . . .'

There were nine of them. Paddy, Wiki, Jibber-jabber, Zohra, Froggie, Blu-Tack Bill, Small Sam, The Kid and Yo-Yo. It was Small Sam that held her attention. He was with them but somehow not with them. There was something haunted about him. Maxie thought back to when he'd arrived here at the museum. Remembering the strange procession that had come in through the doors. Ed, tall and grim with the ugly scar down one side of his face. His friends, Macca and Will and Kyle, coming in with a certain 'show-me-what-you-got' swagger. Then Sam and The Kid and Yo-Yo, clutching her violin case. And, under a blanket, the Green Man. It had all felt so surreal that at first Maxie hadn't registered how amazing it was that Sam was there. A ghost from their past turning up. She'd held back with all of the others, frozen, just watching. Like it was some crazy play. Trying to take it all in.

Trying to get her head round the fact that Sam was alive.

She didn't need to carry the guilt any more – that he'd been snatched by grown-ups on her watch.

Sam gave them hope. If this little boy could survive then maybe they all could. Maybe the nutters in St Paul's who thought he was a god were right after all. Maybe he

31

was special? The secret to their survival. Since then Maxie had made it her special duty to watch out for him, especially now that Ed had gone to look for Sam's sister. Maxie was going to make sure that nothing bad happened to Sam again. She'd asked Whitney to act like a sort of nanny. The big girl was there now, sitting on a bench, watching them. Smiling.

Maxie couldn't get her head round this.

Peace.

London was quiet. No grown-ups on the streets. It was a dream-time. Were there really no monsters lurking in the shadows? Could she really allow herself not to be scared any more? Could it be as simple as just getting from one day to the next? Eat, drink, work, sleep. Survive.

She prayed that nothing bad would happen, that the quiet times would continue and they could grow up in peace and safety. But at the back of her mind was a deeper animal thought. That is wasn't over. That something worse was coming.

She shivered. Looked around for Blue. Spotted him by the fence. Just standing there, alone, staring at the road. She knew he got depressed as well. He kept up a tough exterior, but was more sensitive than he let on to anyone except her. Maxie went over to him and put her arms round him from behind, and he put his hands over hers.

She looked over his shoulder at the empty buildings opposite – flats and offices mostly. One day maybe she could go back to living in a regular house, not having to be surrounded by other kids for safety.

'Will life ever be normal again?' she asked.

'Not until every last grown-up is killed,' said Blue. 'Not until the enemy is gone for good.'

'And how many of us will be around to see that day?' said Maxie.

'I intend to grow old, girl. I wanna see you with wrinkles.'

'You say the sweetest things.'

Maxie felt something nudge her ankle and she looked down to see Godzilla trying to eat her shoe.

Sam came running up.

'Sorry,' he said. 'He got away. He's jealous of the new dog, I think.'

'You got a name for her?' Maxie asked, letting go of Blue.

'The girls all want to call her Bright Eyes,' said Sam. 'Paddy wants to call her Ripper.'

'Ripper's a terrible name,' said Blue.

'I know,' said Sam. 'I said they should call her Ella. Like my sister.'

'Not a good idea,' said Maxie.

Sam looked at her, sadness in his eyes.

'Why not?'

'Imagine when she comes back,' said Maxie. 'Finds out she's got the same name as Paddy's dog. How weird would that be?'

Sam smiled. 'I just want something to remember her by,' he said, and his lip trembled.

'Hey.' Maxie squatted down to his level. 'I didn't say *if* she comes back, did I? I said *when*. OK?'

Sam nodded, holding back the tears. 'Ed should've let me go with him,' he said. 'She's my sister. I want to see her again. That all I've been doing – trying to get back to her. And now Ed's gone off without me. I feel wrong being here, not looking for her, not helping her. I was supposed to look after her. I promised her I would.'

'Hey, hey, hey,' said Maxie. 'Slow down. Ed did the right thing. OK? Trust me. You're safe here.'

'How do you know?' said Sam. 'What if Ella did the right thing? What if she's safe and *we're* all in danger? What if we get attacked and Ed comes back with Ella and I'm dead? She'll be sad.'

'Look out there, shrimp,' said Blue, pointing to the empty road. 'Does that look dangerous to you?'

'To tell you the truth,' said Sam, 'everything looks dangerous to me.'

6

David was getting impatient. *Was this ever going to work?* He very much doubted it. Right now he wanted to hit the strange, sick-looking boy. What a waste of space he was. Paul Channing. He'd turned up from the Natural History Museum, babbling on about how he could talk to grown-ups, or strangers, as David called them. Paul had claimed he could even control them. *Yeah, right.* Every time he tried to demonstrate his amazing abilities it ended like this. A ridiculous failure.

Talk to them? They were all just ignoring him.

David had his own captive strangers here at the palace. The remains of the royal family. A diseased and rotting bunch of ratbags who lived in a room at the top of the palace where their stink wasn't as noticeable. David hated coming in here. So, to be constantly dragged up here by Paul – 'This time it's going to work, I promise you!' – was a right royal pain in the arse. He kept a handkerchief clamped over his nose and mouth. It had been soaked in rosemary oil, but the stench of the captive royal family got through. They had no standards of personal hygiene. They sat there dumbly in their tattered, rotting ball gowns and dinner suits, leaking into the furniture. It stank worse than the elephant house at the zoo. At least they'd stopped

doing their stupid statue thing. For days they'd just stood there like scarecrows, arms outstretched, faces turned to the ceiling, not moving.

Since then, though, they'd been more lifeless than ever. David wasn't sure how much longer he could keep these vile specimens alive. Bits kept falling off. One minor princess had lost most of her face. All the flesh had been eaten away, leaving her thin, boil-studded skin stretched over her skull. Her blue eyes staring out, lidless and weeping.

They'd been his great hope. He'd wanted to show them off, parade them in front of other kids, to show that he was the right man to rule London.

'Look at me, folks, I've got the royal family! I'm the rightful heir to the throne of England!' But they were worse than a joke now. On top of it all, they'd been let out recently and a couple of the more lively ones had been killed before they'd been safely rounded up.

That had not been a good night.

He'd really been hoping that things were going his way when Jester had turned up at the palace with a small army of tough north London kids. David had wanted them to fight for him and help him make his point about being in charge. But they'd wanted none of it, and after eating half his food they'd just left one night, freeing the royal family on their way out. They were on his shit list. Right at the top. One day, when he was in charge, he would punish them very publicly and very painfully.

So when Paul had arrived, claiming he could communicate with strangers, it had felt like a gift from above. Paul was going to be their secret weapon. Their nuclear device.

Only he was proving to be a dud.

'You can't do it, can you?' said David and Paul looked at his shoes. He was tall and thin and very pale, his skin the colour of paper. He was dressed all in black with a greasy roll-neck jumper covering his scrawny neck. He was nearly as bad to be around as the strangers. Sweating all the time, his eyes darting around like nuts. Yeah. Let's face it, he was a nutter. Why had David ever believed in him? For one moment? Talk to strangers? Talk to the moon more like, you useless nutter.

Why had David believed in him? Easy. Because he'd *wanted* to. Because he needed *something* to give him an edge.

'How many times are you going to drag me up here to watch this stupid, pathetic bloody pantomime?'

Paul mumbled something and shrugged. Stared at the wall as if there was an interesting message for him written on it. David looked at Jester, his second in command. Jester grinned and circled his finger round his temple – the universal sign for a loony.

Paul scratched his chin, very fast, like a dog, leaving red marks, then turned to face the royal family. They sat there, on beds, on chairs, on the floor. Slumped and life-less. Drooling, dead-eyed, covered in boils and sores and terrible growths. One of them belched, a long, deep rattling sound that turned into a gurgle as thin brown liquid bubbled out of her nose and mouth. She was some sort of duchess, David seemed to remember. He'd looked her up when she'd been a bit more recognizable. She was the oldest of them, had a tiara in her tangled white hair.

Paul stared at them, red-rimmed eyes shining and manic. He was grinding his teeth and muttering under his breath. His head twitching and jerking occasionally as if someone was jogging it.

'Well, this is brilliant,' said David. 'Better than the theatre. People would pay to see this. You really know how to put on a show, Paul. You dingbat.'

Paul growled like an animal, closed his eyes, his fingers groping at the air, as if he was trying to grab hold of something invisible. His body began to shake, a high-pitched whine coming from between his clenched teeth. The royal family sat there. Vacant. Half dead. David had a powerful urge to walk over and strangle the lot of them. They didn't scare him. They were fed regularly, but were too weak now to do any real damage. Even so, he always brought in at least two of his red-blazered personal guard with him. George Halley and Andy Kerr were standing near the door, watching the show and giggling, leaning on their rifles.

David caught Jester's eye again.

'Come on,' he said. 'Let's go. And Paul. Don't bother again, yeah? OK? I'm too busy for this crap. If you want to stay at the palace you can find something useful to do, like growing potatoes. Might be easier for you, as long as you use a spade to dig with and not the power of your mind.'

George and Andy laughed and David walked towards the door. Realized none of the others had moved. Stopped. Something was happening: he could feel it.

His head was hurting, as if it was being squeezed; there was a buzzing and a humming at some frequency that David could register but not really get a fix on.

He turned back to look at the royal family. A light had come on in their eyes. A light of intelligence and understanding he'd never seen there before. And then slowly, one by one, they all turned and stared at Paul. Eight faces, all paying attention. Those that were sitting down stood up. The ones on the floor struggled clumsily to their feet.

George and Andy became alert as well now, rifles at the ready, looking to David for guidance.

Paul was still clutching at the air, mumbling and working his jaw, the grinding of his teeth startlingly loud, like a machine. He was making an immense physical effort. Sweat was pouring off him. And now David swallowed and stepped back as the royals swivelled their heads towards him. He felt uncomfortable in the beam of their unreadable eyes, usually so dull and dead, now shining and intense. Were they going to attack? He had nothing to defend himself with. He made a vague signal to George and Andy. *Be alert. Don't let me down. Deal with this.* Suddenly two guards seemed inadequate. Should he make a run for it? Order the boys to start shooting?

The royals advanced towards him on shuffling feet. David instinctively put his hands up to protect himself, not wanting to appear weak or frightened. They came closer, closer . . .

'Back them off,' he said, his mouth dry, but it was unnecessary. Paul made some freaky head movements, coughed and went limp, looked like he was going to fall. Jester caught him and held him up as the royals went out of focus, lost the signal, relaxed, slumped, wandered off.

David snapped at his guards, who were standing there open-mouthed, like a couple of zombies themselves. 'Take Paul downstairs and get him some food and water. The good stuff, not the crap we've been giving him. Look after him. I want him well.'

The two guards nodded and took Paul off Jester, heading for the door. The royals had gone back to being mindless lumps of rotting flesh. They weren't important, though. It was the *others*. The ones out there all round

London. If Paul could control the ones in here maybe he could control them too.

David clapped his hands and rubbed them together. An old man's action.

'You know what this means, don't you?' he said to Jester as they went down the grand staircase to David's office.

'Do I?'

'It means that potentially we have all the power in London.'

'Let's not get carried away,' said Jester, always cautious. 'Paul did a party trick with a few useless royals. Might just've been luck. It's a bit of a jump from there to taking over the world.'

'Great leaders jump high,' said David. 'You have to think big, Magic-Man. You're so suspicious, so careful, tiny steps. You've got to see in widescreen.'

'Oh, I can see the bigger picture all right,' said Jester, smiling. With his hair sticking out in all directions and his coat made of bits of patchwork material, he looked wild and scruffy and all over the place, but he was the smartest kid David knew. The opposite of how he looked. Almost as clever as David himself. David relied on him.

Relied on him too much.

'And what do you see in this bigger picture?' he asked.

'I see you sitting on a big white horse that's rearing up, a crown on your head, cloak billowing, a sword in your hand, your defeated enemies dead at your feet, and behind you – London in smoking ruins.'

'Well, apart from the bit about London in smoking ruins, I'd say that was a pretty accurate picture,' said David. 'I'd watch that show.'

'Actually I thought that was the only accurate part,' said Jester. 'I mean, can you even ride a horse?'

'No idea,' said David. 'But I can wear a crown. And that's the most important bit.'

They met Pod halfway down the stairs. Collar turned up. Hair brushed forward, glossy and immaculate. Always immaculate. Pod had the best hair of anyone at the palace. David often wondered what his secret was, how he kept it so clean and perfect, better even than the girls. Pod was his head of security, a little bit stupid, to be perfectly honest, but reliable. Loyal. Very different to Jester. But what was more important? To have people around you who were loyal, or to have people around you who were clever?

'There's someone here to see you, Jester,' said Pod.

'Someone? Who?'

'Er. You know. That *hunter* dude. The spotty one with the ears.'

'Ryan Aherne?'

'Yuh, that's the guy.'

'I thought he'd stopped coming here.'

'Well, he came back,' said Pod. 'Definitely him. Gave a message to the guys out front. Wants a word about something, yeah?'

Jester looked at David.

'Do you need me for anything?'

'No.' David watched Jester and Pod go downstairs. Wondered what this was all about. You never knew with Jester. Whether he had his own thing going on. Too clever to be trusted.

One day David was going to have to get rid of him.

There was only room for one clever person around here.

Jester followed Pod through the inner courtyard of the palace towards the front. He was going on about some problem in the kitchens, but Jester wasn't listening. The kitchens were someone else's problem. Jester was thinking about the strangers upstairs, and how they'd responded to Paul. How had he done it? He hadn't said anything to them. It had looked like some kind of Derren Brown mind-control thing. But how was that possible?

There had been a hum in the room, a throbbing, as if the air was vibrating. Had it been something to do with that? Had Paul somehow generated high-frequency ultrasound waves? And had the strangers somehow responded to them? Paul was just a boy. OK, a fairly messed-up boy, but a boy all the same. And the strangers? Well, they were just mindless pus-bags. How could they all suddenly learn to communicate with ultrasound? Maybe it was something else. Jester knew that not all animals used sound to communicate. Insects sometimes used scent and hormones. Bees danced. But the royal family weren't insects, were they? They were human. Paul was human. Sure, the royals were infected with the sickness, but that didn't stop them from being human, did it? And Paul? He was definitely one sick bunny.

Something had happened to that boy. He wasn't all there. He was warped.

Still human, though. Had to be.

It was hard keeping up sometimes, the way the world was, how it had changed. Sometimes Jester wished he was more like Pod. Pod never really thought deeply about anything, just accepted how things were and got on with it. Not bothered. Why try to figure stuff out? Why not just be happy?

That was the thing about Pod – basically he *was* happy. Wasn't much more you could say about him. Thick but happy.

And was Jester himself happy? He couldn't really tell. Most of the time he just *was*. Not happy, not sad, not depressed, not anything really, just existing. Occasionally there'd be moments. Maybe five minutes when something good was happening – they'd got hold of some new food. Or he was hanging with his mates. Somebody was telling a good joke. And – *bang* – it hit him: *I'm happy now – this is good.* And, as soon as he registered it, it would pass.

So was he happy right this minute?

Neither happy nor sad. The day could go either way.

'What's Ryan want?' he asked Pod.

'Didn't say.'

'What's he doing here? Did he bring some stuff? I thought we never dealt with him any more.'

'Nope. Don't think he brought anything to barter. He just turned up with his hunters. They were going past or something, I guess. All he said was he wanted to talk to you.'

'Didn't say what about?'

'Nope.'

And Pod hadn't thought to ask. Happy but thick. Jester idly wondered what Ryan might want. He used to come here all the time. Always brought good stuff he'd scavenged. Or useful information. Jester hadn't seen him in ages, though. Jester seemed to remember there'd been an argument. Some bullshit thing. David didn't give Ryan what he'd promised him. Said Ryan hadn't fulfilled his side of the bargain. Something like that. Usual David stuff.

He wondered what was so important that Ryan would come now.

'Where's he waiting?' he asked as Pod went towards the front doors.

'Wouldn't come inside,' said Pod.

'Figures.'

'Spoke to one of the guards in the parade ground. Wants to meet you over by the statue of Queen Vic. You want me to, like, send someone out with you, just in case?'

'Nah,' said Jester. 'It'll be cool. No reason Ryan would want to do anything to me. I've got no beef with him.'

'What about strangers?'

'You know what?' said Jester as they went out into the sunlight. 'Apart from that sorry bunch upstairs, I haven't seen a stranger in days.'

'Me neither, now you come to mention it,' said Pod. 'Even those scarecrows have moved on. It's been really quiet lately. Boring.'

Be just David's luck, thought Jester, and he smiled to himself; just as he'd worked out a way to control the strangers they'd all buggered off.

Pod went back inside and Jester crossed the parade ground towards the gates that led out into the street. As ever, two of David's boys were standing guard in the

sentry boxes. Well, sitting, to be more accurate. One was reading a book; the other seemed to be asleep. They were prefects from David's old school and still wore their red blazers. Had rifles they'd taken from the Imperial War Museum. Probably didn't work. Couldn't waste ammunition practising. They must be bored out of their minds.

It really had been so quiet lately. In a way that made you long for something to happen. Summer was coming on. It was getting warmer. Everything would be easier when it was summer. There'd be more fresh food from the vegetable beds, less need to huddle together at night to keep warm. You could sit outside and warm your back in the sun. Jester remembered summer holidays from before. Hanging out in the park. Doing nothing. Long, lazy days.

Maybe this summer would be like that?

Perhaps the world *had* taken a turn for the better.

He realized with a kind of physical pulse that he was happy.

He got to the big iron gates. Looked for any sign of Ryan and his hunters. Didn't see anyone. He called over to the guard with the book.

'You gonna let me out?'

The guard looked at him expressionlessly for a second, trying to compute the information.

'I gotta go out,' Jester shouted, gesturing at the gate. The boy finally got it. Stood up. Strolled over, taking some keys off his belt.

'Where you going?'

'It wasn't you that spoke to Ryan then?' Jester asked.

'Was actually.'

'Well then, you know where I'm going.'

'Suppose so.'

45

Dumb idiot.

'He said he'd meet me at the statue. That right?'

'Yeah.' The boy made a dismissive noise. Swung the gate open.

'Can't see him,' said Jester.

'Maybe he left.'

'Thank God we've got you guys looking out for us,' said Jester as he walked out of the palace grounds.

He crossed the road towards the statue of Queen Victoria. It was a big thing, her on her throne, the top covered in gleaming gold leaf. Sat up there, staring into the distance, on top of a big white plinth. One of the Holloway kids had sprayed some graffiti on the stonework when they'd left.

FREAK LIVES. And underneath someone had added AKKIE DEAKY.

Some kind of pathetic, mindless memorial to one of their gang who'd got killed. Jester was pretty sure it had happened when David had sent them down to attack John's squatter camp at the other end of St James's Park.

Back then David had sort of been at war with John. But now they had an alliance. John's squatters were cooperating for the time being. David was promising them all sorts of rewards, gold and silver and jewels, or at least the modern equivalent – potatoes, cabbages and clean water. So John was behaving.

Jester stopped on some steps by the statue and squinted off down towards the far end of St James's Park. Couldn't really see anything from here. But they were there all right. Living like pigs in their dirty little camp. Maybe that was why it was so quiet lately. Maybe John's guys had been out and about whacking the local strangers.

So bloody quiet.

No sign of John's squatters. No sign of any strangers. No sign of Ryan and his hunters. Maybe they'd got bored waiting and gone home. Jester walked round to the far side of the statue.

'How's it going?'

Jester recognized that voice. It wasn't Ryan, though. Someone much more familiar, but it wasn't registering. Who was it?

A boy came round the side of the plinth, limping slightly, propped up on a staff.

Holy Christ. It was Shadowman.

That was why it hadn't registered. He'd wiped Shadowman from his mind.

Shadowman was dead.

8

'Whoa. Shadow. Great to see you, man.'

'Yeah.'

'Christ, bro, I was worried.'

'Right.'

'When did you get back? Why didn't you come see me?
I lost you out there. Worried I might never see you again.'

'Yeah,' said Shadowman. He was peering at Jester's
coat, covered in its multicoloured patches. Each one cut
from the clothes of a friend who'd died.

'Looks like you got a piece of my T-shirt there?' said
Shadowman.

'What? Nah. Looks similar. Granted. But that was
someone else's shirt.'

'Right.'

Shadowman didn't say anything else. Just stood there
and stared at Jester. Emotionless. Studying him.

Jester broke the silence.

'It's so good to see you.'

'I think you really mean it,' said Shadowman with a
look that was half a frown and half a humourless smile.

'Mean what? What are you saying?'

'You're genuinely pleased to see me, aren't you?'

'Course I am. We're mates.'

'Yeah. Like all that other stuff never happened.'

'Other stuff?'

'The leaving me behind stuff, at King's Cross, when the strangers attacked and you nearly knocked me out trying to fight them.'

'Oh man,' said Jester. 'That was bad. That was chaos. Carnage city. We had to cut and run.'

'You had to cut and run and leave me behind.'

'What could we do, man?' said Jester. 'You couldn't walk. You couldn't hardly even stand up. You were concussed.'

'I was concussed because you'd hit me.'

'Yeah. Accident. I mean, come on. You'd have done the same, Shadow.'

'Would I?'

'But never mind all that,' said Jester. 'What happened? How'd you make it home? How long you been back? So many questions, man.'

'I've got one question for you,' said Shadowman. 'What do you reckon I've thought about ever since that day?'

'I dunno.' Jester grinned. 'Girls? Food? The meaning of life? Who shot first? Han or Greedo?'

'*You*. I've thought about you.'

'I'm touched.'

'I've thought about what I'd do if I ever saw you again.'

Jester was starting to get nervous. Not liking the way this conversation was going. He'd put Shadowman out of his mind. The two of them had been friends since before the sickness. Dylan Peake was Shadowman's real name. Shadowman was his rock-star name. They'd grown up together. Tried to start a band together.

That was all a long time ago. Shadowman had grown

into a tough, mean survivor. Jester got by on his wits. He wasn't a fighter. If Shadowman was out for revenge Jester was going to have to talk him out of it. Sure, he could probably have done more when they'd been attacked on the railway tracks behind King's Cross station. But survival was key. Survival was all.

'We had no choice,' he said.

'So you left me for dead?'

'Yeah, but you're not dead, are you? Unless you're a ghost or a zombie or something – wouldn't put it past you.'

'You always were funny.'

'So all this thinking you've been doing?' said Jester, not wanting to let Shadowman get the upper hand. 'About what you were gonna do to me. What was the conclusion? Is this it? You were gonna have a nice friendly chat, shake hands and make up?'

'I thought of a lot of ways to hurt you, Jester.'

'Listen,' said Jester. 'It wasn't just me back there. I had to look after the others. Staying to help you would have put them all in danger. It wasn't my fault. Wasn't my fault you got in the way when I was swinging my club. You want to blame someone, blame the bloody strangers.'

'Don't blame you, yeah? None of it was your fault?'

'No. I was just trying to survive, Shadow. Save the group.'

'Save the group? I thought you were the only one made it back here,' said Shadowman. 'The others? Tom and Kate and Alfie. What happened to them?'

'Kate and Tom left me, if you really want to know,' said Jester. 'Never saw them again. Alfie was killed by strangers. I tried to protect him.'

'All dead then. Well done. You're a hero.'

'I did my best. Come on. How many kids have died? You know how hard it is out there.'

'Took me a while to get back,' said Shadowman. 'Got a bit mashed up on the way. And when I found out you were alive . . .'

'Yeah, I know. You thought of a hundred and one ways to give me a hard time. Jesus, Shadowman, this isn't school, this isn't the good old days; this is now, this is dog eat dog, this is survival of the fittest. The rules have changed. You were concussed. I made a decision. If I'd stayed to fight we'd have all been killed.'

'As opposed to everyone else getting killed but you surviving?' said Shadowman. 'If you'd helped me I could have helped you all. Tom and Kate and Alfie might still be alive.'

'Yeah, right,' said Jester, figuring that attack was the best form of defence. 'You could really have helped us. You couldn't even stand up. Be serious, man. And besides, look – here you are. You made it back in one piece. Except for your limp. You all right?'

'Sprained ankle. Nearly healed. Can't go too fast, though.' Shadowman paused, looked away down the road. 'I came to a conclusion in the end, you know,' he went on.

'About what?' As if Jester didn't know.

'About what to do with you.'

'Yeah? Better be good.'

'You didn't like it out there, did you?' said Shadowman. 'In the real world. Outside your palace walls. The world of the strangers.'

'Sorry. Was I supposed to like it?'

'You know, if I didn't hate you so much I'd quite like you.'

'Nice.'

'So you wanna hear it?'

'Not particularly. Listen, Shadowman.' Jester's throat had gone tight and dry. This wasn't going to end with a fist bump and 'no hard feelings'. He started to back away, ready to make a run for it. Wishing now he'd told the guards to come with him. Not that they'd have been much use against Shadowman.

Well. Jester's happiness hadn't lasted very long at all this time, had it? He'd been fooled by the sun and the peaceful atmosphere. The world was still crap.

'Listen,' he said. 'OK. You've made your point. I'm sorry you blame me for what happened, yeah? I panicked. As you say, I'm not used to life on the streets. I'm not you. I'm not a hero. I'm just an ordinary kid. And maybe I messed up that day. Fine. Mistake. Apology. So I'm going back inside now.'

Shadowman lifted up a crossbow that was hanging from his belt, hidden by his cloak. The tip of a thin, sharp bolt was sticking out of the end.

'I haven't finished,' said Shadowman, his voice flat and calm.

Jester didn't take his eyes off that cruel steel point.

'You wouldn't . . .'

'I would. Of course I would. You said yourself this isn't school. Times have changed.'

'Shadow . . .'

'Haven't you been listening to a word I've said?'

He raised the bow and aimed it squarely at Jester's gut. 'You hear me out now. Try to walk away and I fire this into you and that's that.'

'Oh, come on. *Really?* This is your plan that you've

spent weeks thinking about? You shoot me with a cross-bow?'

'No, this is just insurance. To make sure you listen to me and do what you're told.'

'Go on then,' said Jester. 'Surprise me.'

'You noticed how there's no strangers around here?'

'Yeah. Blue skies, Shadow. Things can only get better.'

'You think? There's an army out there, Jester. An army of strangers. They're massing. That's why you don't see any. They've all gone north. After you left me at King's Cross I stumbled across them. Tracked them across London. They weren't so many at first, but they grew, more and more of them, became a bigger and badder army. They're organized as well, in a way you wouldn't believe. They must be pretty near unstoppable by now. I had to leave off tracking them when I nearly busted my leg. Only just made it back into town. But now my leg's nearly better. Can't go as fast as I'd like, but it'll do. Thing is, I need to get back out there and find where they are, find out what's happening, where they're heading. You see, if it's as bad as I think I've got to come back and warn people. We have to get organized, but for that I need information, I need up-to-date news.'

'And you want me to pass this information on for you?' said Jester. 'Is that it?'

'Yeah. That's it.'

'Well, I can do that. You come straight to me when you get back.'

'Yeah, but my ankle's not *quite* strong enough yet for me to risk going it alone. I need help. I need a right-hand man.'

'You don't mean . . . ?'

'You and me, old buddy, heading back into the badlands. I'm going to show you first hand what we're up against. Might help you deliver the message more forcefully, you know, more convincingly. And this time you won't be able to leave me behind because it'll be just the two of us. I'll be the only thing keeping you alive.'

'What if I say I don't want to come?'

'Then I shoot you in the guts and you die a long, slow, agonizing death, smelling of shit.'

'Hmm. Decisions, decisions . . .'

'I'm glad you think this is a joke. But I'm warning you. The army out there? It's not a joke on any level.'

'OK, listen. I'll need to get my stuff together.'

Shadowman swore at him and Jester stopped talking.

'You know I'm not stupid,' Shadowman went on. 'You go through those gates, Jester, and you won't come back out again.'

'Look, Shadow, I can't just go off like this. No other clothes, no weapons, no food or water.'

'No make-up and security blanket. I've got all we need, except a change of boxers.'

'No, listen, Shadowman, no way. OK? No way am I just walking off up there now.'

'Wanna bet?'

'You try and force me, they'll see you from the palace. They'll come out and rescue me.'

'Those two dozy bastards? They can try. When did they last leave the palace grounds? You think I'm scared of them? No, you and me, we're going to take a nice easy jog over the road into Green Park, and then we're gone. All being well, we'll be back by dark. Of course, if it all goes tits up you'll never be back and they'll all wonder what-

ever happened to Jester, the way he disappeared like that. Oh well, never mind. Survival is key. Survival is all. We're all right. Let's forget all about him and his stupid patchwork coat. Now walk.'

'No.'

Jester suddenly rocked back, his whole head singing, his cheek burning. It took him a moment to work out that Shadowman had hit him. Slapped him hard round the face. Jester swore and Shadowman hit him again, too fast for Jester to react, to protect himself.

'Stop it,' he said, his voice sounding more whiny than he would have liked. There were tears in his eyes. He wasn't used to being hit.

'No,' said Shadowman. 'I'm not going to stop it, not until you understand what's going on here.'

'All right. I understand. You go. I'll follow . . .'

Wham. Shadowman hit him again and now the tears had left Jester's eyes and were crawling down his cheeks. He felt ashamed of them.

'*You* go, I'll follow,' said Shadowman. 'And I'll have this crossbow aimed at your back every step. You know I never miss. That's how I've stayed alive. Head for the gates over there. Walk steadily, not slow, not fast. Anything you do that I don't like you've got a crossbow bolt sticking out of your arse.'

Jester had no choice. He started to walk. Legs trembling, knees weak. His back muscles twitching and clenching, expecting at any moment to feel a sharp jolt in his spine. Tears of self-pity stinging his eyes.

9

Maxie was trying not to stare at Wormwood. She couldn't help it. He was just so *freaking* weird. Covered from head to foot in a fur of green mould, he wore only an old blanket, loosely wrapped round his body, and a stupid green bowler hat, his long, stringy hair hanging down from underneath it. He had very pale eyes and, if they looked at you, you felt it. Like he thought you were nothing, less than nothing, a tiny speck of dirt, even though he himself smelt pretty awful. He had long yellow fingernails that he liked to click together, making a dry rattling sound. Justin, who was in charge here at the museum, had asked him several times to cut them – everyone has asked him to cut them – but Wormwood refused. It was difficult to get him to do anything. He was sitting there now, his hands dangling between his knees, fingers wagging, fingernails clicking. *Click-click-clack.* Maxie wasn't going to tell him to stop, even though it irritated the hell out of her, and put her on edge. She didn't want to risk him turning those old, cold eyes on her. She was keeping a safe distance. He was, after all, a grown-up. And for the last year the kids had killed any grown-ups on sight. The alternative was to let them eat you. OK, so you could have a conversation with this one, but the sickness was still in him. He wasn't

to be trusted, and he was never allowed anywhere without an armed guard.

So far Wormwood had behaved.

He hadn't attacked anyone.

But the kids hadn't got this far by being sloppy. Right now Maxie and Blue and a big-nosed kid called Andy they'd picked up at Buckingham Palace were guarding him. Maxie had her katana at her side. It was sharp as a razor. If Wormwood decided to get jiggy it would be a race between her and Blue to see who could gut him first.

Wormwood's favourite place in the museum was the Darwin Centre in the orange zone, a modern addition to the museum that housed several laboratories. A science nerd called Einstein ran the place. Maxie didn't like Einstein much, but had to admit that he was probably the cleverest kid she'd ever met. He and some other smart kids were trying to find out how the disease worked, whether there might be a cure for it.

Wormwood was helping. His real name was Mark Wormold apparently, and he'd been a biologist before he got the disease. Had worked in a research centre called the Promithios Institute. When he could focus, when he had a window of sanity and stopped spouting nonsense, he talked fairly rationally to Einstein about his work. Maxie had got used to grown-ups being drooling idiots, so it had been a shock to find one like Wormwood who could talk and think and appear sane for brief spells. Well, not exactly *sane* – insane would be closer to the truth – but able to communicate at least.

So here he was. In the labs, trying to act like a scientist. It was unreal. Right now he was deep in conversation with Einstein. Maxie didn't understand a lot of what they were

talking about and she reckoned Einstein was pretty much in the dark as well. Much of what came out of Wormwood's mouth was pure gibberish. Somewhere in the stream of nonsense there was sense, though, there were facts about the disease, if only Einstein could figure it out. The one phrase that Wormwood kept coming out with was, 'Good blood will drive out the bad.'

'I know, I know,' said Einstein, shaking his head. 'You've said it a hundred times. But what does it mean?'

'You must listen to me,' said Wormwood.

'I *am* listening.'

'No, you're talking. Always talking. Just be silent and listen. Hush . . .' He put a bony finger to his lips, stared at Einstein, who looked away. 'You're like the bugs back in the big green, buzzing, buzzing, buzzing, never sitting still, never listening. Impossible to have a conversation with bugs.'

'And there *you* go again,' said Einstein. 'The big green. You always come back to the big green. The big green this, the big green that. The big green what? The big green giant? The big green house? The big green bogey?'

'And there *you* go again,' said Wormwood. 'Always talking, never listening.'

'He means the jungle,' said Blue. He hadn't looked like he was really listening. He never did. He looked bored most of the time, not interested. A hard man. But there was a lot more going on inside him than he let on.

'Don't pretend you weren't there when the Twisted Kids told us all about it,' Blue went on. 'About where the disease came from. About the rainforest. South America. The jungle.'

'That's one theory,' said Einstein. 'I don't have to believe it.'

'Feels a whole lot like the truth to me,' said Blue, and he turned to Maxie and the others. 'There was a tribe, the Inmathger. They had the disease, only they've never met any other humans, and when they did – *pow!* It spreads all over before anyone can stop it. Wormy here was one of the scientists who was out there studying them. Carried the sickness home with him. Ain't that right, Wormy? You was out there in the big green?'

'I was there for thousands of years,' said Wormwood without looking at Blue. 'And before that I was a Starchild. And look at me – I still am a star.'

He did a little prima donna thing, raising his chin and combing his hair back on one side with his fingernails.

'Yeah, right,' said Blue, shaking his head.

'Bang goes your theory,' said Einstein. 'Unless we accept that our Mister Wormold here is thousands of years old and came from outer space or something.'

'Just because some of it's bullshit,' said Maxie, 'doesn't mean it *all* is.'

'But how do we separate it out?' said Einstein. 'How do we know which bits of it, if any, are the truth?'

'He definitely worked in the rainforest with the Inmathger,' said Blue. 'For Promithios. You should properly talk to the Twisted Kids some time, Einstein. They know stuff.'

'They give me the creeps,' Einstein said dismissively.

'Yeah, well, I'm sure you give them the creeps an' all,' said Maxie. 'You give *me* the creeps sometimes.'

'That's because I'm creepy.' Einstein laughed. He had thick skin. You could say what you liked to him. To be honest, he was slightly weird-looking as well, with his mad hair and yellow teeth. He didn't have any social skills, but it obviously didn't bother him.

'I've talked to the Twisted Kids too,' Maxie went on. 'They grew up in the institute. Blue's right. You should be asking them stuff.'

'As they tell it,' said Blue, 'Wormold came home and when his wife got pregnant the disease mucked up the embryo and Fish-Face came out.'

'Very scientific, I'm sure,' said Einstein. 'You should write a paper: "Mucked-up embryos leading to fishness of the face".'

Maxie sucked in her breath. Einstein could be a real douche sometimes. Didn't worry at all about hurting anyone's feelings. Blue wasn't about to let Einstein get to him, though. As ever, he showed nothing.

But Maxie was glad Fish-Face wasn't there. She was the Green Man's daughter. She had a bizarre flattened head, her eyes forced round to the sides. Maxie didn't even know what the girl's real name was. It felt demeaning to call her Fish-Face, but that's what she chose. 'The Twisted Kids', as they called themselves, carried their mutations with pride. Blue said they even had their own song, but Maxie hadn't heard it. Wasn't sure she wanted to.

'If you don't listen,' Blue said to Einstein, 'how you ever gonna learn?'

'Theories, theories, theories,' said Einstein. 'There's no proof in any of this.'

'Didn't Einstein have a theory?' said Blue. 'The real Einstein? You gotta start somewhere.'

'Well, let's start in the big green, shall we?' said Einstein. 'Up the jungle without a paddle.'

'I was there,' said Wormwood. 'In the big green. I was there before I was the Green Man. I was there when I was wormwood the poison star, fallen from heaven.'

60

'Wait, stop, let me get this down,' said Einstein. 'This is scientific gold.'

'What is wormwood anyway?' said Blue.

'It's a poisonous plant,' said Einstein. '*Artemisia*. Brings on hallucinations if you eat it.'

'I reckon he must have eaten a whole forest of it,' said Blue, looking at the Green Man.

'It's in the Bible as well,' said Andy. Maxie had forgotten he was even there. She saw that he had a little Bible open in his hands. He must carry it around with him. She'd had no idea he was a God-botherer.

'The Book of Revelations.' Andy turned a page and began to read. '*The third angel sounded his trumpet, and a great star, blazing like a torch, fell from the sky on a third of the rivers and on the springs of water – the name of the star is Wormwood. A third of the waters turned bitter, and many people died from the waters that had become bitter.*'

'That kinda makes sense,' said Blue. 'Could be a description of the sickness.'

'That is not science!' Maxie had never seen Einstein get genuinely angry before. 'That's just a book. It's made-up stories. His name's Mark Wormold and his scrambled brains have picked up on a load of claptrap from the Bible and so now he's Wormwood, the death star.'

'Poison star,' said Andy.

'I was Wormwood, the exterminating angel, the great flea. I was king of the bats and bugs. That was long before I got into this broken body and stepped down from being a Starchild, became a human bean.'

Maxie had noticed the way the Green Man talked about himself almost as if he was two different people: the Mark Wormold part and the Green Man part. He was

like someone possessed, switching between two minds. A man possessed by the disease, as if it had a voice, a mind of its own.

'Forget all that,' said Einstein. 'Forget the jungle and the birds and the bees. Forget about the big green for a minute, can't you? Tell me about the blood.'

'My blood,' said Wormwood, 'is bad blood.'

'You can say that again.' Einstein had his eyebrows raised in a slightly camp way. 'And my blood?'

Wormwood made a dismissive noise.

'Not good. Not bad. It's just blood. It's everyday quaffing blood. A nice snack is all.'

'Charming.'

'Your blood couldn't drive out anything.'

'What about me?' said Blue. 'What about my blood?'

'The same, the same, the same. All of you. You need to find the good blood.'

'What for?' said Einstein. 'For you to drink?'

'No. To drive out the bad blood.'

'Do you mean like a kind of vaccine?' said Maxie. 'Are you saying that if we could find the right blood, the right kind of healthy blood, we could use it to fight the disease? Make a cure?'

'Oh, the girl's smarter than she looks.'

'Thanks,' said Maxie sarcastically.

'The girl's got the right idea,' said Wormwood. 'The good blood will drive out the bad.'

'Yeah, you can stop the love-in,' said Einstein. 'It's not like that's a new idea or anything. What do you think I've been doing here? Making cupcakes? All I need is some kid who's survived being bitten by a sicko. But so far I can't find any. Not any that stay alive.'

'There was one here,' said the Green Man. 'I could smell him when I arrived.'

'You mean Paul?' said Maxie. 'The kid who went crazy?'

'I don't know names. I'm just a wormy old ratbag of rot and decay. Don't throw names at me.'

'Is it possible Paul was bitten by one of your sickos?' said Maxie, using the museum kids' term. She knew that Einstein had kept some grown-ups for research, locked up out in the old car park, and it had been Paul's job to look after them.

'Possible,' said Einstein. 'That could explain why he went postal. But he's buggered off.'

'His blood was better,' said the Green Man. 'Smelt pretty good. But not the best. There's another, though.' He gave a sly smile. 'Best blood of all. Sweet and clean and pure and . . .'

'Another kid who was bitten, you mean?' said Blue.

'Not bitten, no. Born with the good blood.'

'A kid born with immunity?' said Maxie. 'Is that possible?'

'Anything's possible,' said Einstein. 'But the question is – who is it?'

'Not telling.' Wormwood twisted away, like a little boy with a secret. 'Not unless you give me something to eat.'

'We give you plenty to eat, you greedy bastard,' said Einstein. 'We've been feeding you three meals a day since you got here.'

'No,' said Wormwood petulantly. 'Something good to eat, the real sweet stuff.'

'That's enough,' said Blue moving towards the Green Man and raising the club he had with him. 'No way, man.'

63

'What's the matter?' said Andy, coming alive, sensing danger.

'He wants to eat one of us.'

'You must be able to spare one, a little one, a weak one. I need the flesh. I need the blood. My brain is going cloudy. Can't help you any more. The other ones. They fed me. They gave me sweet flesh.'

'Ed told me how he was kept locked up by the religious freaks at St Paul's,' said Maxie. 'Like you kept your grown-ups here. Only they fed him children.'

Einstein laughed. A couple of the other kids swore.

Maxie went over to the Green Man. 'We'll give you blood,' she said, feeling almost sorry for the pathetic creature. 'We'll give you the good blood, yeah? We'll try to cure you. You can be our guinea pig.'

'Yeah,' said Blue. 'You can be our crash-test bunny. But you're not eating no one. You so much as sniff one of our kids and I will cut your head off with a blunt knife. We'll inject you or whatever we have to do – you tell me. I ain't no scientist.' He gave a questioning look to Einstein. 'Help me out here. What do we do, make a serum?'

'Something like that.'

Blue walked closer to the Green Man, his club still raised, giving him the hard stare. 'You got that, wormhole?'

'You're cruel.' The Green Man shrank away, looking hurt and self-pitying. 'It's not fair. I'm an important person.'

'You're a tool. A green stain. Now tell us who it is. Who's got the good blood? Who was born with immunity?'

'I'm not telling you. You've been mean to me. I'll never tell you. Not unless you feed me properly.'

'I'll tell you,' said a voice and Maxie turned. It was Fish-Face. She'd come up to the Darwin Centre with some of

the younger kids. She was the shyest person Maxie had ever met. She twisted herself into contortions to keep her head turned away, staring at her shoes.

'Don't tell them,' said Wormwood. 'I need my good stuff.'

'You need a good kicking,' said Blue.

'How do you know?' Maxie asked Fish-Face. 'Did he tell you?'

'He didn't need to. I know everything he thinks. It's almost like we share one brain.'

'So who is it?'

Fish-Face didn't say anything, but Small Sam stepped forward.

'She says it's me,' he said.

Shadowman was shocked how close the main body of the grown-ups was. He and Jester hadn't gone far past the Bayswater Road, that ran along the north side of Hyde Park, when they'd come across the first sentinels standing, waiting patiently, unmoving, burning in the weak sun. Jester went a sickly pale green colour and started babbling about running, or fighting, or getting help – scared silly by these harmless outliers.

'These are nothing,' Shadowman said. 'You wait. These losers aren't anything to wet your knickers over.'

'You make me jumpy.' Jester's voice was tight and high-pitched. 'Pointing that crossbow at me all the time. I keep expecting at any moment to feel a bolt in my back.'

'So it's me you're scared of, yeah? Not the strangers?'

'I just wasn't expecting them so soon. It's been so quiet lately. We never see them round the palace.'

'That's why I wanted you to come and see,' said Shadowman. 'Or you wouldn't have believed me.'

'OK, well, I believe you now, so can we go back?'

'Nope. I want you to really see.'

So they pressed on, Jester moaning every step of the way. Half an hour later the two of them were peering round a corner and looking down a long, straight stretch

of Kilburn High Road, which ran roughly south to north. There were sentinels strung out all along it, closer together than Shadowman had seen before.

'OK. Point made,' said Jester. 'I can really see.' And he pulled back, worried about being spotted, even though the sentinels were completely ignoring the two of them.

'You don't listen,' said Shadowman, giving Jester a playful slap. 'This is nothing. I want to show you the hard stuff. I want to show you their army.'

'Do you have to?'

'There's a reason it's been quiet, Jester. There's something going on, man. We got to work out what.'

They'd been skirting round the edge of the main body. Moving slowly east and north, then west, in a wide circle. So far Shadowman's bad leg was holding up. He was only limping slightly and apart from a dull ache he could ignore it most of the time. He was trying to get a fix on how many strangers there might be and exactly where their centre was. He was also looking for a high point where he could get a good view of them. He didn't want to go blundering in any deeper without full reconnaissance. The outliers were harmless. He knew it wouldn't be the same story when they got closer to the pack.

It had been the same all the way, for street after street – sentinels standing facing outwards. Occasionally they came across a lone stranger, or a small group of them, stumbling in past the sentinels, drawn from God knows how far away. These walkers might be more dangerous, so Shadowman kept Jester well away from them, hiding in gardens, behind walls, watching. As far as Shadowman could see, though, even the walkers weren't interested. They just wanted to get to where they were going. Like

festival-goers heading for the main stage. Except there was no noise. No sense of a huge crowd. It was like there was just a big black hole. Shadowman knew they were there. The main body of them. They had to be. And there had to be a lot of them. But what were they doing?

'Why's it so important to see them close up?' Jester asked for the tenth time, and Shadowman decided to answer him.

'Why, why, why? Don't you get anything, Doctor Why? You're so tied up at the palace with your plans and your schemes and worrying about what other kids are doing, you've not been watching the match. You're on the wrong channel even. You've forgotten who the enemy is. But they're in there. Grown-ups, strangers, oppoes, sickos, bastards – whatever you want to call them – to me they're just the enemy.'

'And when we've seen the enemy?' Jester whined. '*Then* what?'

'I'll let you know. I'll text you, yeah? For now you're safe, though. OK? This lot aren't gonna attack. They're too busy talking to God. Even the ones in there . . .' Shadowman nodded towards where he knew the main body must be. 'Even they must be sleeping now. We've only seen sickos heading into the centre – none coming out.'

'You're enjoying this, aren't you?' said Jester. 'You're getting a big kick out of it.'

'Not really. But at least I feel at home here. Since you abandoned me at King's Cross, apart from the last few days when I've been resting up and waiting for my leg to stop hurting, this is where I've been, out on the streets, with this lot. Living alongside them day after day, watching them grow stronger, grow smarter. I understand them, yeah? I

understand how they live, how they hunt, how they work together. I understand how dangerous they are.'

'So do I,' said Jester wearily. 'OK? I mean, you've, like, made your point.'

'No, I haven't. I keep telling you – these ones are dopes. They're not dangerous.'

Shadowman had spotted a tall building some way along the Kilburn High Road. He wanted to get a better look at it.

'There,' he said. 'That's what we've been looking for.'

'What?'

Shadowman pointed to where a tall grey tower jutted up into the sky and they started to walk. Pushing past the still and silent sentinels. Jester stuck close to him, muttering under his breath, shaking with fear. They saw evidence of feeding, bones and bits of skin and hair, bloody clothing, lying in the streets, but the scraps looked old and there surely wasn't enough food around to feed them all. They must have cleaned out the area for miles around.

And then stopped.

As they got closer, Shadowman saw that the tower was part of an old building that looked like it might once have been a cinema, built in the days when cinemas were a big deal. The tower must have been at least thirty metres high, and the word STATE, in big red letters, was spelled out on each face. Indeed, it looked like a miniature version of the Empire State Building in New York.

The building hadn't been a cinema for some time by the look of it. Its last incarnation had been as a church of some sort, and the doors at the front were boarded up. Shadowman took his crowbar from his pack and easily removed a

couple of boards, then used the bar to smash the glass doors behind. The sentinels standing nearby ignored them completely, just stood there, blissed out, at one with the sky.

'You don't think all this noise is going to attract more of them?' said Jester. 'I mean, you're the one keeps going on about how dangerous they are.'

'I can feel it, Jester,' said Shadowman. 'They're not buzzing. It's like they're dormant. Waiting.'

'What for?'

'Keep telling you. I don't know.'

'And I thought you knew everything.'

'I know enough. Come on.' Shadowman took out his friction torch and went through the broken door. Inside it was like a palace, with painted walls and ceilings, columns and pillars, chandeliers and a great marble staircase. The vast auditorium was even grander, large enough to seat at least four thousand people. Shadowman's torch could only give them glimpses of it.

'Cool,' he said. 'This is like that scene in *Alien* where they go inside the alien spaceship, and they're like ants in there.'

'Nice image,' said Jester sourly. 'Alien, yeah. And next minute some face-hugger is gonna jump out and rape us.'

'There's no strangers in here,' said Shadowman. 'I'd smell 'em.'

He'd have loved to explore more, but there was work to be done. It took them a while to find their way up into the tower, and they had to break open two more doors. The stairs were dusty and half blocked with old bits and pieces that had been dumped there years ago. They eventually made their way to the top, though, to where the windows gave them a 360-degree view. Once they'd wiped off the

dust and grime and crap, they were able to look out over London.

'There,' said Shadowman after a few seconds of scanning the area. 'That's what I wanted to show you.'

'What?' Jester was squinting and frowning. 'I can't see anything, only . . . Oh Jesus . . .'

A few streets away was what looked like a cemetery, and it was filled with black, greasy bodies, all pressed and huddled together, radiating out from a central spot in great concentric circles. Shadowman knew what would be in the middle. St George, with his lieutenants.

From the cemetery the bodies spilt out into the surrounding streets, densely packed at first, but thinning out the further they got from the hub. That was why Jester hadn't spotted them at first. A black hole was the right description. They were an awful dark stain, like an infestation of insects, packed in so tightly they must be on top of each other.

'Jesus,' said Jester again. 'There must be a thousand of them. Five thousand. Ten. How could you even count them? It must be every stranger in London. But what are they doing? What are they eating?'

'They're not eating,' said Shadowman. 'Food doesn't seem to matter so much to them at the moment. They're getting ready for something. Something more important.'

'Like what?'

'Next stage of the disease maybe. They're massing. For some event. Like salmon before they spawn.'

'You talk like they're organized.'

'They are,' said Shadowman. 'In the middle of all that, like a queen bee in her hive, is the king of the strangers. A mean, ugly, vicious killer I call St George. He has the

71

power to make them do whatever he wants. They'd follow him over a cliff if that's where he was going.'

'No such luck, I guess.'

'He's planning something, and walking off a cliff isn't it.'

'So he's intelligent?'

'It's a sort of intelligence. An animal intelligence. A hive mind.'

'How does he do it then?' said Jester. 'How's he communicate with them? Can he, like, talk?'

'It's more of a mind-control thing. Secret signals, ultrasound. I don't know. I haven't figured it out.'

'But we might be able to communicate with him?'

Shadowman looked at Jester. 'Why would you want to do that?'

'I don't know,' said Jester. 'We could negotiate with him.'

Shadowman let out a burst of laughter. 'Negotiate?' he snorted. 'What are you talking about? You don't negotiate with dangerous animals. You kill them. It's simple.'

'Or we could just leave them alone. Let them do their thing and die.'

'Didn't you hear me?' Shadowman shook Jester. 'They're getting ready for something. And you've seen enough of how strangers are to know that it won't be nice. We have to stop them.'

'Stop them? Stop that lot? Are you nuts? Look at them. They're an army.'

'And how do you stop an army?' said Shadowman.

'You don't,' said Jester. 'You run away.'

'No,' said Shadowman, wishing Jester wasn't being so deliberately dumb. 'You create your own army, and you take the battle to them. You beat them, Jester. Imagine that, if we could destroy this lot. You said it yourself –

that's every stranger in London. And we could wipe them out. They've made it easier for us. They're all in one place.'

'Except,' said Jester, 'we attack them, they're liable to get up off their arses and fight back.'

'We can do it,' said Shadowman. 'We can take them down.'

'What?' said Jester mockingly. 'Us two?'

'It's possible,' said Shadowman, ignoring Jester's joke. 'If we got an army together.'

'Don't be stupid. Look at them.' Jester banged the window. 'Look at them . . .'

Shadowman looked. The thought of taking on that lot was terrible. He could imagine the stink they generated. The heat. All those rotting bodies oozing pus. He pictured himself standing with a pitifully small army of children as the sickos came on.

Too many to count, Jester had said. Too many to kill . . .

'We can't fight them,' Jester whispered, shaking his head.

'We can,' Shadowman shouted, trying to drown out his own doubts and fears. 'Scattered around London there are hundreds of kids. They just need to be united, persuaded to join together. If we did that we could win.'

'Where do we start?'

'Come on. Let's go.' Shadowman jerked his head at Jester and they made their way back down the stairs, through the cinema and out of the front.

There were two sentinels outside, who hadn't been there before. Shadowman ignored them. Started walking north. The rotten stink of strangers seemed heavier in the air.

'What about David?' Jester asked after a couple of minutes. He'd obviously been thinking about what Shadowman had said.

'What about him?' said Shadowman.

'He's gonna want to be in charge.'

'That jerk?' Shadowman laughed. 'He knows sod all about war. He lucked out getting into the palace before anyone else. Took control by lying and cheating and dumping on other kids. What would he know about taking on an army like that?'

'That's what I meant,' said Jester. 'He won't go along with it. Won't want anyone else telling him what to do.'

'Then maybe I'll sneak into Buckingham Palace and slit his chicken throat one night.'

'You wouldn't . . .'

'Wouldn't I? You'll need to watch your back, Jester. Sleep lightly. This isn't over.'

Jester stopped walking. 'Leave it out, Shadow,' he said. 'I know you're kidding.'

'Do you?' Shadowman raised his crossbow.

Jester sighed. Blew his breath out from between puffed cheeks. He'd had enough.

'Let's go back now, yeah?' he pleaded.

'Nope. We've one more thing to do today.'

'I am *done*,' said Jester wearily.

Shadowman spotted something over Jester's shoulder and walked close to him, put his face right in the boy's face.

'This isn't about you,' he hissed.

'No? I thought this was national kick Jester's arse day. What *is* it about then?'

'That.' Shadowman pointed back down the road and Jester turned to look.

A group of strangers was walking towards them, their stink filling the street, thick and almost physical. Jester swallowed, looked like he wanted to puke.

'We need to run,' he said.

'Uh-uh.' Shadowman held him in place. 'Look at them. They're rubbish. They don't want to eat. They're catatonic. Zombies.'

'Zombies . . .'

'Harmless ones.'

The strangers seemed to be wandering aimlessly. Shadowman stood his ground. Testing them. Testing Jester. He wanted to rub his face in it. Make him understand – This was it. This was this.

The strangers, a mix of mothers, fathers and older teenagers, were filthy, black with grease and dirt. Most of them were bald. One or two had clumps of hair that was long and matted. All were diseased, bits missing, skin made inhuman by boils and growths and sores – eaten away by open, weeping wounds. How they were still alive at all was a mystery. Some sort of invisible puppet strings were keeping them upright as they came shuffling on.

'OK,' said Jester, and he was trembling, his face covered in sweat. 'You've made your point. This is crazy. We need to fight or we need to run. Let's run, yeah? Let's go home.'

Shadowman held him still until the strangers were right upon them. They parted as they came close and then brushed past. Not interested.

'We're going,' said Shadowman. 'But we're not going home.'

'Where then?' The relief on Jester's face when the strangers had simply walked past was comical.

'We're going shopping,' said Shadowman.

'Shopping? Where?'

'IKEA.'

Ollie was in the library at the museum, sitting on the floor reading a book, or at least trying to read a book. Actually he was doing no more than pretending to read a book. He was listening to what was going on at the big central table. The boy in charge here, Chris Marker, who was dressed a bit like a monk, was quizzing Small Sam.

'I'm trying to get your story down,' he was saying, a hint of exasperation in his voice. 'It's important we collect everybody's story. We have to keep a record for the future. But I'm finding it hard to believe a single word of what you're telling me. You mustn't make stories up.'

'It's the God's own truth,' said Sam's peculiar friend, The Kid. 'The God's own, boy's own, frogspawn truth. Straight from the horse's arse and smelling of roses. This boy couldn't lie if you paid him. He is a truth machine.'

Ollie grinned to himself. He liked The Kid, even though he talked in his own weird way. In fact, that was probably *why* he liked him. The Kid looked at the world differently to everyone else. Maybe that's why he was still alive.

Ollie was only here because he was looking after Lettis. He'd saved her life and she'd latched on to him, wouldn't let him out of her sight. Wherever he went, she had to go.

And wherever she went he had to go. She liked coming here. To the library. She'd been helping Chris Marker write down the stories before, but now, although she wrote obsessively in her own leather-bound journal, she never let anyone else see it.

She'd been nearly mute since the attack, when a bunch of grown-ups had cornered her in a church, and had a permanently haunted, broken look in her eyes. Ollie wasn't sure she'd ever really recover. She was sitting next to Small Sam at the table, staring at him with her big, black-rimmed eyes. Next to her was The Kid, and next to him was another girl, who was called Charlotte or by her nickname, Yo-Yo. She carried a violin around with her in a case all the time. She'd played it one night, in the main hall before bedtime. She wasn't bad, not exactly a child prodigy, but good enough to make everyone stop what they were doing and applaud her. You never heard much music these days unless someone played a real instrument. Without electricity, all the world's digital music had disappeared.

That night, in the main hall, Ollie had sat out of the way in the shadows and wept when he'd heard the violin, the notes echoing up and away into the vast open space of the hall. He'd wept for everything they'd lost, and he'd wept for how clever mankind had once been, composing beautiful music, creating beautiful instruments, teaching children to play, creating machines to preserve it . . .

'Let's go back over what you've told me.' Chris Marker was looking down at the big book he'd been writing in. 'You were captured while you were playing in the car park behind the Waitrose supermarket.'

'Yes. Some grown-ups got over the wall.'

'And they took you to the Arsenal football stadium, where you managed to escape by starting a fire that burned the whole place down.'

'I didn't mean to,' said Sam. 'It just happened.'

'OK. Then, trying to find your friends, you went down into the underground tunnels at Camden Town tube station, where you were taken in by two people who weren't diseased but turned out to be cannibals.'

'That's where I come in,' said The Kid. 'To the rescue remedy! Look up! Look down! Is it a plane? Is it a James Bond? Is it Superman? No, it's the mighty Kid! Bravo! He'll save Sam from the clutches of the evil child-eaters!'

'They were horrible,' said Sam. 'They pretended to be friends. They only stayed healthy by eating children and keeping out of the light.'

'I got him out of there,' said The Kid. 'Make sure you write that bit. I ain't never been in no reading book before, skipper. I was the hero, Robert De Niro, William Shakespearo! Walking on the beaches, looking at the peaches.'

Chris Marker gave The Kid a look that said, 'You're not really helping.'

'And so you both went to the Tower of London,' he said. 'I wish I'd been able to talk to Ed before he left, and get his side of the story.'

'It's the greatest story ever told,' said The Kid. 'It's got thrills and spills and kill bills. And it's got *me* in it. That's the good bit. You are writing it, aren't you?'

'Ed would've told you the same story,' said Sam. 'I'm not making it up. He found us and took us in at the Tower of London.'

'OK,' said Chris, looking at his book again. 'And you say you left the Tower to go and look for your sister, but

some kids at St Paul's took you in because they thought you were a god.'

Sam giggled. 'I know it sounds stupid.'

'You had to be there,' said The Kid.

'I *was* there,' said Yo-Yo. 'It's all true. Mad Matt was in charge. He's made up this, like, crazy religion.'

Chris put down his pen, rubbed his face.

'You know what, Chris?' said Ollie, getting up and walking over to the table. 'This whole world's gone crazy. Sam's story doesn't sound any more nuts than what the rest of us have been through. It's just we've sort of got used to it. We've accepted that this is how things are now.'

'Maybe.'

'And now they're saying that Sam might have the cure for the disease in him,' said Yo-Yo.

Ollie looked at Chris with raised eyebrows and Chris started to laugh. It was an alarming noise, like a donkey sucking in air to breathe. It was a rusty, sticky, awkward laugh. The laugh of someone who hardly ever used it. Chris was usually so serious, quiet and introverted; now he looked like any other boy. Just laughing.

'This whole thing's a massive wind-up, isn't it?' he said once he'd taken control of himself.

'Fish-Face and the others said it,' said Yo-Yo.

'Fish-Face!' Chris blurted and that set him off laughing again.

Yo-Yo looked upset, as if she thought Chris was laughing at *her*.

'She did!' she pressed on angrily. 'She said her father, the Green Man, had seen it in him when he first met him. He's scared of Sam.'

'Sam has it in him,' said The Kid. 'Was born with it.

Like some people are born with immunity to the plague, or the yellow fever, or the red death or the purple rose. He has the cure, the magic medicine; he's got the immunity in his blood . . . He's bloody fantastic.'

Chris looked at Ollie, suddenly serious, a kind of desperate hope in his eyes.

'Do they know how to make an antidote out of it?' he said.

'I don't know,' said Ollie and he shrugged. 'If the Green Man and Einstein and everyone else can work together maybe they can do it. We just have to hope nothing happens to Sam in the meantime. And the way his life has gone . . .'

Chris stared at Sam. He was sitting there, looking terribly young and breakable. Did everything rest on this little kid?

'I hope this is a true story,' said Ollie.

'It is,' said The Kid. 'With a happy ending and everything. The End. Kiss goodnight. Out goes the light, sleep tight, don't let the bedbugs bite.'

'Don't worry,' said Ollie. 'We're gonna turn this thing around. You make sure that's a book about winners, not losers, Chris. About heroes who save the world!'

'It's not up to me,' said Chris. 'I just write stuff down.'

'Either you tell me what we're doing or I'm going back by myself,' said Jester.

Having survived his close encounter of the scary kind with the strangers outside the cinema, now that they were on emptier streets with only the odd stray sentinel to remind them of the threat, Jester was growing brave. Brave and whingey. Moan, moan, bloody moan. Shadowman was tempted to shoot him in the leg with a crossbow bolt and really give him something to moan about. What made it worse for Shadowman was that his own leg was aching, his ankle sore as hell and throbbing with every step. He was worried that he was overdoing it and would be crippled again when their little expedition was over. He had to press on, though. He wasn't coming up this way again in a hurry if he could help it. He had to get everything sorted now.

'You're not going anywhere without me,' he said.

'No?'

'No. My city, my rules, Magic-Man.'

'At least tell me where we're going.'

'I told you. We're going to IKEA.'

'Well, that's just fine. I really need some tea lights, a bookcase called Twat and a lamp you can't fit any normal bulbs into.'

'Just shut your mouth for a bit, yeah?'

'Look, you've made your point, Shadow. You've given me a big scare. Well, I'm sorry I didn't dump a load in my pants, but I hope you feel we're quits now.'

'Quits? Are you joking me? Quits? How can we ever be quits? You left me to die. All I've done is show you the enemy. If I didn't need you to spread the word I'd happily kill you, brother.'

'That would be *so* unreasonable,' said Jester. 'You are so totally overreacting.'

'Overreacting, my arse.'

'Yeah, overreacting, your arse.'

Shadowman strode up to Jester and threw him to the ground. Aimed his crossbow at the middle of his smug face.

'How about I make it proper quits?' he said. 'How about I club you round the head so you can't stand up? And then drag you back there and leave you with the stranger army as a plaything? Would that make you happy? Would that be a reasonable response?'

'I didn't do anything on purpose,' said Jester. 'I was thinking of the good of the majority . . . and anyway.' He looked properly angry now. 'And anyway *you survived*. You're all right. So can we just get this over with and go back to civilization?'

'Can I trust you, Jester?'

'Of course.'

'Can I trust you to back me up? To tell David what we've seen. Get him to unite with the other camps around London?'

'Yes.'

'Right. It's just if you ever let me down again, if you

turn this around somehow, if you don't do the right thing, I will definitely kill you. OK?'

'I believe it. So will you tell me why we're going to IKEA?'

'There's someone I need to talk to. Only problem is, he's a bigger jerk than you.'

The two museums were side by side. The Natural History Museum was crammed with the wonders of the natural world. The Science Museum was crammed with the wonders of the man-made world. And Ben and Bernie were in no doubt about which one they found the most interesting.

The Science Museum was like Disneyland for them. They'd come through the 'Energy Hall', 'Exploring Space', and were now in 'The Making of the Modern World', bug-eyed at the technology on show. Cars and engines and planes, clocks and computers, spaceships, steam trains and motorbikes. Jackson had shown them the way through from next door and was escorting them, just in case. Nobody from the Natural History Museum had come in here for ages.

'Is this where this stuff belongs now?' she asked them. 'In a museum? Will we ever be able to get back to where we were? Make all this stuff and get it to work again?'

'We can do it,' said Bernie. She was dressed all in black. They both were, with goth black hair hanging over their faces. Some kids called them the emos, but Jackson didn't think that many emos were into science and engineering. As far as she was concerned, they weren't emos or goths. They weren't punks or pinheads, nerds, geeks . . . they weren't

anything. They were just themselves. Two kids who got off on technology and how things worked. And what was wrong with that? Kids like Ben and Bernie were going to be just as important as fighters like Achilleus and herself if they were ever going to put the world back together again. So she was staying close. Looking after them. Making sure they didn't wind up as some sicko's breakfast.

She smiled as they ran from one exhibit to another, like two kids in a sweet shop, their faces beaming.

'So you can make this stuff work, then?' she asked.

'Some of it,' said Ben. 'The rest we can figure out. There are books here, papers, files, manuals.'

Jackson couldn't help making a face. She'd always hated reading manuals. Not that she ever *did* read them. They filled her with horror. But she was glad that there were some people who liked them. Positively enjoyed studying them.

'There's everything we need here to rebuild,' said Bernie.

'As long as we don't get wiped out,' said Jackson.

'That's where you come in,' said Bernie. 'You fight off the enemy while we try to get the engine started. We've all got jobs to do. We'll look after the technology – you can look after the ass-kicking.'

Jackson laughed. 'Is that all I'm good for?'

'We need all the skills there are,' said Ben. 'That's how it works. No use us all being engineers, and no use us all being warriors either. But one's no use without the other.'

Jackson wasn't listening. Her radar had come on. Months of being at the ready, of tracking and killing sickos, had sharpened her senses, conditioned her. She was a dog with its ears up now and realized that Bernie was looking at her funnily.

'You all right?' she asked. 'What's up?'

Jackson sniffed, closed her eyes to concentrate better.

'No,' she said. 'Not all right. They're in here. They've got in.'

Bernie swore. Jackson opened her eyes and quickly scanned the area.

'Do you want me to take you back?' she said.

'No,' said Ben bluntly. 'We don't. It has to be safe in here. We have to be able to come in when we want. We've got work to do. We need to figure out how to use these machines. If there are grown-ups in here we're going to help you get rid of them.'

'Are we?' said Bernie. '*Really?* Don't you think you might have checked with me first?'

Ben and Bernie were both armed with clubs, Jackson had insisted on it, but they weren't fighters.

'We'll find out what we're up against,' said Jackson. 'But if there's too many of them we'll get out fast and come back with a proper fighting unit.'

'How many's too many?' asked Ben.

'Like, *one*,' said Bernie.

'I'll let you know,' said Jackson. 'But if I start running you get right behind me.'

'Don't worry,' said Bernie. 'We'll be in front.'

Jackson followed her nose and her instinct and they slowly, slowly, moved through the museum. They passed a display of computers and an ancient Mini that had been cut in half to show its workings, a porcelain bowl rescued from Hiroshima after the first atomic bomb dropped . . .

She had to admit she felt nervous, not so much for herself but for the other two. She didn't want to be responsible for losing their engineers. If it kicked off big time they wouldn't be as fast as her, despite what Bernie

had said. The emos had made it this far without coming to any harm, so they couldn't be completely hopeless, but, even so, she wished she'd brought along more backup.

What she really wished was that she could have brought Achilleus along. Perfect excuse. *No.* She had to stop thinking about that boy. He was bad news. Arrogant, rude, ugly. Why was she so attracted to those types? The bad ones. Was it that she thought the nice, good-looking ones wouldn't be interested in her? Except Achilleus wasn't interested in her either. Good joke. She'd keep on trying, though. It had driven her mother spare, the boys she came home with. One had been four years older than her and had stolen her mum's purse.

'You are not to see him again!'

Jackson had always ignored anything her mother had to say. She'd been a bit of a bitch to her, if you wanted the God's own truth. And after Dad had left home her mum hadn't ever really had any control over her. The harder she'd tried to put Jackson in pretty dresses and get her to grow her hair long, the more Jackson had dressed like a boy and cut her hair short. She did it herself in the bathroom mirror with a pair of scissors. She'd always fancied getting a razor cut like Achilleus; maybe she'd ask him to do one for her.

Concentrate, girl. Mind on the matter.

'There.' Jackson stopped and pointed at an Apollo rocket capsule.

Something had made a nest in there. There was movement. Whatever it was – and Jackson had a pretty good idea what that might be – it appeared to be sleeping.

She carefully checked out the nearby area. Seemed all clear. You could never be too careful, though.

'We're going to scare it out,' she said.

'Are we?' said Bernie.

'You know you asked how many was too many?'

'Yeah.'

'This isn't it. *This* I can handle. Best to get it now while we've got it cornered.'

'If you say so.'

Jackson could see both kids shaking. The emos were scared. She was scared. It never went away.

'What do we do?' said Bernie.

'Like I said. Scare it out. Wake the mother up.'

Ben and Bernie started to bang on the sides of the pod. At last a head appeared at the open door, confused more than dangerous. It *was* a mother, with a puffy, swollen head, all her hair missing, most of her teeth – which they saw when she opened her mouth wide at them, half a yawn, half a silent snarl – one eye gone and half her nose. She crawled out from her nest. She had a big upper body but shrivelled, skinny legs that could hardly support her. Her arms had swollen up like balloons. She was a balloon animal with deflated legs.

Luckily she appeared to be alone. Abandoned. She limped and shuffled towards Jackson, mouth stretching open and closed, open and closed. She stank. All she had on was some filthy underwear, unchanged in a year, and her body was a mess. Jackson didn't want to look at her any longer than she had to.

Jackson didn't want to touch her either, if she could help it. Didn't want to have to heave her horrible, diseased body outside and dump it in some far back alley to rot in peace.

'Come on,' she said, beckoning to the mother. 'Come to Jackson. There's a good mother. Follow me.'

As she backed away, spear held out at the ready, she called over to the emos.

'Check the pod for any more of them.'

They moved in quickly, prodding and poking around.

'Nothing.'

'Then let's get out of here. We're going to walk this lady into the courtyard where we can get some help to deal with her.'

'We're with you.'

They went back down the length of the galleries, the mother blinking in the light from the tall windows at the end of the building. But still she came on, a rope of saliva slowly lowering from her mouth, swaying from side to side as she walked. Ben and Bernie followed along behind, keeping a safe distance from her, but prodding her if she stopped.

Jackson made her way to the door that led outside. She wasn't sure the mother would want to go out into the daylight so once she'd opened the door she switched places with Ben and Bernie. They went out as bait and she persuaded the mother to follow them by sticking the point of her spear into her back, causing little buttons of blood to well up.

At last the mother stumbled out and stood there in the courtyard between the two museums, shrinking from the sun, screwing up her face. Blisters were already starting to appear on her forehead. She was burning easily.

'She needs to put some sunblock on,' said Bernie and she giggled with relief. There were other kids around and already some were walking over to see what was going on.

There was a small group of younger kids over by the chicken runs, holding back. Some bigger kids were hanging round the lorry where Einstein had kept the captive

sickos he used for his experiments. Before they'd got out and caused havoc in the library, that is.

Jackson called over to the younger kids. 'Get inside. We've got a live sicko here.'

The little kids didn't need to be told twice, but two of the older ones from the lorry joined a group that was approaching.

'Give me a hand here,' Jackson shouted to them. 'We need to kill this mother.'

'No, wait!' said one of the kids. 'We need sickos. Can you get her on to the lorry?'

'Not without some help.'

'I'll round up a team. How many do you need?'

'The more the merrier.'

'No prob. Keep her here and don't damage her if you can.'

Damage her? Jackson hated sickos. Killed them whenever she had the opportunity, but she had to admit she felt almost sorry for this one. How much pain must she be in, her body wrecked and ruined like that? And now she was going to be held captive like an animal. Einstein would take her blood, inject her with stuff and generally use her like a lab monkey.

'Are they sure about this?' said Ben, staring at the mother, who was whimpering and cringing from the sun.

'Nothing to do with me,' said Jackson. 'You said it. I'm just a warrior. I'm not an engineer like you, and I'm certainly not a scientist like Einstein. It was down to me I'd put her out of her misery. But it's not. She's Einstein's baby now. Once she's safely locked up on the lorry I'll take a crew in and we'll make a proper sweep of the Science Museum. And after that . . . ? The future's all yours.'

This guy, Saif, was slumped in a big armchair like he was some doomed king sitting in his throne on the cover of a fantasy novel. His long, curly black hair was hanging down around his dark face which wore an expression that was presumably meant to be brooding and slightly menacing but came across as grumpy and just a little stupid.

He was eyeing up Shadowman and Jester. Had been for some time. Being dramatic, theatrically stringing out the wait. Jester was trying not to laugh.

'So you're back,' Saif said at last, fixing his eyes on Shadowman.

They were in the main living quarters inside IKEA. The local kids had used all the furniture here to make a recognizable sort of home, and this more open, central area was done out like a throne room.

'I'm back,' said Shadowman. 'And this is . . . someone who's come with me.' Jester smiled. Shadowman couldn't bring himself to describe him as his friend.

'Someone who's come with you?'

'Pleased to meet you,' said Jester, putting on his most open smile. 'Shadowman's told me all about you.'

Indeed, he had. He'd told Jester all about how he'd

brought one of Saif's fighters back here after he was wounded by St George's army. How he'd tried to warn Saif about St George and how Saif had ignored him and attacked the grown-ups anyway. Like Jester, he hadn't believed that 'zombies', as he called them, could get organized.

And then Shadowman had told Jester how he'd watched the whole thing unfold from a vantage point high up on a crane. Watched Saif's guys being massacred. Hadn't even been sure whether Saif himself had got away.

Well, he had. And here he was. Large as life.

'What did he tell you about me?' Saif said.

'He told me what a great set-up you have here,' said Jester. 'What awesome fighters you are.' Jester was good at this sort of thing. Diplomacy. Shadowman had agreed to leave him to it.

'You got a name?' Said asked.

'Most people call me Jester.'

'That right?'

'Yup.'

'Well, "*Jester*", did he also tell you how we didn't listen to him?'

'He did, yeah. He saw what happened to you actually.'

'That right?'

'Yeah.'

'And he's come back to rub it in, has he? "I told you so," and all that crap?'

'No,' said Jester. 'Not at all. He's come back to offer you revenge, as it goes.'

'Revenge on what?'

'Revenge on the zombies who killed your friends.'

'You two are an army, are you? You some kind of superman, Jester? You gonna take them down all by yourself?'

'No,' said Jester. 'But there are lots of kids in the centre of town. And they all want the same thing as you.'

'That right?'

'Yes,' said Shadowman. Jester could see that he was growing impatient. 'That's right.'

Jester read the situation. Saif had shown himself to be a fool last time. Hadn't listened to Shadowman. And now he was trying to save face. Shadowman was running out of patience. Perhaps the time for diplomacy was over.

'We can make our own army,' said Shadowman, 'and destroy St George once and for all.'

'We've been keeping spies on them,' said another boy, and Shadowman nodded at him in a friendly way.

'You all right, Dan?' he said.

'I'm cool.'

Shadowman had told Jester that Dan had been about the only kid here who'd been nice to him, after Shadowman has rescued Dan's friend, Johnny.

'So you know they've stopped moving?' said Shadowman.

'Yeah,' said Dan. 'They been camped up in Kilburn cemetery for days now. They ain't going nowhere.'

'They will, though,' said Shadowman. 'When they're ready.'

'Yeah?' said Saif, with a sneer. 'You know that, do you? Oh, I forgot. You close with them suckers. You almost one of them.'

'I know them,' said Shadowman. 'And, yeah, maybe I will rub it in just a little bit. You behaved like an arsehole last time, Saif; you completely ignored me. I was right, and you were wrong. That's the truth. I'm surprised they let you stay in charge, to be honest. How many of your people did you get killed?'

Saif jumped up from his chair and stalked over to Shadowman. He ended up about a centimetre away, eyeballing him, trying to make him back down. Jester would have lasted five seconds. Shadowman didn't even blink.

'Well, I *am* in charge here,' said Saif. 'Was never any argument. Because there's no one better.'

'In that case you're gonna be smart enough to listen to me this time,' said Shadowman. 'You show me some respect, I'll show you some.'

Shadowman held his hand out to Saif. Saif stared down at it for a long moment, then laughed and shook it hard and quick.

'What you want from me, hard man?' he said.

'Right now St George is waiting for something,' said Shadowman. 'He's not given up. He's growing stronger. Getting ready. I just know that when he's ready he's gonna make his move.'

'And do what?'

'That I don't know. But I hope that before he does we've got time to unite all the kids in London. To create our own army and be ready to take him on.'

'And where do I come in?'

'There may be things that come up and we'll need your help, but for now I want you to carry on doing what you're doing. Keep watch on him. And when he does move I want you to come into town and tell us. And then I want you to stand next to us. Stand up and fight them.'

15

'Come on, line up straight. You don't look like soldiers, you look like a useless bunch of little kids.'

Wiki giggled. 'I don't mean to disrespect you, Paddy,' he said. 'But we *are* a bunch of little kids.'

'You won't be when I've finished with you,' said Paddy. He hated his troop talking back to him. 'We're going to lead the children's crusade and help wipe the sickos off the planet.'

He was strutting up and down in front of the ragged line of kids, waving one of Akkie's spears around. Trying to act like an officer. Trying to kick them into shape. His troop. The troop he called the Youngbloods.

His dog was sitting patiently nearby, watching him as he walked up and down, her tongue hanging out. It was a warm day.

For now he was calling her Bright Eyes, because most of the others refused to call her Ripper. When he thought of a better name for her, he'd change it.

Standing in the front line of his troop were Sam and The Kid, then Yo-Yo, and Zohra with her little brother, Froggie. Then Jibber-jabber and Wiki and Blu-Tack Bill. Behind them, in a second rank, were some of the other kids who'd come from Holloway and a bunch of the

smaller kids from the museum. They were twenty in all, and none of them were any good at being soldiers. Blu-Tack Bill was the worst. He had no interest in drilling or fighting, or even standing still. He kept wandering off or sitting down. Paddy had got quite cross with him at first and shouted at him several times. Once he'd realized it wasn't going to make any difference, and that nothing he said or did was going to make Bill keep in step with everyone else, he'd just been ignoring him.

The Kid was probably the keenest, but that didn't make him the best. Somehow he got everything wrong or misunderstood or took it the wrong way, and the harder he tried, the keener he was, the worse he got. Paddy was ignoring him now as well. The thing was – Paddy didn't really know what he was doing himself. He tried to give orders, but he'd only picked them up from watching war films and playing computer games. He didn't really know what most of the commands meant and he kept forgetting how he'd used them before, and ended up giving the same command to mean something completely different. He just hoped the troop didn't notice.

He got them marching, shouting things at them like 'assume the position', 'blue on blue', 'present arms', 'extraction point', 'watch your six' and 'fubar'.

'Can't we just do some fighting?' Sam asked when they stopped for a rest. 'Drilling's boring and a waste of time. What difference does it make if we can march in step with each other? Or put our spears on our shoulders at the same time? That won't help us in a battle.'

'It's all about discipline, soldier,' said Paddy. 'It's about making you obey orders quickly without having to think.'

'But if a grown-up's attacking me I can't wait for an

order to defend myself. I'll just do it, surely? And anyway the orders don't make any sense. Eyes right and slope arms and fire in the hole. What we need to learn is how to use our weapons properly.'

'All right, all right. We'll do that. We'll do some more drilling tomorrow.'

'Tomorrow?' said Wiki. 'You mean we've got to do this every day?'

'Of course we've got to do this every day. How else are you going to learn to be soldiers otherwise?'

'Actually I don't really want to be a soldier,' said Wiki.

'Me neither,' said Jibber-jabber. 'It's boring.'

'But we're going to fight now.'

'Fighting's boring too.'

'I like fighting,' said The Kid. 'The old one two, in out in, snickersnee, snickers bar, have at thee, varlet, I regret that I have but one life to give, they don't like it up 'em, Ken clean-air system, whammo!' The Kid illustrated this outburst by throwing some fighting moves and fake punches that scared no one.

'Yeah,' said Paddy. 'What he said. Probably. Let's do it then. Fall in!'

Nobody moved.

'I'm really confused now,' said Sam. 'I can't remember what we're supposed to do when you shout "fall in", and the more you shout it, the less sense it makes.'

They were outside the museum, over to the west side, in front of the new extension. Sam could see the huge white concrete pod thing behind its high glass wall, and right up there at the top was where Einstein and his team of scientists were trying to find a cure for the disease.

Sam had been really freaked out when the Green Man

had said that he was the one who would save them, that he had something in his blood that could fight the disease. The Green Man said he could smell it. Had known it from the start. Sam had never wanted to be special, never wanted to be different. All he wanted was to find Ella and for the two of them to be safe together. Other kids looked at him funnily now, and he knew the older ones, the fighters, were trying to protect him. Einstein had taken some of his blood. He hadn't liked that at all. He didn't like needles. He didn't like blood, even though he'd seen buckets of it this past year. And worse. Somehow it was different when it was your own. Einstein had made very sure everything was clean and sterilized and used a load of antiseptic and a brand-new needle. Sam had no idea what they were going to do with his blood, but they were up there now, working away.

Making a cure.

Was that even possible? And, if it was, how were they ever going to use it? How were they going to get close enough to the grown-ups to inject them? It made no sense. How much blood would Sam need to give? There were so many of them. He'd be drained dry.

'Eyes right!'

Paddy had spent ages setting up a fighting arena in a sunken terraced area surrounded by steps you could sit on. He had some stuffed dummies and a sort of assault course thing. Ben and Bernie, the emo engineers, had helped him, but Paddy had made most of it himself. He'd been fired up ever since rumours had got out that there was a grown-up army camped out up in Kilburn. All the talk now was about the London kids needing to build their own army. Paddy wanted to make the Youngbloods into

a proper fighting unit, although Blue and Maxie had already made it very clear to Sam that if there was any fighting he would be nowhere near it. He was going to be safely guarded behind the lines.

There was no harm in learning how to fight, though. In the short time he'd been at the Tower of London he'd done some regular combat practice and had learnt a bit. Not that he could remember much of it now. The training at the Tower had been well organized, and run by kids who really knew what they were doing. This was different.

The Youngbloods were hopeless.

The next half-hour was mad – kids running and climbing and shouting, swiping at the dummies and each other with the wooden poles wrapped in rubber tubing that Paddy had given them to use as weapons.

Bill sat on the steps and played with his lump of Blutack, moulding it into all sorts of complicated shapes, his fingers working away too fast to follow, and then just as quickly he'd squash his little models and shape them into something else. Wiki and Jibber-jabber stood off to one side, talking about something in a very serious way. Froggie broke off to play with Bright Eyes. Sam did his best to join in, but the fighting wasn't really organized and he was small and not very strong and he kept getting whacked. Once on his fingers, which made him cry. He decided he was better at hiding than he was at fighting.

The Kid really went for it, charging about and yelling and swinging his weapon like he was in some kind of pole display team. Yo-Yo turned out to be pretty good. Twice she let The Kid exhaust himself, waving his pole like a maniac, and then just thumped him with her own pole. And each time The Kid went into a fancy dying routine.

'Aaargh, I am killed! My lifeblood ebbs away. You slay me, daddio. Bury my heart at wounded knee . . .'

After they'd been at it for some time, and Sam was thinking of giving up, he heard laughter and looked over to see Jackson and Achilleus watching them.

'You're gonna really scare them grown-ups, Paddy,' said Achilleus. 'They'll be filling their nappies in fright.'

Achilleus was holding a pile of gear. Armour and weapons and clothing. Sam knew that he and some other kids had been over to the Victoria and Albert Museum to pick up equipment. Sam spotted an enclosed iron helmet, big and ugly and mean-looking.

'It's only our first day,' said Paddy. 'You wait and see, Akkie. We're gonna be the best-trained unit here.'

'I'm sure you will, caddie.' Achilleus walked over and plonked the helmet on Paddy's head. It was way too big and way too heavy. Sam saw Paddy sort of sag down. It was like someone had put a giant bucket on his shoulders.

'I can't see anything,' he said, his voice muffled.

'You look great,' said Achilleus. 'A proper warrior.' He whacked the helmet with his spear and it made a dull *clonk*.

Paddy said, 'Ow,' and took the helmet off. He studied it, grinning.

'Cool bucket helm,' he said.

'Actually it's called a sallet,' said Wiki, who knew everything. 'Fifteenth century.'

They were joined by Ollie and some of his missile team, Lettis tagging along behind, looking sad and far away. She reminded Sam a little of his sister, Ella. Paddy had tried to get her to join his Youngbloods, but she'd refused, and when he'd tried to push it Ollie had told him to get lost.

Ollie's guys were carrying stuff as well – bulging bags and bundles of sticks.

'Arrows,' said Ollie, dropping his bundle to the ground. 'You lot can do something useful and help us make them. We need as many as possible. I'll show you how to do it.'

Wiki and Jibber-jabber hurried over. This was more their thing. Soon half the kids were sitting in a circle as Ollie gave them an arrow-making workshop.

Paddy tried to give the sallet back to Achilleus.

'You can keep it for now,' said Achilleus, walking away. 'I got to go to some boring meeting. Bring it me back later when you're done.'

A meeting. They were all getting ready for a big fight. Sam was trying not to think about it. But there was a feeling in the air. People were on edge. Waiting.

Sam went over and sat next to Lettis, who was with Ollie on the top step. He smiled at her.

'Shall we make some together?' he said. Lettis turned to him, but said nothing.

Sam felt a whack across his arm and turned angrily to see that it was The Kid.

'Come on,' he said. 'Stop your daydream believer, private. Get your head down from the clouds and concentrate on the matter in hand. This is a battle without humour or humanity. The last battle. The apocalypse disco. We're going down with all hands.'

Sam laughed and belted The Kid with his pole and soon they were chasing each other around, laughing and yelling, and Sam had forgotten all his worries.

'So that's why we got you all together.' Jester looked around at the assembled kids. 'Why we're all here. So I could tell you about what Shadowman showed me . . .'

Maxie felt out of place here. She'd never realized quite how posh the Houses of Parliament were inside. She'd seen the place on the television, bits of boring debates on the news, MPs shouting at each other about stuff she didn't really understand. You never really looked at the building when it was on TV, but it was like a palace inside. One of the local kids had told her that's what the place was actually called – the Palace of Westminster.

They were in the big chamber where the lords used to meet – the clue was in the name, the House of Lords. There were red benches, a huge golden throne down one end, wood panelling and carved stone everywhere, stained-glass windows, giant paintings and fancy hanging lights. It was like a cross between a cathedral and a throne room.

And a girl called Nicola was sitting on the throne. When Maxie arrived, Nicola had told her that she was the prime minister, which Maxie had thought was a joke. Apparently it wasn't, even though Maxie didn't remember voting for her. Nicola had long red hair and was one

of those confident, clever girls who made Maxie feel a bit stupid and useless. She was glad she had Blue with her. Blue didn't take any bullshit and wasn't impressed by the set-up.

Nicola stood up again. She'd been running the meeting, using phoney adult language.

'Thank you, Jester,' she said. 'There's a lot to debate. But, before we do, I'd like to say a few words . . .'

Blue leant over and whispered to Maxie. 'You could take this lot out in a second if you wanted, babe,' he said. 'This is all just play-acting.'

Maxie couldn't take any of it seriously either – the OTT decoration, the titles everyone gave themselves, the idea that anyone could claim to be prime minister . . . What she did take seriously was what they were actually talking about.

An army of grown-ups.

She didn't know whether to be scared or excited. The idea was pretty intense. The picture Jester had painted of the army – how many they were, how organized they were – had been way too vivid. But the idea that the kids might actually be able to beat them had given her a tiny shiver of hope.

Jester had managed to get most of the local London kids to turn up. Or at least a representative from each camp. David was here with some others from the palace. Maxie recognized Pod, who was in charge of palace security; Franny, who looked after the gardens; and Rose, who ran the sick-bay. They sat apart with some of David's red-blazered boys, his personal guard. Maxie, Blue, Whitney, Jackson and Achilleus had come from the museum, escorting Justin and Einstein. Maxie had tried to persuade Ollie

to join them, but he'd explained that little Lettis wasn't strong enough yet to leave the museum grounds and he couldn't leave her behind by herself. Will and Finn, two of Ed's friends from the Tower, had also come along. They were representing the Tower kids, since Ed himself had gone west to look for Ella and nobody had been in a hurry to go all the way out east to the Tower through the badlands to let anyone there know what was happening.

There was a strong contingent from the Houses of Parliament. They didn't look much like fighters, but they did look smart and sensible. From what Maxie had picked up they paid Ryan and his guys to do all their dirty work for them. The hunters were here, sitting quietly in a group under the windows. They were clearly more civilized than they looked.

The only settlement not represented was Just John's squatter camp. Maxie was glad they hadn't showed up. They were a grubby, hyper, disruptive bunch, and they had reason to hate Maxie and her friends. Achilleus had beaten Just John in single combat. Smashed him to bits. It would be a long time before John would forgive him for that. John's squatters were apparently still in a sort of truce with David – which was what the fight had been about – but the thought that John and his chaotic gang would be able to sit still and help make plans was ridiculous.

Sitting alone, out of the way, was the boy called Shadowman. He was in the darkest, quietest corner and had a hood half covering his face. Maxie sensed that he didn't want to be here, didn't want to be seen. She was intrigued by him. Most of Jester's information about the grownups' army had come from him. He seemed happy, though, to allow Jester to do his talking for him.

Nicola was still bigging herself up, saying how important it was that they'd come to the Houses of Parliament today, that it was democracy in action, how they would have a fair and open vote on what to do.

'As far as I knew,' Blue muttered under his breath, 'we came here because it's neutral territory. Safe. Ain't no chance that Nicola and her wimps are gonna suddenly pull some crazy stunt, assassinate all the other leaders and take over.'

There had been a lot of discussion about this. About where to meet. David had of course wanted everyone to come to the palace. Nobody else had thought that was a good idea. Justin, on the other hand, hadn't wanted anyone to come to the museum. He didn't like the idea of outsiders being there, didn't want the risk of things going wrong. So that left this place. The soft option. The safe option.

Parliament.

'So I assume we all want the same thing,' Nicola was saying.

'Yeah,' said Blue quietly. 'World peace and free Wi-Fi.'

'Stop it,' Maxie whispered, trying not to giggle. 'This is serious.'

And this *was* serious. The fact that everyone had come here today was proof of that.

'So we need to work out a plan of what to do if the oppoes attack,' said Nicola.

'Objection, Your Honour.' Achilleus was slouched in his seat and had his hand up.

'You don't have to call me Your Honour,' said Nicola patiently. 'But can you please not interrupt until I've finished speaking?'

'Nah,' said Achilleus. 'That don't work for me. I'll say what I want when I want to, Your Honour, all right?'

'All right, yes, go on then.'

'First thing we gotta do is work out what to call the enemy. It's confusing the crap out of me. I only just worked out what you meant by oppoes. Didn't have a clue before. It's grown-ups, yeah? That's what you call them? Oppoes.'

'Yes,' said Nicola. 'Oppoes, short for the opposition.'

'Yeah, OK, I don't need the Wikipedia entry. And it's a stupid name anyway. Thing is, *you* call them oppoes, David's mob call them strangers, Ryan and his crew just call them bastards – which I personally like, at the museum they call them sickos, and us lot from Holloway just call them plain and simple grown-ups. Can we decide what we call them, and all stick to it, yeah? Gonna make it a whole lot easier when the battle commands start flying. So I'm not, like, "Attack the oppoes? Which one's an oppo again?"'

'Can't we stick to the important stuff?' asked Justin, who didn't like Achilleus one bit.

'This *is* important,' said Nicola and Achilleus raised an eyebrow in appreciation. 'I think it's a good idea. It's the first step towards us all working together and it shows unity and will avoid confusion in the future.'

Now Finn stuck his hand up.

'We call them sickos at the Tower too. Can we just go with that?'

'I prefer *bastards*,' said Achilleus, and he laughed.

'We'll take a vote,' said Nicola. And so they did.

One vote per unit. Maxie and Blue overruled Achilleus and chose sickos, which, with the Tower boys' and Justin's vote, made three, and that swung it. Not surprisingly, all

the others voted for their name and not surprisingly David moaned and grumbled when the vote went against him, but sickos it was.

With that out of the way, Nicola carried on.

'OK,' she said. 'Next we need to decide exactly what we do when the sickos arrive.'

'It's obvious, isn't it?' said Ryan. 'We fight them. We hit them hard. What we need is a battle plan.'

'What we need is an army,' said David, standing up and raising his voice. 'A properly organized army with a strong leader. Someone who knows how to take charge and give orders.'

'And who might that be?' said Achilleus. 'No, let me guess . . . it's you, isn't it!'

'Yes,' said David. 'And what's wrong with that? Who would you rather took control? Nicola? Justin? Ryan maybe?'

'Prefer Ryan to you, to be honest.'

'No way,' said Ryan. 'I ain't no general. I can look after my lot, but I don't want to take on running the whole show.'

'Exactly,' said David. 'So it should be me.'

Maxie didn't know what to think, seeing David again. They'd walked out on him after turning down his offer to stay at the palace. He'd been relying on them to improve his fighting force. They'd had other plans.

So far he'd been aggressively ignoring them. Refusing even to look at her and Blue. He had that awful snooty look about him that made you want to slap him round the face. Blue had already hissed nearly every insult he could think of to Maxie. Now he added a couple more.

David couldn't ignore Achilleus now, however. Achilleus was on his case.

'Might as well be Justin in charge as you,' he said.

'Justin?' David scoffed. 'You're joking. What does Justin know about military tactics and leading troops into battle?'

'Is my point exactly,' said Achilleus. 'You two is pretty similar, to be frank. Neither of you is my idea of a general. If I was going to vote out of anyone here I'd vote for Blue. He knows what he's doing. He's got experience out on the streets. He's a hard man, not a talker.'

'David is the most natural leader here,' said Jester. 'He's used to giving orders, and he already has a well-disciplined fighting unit in the personal guard.'

'He's also a dick,' said Achilleus to a scattering of laughter. Maxie saw that even Nicola was trying to hide a smile. 'You need a general everybody's gonna respect and listen to or your great army is just gonna fall apart and do their own thing.'

'Can I say something?' This time it was Will who had put his hand up.

'Go on,' said Nicola.

'If you want a general we have a general. No disrespect to Blue, but the guy that runs the Tower, Jordan Hordern, knows more about battles and military tactics and giving orders and organizing an army than anyone else in London.'

'Yes, well, he's at the Tower, though, isn't he?' said David as if he was talking to an idiot.

'Doesn't have to be,' said Will patiently. He wasn't going to get flustered by David. What Maxie had seen of Will she liked. He was smart and a good listener. 'Surely we need all the kids we can get?'

'That's true,' said Nicola.

'And maybe . . .' Will went on. 'It would mean you lot here wouldn't argue among yourselves so much. Jordan's

someone from outside. Someone neutral. Me and Finn, we could maybe go to the Tower and fetch him, bring back a really strong fighting force. Well armed, well disciplined. A proper army.'

'That sounds like a great idea,' said Nicola.

'Not to me it doesn't,' said David. 'This is what you've been planning at the Tower from the start, isn't it?'

'What d'you mean?' said Will. 'I'm not with you.'

'That's always been your idea,' said David. 'I knew it. First that boy DogNut came to spy on us, and now you're here, all innocent – "Oh, we can bring Jordan, he'll help you." We're not stupid. We know you've been trying to take over here from the start.'

Will was laughing. 'Are you serious?'

'Yes.'

'Come off it. If Jordan had wanted to take over here he could have marched in any time he wanted. He doesn't have to be invited. He could just walk right over the lot of you.'

'No,' said David, going slightly red in the face. 'We don't need any outsiders here . . .'

'We do,' said Blue. He didn't put his hand up. Didn't need to. People listened to him. 'Will's right. We need as many kids who know how to fight as possible. I mean, how many soldiers we got between us? A hundred and fifty? Sixty maybe? I don't mind some other kid coming and taking charge if he's better than me. Makes sense.' He looked round at Will. 'How many can he bring?'

'At least another hundred.'

'Gets my vote,' said Blue.

'Mine too,' said Ryan.

'We should have a proper vote on it,' said Nicola.

'Wait a minute.' Pod put his hand up. He was a good-looking boy, but not the brightest pixel on the screen. He also always wore his collar turned up on his shirt, which Maxie found really irritating. 'Can I, like, *ask* something?'

'Go ahead.'

'Well, even with Jordan's kids, yeah? If I figure this right we're talking two fifty, maybe three hundred tops, trained fighters? Is that right?'

'I think so,' said Nicola.

'And how many sickos are out there?' Pod went on. 'How many are we expecting?'

'At least twice that, probably more like five times,' said Jester. 'We didn't get close enough to count them. But there's maybe up to a thousand.'

'Jesus.' Blue shook his head. 'That ain't great odds.'

'They won't be armed, though, will they?' said Ryan.

'No . . .' Jester didn't sound too sure.

Now Shadowman spoke for the first time, surprising the other kids who had forgotten all about him.

'Some might be,' he said. 'They're changing, growing smarter. They're not just mindless zombies any more. They can communicate with each other. They could wipe the lot of you out. They're getting organized, and you have to be organized too if you want to defeat them. So stop your arguing.'

'Exactly,' said Nicola. 'We all want the same thing – to defeat the sickos. Get rid of them once and for all. So let's vote on whether Jordan will be our general when he gets here.'

And so they voted again, and there was only one vote against – David's.

'Don't think you can vote for me to join you,' said

David afterwards. 'That's my decision and you can't make me change my mind.'

'But it's Jester who called this meeting,' said Nicola.

'I thought it would be obvious that I am the only natural leader here,' said David and Jester shrugged. 'I didn't think you'd all be stupid enough to invite some unknown outsider to come in and take over.'

Maxie had always known that David was going to be a problem, and she wondered how important he was to this. How much of a difference would his troops really make? They had a few guns, but how many bullets? They had fighters like Pod and the boys in the red blazers, but how many in all? Twenty-five, maybe thirty? And then she remembered the squatters. Just John's guys were mean and streetwise. You wouldn't want to go to the prom with any of them, but you might want to go into battle with them. Whatever else you said about them, they knew how to fight. They could tip the balance. Make the difference between winning and losing. And losing didn't bear thinking about.

'David could cause problems,' she murmured to Blue.

'You don't say.' Blue was sucking his teeth. 'He could keep his lot and John's guys out of the fighting. Stay safe inside the palace until it's over.'

'Is it worth trying one more time to persuade him not to be an arse?' said Maxie.

'One last time.'

Maxie stood up.

'We have to remember what this is all about,' she shouted. 'This is bigger than all of us. We've got the chance of a last battle. To make an end. Make London safe forever. We have to forget our differences. We have to accept a vote.' She turned to David. 'We really want you with us.'

'Like I can trust you,' he sneered.

'We fixed your problems,' said Maxie, trying not to lose her temper and swear at him. 'We beat Just John for you. As I understand it, he's still in a truce with you. We left you stronger than when we arrived. OK, so maybe we didn't stay at the palace, but all we did for you came out good. So yeah, you *can* trust us. In fact, you could thank us.'

She wished she had more to say, could make a proper argument, but she was convinced now that nothing she said was going to have any effect on David.

She stared at him a moment longer and when it was clear he wasn't going to say anything she sat down. Nicola had a few quiet words with a boy next to her who was writing in a big book, and then she addressed the assembled kids again.

'I don't think there's a lot more we can say or do until Jordan gets here,' she said, and looked to Will and Finn. 'You're sure you're all right to go back out to the Tower and get him? It'll be dangerous.'

'We know,' said Will. 'We've done that journey before. But we're prepared to try. From what we've heard today most of the streets around here are clear of sickos. We'll need backup all the same. No way are just the two of us going out there alone. I know Ryan won't want to come. He said before he was too scared to take his hunters into the badlands, so maybe someone else here can . . .'

'Hey, whoa, hold up there, bro!' Ryan was on his feet now. Maxie smiled. Clever boy, Will.

'Never said we was scared,' said Ryan. 'Just *careful*. Never been no need for us to go out that way. From what I seen, though, people coming and going along the river

to the east, it's cool over there now. We'll go with you. We'll keep you safe.'

'You sure?'

'Yeah.'

'As I remember, it was your dogs,' said Will. 'You said they were nervous of going that way, into the no-go zone.'

'My dogs are cool,' said Ryan. 'They'll do what we tell 'em. You can rely on us. No one says Ryan the hunter is a wuss. We'll get you to the Tower. When will you be ready to go?'

'We're ready now,' said Will, checking with Finn, who nodded. 'If you are. We can walk it in a couple of hours.'

'Yeah,' said Finn. 'So long as there really *aren't* any sickos out that way.'

'We'll see,' said Ryan, starting to walk out of the hall. 'Saddle up, guys, we going to work!'

'How long's she been like this?'

'An hour or so, maybe longer.'

'You should've got me sooner.'

'Didn't know how serious it was.' The girl, Geta, was sheepish.

'Look at her,' said Einstein. 'Doesn't that look just a little serious to you?'

The captured mother was lying on the floor of the lorry that the museum kids used as a cage. She was writhing and screaming as if something sharp and toxic was inside her, fighting to get out. Brown bile was dribbling from her mouth and she kept coughing up fat lumps of vile grey phlegm. The stench coming off her was worse than the usual grown-up stink. There was a choking edge to it, like the smell of burning hair. Her eyes had gone a nasty yellow colour.

Ollie had been out in the car park with Lettis when he'd heard the screaming and yelling coming from the lorry. Lettis had been feeding the chickens. She enjoyed looking after other creatures. It seemed to calm her down and make her forget her own problems. She sometimes managed to catch a hen and pick it up like a pet. If she held them tight and stroked them they

stopped struggling and went into a sort of peaceful trance.

Lettis had looked scared and haunted when she heard the mother thrashing about and wailing. She'd dropped the chicken she was holding and clung on to Ollie's shirt. Luckily there were some other kids around who offered to look after Lettis, and Ollie had assured her that he was only going a little way away. When he'd got to the lorry, he'd found a cluster of kids there, mainly the ones in white coats who worked in Einstein's lab, but also one or two of the Holloway kids and, standing at the back, the Twisted Kids, Fish-Face and Skinner, looking anxious. Einstein was quizzing Geta, one of the kids whose job it was to look after the mother.

'What's going on exactly?' Ollie asked, climbing on to the lorry. 'Is she dying?'

'I hope not,' said Einstein. 'We injected her earlier.'

'Injected her? You're joking. Injected her with what?'

'With the first batch of serum we've been working on,' said Einstein.

'Serum?'

'Serum, antidote, formula, drug, elixir, remedy, George's Marvellous Medicine . . . whatever you want to call it. It was based on some of the blood we took from Small Sam.'

'Looks like kill or cure to me,' said Ollie as the mother screeched and arched her back so far it looked like she might break in two.

'That's pretty much it,' said Einstein. 'It's a shot in the dark. Obviously I hope it's cure rather than kill. The Green Man's been trying to help us. The problem is we don't understand most of what he's talking about. If this works,

though, if this makes her even a little bit better and doesn't kill her then we could try the antidote on him. If we could clear his mind a little he might really be able to help us.'

'He's your best hope,' said Ollie. 'You kill him, you're stuffed.'

'We'll keep using this one as a guinea pig,' said Einstein. 'Until we perfect it.'

'Good luck with that,' said Ollie. 'She looks about ready to peg it.'

Fish-Face mumbled something so quietly that Ollie couldn't tell what it was, and then she peeled off and went back towards the museum buildings. The mother's eyes opened wide and she looked around fearfully at the kids. She was chained to the side of the lorry. One chain round her neck, another round one ankle, her hands cuffed in front of her.

'We had her mouth taped shut with gaffer tape,' said Geta. 'So we could get close to her and inject her without getting bitten. We had to pull it off, though; it looked like she was going to choke to death.'

The mother's eyes darted from one kid to another. Ollie wasn't used to seeing a grown-up show any emotion, but she was going through the lot – horror, pain, sadness, confusion, fear. She reached out her hands towards Einstein. He ignored her and she turned and reached out towards Ollie. She looked desperate and strangely intelligent, like someone coming out of a mad fever waking up to the cold light of day. Ollie stepped forward and took her hands. She smiled at him, pathetically grateful, but it only lasted an instant. The smile was suddenly replaced by a look of animal fear and aggression, like a dog with rabies, and she lunged at Ollie, teeth bared. Ollie was ready for her. He was

always ready. Hadn't got this far without being careful. He drove the palm of his free hand into her forehead, knocking her back and stunning her.

'You can't leave her like this,' he said to Einstein. 'I mean, what if you don't kill her, but drive her into some sick hell? You'll need to put her out of her misery.'

'I can do what I bloody well want, thank you very much, ginge,' said Einstein. 'She's useful to us for our experiments. She's the only one we've got.'

'No, she isn't,' said Ollie. 'She's not the only one. You said it yourself: you've got the Green Man.'

'And, as you said, we can't risk harming him in any way. So can you please just back off? I don't need you interfering. All of you, back off. I need room here.'

Ollie climbed down, looked back. Einstein was standing over the mother, who suddenly sat up and stared at him.

'Help me!' she shouted. 'Please help me!'

Einstein laughed and clapped his hands.

'Jesus, she can speak,' he said. 'She can bloody speak.' He was grinning like a madman. Ollie wondered if this was his eureka moment. Had months of working in the lab finally paid off? It looked like his antidote had had some positive effect on this woman, cleared her mind, driven the sickness out. But she looked miserable, utterly miserable. Her reason was returning and so was her memory. You could see it in her eyes.

That was the worst, most terrible thing of all. Understanding.

The memories of all she'd been, all she'd done, were bubbling up inside her. Ollie wondered how you could ever deal with that.

'I will help you,' said Einstein. 'I'm a doctor. I'll make you well.'

'Help me, help me, help me! They're doing things to me. You have to make them go away. You have to make them stop. It's not right. They're in me. What have you done to me?'

'Nothing. I've just made you well,' said Einstein.

'Bastard!' And then the mother flung back her head and screamed, so loudly that Ollie had to step back and cover his ears. It was a deep yell from the depths of her misery and pain. And then she was an animal once more. What was left of her humanity had struggled to the surface. She'd got her face above the water, for just one moment, seen the sky and the sun shining on the beach – a beautiful tropical island just out of reach – and she'd been too weak to swim there and had sunk back beneath the waves.

She jiggled and shivered, trembled and ground her teeth together noisily. She jerked against her chains, flung herself against the side of the lorry, attacked her face with her fingers, pulling away the skin where it had gone soft around the growths and boils that covered it. It came away like soggy newspaper, exposing the muscle and bone beneath, and then she gave one final cry and went rigid, her arms and legs stretched out. Grey jelly oozed out of her mouth, her nose, her ears, from under her eyelids. Her body spasmed and jerked as boils erupted all over what was left of her skin.

Ollie swallowed hard. He recognized the symptoms.

'She's a burster!' he shouted, stepping away from the lorry. 'She's gonna blow!'

Some of the kids around him jumped back as well. Those who knew what was about to happen. Einstein

didn't move. He was staying close to the mother, studying her.

'What are you talking about?' he said. 'I'm going to help her.'

'Good luck,' said Ollie.

'The injection's working,' said Einstein. 'She's just getting rid of the sickness.'

And then it happened. The mother's body erupted, slowly at first, the skin disintegrating, her insides pushing out, and then it accelerated fast. There was a horrible gurgling sound and she burst, spraying Einstein with a foul, stinking liquid.

Ollie couldn't help it. He started to laugh. And the others joined in.

'I guess it's kill, then,' he said.

'You saw it!' said Einstein, ignoring the mess, his face spattered with gunk. 'You saw it yourselves. For a moment she talked. For a moment she was human. It's a start. We're getting there. It's a start.'

'Yeah, right,' said Ollie. 'All you got to do is inject every grown-up in the world and wait for them to either burst or be cured.'

Wormwood was standing in the library, staring out of the windows that overlooked the car park. He hadn't been able to see exactly what was going on in the lorry, but he could tell from the kids' reactions and from the vibrations in the air what was happening. Two of the museum kids were acting as his minders today. Some boy with a big nose and another one with a scarred neck who he thought was called Cameron. They never let him out of their sight, but kept their distance. He'd come in here to find some books and been distracted by the noise from outside.

There was one of his kind down there. A woman. At least there had been. He could feel that her light had gone out. He couldn't hear her whining noise in his head any more. It had got very loud and then . . . *poof.*

Nothing.

'Daddy?' He turned from the window and there was his twisted treasure, his little girl, who had come out wrong. She was walking round the big table in the middle of the room where his minders were sitting looking bored – bored and just a little bit scared.

His baby. She put her arms round him and he held on to her. She was crying.

'Daddy. They're going to hurt you.'

'No,' said Wormwood, his mind fizzing and spinning. 'I'm hurt already.'

'I saw her. On the lorry. What they did to her. They want to do it to you.'

'I need to help them,' said Wormwood and he held her where he could see her. 'You see? You understand? I came from the big green and already I can feel it slipping. The blood is rising. Good blood will drive out the bad. Wormold is getting stronger while Wormwood grows weak.'

'I wish I understood, Daddy. I never did. But I need you.'

'Then let me help them,' said Wormwood. 'I don't want to go back to the big green. I don't want to go back to the stars. I only wanted to be happy here. You see? I only wanted to live. I was never strong enough to be alone, though. I'm sorry. The thoughts are there, but my brain is slippery. They can't hang on. In the green, before all this, I wanted to ride the monkeys. Books and bees and fleas – they were my friends. I never meant to kill them.'

'Books, Daddy?'

'Books or birds or baboons. Beasts. The beasts of the big green. I never meant to harm them. I just wanted to ride in them. Back there.'

'The jungle? South America? You weren't there for that long, Daddy. You're getting confused.'

'I was there for a hundred thousand years. Not me, not Wormold, but this thing inside me. You see? The bug, darling. The sickness. It lived there, moving from beast to beast, working its way up, from bugs, to fleas, to bats, to monkeys, to men and women. Finally it found people. It never meant to hurt them. Only to live. We never meant to twist them and make them sick. Honestly I didn't, I

didn't. But I can feel the big green dying in me, the leaves falling from the trees, my home from home from home from home. This is my home now, but my house is on fire. You see? Or do you not see?'

'You talk as if you're two different people sometimes,' said his girl.

'Not two,' said Wormwood. 'Two million. There's me, your father, Mark Wormold, and there's the others. The bugs in my pipes, the stars inside me, a constellation. A universe. I'm plugged in. They were strong, but they are growing weak. They can be beaten, but only if we protect him. And the others.'

'Protect him? Protect who?'

'The boy, the bogey boy, the golden boy.'

'Small Sam?'

'Yes. Yes, him. They're scared of him; they'll try to stop him, to kill him. Because his blood is the good blood. And he is not alone. Not here, not near, but there are others. They must be saved, you see? They must be protected. So that we can use their good blood. Starboard staff for dead star . . .'

'What?'

'I used to be a star. I used to be a god. They used to sacrifice to me. I lived in a palace. A dark palace. There was no light in there. It was my world. After I'd left the big green this was, must have been . . . I went to the dark palace. They fed me what I needed. Only the boy came, not the golden one, the mad one. He turned on the lights. He showed me that I wasn't living in a palace, I was living in a prison. They fed me scraps to keep me happy and told me it was ambrosia and nectar. It wasn't. It was children. I needed what was in them.'

'Daddy, don't. I don't want to hear. You've done bad things, but I never want to hear. They told me how they found you, underground, and how Sam's friend, The Kid, rescued you. Make it a happy story, Daddy, with a happy ending.'

Wormwood laughed.

'They got it wrong,' he said. 'They were confused. They tried to sacrifice the wrong one. Ha, ha, ha! The stars were calling to them; the shout went out and they got it wrong. The boy there, the one who gave the orders, he's got the bug in him. He's halfway to the stars. You'll see! You'll see it. But he didn't listen properly. He didn't send me the golden boy. He sent me the mad one, madder than me. I so wanted to eat him . . . I was so hungry . . .'

'Daddy, stop!'

'Darling girl. You're my angel. You came out wrong, but you were still my girl. I should have loved you. I should have saved you. I should have protected you and instead I became one of them. I let the green in – the bugs and bees and stars went in me until I was mad. I became Wormwood the poison star, out to spread the word, to bathe the world in bad blood. I became the Green Man. And the Green Man can destroy everyone, or he can save everyone, but only if you let them use the boy's blood in me. Then the Green Man can save the world.'

'No, Daddy, they'll kill you.'

'I deserve to die. I killed so many of them. So many children. In my palace prison under the ground, my dark home from home. And I abandoned you. My own little girl. But you were stronger than you looked. Weren't you? Look at you. You're my angel. How many brothers and sisters do you have out there? Around the world.

Children of the green. My children. I will do it, for all the children of the world. I will make the blood be good, and it will drive out the bad. You'll see.'

'And will it kill you?'

'I don't know, darling girl. But I must let them try.'

'You tricked me, didn't you?'

'Did I?'

'You tricked me well bad. Saying I was too scared to come out this way.'

'So you're not scared then?'

Will and Finn and Ryan's hunters were crossing Westminster Bridge towards the south side of the river. This was the route Will had taken with Ed when they'd gone back to St Paul's to rescue Small Sam. Will could have gone the more direct route, along the Embankment on the north side, but he figured this route had been lucky for them last time.

Stick to what worked.

Whatever the case, there were definitely fewer sickos around. They'd seen none on the way to the Houses of Parliament from the museum, and none since. The streets felt eerily quiet.

'Scared?' Ryan grinned at him, his acne-covered face ugly and raw-looking. Maybe that was why he usually wore the horrible mask he'd made out of a sicko's face.

'Not scared, soldier, no. I mean, if what Jester was saying back there is, like, the *truth* then all the – sickos – that's what we got to call them now, right?'

'Yeah.'

'Yeah. So all the sicko bastards is now down Kilburn and this part of town is clear. We're free to roam. Tell you the truth, bro, I'm well curious to find out what's out your way. I never gone east since all this started. Those streets were always bad. The dogs was always spooked. But look at 'em now. Chilled.'

Indeed, the dogs were trotting along happily at the hunters' sides, wagging their tails, happy to be on the move. Sniffing and weeing and doing everything that normal dogs did.

Will hoped they'd stay that way. It meant they were safe.

'That's why we call it the no-go zone,' he said. 'The badlands. I'm hoping Jordan's gone in there and cleaned the sickos out. Last I saw of it, it was mental, though. A whole army of sickos was, like, *besieging* St Paul's Cathedral. We got to pray they've all moved north.'

'That's where the greens live?' said Ryan. 'St Paul's?'

'Yeah,' said Will. 'That's where Mad Matt and his religious freaks hang. Provided the sickos haven't killed them all.'

'Is true he tried to sacrifice Sam's friend?' Ryan asked.

'Yeah. Mad times, man.'

Will thought back to that night. When Adele and Tish and Brendan had died holding the bridge. Will had hoped that it had all been for a good reason. That Sam was worth it. With everything that had happened at the museum, the new antidote that Einstein was working on, he reckoned it probably was.

He stared down at the churning grey waters of the Thames. That night the river had been thick with the fallen bodies of sickos, like black seals in the water. And he

remembered early days at the Tower. How you'd look out and see the river clogged with crap – dead, bloated bodies, all kinds of rubbish, foam and oil, boats that had slipped their moorings – but it had had a year to clean itself, to dump all the crap out to sea. Must be the cleanest it had been for hundreds of years. A flock of seagulls came swooping and squawking and squabbling. Something splashed in the water. Might have been a fish, might have been anything.

'We rowed up this way with DogNut on a boat,' said Finn. 'If we'd've had one now we could have gone back that way. All the way to the Tower. Our boat sank, though. When this is over, we need to get back on the river.'

'You never tried to go home?' Ryan asked.

Finn raised his right arm. It was bandaged.

'I could run but I couldn't fight,' he said. 'Wasn't any use to anyone. Didn't want to put mates in danger by having to look out for me.'

'How's it now?' Ryan asked.

'Nearly better.'

'Nearly's not good enough, man!' said Ryan. 'You saying you're still useless? You're telling me you can't swing that axe you carrying?'

Ryan was only half serious.

'I can swing it if I need to,' said Finn, settling his axe comfortably on his shoulder. 'Don't worry, I won't stand back and watch you get killed. I used to be good with a sword. It's gonna take a bit of practice and a bit more healing to get back to where I was.'

'Well, you plenty big enough,' said Ryan. 'We'll use you as a human shield, yeah?'

'Deal.' Finn laughed.

Will smiled. The weather was holding up. The sky was half cloud, half blue. Not hot. Not cold. A neutral kind of a day. Will hoped it would stay that way. Neutral. Nothing. Nothing to tell anyone. Boring.

They reached the south side of the bridge and started to work their way eastwards. Then they could either cross back over at the Millennium Footbridge, as they'd done before, or carry on along to Tower Bridge. Will decided he'd wait and see what it looked like when they got there. This part of London south of the river had been badly damaged in the big fire and there had always been fewer sickos down this way. The buildings were cracked and blackened, quite a few had collapsed and sometimes the boys had to make their way round piles of rubble and debris.

They'd been walking for about ten minutes when they saw their first sicko. A sentinel. He was unmoving. Like one of those living statues that used to hang around Covent Garden. Arms held out, face tilted to the sky. His skin was grey and ruined and bloodless, stretched tight over his skull. He looked dead. And as they got closer they saw that he was oozing grey jelly from his mouth and nose and several burst boils on his face. The jelly was moving a little. It looked more alive than him.

'Jelly bugs,' said Zulficker, one of Ryan's hunters.

'You want to chop him down like a tree?' Ryan said to Finn, who smiled but shook his head. His axe stayed on his shoulder.

Zulficker stepped right up close to the sentinel and yelled into his face.

'You are in our way, sir! Kindly move or I will kick your arse into the river.'

He laughed, and then jumped back as the sentinel opened his eyes. Glared at the boy.

'Whoa!' said another boy who moved quickly, cutting the father's head from his shoulders with a machete. He then walked over to the fallen head, knelt down and started to cut the ears off with a sharp knife. Will looked away.

'Let's keep moving,' he said and they carried on, the boy catching up with them when he was done.

They only saw two more sickos before they got to the footbridge. Sentinels, off in the distance, looking as dead and dry as the first one. When they got to the bridge, they found two kids from the Tower standing at the barricade that guarded the entrance. A girl and a boy whom Will recognized. They were amazed to see him and Finn and they opened the barricade to let them through.

'We thought you was both dead for sure,' said the boy, Abdullah.

'Well, we're not,' said Will. 'Disappointed?'

Abdullah grinned, gave Will a big hug.

'What is all this?' asked Finn. 'What are you doing this far from the Tower?'

'There's been some changes around here,' said Abdullah. 'Big changes. Come on. We'll show you.'

And so they crossed the bridge towards St Paul's. And Will felt safe. Felt like he was nearly home.

20

St Paul's looked very different to how Will had last seen it. Under siege. Back then the whole area in front of it, and all the way up the wide steps leading to the entrance, had been swarming with sickos. They'd been battering at the doors, trying to get at the kids sheltering inside. As Will and his friends had fought to escape, he'd been sure that they'd never see any of the local kids again. At least not alive.

Will was amazed. Looking around now, you wouldn't have any idea what had gone on that night. There were no signs of a battle and the locals all looked fit and well and happy in their green outfits. Will had forgotten about the green. How Matt made them all wear it.

He grinned. The area was a model of peace and calm. A row of kids was sitting on the steps, eating, like school kids on an outing. Other kids were walking purposefully in all directions, carrying supplies. The secret to Matt's success had been discovering a huge underground warehouse stocked with food and other useful stuff. There were several faces Will recognized from the Tower – guard units keeping watch – and there was an air of military efficiency. No sickos were going to get in here and spoil the party.

No, not sickos. What was it Matt called them? *The Nephilim.* That was it. He'd got the name from the Bible. Matt was obsessed with the Bible. Had written his own garbled version.

Will heard a cry, and there was Hayden running across the road towards them. She crashed into him and gave him a hug that nearly popped a rib.

'You're alive!' she screamed into his ear and he laughed.

'So don't kill me,' he said. 'You're crushing me.'

When Will and Ed had carried on into town, Hayden had been sent back to the Tower to let Jordan know what was happening. Will was relieved to find her alive and well.

Hayden let him go and looked at him, then gave the same treatment to Finn. Who winced as she squeezed his sore arm. She even hugged Ryan, who looked very uncomfortable. He had his armour of leather and fur and studs. He was the big man on the street and didn't want to show any vulnerability. Will knew the armour was as much to keep other kids out as it was to protect him from sickos.

Will began to explain everything that had happened since they'd left her on the South Bank that night. And when he was done it was her turn to tell him what had happened here.

'Jordan Hordern got an army together,' she said. 'As soon as it was light, we marched. Matt was just holding on inside. It was bare nasty, there were just so many sickos, but Jordan managed to drive them off. We should go to the Tower. He'll be pleased to see you.'

'Really?' said Will. 'Pleased? I've never seen him show any emotion.'

'OK, yeah, maybe not pleased. Let's just say "interested".'

'That's the best we can hope for. But there's more. A lot more I need to talk to Jordan about. I'll tell you on the way.'

As they headed off towards the Tower, Hayden pointed out where they'd strengthened and repaired the barricades Matt had built to keep the sickos out, but also where they'd made an opening and a protected walkway, so that there was a safe route all the way to the Tower, with newer barricades blocking off the side-streets.

'The no-go zone has gone,' she explained. 'But in fact, to be honest, nearly all the sickos have disappeared from around here. We hardly ever see any. We've been shifting a lot of the supplies back to the Tower. Matt doesn't like it, but he had no choice. Jordan made it clear when we showed up to save Matt's bony arse that there was a price to pay. Quite a lot of the cathedral kids have moved in with us as well. It's only really the full-on religious fanatics who stayed behind. Matt comes up to the little church at the Tower to hold prayer meetings sometimes. It's weird. Like the world's going back to normal.'

'Funny kind of normal,' said Will and Hayden smiled.

'It's good,' said Hayden. 'Can't you feel things changing for the better? Like we may be winning at last. Getting rid of the sickos.'

'Well, I hate to burst your bubble, girl,' said Will. 'But we didn't come here on the tour bus to go sightseeing.'

'You came to burst my bubble.'

'To burst everyone's bubble. You know how Jordan's always wanted to be a real general, in a real battle? Well, there's a shitstorm coming, Hayden. And we're going to be right in the middle of it.'

21

General Jordan Hordern was sitting in the council room in the White Tower that stood at the centre of the castle. He'd made sure he was settled in his big throne before any of the others arrived. He hadn't wanted them to see him groping his way up the stairs and across the room. Only his two young helpers, Jim and Hugo, knew how bad his eyesight had become. And they were scared enough of him to keep their mouths shut. The centre of his vision was a brownish-grey blur so that he could only see round the edges if he looked at things sideways.

On one level he didn't mind. The world in his head was much neater and more ordered than the real world. There weren't so many distractions this way. The universe was made of numbers. If he just knew what the numbers were everything was fine. But he still needed to be able to fight. He was meant to be a warrior, a leader, a general. How could he lead an army if he couldn't see? How could he command any respect? If the kids here knew they'd probably try to get rid of him. There'd be a struggle for power. He mustn't show any weakness.

Jim and Hugo had helped him get seated, and had murmured in his ear as the other kids who made up the war council had come in, telling him who they were. Not

that he really needed to be told. He had a pretty good idea because he insisted that everyone always sat in the same place. Everything always had to be the same or he got uncomfortable. But, even so, he wanted information. He needed to be informed of everything going on around him. He needed control.

'And this lot are the boys who went with Ed to the museum,' said Jim. 'Will and Finn.'

'Who's that with them?'

'They call themselves hunters. They look like good fighters.'

'Oh yeah. Hayden told me about them before. What they look like?'

'Pretty crusty,' said Jim. 'Some of them have masks made out of the faces of dead sickos. They've got dogs with them as well. A pack of them. Big bastards.'

'Dogs?' said Jordan. 'We could do with some fighting dogs.'

'I don't reckon they'll sell you any of theirs.'

'We'll see. I want to talk to them after. Sort it for me.'

'OK, boss.'

Jordan was thinking. With a dog at his side, he'd be safe. A dog could be a real help and would make him look tougher instead of weaker. Nobody would question him having a dog. They needn't know that he'd be using the dog's eyes.

At last everyone was in place and settled. Jordan turned to the blurred silhouette that he recognized as Will.

'So you got news for us?' he said.

'There's a war coming.'

Jordan liked Will. He was smart. Didn't muck about. Knew that Jordan always wanted to get straight to the point.

'A war?'

'If we're lucky then maybe not a war, but at least a battle.'

'You saying if we win the battle the war's over?'

'Yeah,' said Will. 'But if we lose . . .'

'We'd better win it, then. So who exactly do we fight . . . ?'

And Will told him everything, Jordan listening carefully. Taking it all in. Remembering the names. The numbers. Storing all the facts. He was good at that.

'I'd been wanting to push west,' he said once Will was finished. 'As soon as I was sure the whole area between here and St Paul's was safe, I was gonna send troops into town to find you and Ed and everyone. I guess now we need to move quicker than I thought. If this goes right we can unite the whole of London.'

Jordan was thinking fast, plans forming in his head, supply lines, battle plans, rows of soldiers, neat and orderly. He could see London as a vast map, with people moving around on it. In his mind it was simple and clear. And what had to be done was simple and clear as well.

It was time to start giving orders.

'Tomoki, you'll be in charge here at the Tower, yeah? It's quiet round here now, 'specially if what Will says is the truth. You stay here with all the non-fighters. Be safe inside the walls. I'll take everyone else. I'll take an army and we'll march on Buckingham Palace and I'll be the liberator of London.'

'Might not be quite that easy,' said Will. 'There's other kids want to be in charge. David King at the palace. You remember him? Kid who rocked up at the Imperial War Museum with a load of kids in red blazers all that time back? Wanted all our guns.'

'Yeah. I remember him. Smart but slippery. He's in charge there, is he?'

'Not happy about you coming in and taking control.'

'I don't give a monkey's about no David King,' said Jordan. 'If he don't want to do what he's told he can sit in his palace with his thumb up his arse. There's no general better than Jordan Hordern. We'll take anyone from the cathedral as wants to come as well, anyone who can fight. Hell, they can even bring their musicians if they want. Like a proper army marching with a band. This is what we been waiting for. Training for. This is what I been planning for. We gonna end this once and for all time.'

Jordan could see the coming battle as an illustration in a book – a grand painting, soldiers locked in combat, Romans against barbarians, Henry the Fifth cutting down the French knights at Agincourt, Wellington's red against Napoleon's blue. One day someone would paint a picture of him, leading his army into battle, destroying the sickos . . . Only thing was – he'd probably never be able to see it.

'Why should we believe them?' David slapped his hands on the stone balustrade that ran along the balcony at the front of the palace. 'Why should we do what they say? Why should we even listen to them?'

'But Jester saw the grown-ups.' Nicola looked at David. He had a big angry spot on the back of his neck. 'And Jester's one of yours.'

'Yes,' said David. 'And I don't always trust him.'

'What do you mean?'

'I've never really been sure about him, to tell you the truth. He'd take over here given the chance. That's the problem with people who are second in command – they want to be first in command. Stalin regularly killed all his generals.'

'Really?' said Nicola. 'I never knew that.'

David turned to face her. He was blushing slightly, a little overexcited, showing off as usual.

'Jester's always been sneaky,' he said. 'But something happened to him out there. That creepy kid, Shadowman, got to him. They've made some sort of a plan together. I just know it. I can't trust anyone.'

'What about me?' said Nicola. 'Can you trust me?'

'I think so, yes,' said David. 'You're a girl. Girls aren't so devious.'

Nicola had to suppress a laugh. David was such a mix. On one hand he was really clever and on the other he was unbelievably stupid. He had school smarts, not street smarts.

She stared directly at him, seeing if he dared make eye contact. He didn't. He may have been scarily clever and ruthless, he may have taken over here, running his little empire and getting rid of all the oppoes, but there was one thing he was scared of. There was one thing he didn't know how to deal with.

Girls. *And this girl in particular*, thought Nicola. *He thinks he's the one in charge, but right now I'm the one with all the power.*

She joined David at the balustrade, looking out over the parade ground towards the golden statue of Queen Victoria and, beyond that, St James's Park. She knew that out there were the squatters, the unruly rabble of unstable dropouts who'd made an uneasy alliance with David. How long it would last in the face of real trouble she had no idea. She'd always felt uncomfortable being part of this three-way coalition. She'd visited the squatter camp one time with David, soon after they'd made their treaty. She'd felt very nervous. The kids who lived there were half wild, dirty, disorganized, living on the edge. Some of them were drunk, fighting among themselves. Some had found a giant Union flag and their leader, John, had gone on about how great England was and how they were going to make it right. Make England the most powerful country in the world again.

'This was all meant to be,' he'd ranted. 'God has wiped out everyone else so we can start again and build it right this time. Build a new England.'

How they intended to do that when they couldn't even organize their grubby little camp was beyond her.

So this was her team. David with his dreams of becoming king and John with his dreams of . . . what? A new world ruled by drunken thugs. Nicola knew she'd made a mistake joining with David. She should have made an alliance with the museum kids. Now that they had Maxie and Blue and the Holloway gang with them they were the group best placed to sort things out. And David was never going to admit that. He hated them.

'Come on,' she said. 'Why wouldn't we believe Jester and Shadowman?'

'Because they're just like all the rest,' said David. 'They don't like me, and they don't like the idea of me being in charge.'

'I don't think so,' said Nicola, who thought he might actually be right.

'They're scared of me, you see,' said David. 'And people hate what they fear. The truth is – they're all plotting to get rid of me, to take over for themselves; they always have done. They're jealous of what I've got. But before now they haven't been strong enough to do anything about it. Those museum nerds aren't fighters, led by chief nerd Justin. They've got together and made up all this stuff about an army of strangers just so that they can try to get rid of me. They've been plotting it. It's so obvious. Plotting to call in those bastards from the Tower of London. I mean, it's stupid. Why would we let a bunch of complete strangers come strolling in here and tell us what to do? This is our part of London.'

'Have you ever considered,' said Nicola calmly, 'that this might be nothing to do with you?'

'What do you mean?'

'That they're not plotting against you? That they couldn't really care less about you?'

'Look!' David waved his arms towards the park. 'Look at that! There are no grown-ups! There are no strangers. There are no oppoes or whatever it is you call them. No *sickos*. There is no threat. They've got rid of the enemy and now they want to get rid of me. It's so obvious it's laughable.'

'It's not obvious to me,' said Nicola. 'And, to tell you the truth, if anything's laughable it's you.'

'You can't say that to me.'

'Why not? We're equals, aren't we? We have an alliance. A coalition.'

'Yes, we have a coalition, but I am the senior member. That's always been understood. I have the bigger army. I have guns. I have the royal family.'

'So what am I to you then?'

'I told you,' said David, and he flushed deeper, his face going the red of his boys' blazers. He looked away. Forget eye contact, he couldn't even look in her general direction. 'Make a proper alliance with me,' he mumbled. 'Be my girlfriend.'

'Oh, you're so romantic, David,' said Nicola sarcastically. 'Are you proposing marriage?'

'Don't be silly,' he said. 'I just want to . . .'

'Just want to what?' Nicola moved closer to him.

'You know.'

'No, I don't know. Spell it out for me.'

'I want to do all the things that boys and girls do together.'

'Like what?' said Nicola. 'Play cards? Go for a bike ride? Sing close-part harmonies . . . ?'

'Would you let me kiss you?' David asked and Nicola almost felt sorry for him. He was so utterly clueless. She wondered if he'd ever kissed a girl.

Not that sorry, though. He couldn't bully her into it. And the thought of kissing him was . . . Well, it didn't exactly turn her stomach. She just couldn't picture it. Couldn't imagine any scenario where it would feel right. Not even if she was dying and needed mouth-to-mouth. She'd been stringing him along because it made him easier to handle. It made him nicer to her. More open. But she wondered now whether she shouldn't just let him down easy and tell him the deal was off. No kissing. No girlfriend stuff. No alliance. She could do without the extra food he'd been regularly sending over to the Houses of Parliament. What else did she get out of their arrangement, other than keeping him and the squatters off her back, and stopping them from trying to take over her little corner of the world?

Nicola had gone through a craze of playing Risk with a group of friends before the disease had struck. They'd play for hours in her bedroom. The trick to winning was to make alliances – 'Don't attack me in Australia and I won't attack you in South America . . .' And she always knew the alliances were nothing to do with helping the other person; they were simply a way of getting what you wanted. Once you'd done that, it was time to ditch the alliance and screw the person you'd made it with. Well, maybe it was time to do that now? Only thing was – she bet David used to play as well. He was just the sort. Probably won every time. So was he getting ready to dump on her if she looked like getting the upper hand?

Best to wait. Make sure Jordan's army arrived from the

east first. When everything was all in place, she could break the alliance, take Australia and leave David alone and floundering. In the meantime best to keep him happy.

'Not now, David,' she said, and gave him the sort of smile she thought he'd like. 'Not here.'

'We could go inside,' he said, pathetically eager, like a little boy. Which after all – let's face it – was exactly what he was. Most of the time you forgot that. But now Nicola could see him clearly. An insecure fifteen-year-old.

'It doesn't work like that,' she said. 'You can't just tell me what to do and march me inside like some kind of hooker or something. You need to build up to it.'

'What, like, give you flowers?' said David sarcastically. 'I can't wait, Nicola. I *have* built up to it. I think about you all the time.'

'Well, it's different for girls,' Nicola lied. 'We can't just go from nothing to sixty in three seconds. You need to . . .'

'Need to what?'

'You need to *woo* me.' Nicola almost laughed at the silly, old-fashioned word that she couldn't remember ever having used before.

'How?' David asked.

'Oh God, David. If I have to tell you!'

'Well, I mean . . .' David was struggling. 'The world's changed. We can't exactly go on a date, can we? Go to see a film, or out to dinner or something.'

'A school disco,' said Nicola. 'Did you ever go to one?'

'No.'

'That figures.'

'So what would count as a date these days?' said David. 'Digging up potatoes? Killing sickos? There isn't time, Nicola. Not any more. Not for all that nonsense. Life is

short and pretty intense. We *do* just have to go from nought to sixty in three seconds.'

Nicola thought about that. He was right really, wasn't he? She just didn't like his car, though, never would. And she didn't like the way he drove.

'I'll think about it,' she said. Lying again.

'Oh . . . OK.' David looked so completely broken. So young and helpless.

'Maybe next time, yeah?'

'OK. Do you promise?'

'I don't promise anything. But David, if you want me to go along with you, you're going to have to listen to what everyone else is saying. You have to join the alliance. Otherwise it's not going to work.'

'OK,' said David. 'I will. I'll properly think about it.'

Great. So who was the bigger liar? Him or her?

'David?'

Nicola turned to see Pod. How long had he been lurking back there in the room that led out to the balcony? Had he been watching the sad little show?

'What is it?' said David.

'There's something you need to come and see. And you, Nicola . . .'

Matt had a slight limp. Will had never noticed it before. Not sure he'd ever seen him walking around that much and, if he had, Matt had always been surrounded by his acolytes. A group of boys who kept close to him, like flies round a cow's arse. But, marching alone like this, Will was able to get a good look at him. Matt was painfully thin, his bones showing. He was just muscle and gristle, no fat, like a walking skeleton. His skin was so pale it was almost transparent, his hair cropped short. Like all his followers, he was dressed head to foot in green, with some kind of green dyed religious robes flapping about his scrawny frame. He must have found them at the cathedral.

He was loving it. Marching with his musicians and his banners. A holy man going on a crusade. When Will had announced the news about Sam, and the idea of using his blood to make an antidote, it had quickly got to Matt. He'd gone into overdrive, rocking up at the Tower, ranting and yelling and rolling his eyes up in his head.

'We will wash our robes and make them white in the blood of the Lamb! He is the firstborn from the dead. He will free us from our sins by his blood. He is coming with the clouds, and every eye will see him . . .'

So here he was now, limping along, head held high, at

the front of his crusaders. At the head of the procession were the musicians, trumpets blaring, drums banging. Will wasn't sure they were exactly playing a tune, but it still sounded pretty awesome. Next came Matt's acolytes, holding up several huge banners. One of them Matt had had made over a year ago, back at the Imperial War Museum, and which had caused much laughter. It said 'Angus Day' in big letters, and underneath were the crudely painted figures of two boys, one shining and bright, the other dark – the Lamb and the Goat. The other banners were newer. Will hadn't seen them before. 'Blood of the Lamb', 'God's Hand' and one with a much better painting on it than the Lamb and the Goat. It showed a battle between children and monsters, with the words 'Death to Nephilim' across the bottom and 'Army of God' across the top.

Then came Matt himself, keeping clear of everyone else, even his right-hand man, Archie Bishop. Archie was off to one side, taking in the view along the Thames from the bridge. Behind Matt were the rest of his troops, trying to march in step and failing. Will was among them. He'd moved forward to be near the front, to see what was going on. Jordan had been happy to let Matt and his green party lead them into town. He was heading up the second body of kids, the ones from the Tower, heavily armed and armoured.

Will would have liked to have spent more time at the Tower. He'd only been at home for two nights, just long enough for Jordan to get everything ready. He would have loved to properly catch up with his friends. They all had so many questions. He felt like a real hero – someone who'd been out there, gone past the no-go zone, brought back news from the wider world. He was Columbus, and

Drake, and all the other great explorers rolled into one. And now he was leading his friends into this new world.

They'd come along the South Bank, making a detour to the Imperial War Museum on the way. Jordan had always wanted to go back there, ever since they'd been forced out by the massive fire that had destroyed half of south London. Jordan had wanted to know if the flames had left any part of the buildings and its collections of weapons undamaged. There was a strongroom underground, with a reinforced door and walls, where the museum's pile of functioning weapons and ammunition had been stored. The fire had ripped the place apart, and the roof had partially collapsed. There were fallen planes and blackened tanks in the remains of the main exhibition hall. Weeds and small shrubs were already growing in the ruins, but the kids had managed to find a way downstairs, hauling rubble and bits of ruined exhibits out of the way. Scorched display dummies in their uniforms lay all over the place, like corpses. They'd broken into the strongroom and, while their haul hadn't been all that Jordan had been hoping for, they did still manage to find some new gear — swords and spears, bayonets, even a few old guns with working ammunition.

Once they'd stocked up they'd headed north towards Westminster Bridge, and were now crossing towards the Houses of Parliament. Will felt proud. You had to admit they were an impressive sight, like a real army. At school he'd read about the Children's Crusade in the thirteenth century, when children from all over Europe had joined together to march to the Holy Land and free it from the Saracens. At least that's how they'd seen it at the time. Will hoped this army would fare better. Most of the kids

from the Children's Crusade – those that hadn't died from disease or starvation – had ended up boarding boats owned by slavers and being sold into slavery.

There was a good crowd of local children waiting for them on the north bank. Ryan and his hunters had gone on ahead to whip up some excitement. Jordan wanted to make an entrance. A show of strength. He'd told Ryan to spread the word – at midday, when the sun was at its highest, Jordan would bring his troops across the bridge. And he didn't just want cheering locals. He wanted all their leaders there as well. He wanted a proper welcoming party. He wanted to make a point.

Will pushed ahead, past Matt and Archie, past the flapping banners, up into the front rank of musicians. He felt slightly out of place not being dressed in green, and hoped he wasn't spoiling the look of the army, but he wanted to be sure that the right people were ready and waiting. He knew how important it was. If the locals didn't all accept Jordan being commander-in-chief it would lead to days of arguing. And it might piss Jordan off. Which wouldn't be a good idea.

Will spotted Justin in the crowd of waiting kids, with Jackson, Blue and Maxie from the museum. They were standing close to Nicola and a big group from the Houses of Parliament. No surprise as this was right on their doorstep. On the opposite side of the road were David, Jester and Pod, with a group of David's boys in red blazers forming a personal guard. And there were Ryan and his hunters, with their dogs, whooping and cheering.

So that was pretty much all of them. Jordan had planned this well. The locals were wide-eyed and slack-jawed.

When the front of the column reached the end of the

bridge, Matt shouted a command as arranged and his musicians gave a sort of ragged fanfare that signalled to all the army to stop where they were. They halted and there was a sudden and unexpected deep silence. Will smiled. This was working so well. The front ranks parted, lining up on either side of the bridge, and they all turned to face the centre as Jordan came forward, walking slowly and steadily between them, his own guard flanking him. It was designed to be a long walk. To let the power of the moment really sink in and crank up the tension. If Jordan organized the battle this well, how could they lose?

When he got to the front, Jordan stopped. Standing there for a long while, not saying anything. Keeping very still. There was dead silence. The local kids watching him, waiting, wondering. Will remembered how some teachers could keep order in a classroom without seeming to do a lot. Others would shout and throw out threats and still nobody listened.

Finally Jordan spoke. Didn't have to shout. Everyone was listening.

'My name is General Jordan Hordern,' he said. 'And I've come to help. If you accept my help I will lead your army and we will kill every sicko in London. If you don't accept my help I will turn round and march back to the Tower and leave you all to die. If you speak for your people come forward and talk.'

Will waited. There was a moment's hesitation while this sunk in. And then Justin came over, nodded at Jordan, told him who he was. They hadn't met in a long while. It had been over a year since they'd split up during the battle of Lambeth Bridge. They exchanged some words. Then Maxie and Blue joined them, Nicola close behind. Ryan

sauntered over, not wanting to be left out. Only David hung back. Too proud. But, when he saw that he was in danger of being left out altogether, he walked over with Jester and Pod. Some agreements must have been made because the next thing they were all shaking hands and nodding. Again the only one who didn't instantly join in was David. He was still keeping his distance from the main group, muttering to Jester and Pod.

Will had been expecting this, and he'd warned Jordan that David was going to be trouble. This whole show would let him know that Jordan wasn't to be messed with, but there was a big danger it would scare him and make him less keen to accept Jordan as the boss. Finally Jordan turned to David and gave him the stare. This was the moment. Jordan hardly ever looked at you square on, and when he did it freaked you out. It was time for David to make up his mind. He tried to return Jordan's look, but only lasted a few seconds before turning away and walking off. Jordan cut him out, barked a couple of commands and his kids reformed into a column and marched on. Nicola, Justin, Blue and Maxie fell in. Part of the army now. Enjoying it.

Will glanced over at David as they marched past him. He didn't look happy. His eyes darted about. Was he trying to count the number of kids in the army? Will smiled. David would probably be feeling pretty foolish now. Jordan had outplayed him.

This part had gone well. The easy part. What next? Were they really going to face up to a whole army of sickos?

Will didn't want to think that far ahead.

Maxie turned to smile at Blue. This felt good – like they had a chance. Blue wasn't showing anything, though. They'd all just been through a macho, bullshit ritual. It had been all about 'face', and Blue had kept his blank. He was marching in step, though. Maxie had been in the football team at school and remembered what it had been like when the other schools turned up to play. That wariness. Checking each other out. Sizing each other up. Which team was likely to win? Who were the players to watch out for? They were all on the same side here, but it had still been awkward. Quite frankly, she wasn't that bothered who was going to lead the army in the coming battle. Blue would have been as good as anyone else, Achilleus even, or Jackson. It was going to be a messy scrap whatever. A brutal hand-to-hand with a load of diseased grown-ups.

Hardly Waterloo.

It wouldn't need the planning of, say, the D-Day landings.

Maxie had no interest in doing it herself, mind you. She'd never really even wanted to lead the Holloway kids. It had just sort of happened after Arran had died and nobody else wanted the responsibility. Achilleus was a

better fighter, but he didn't want to be in charge. He liked doing his own thing and sneering from the back. Now she sort of shared the job with Blue. The two rival Holloway gangs had merged into a single unit on their way to the palace. Blue had that male pride thing going on. Stuff like that was more important to him than it was to her. All Maxie really cared about was surviving, and making sure her friends survived. She didn't mind how, and she didn't much care how she looked, what other people thought of her. Blue was different. He'd grown up in a tough world where the impression you made was the most important thing. A world where status mattered. She'd talked to him, though, and deep down he was happy to let someone else take overall charge, so long as he kept control of his own troops.

She knew that Justin was cool about it too. He was happy to let Jordan be general. Justin was a thinker, an organizer, not a fighter. Nicola too. She wasn't a military type. She got power in other ways.

David, though. David was an arse. If he didn't want to play ball then he was going to be on the sidelines. Were his troops even that important? This new lot from the Tower looked like proper fighters. Maxie had never been convinced by David's gang in their posh red blazers. She'd smiled at the way David had backed off, slunk away. They'd marched past him standing by the side of the road, sulking. He knew he was beaten.

She was impressed by how well drilled the Tower kids were, how well organized, but she was most impressed by the weapons they'd brought. They had guns and proper spears and swords and armour, not the home-made, improvised stuff the Holloway kids had scavenged off the

streets. And then there was Jordan Hordern. He was properly hard. It was funny – boys who tried to look tough, to act deadly, usually ended up just looking silly, like they were playing a part. Kids like Jordan didn't have to put on an act because they were sure of their power. Nobody was going to argue with Jordan.

Maxie really thought they could do it now. Take on the grown-ups and win. It was such an abstract concept, though. She found it hard to believe that there really was an army of them out there. It had been so quiet lately. If there was going to be a battle, then when? How long were they going to have to wait?

Some of Matt's green troops peeled off. He'd insisted that he take his most hardcore religious fanatics to rough it in Westminster Abbey, which was right behind the Houses of Parliament. The rest of his group, the younger ones, the less devout, the fighters who wanted to join in the training, had chosen the relative comfort and safety of the museums. The new arrivals would be staying in the Victoria and Albert, where there was a lot of free space. Maxie and Blue had spent the last three days working with a crew, dragging beds and bedding in there from nearby houses. It looked like the new arrivals had brought supplies with them, but how long would they last before food began to run out?

There had been talk of drawing the sicko army out into the open somewhere. Choosing a battlefield. David had had some thoughts. Not great ones. But he wasn't part of it any more. So what would he do now? He could stay in the palace and miss out on all the glory, but could he do anything to upset the other kids' plans? To make life difficult for them? Not in any way Maxie could think of.

No. He was just going to make himself an outsider. If he wasn't a part of this, then he was going to be ignored when it was all over. Insignificant. She knew the battle was going to be one of those things – if you weren't there, then . . .

Well. You weren't there.

25

He was singing at the sky and the sky sang back. A blue song. He smiled. That was a new thought. And an old thought. Yesterday he hadn't had the word – *blue*. Didn't know that all that up there was the *sky*. The words were coming back to him. Filling him up. The thoughts becoming clear and straight in his mind. Blue. Sky. New. Thoughts. Words. Mind . . .

He remembered things from his life – that was new as well – memories, coming back to him. He could list them all. A long string of them. Starting up there in the sky. In the blue. On a far-distant star. That's where it had all begun, his life. Yes, he was sure of that. And then he'd come here. To the green. To the jungle. And, my God, that had been a long time ago. More than a hundred years. Thousands of years even. Longer. Dear Lord, he'd lived for a long time. He must have done, to remember all that so clearly. The blue, the green, the jungle, the trees, the bats and the birds and the fleas. And the people . . .

He'd been one of them. He'd been pretty sure of that. Living in the jungle. And then he'd come here. To . . . what was the name?

London!

Yes.

And then . . . How did that work? How did that fit together? This was where it all got confusing. He somehow must have lived two lives. His life up there, in space, and then in the jungle, and his other life here, as a butcher. His life with his boy. His Liam. His little boy. Taking him to watch the Arsenal play at Highbury. The old stadium. The new stadium. Near home. It had burned down, hadn't it? And Liam . . . Someone had killed Liam. Someone bad. He knew it. A bad man. With a big head and a cross on his front. He knew him so well. What was his name? No. He couldn't remember everything – *give me a break* – not all in one go. It was too much, too fast.

Liam was dead, though. He was sure. He remembered that. And he had to make it right for him. Yes, it was all coming back. Working hard. Visiting the farms to see the animals with Liam. That was when it had happened. The disease. Yes, he'd forgotten about the disease. That had been bad, hadn't it? And what had happened to it?

It had got inside him. It was living in there. He had a dirty foreign squatter inside him. You see, that's where it all got mixed up. He'd been doing so well. Clear blue skies. Not a cloud in his head. And now? Was he a bug or was he not a bug? Was the bug inside him? Was that it? Millions of bugs – all squeaking and twittering at each other – sending him mad. He was the bug and the bug was him. I'm George. I'm me. The butcher, the baker, the candlestick maker . . .

No! Shut up! I'm Greg.

I'm Greg. That's who I am.

It was clear to him now and clear what had to be done. It was time for the eggs to hatch, for the bugs to come out and play. But first they had to kill them all. Not the bugs.

The children. Kids. They'd caused all the trouble in the world, and they were trying to cause more, trying to stop the eggs from hatching. And if the bugs couldn't hatch then it would all be over.

He scratched his head. It was hot and tangled in there, full of battery acid. He had to drain it. He had to try to GET THINGS STRAIGHT.

He wanted help. Help to kill the children. Because the children wanted to kill him. Yes, they did. Him and all his kind. And they had the boy, the one with the strong blood. They must not give the children time. Time to make their medicine. He must strike hard and stop them all. And only then would it be time to emerge.

Emerge. That was a good word.

A new birth. That was it. He was sure he had it straight now.

So he needed help. And he was sending out the call. Come to me. Come and finish what we started. All of you who can hear me. Come and we will be an army and I will lead you and we will kill them all.

He was one giant being, as big as London – bigger – with arms stretching out in all directions, hundreds of fingers reaching out, and hundreds of mouths all calling out. Come to me if you can hear me.

He felt so strong now. And peaceful. Not hungry any more. They didn't need to eat; they had all the energy they needed, stored inside them. They just had to do this one last thing – this great push – and then ... peace. Nirvana. Eternity. At one with the universe.

His army was quiet and still. Waiting for the others. When the others came, they would move. They would attack.

First. First things first. They had to take the boy. The small one.

He'd seen the tiddler, the sprat, back at the stadium. All that time ago. He'd seen the boy, but back then he hadn't known. Hadn't realized who he was. He knew now. Because the voices had been screaming it in his ear. And he knew what he had to do. Find the boy. Kill the boy.

He stared at the sky, still singing in his head, still calling, and all his army calling come to me, come to me, come to me . . .

And they were coming. He could feel them. Moving closer.

He turned from the sky and looked at his people. All packed in together in a dark and greasy heap, lying on top of each other, spreading out as far as he could see in all directions.

He walked, and as he walked his people got up and made way for him, parting to make a path. They all looked to him. He was in all their brains and they were in his. They were one being. A giant bug colony with only one thought. He loved them. They would do whatever he said. One came over, a mother, threw herself at his feet, her mouth moving, no sound coming out, just a soft call in his brain, his inner ear. He loved her. She was his. Utterly devoted to him. He looked at her. And he put thoughts into her mind and she smiled and put her fingers to her face, hooked the tips into her lower eyelids, and pulled and pulled and scraped until her whole face had come off. He made her do it because he could. How she smiled at him now. You'd never seen such a big grin.

And then he told the others to eat her. Not because

they were hungry, but because he could. And she never stopped smiling. She loved him so much.

These people were his. They were his hands, his eyes, his heart.

And here were his soldiers walking towards him, the ones who had been with him from the start. They'd brought what he'd asked for, the tools to finish the job – blades and points and hammers. Sharp things. Hard things. Cold things. Things to do harm, to cut and club and smash. He chose one – a cleaver. The name came back to him. *Cleaver*. A good word that. He had used that word before; he had used the tool. He'd been a butcher after all, hadn't he? He'd already established that. The cleaver was a good tool. It cut through meat and bone and fat and gristle and sinew and veins and arteries. Clean.

He held it above his head and showed his people and they understood. They started to move away, to spread out. They were going out into the city to find whatever tools they could. No, not tools. There was a better word. It was there. Waiting for him. It was a word that had made his kind kings of the planet.

He just had to let it come.

Seven.

Weeping.

Wept on.

Slept on.

Went on.

Weapon.

I am St George and I will slay the dragon with my cold weapon.

26

'So what am I then? What rank?'

'I don't know. What rank do you wanna be?'

'Corporal, no, captain, that sounds good – Captain
Achilleus, like Captain America . . . Colonel? Could I be a
colonel? Maybe a lieutenant, not a sergeant or sergeant
major. What about major? Is that above captain? What's
one rank below general?'

'Brigadier maybe?'

'Nah, sounds crap.'

'You can be whatever you like,' said Maxie. 'Just not a
general.'

'Oh no, not a general. That job goes to the high-and-
mighty Jordan Hordern. He is our Führer.'

'Don't make this hard, Achilleus.'

'I ain't. I told you. I don't want to be no general. Generals don't fight. Generals don't win medals. Nobody used
to make films about generals, because generals were
boring. Giving out orders all day and sitting on horses and
looking at maps. No thanks. I want to be on the frontline,
kicking butt, living it, yeah? My spear slippery with their
blood. So who do I get to be captain of?'

They were in Hyde Park. Jordan had chosen it as the
best place to practise manoeuvres, and if possible he was

159

going to have his battle with the sickos here. He had it all planned. There'd been another big meeting at the Houses of Parliament, with maps and everything, just as Achilleus had described the life of a general.

'Wellington beat Napoleon and his armies because he was very good at picking battle sites,' Jordan had explained. 'Choosing the right site means the battle's halfway won.'

The meeting had gone on for ages. They'd discussed every aspect of the plans. Everyone had been there except, of course, David. He'd sent Jester with a letter explaining that unless he was general then he wouldn't be sending any troops. But Jester had stayed all the same and joined in. He wanted to know what was going on. Maxie had taken him aside at one point and had a go at him. He'd tried to defend himself, said that if it was down to him he would have accepted Jordan taking charge, no problem, and brought the fighters from the palace with him. But it wasn't his call. There was no democracy at the palace. What David said went.

'So why don't you have a coup?' Maxie had asked.

'Don't think I haven't dreamt about it,' said Jester with a sly grin. 'Imagined David's head on a pole. But the thing is — David might be a prick, and a pompous jerk, but he holds things together. People feel secure and happy at the palace. I couldn't rule in the way David does.'

Yeah. Jester was a right-hand man, a lieutenant, not a leader. An ambassador. An adviser. In that he was like Achilleus. Who didn't want to be in charge.

So what was Maxie?

She was just someone who wanted to make things right.

And now it was down to her to explain to everyone what their duties were.

'You're in charge of the right flank infantry,' she explained.

'The right?' Achilleus sounded theatrically indignant. 'What if I want to be in charge of the left flank?'

'What if you want to be a douche? It doesn't make any difference.'

'Yeah? Would of been nice to have been asked, all the same.'

'You don't want to be a captain? Fine. You can be a private if you want?'

'No. Is cool. I'll take the right flank infantry.'

'OK. Ollie's in charge of artillery.'

'Artillery now, is it? Not just throwing shit?'

'Got to call it something.'

'And who takes the left flank?'

'Matt and his green kids.'

'That it?'

'Jordan holds the centre. That's where me and Blue will be, sticking close to him. Making sure what he wants to happen happens. Ryan and his hunters are going to patrol the streets round the perimeter, make sure no sickos try to get past us. And there's a reserve unit at the back, the less strong fighters. They're under the control of that Boggle kid from the museum. They'll be fed into the other units as needed.'

'OK. Sounds organized. So Boggle's the only museum kid who gets to be a captain. What about Jackson? She's good.'

'Jackson was offered it, but she said she wanted to be in your unit.'

'Yeah? Crazy girl. She can be my corporal or whatever. So do I get to pick all my own officers?'

'I guess so.'

'What about Will?'

'What about him?'

'I reckon I'll take him. He knows what he's doing.'

'Yeah, he's OK.'

'You think he's good-looking?'

Maxie hadn't been expecting this question.

'He's all right,' she said. 'Why?'

'You're a girl. You think about these things.'

'Not necessarily.'

'Oh, come on, Maxie.'

'Are you asking me if I fancy him?'

'Well, do you?'

'I've got Blue. You know I do. I don't think about anyone else.'

'Bet you do.'

'Bet I don't.'

'Well, if you didn't have Blue. If you were a free agent. A girl about town. Would you go for Will?'

'He's OK. I don't know. Maybe. He's nice. Clever. Civilized – unlike you. And yeah, he's OK-looking.'

'Does he have a girlfriend?'

'I don't know.' Maxie was confused. She'd never had a conversation like this with Achilleus before.

'Ask him.'

'Achilleus . . . ?' Maxie looked at the boy. He was sitting on the grass, spinning his spear in his hands. 'I am not interested in going out with him. OK?'

'I'm just making conversation. I'm a captain now. People got to listen to me.'

'You *will* take it seriously?'

'Up to a point.' Achilleus spat. 'In the end all this organization ain't gonna account for much. It's just gonna

be fighting. Hard and nasty. Makes no difference whether I'm called captain, head honcho or chief cheerleader.'

'The thing is,' said Maxie, 'it's an important position, yeah? Everyone said you were the best guy for the job. You should be proud.'

'You sound like my science teacher when I got a D.'

'I mean it. We don't always tell you, Achilleus, because, well, frankly you're a pain in the arse, but we appreciate all you've done. OK? We'd probably none of us from the Holloway crew be here if it wasn't for you. You're far and away the best fighter around.'

'Aw. I'm touched.'

'See. Arsehole.'

'Maxie?'

'Yeah?'

'Maybe nobody tells you things either.'

'What do you mean?'

'After Arran died we could've fallen apart. But we didn't. Because you held it together. "*Arran Lives*" – you remember that?'

'I remember.'

'He lived on in you, Max. You done well. I like you. You're cool.'

Maxie didn't know what to say. She was waiting for Achilleus to pull the chair away, to laugh at her as she crashed to the floor. But he didn't. In the end it was he who spoke next.

'So? We gonna win this thing?' he asked.

'We've got to,' said Maxie. 'Otherwise it's the end for all of us.'

'The Last Battle . . . We'll do it. Arran Lives. We all live.'

Now Achilleus did laugh and Maxie was going to say something when she realized that he wasn't laughing at her. He was watching the smaller kids who were drilling in an area away from the main block. Paddy was shouting orders, his high young voice carrying in the still air.

'Look at them little mugs,' said Achilleus. 'What's Jordan gonna do with them? Use them as cannon fodder?'

'No bloody way,' said Maxie. 'Sam's too important. 'Don't tell them, but they're gonna be nowhere near the fighting when it kicks off. They're staying back at the museum, under guard. Whitney's got the job of keeping them away and keeping them safe. That what we're fighting this battle for after all, to protect Sam long enough to make a cure. If he dies this is all a waste of time.'

'Should I be scared?' Achilleus asked.

'You don't ever get scared.'

'You're right.' Achilleus laughed. 'I don't have the imagination. You know me. Point me at the enemy and I'll fight. All this stuff, it's way complicated.'

'Not really,' said Maxie. 'When it comes down to it, you've got the right idea – all we gotta do is kill more grown-ups than they kill of us.'

'That I can understand,' said Achilleus. '*That* – I can understand.'

Paddy felt ten feet tall. Out here with all the big kids, shouting orders, being in command, with his own troop. An officer. Jordan Hordern had even sent over a marshal, Hayden, to help with his training. She was a girl, but that was OK. She was a cool girl. Paddy used to do football training at the weekends, with a club, and there'd been lots of girls like Hayden helping out. She knew proper weapons drill and, when Paddy had shown her what his troop could already do, she'd been well impressed, Paddy could tell. She'd even clapped and whooped a couple of times. She'd been impressed by all of them except Blu-Tack Bill. Bill did this thing where he'd just stop what he was doing. He'd stop marching, or drilling, or mock fighting or whatever, and wander off to the side, saying numbers out loud. In the end Hayden had asked him what the matter was. Bill said nothing was the matter, he was just counting.

'Counting what?'

'Stuff.'

'What stuff?'

'Trees. People. Railings. Mostly people. I need to know how many.'

'Why do you need to know?'

Blu-Tack Bill had shrugged.

'He's amazing,' said Jibber-jabber. 'He's a savant. A master of numbers. You can try him on anything. Here . . .'

He'd picked up a bunch of gravel and thrown it on to a tarmac pathway.

'How many stones, Bill?'

Bill had glanced at them. A few seconds was all.

'Forty-eight.'

'Go on,' Wiki had said and Hayden had counted them. Bill had been right. Exactly forty-eight. The other kids had cheered, but Bill had just shrugged again. It was nothing to him. Hayden tested him on a couple of other things to make sure it hadn't been a fluke and couldn't believe it. After that they'd stopped for lunch and Hayden had tried to talk to Bill. He wasn't much of a talker, though.

Hayden worked them for a couple more hours and then left them to it. Paddy was starting to get tired. To be honest, drilling was a little bit boring. He liked the mock fighting, but that made you tireder than anything, and the kids couldn't keep it up for long. Paddy was hoping they were all going to stop soon so he could get back to the museum and rest. He looked at the big kids. They were in huddles, making plans, some of them building defences. Constructing a barricade out of wood and branches and railings. He smiled. He was one of them. When the big battle came, his kids would be right there, fighting alongside the likes of Achilleus, Jackson and Blue.

'OK, troop,' he said, his voice a little hoarse from shouting all day. 'Take five. At ease. Hang loose.'

The others gratefully dropped their weapons and slumped to the grass, started chatting among themselves. Paddy sat with Bright Eyes, Zohra and her little brother,

Froggie. Bright Eyes had been sitting there, patiently watching them all day. Zohra and Froggie made a fuss over him. The two of them were always together. Paddy could tell that Zohra was proud that she'd protected Froggie, got him this far.

'What will happen after the battle?' said Froggie. He was too young really to know what it was all about, what a battle was going to be like.

'After the battle there'll be peace,' said Zohra. 'We can get things back to how they were before.'

Froggie thought about that and nodded.

'Which one of you kids is Blu-Tack Bill?'

Paddy looked up to see Jordan Hordern standing there with Hayden. Paddy jumped to his feet, cursing himself. What had he done wrong? The general scared him. He wore those thick glasses, but he never looked at you straight.

Paddy pointed to Bill.

'That's him. I'm sorry we stopped training. Some of the smaller ones were a bit tired. Not me. We'll carry on if you want. What have we done?'

Jordan looked at him sideways.

'Nobody done nothing bad,' he said. 'I just want to talk.' He turned to Bill who was staring at the ground. 'You Bill, yeah?'

Bill nodded.

'You OK to talk?'

Bill shrugged like he always did.

'We'll walk a ways,' said Jordan. 'Just you and me, yeah? You cool with that?'

Bill shrugged again and got up, and the two of them wandered off, the general doing all the talking. After

they'd gone a little way Paddy saw Bill take Jordan's hand. Paddy hadn't ever seen that before. Bill didn't like to be touched.

'What's that all about?' Paddy asked Hayden.

'The general needs a kid like Bill,' said Hayden. 'He always says that intelligence is your best weapon.'

'Oh,' said Paddy. 'I'm not sure Bill's intelligent really. He can do his number trick, but his brain's a bit screwy.'

'Jordan's brain's a bit screwy too,' said Hayden. 'They make a good pair.'

'He taking him out of my fighting unit?'

'Would you mind?'

'Not really. Bill's not a natural soldier.'

Hayden laughed. 'Jordan will only take him if Bill agrees.'

'We'll be under strength.'

'You'll manage.'

After a while Jordan and Bill came back. Bill sat apart from the others as he often did. Jordan squatted down and rubbed Bright Eyes's head.

'This your dog?' he asked Paddy. Paddy beamed.

'Sure,' he said. 'She's a good dog. She's real clever. She used to be a seeing-eye dog. I'm training her to be a dog of war.'

Jordan studied Bright Eyes, not saying anything. After a while he grunted and stood up. Walked away with Hayden, the two of them talking about something. Hayden glanced round now and then to look back at Paddy and Bright Eyes.

'They're talking about me,' said Paddy. 'She's probably telling him what a good officer I am, what a good job I done with you lot. Maybe he'll even put us in the front

rank of the fighting. We'll be handy. We can nip in there, chop them bastards in the legs.'

Paddy didn't feel tired any more. He was fired up, his head filled with dreams of glory.

'Come on,' he shouted. 'Let's try a double-time quick march!'

Bill shook his head. Looked round at his friends and then ran off after Jordan and Hayden. Fell in next to them and, after a few paces, took hold of Jordan's hand again. He turned once to look back at them all. Like he was saying goodbye forever.

28

This felt unreal. Too weird. Sitting in the back seat of a Land Rover Discovery with Bernie, driving north through empty streets. It even had that new-car smell. Ben had no idea where Shadowman had got it from – it really *was* a discovery. Where exactly they were headed was also a mystery.

Shadowman had come to find him and Bernie at the museum. They'd been working in the kitchens, rigging up a better system for smoke extraction. It was so smoky in there from the open fire they cooked over that it was in danger of ruining the kids' lungs. When Ben had first seen their system, he'd sworn and told the girl in charge – 'You don't have to worry about grown-ups getting you. This'll kill you a whole lot faster.'

Shadowman had been secretive. From what Ben had seen of him he was always secretive. He'd just told the two of them that he had a job for them, more important than getting rid of smoke. He'd led them out along the Cromwell Road to where he'd left the car parked up a side-street some way from the museum. He didn't say anything, but it was obvious he didn't want anyone at the museum to know that he had a vehicle.

So far they'd been driving in silence. Ben and Bernie

were so gobsmacked by the whole experience that they were just staring out of the window like little kids up from the countryside on a day trip to the big city, marvelling at it all. It wasn't like they'd even seen anything spectacular. No Trafalgar Square or Houses of Parliament, no London Eye or Tower Bridge. Just the ugly grey streets of Earls Court and Shepherd's Bush. But it was still thrilling to the two of them. For nearly a year they'd seen nothing except the small area of Holloway around Waitrose. Then there had been that short, intense, terrifying trip into town. Since then – well, since then they'd got used to being at the museum. Took it for granted. And now this.

It was like a trip to the most exotic foreign country. They'd told themselves they'd never do something like this again. Drive in a car. Warm and safe. Not a grown-up in sight. Shadowman had even put some music on. Not something Ben would normally have listened to – it sounded like an old Rolling Stones CD – but just to listen to any music was extraordinary.

Ben couldn't hold it in any longer. He *had* to know what was going on.

'So? What's up?' he said as casually as possible. 'Where we going, dude?'

'North,' said Shadowman.

'More info required,' said Ben.

'Right now we're going round St George's army,' said Shadowman.

'I get that,' said Ben. 'But what's our destination?'

'Did you know Ed at all?' Shadowman asked.

'Not really,' said Ben. 'I talked to him a couple of times, but he wasn't with us for long.'

'I talked to him a lot,' said Shadowman. 'He told me

things. Like what happened to him before he arrived at the Tower of London.'

Ben didn't say anything. He looked at Bernie – eyebrows raised. Bernie gave him a look back. They were both wondering where this was going, but Ben guessed that Shadowman wanted to tell them in his own way, in his own time. Ben reckoned that when people did that it meant they weren't really sure of what they were saying. He figured maybe Shadowman wasn't entirely convinced by their mission. He was kind of creeping up on it, giving the explanation sideways.

'What did he tell you?' said Bernie. 'And what's it got to do with where we're going? You can't just kidnap us, bro. Nice as it is to go for a drive.'

'You know the Oval cricket ground in south London?' said Shadowman.

'Not really,' said Ben. 'We neither of us exactly cricket fans. They all wear white. We tend towards the black.'

Bernie laughed. 'So true,' she said. 'With us, it's all about black. With them, it's all about white.'

'Is there any sport where they all wear black?' said Ben.

'Maybe a team of referees,' said Shadowman. He had a sense of humour at least.

'Wasn't there a rugby team called the All Blacks?' said Bernie. 'From New Zealand or something? Dad used to watch the rugby. I could never understand it, and he could never understand me. Why I painted my room black and listened to Marilyn Manson and My Chemical Romance all the time. But it was him that taught me all about mechanics and engineering.'

'What's cricket got to do with where we going?' said Ben. 'You got to stop being so secretive, dude.'

'About a year ago,' said Shadowman, 'when Ed was travelling through south London, he and some friends broke into the Oval, looking for gear.'

'What did they find there?' Ben asked.

'Bodies mostly,' said Shadowman. 'Dead bodies.'

'Watching the cricket?' said Bernie. 'Just like it always was.'

'You see the government?' said Shadowman. 'Seems like they'd run out of places to dump the dead. The army had started loading them on to trucks and using cranes and diggers and crap to pile them all in the Oval. They'd filled the whole stadium up.'

'Jesus,' said Bernie. 'I wondered what their plan was.'

'Wasn't much of a plan,' said Shadowman. 'They all got sick before they could finish it.'

'What exactly were they gonna do when they ran out of space in there?'

'They were gonna blow the whole place up,' said Shadowman, and he gave a dark little laugh.

'For real?' said Ben. 'Cool.'

'Burn the lot of them,' said Shadowman. 'Had the whole stadium rigged with explosives and stuff to start fires. But, as I say, they all got the disease before they could ever do it.'

'OK,' said Ben. 'Good story, but where is this going? Where are *we* going?'

'*We're on our way to Wembley,*' Shadowman sang. Ben guessed it was some kind of football chant.

'You mean we're going to see if Wembley was rigged the same way?' said Bernie.

'You're on it,' said Shadowman. 'That is exactly what we're doing. Seems to me, if they rigged up one stadium

they might have rigged up more. And Wembley is the biggest of them all. At least around here. See this car? Belongs to a guy called Saif. He's got a powerful settlement up that way. He's got vehicles and he's got troops. Plus, he has a thing going with St George. Bad blood. Wants to kick the guy's ass.'

'Don't we all,' said Ben.

'Well, plan is we can give him the biggest kick up the ass in history,' said Shadowman. 'We boot him with high explosives and incendiary bombs.'

'Won't that be a little . . .' Ben paused, searching for the right word. Hazardous? Risky? Unsafe? '*Dangerous*?' he said. Keeping it simple.

'That's what we got to figure out,' said Shadowman. 'And that's where you come in. You know about this type of stuff. About mechanics and engineering and how things work. Plan is we rig up as many vehicles as Saif can give us and turn them into car bombs. All you gotta do then is work out a way of driving them into the rear of St George's army without getting killed and blow them all into another dimension.'

'That's *all* we've gotta do?' said Ben, with heavy sarcasm. 'Break into Wembley Stadium. Find out whether there's actually any explosives in there. Work out how to get them out without killing ourselves. Rig up a fleet of vehicles as car bombs, and then drive them into the middle of St George's army and blow them up without killing ourselves for a second time. This is assuming that Saif and his guys don't want to become suicide bombers.'

'They certainly don't,' said Shadowman.

'So you thought you'd just jack us, drive us up there and we'd do your bidding?' said Ben.

'I've already got some ideas actually,' said Bernie. 'This could be cool. A challenge. And if we get it right, man, if we pimp those rides and turbocharge them to the max, it could change everything.'

'OK. It looks like we're on board,' said Ben. 'What Bernie says goes.'

'You never had a choice,' said Shadowman. And as he said it Ben got his first glimpse of the stadium. Still some way ahead, but towering over the low buildings of Wembley. The distinctive shape of the massive white steel arch unmistakable.

'What if we get there and it's empty?' said Bernie.

'Then we try Tottenham, QPR, Chelsea . . . We keep looking till we find what we want.'

'What about Arsenal?' said Bernie.

'Stadium burned down,' said Shadowman.

'Cool,' said Bernie. At school the sporty kids had teased and bullied the two of them. They'd become a team, drawing strength from each other, laughing about the macho kids. But when the older kids had found out that Ben and Bernie could fix their, mostly stolen, scooters and mopeds they'd gained some respect and the bullying had stopped.

Now everyone had their place. And Ben and Bernie were going to try to help defeat the enemy in their own way. With skill and ingenuity and knowledge. Sure, in a war you needed foot soldiers, to fire the guns and drive the tanks and fly the planes. But they wouldn't get far without people to design and build the guns and the tanks and the planes, to build the bridges for the tanks to drive over.

Every army had its engineers and, without them, they were useless.

Ben knew how to fix engines, had learnt to fix guns, but high explosives?

That was something else.

The trick was going to be not blowing themselves up before they got anywhere near the enemy.

TV Boy was worried. The Warehouse Queen was having a major weird-out, jerking and gibbering. She was thrashing her head around so wildly that the bony lumps that grew out of her skull in the shape of a crown were bashing against the cardboard cut-out of a throne that was fixed to the back of her wheelchair and threatening to smash it to pieces.

Monstar looked worried. He was hugging himself, his long arms wrapped round his hugely muscled and misshapen body.

'She's getting worse and worse,' he said and TV Boy had to agree. He shuffled closer, loose-jointed arms and legs going in all directions, knees up around his ears. When the Queen had these fits, she was often exhausted afterwards. Sometimes she was even physically sick.

'What's going to happen to us?' he asked. The three of them were on the communal platform, high above the warehouse floor. They felt incomplete, out of sorts, not having the others here – Trinity and Fish-Face and Skinner. They'd lived all their lives together, had shared everything in their own little group, separated from the rest of the world. Pencil Neck had been the first to leave, slithering off to lose himself in the corners and crevices of the warehouse.

But he'd never really been one of them. He was so far gone he was more animal than human. He was still out there somewhere, crawling through the heating pipes, and along the wiring ducts, catching insects and rodents.

It was very different when the others left. It had felt like the end of something. TV Boy often thought about the Inmathger, the rainforest tribe whose first contact with other humans had been the moment the disease escaped their tiny part of the jungle and entered the wider world. They had wandered out of the rainforest into the sunlight, and one day soon the warehouse kids were going to have to come blinking out of their own jungle and mix with other people. They couldn't stay an undiscovered tribe forever. Let's face it, they'd already *been* discovered. Blue and Einstein and their gang had tipped up and turned their world upside down. TV Boy wondered when Skinner and the others would return. That had always been the plan. They were supposed to report back on what was out there. But judging by the messages the Queen was getting from the voices in her head, which only she could hear, it seemed that what was out there was a whole lot worse than they'd feared.

Maybe the others would never return?

The Queen bit the edge of her hand and Monstar went to her, tried to calm her down by holding her.

'What's she hearing?' TV Boy asked and Monstar made a face.

'The usual stuff,' he said. 'She tries to make sense of the voices. I worry about what it's doing to her.'

Monstar may have been a big, muscle-bound hulk, but he was soft inside. Perhaps, like the rest of him, his heart was unusually big as well. Out of all of them he was the one who cared most.

And TV Boy knew that the thing he cared most about was the Queen. Monstar worshipped her. The big, soft, gooey marshmallow.

Suddenly the Queen fell very still and her eyes opened wide. She stared into the distance, looking at something that only she could see. She raised a hand and pointed, horrified, then her hand flopped down and she relaxed, normal again. As normal as she ever could be.

'It was him,' she said at last.

'Who?' asked Monstar.

'Mister Three. I heard him as if he was here with us. He's the loudest of them all.'

'I usually hear him,' said Monstar. 'But he's too far away for me now.'

TV Boy was sometimes jealous of the way the others could communicate like this, but he was quite glad not to have crazy Mister Three yelling away inside his head.

'What's happening?' he asked.

'They've split up,' said the Queen. 'Trinity has gone west with a boy called Ed; they're looking for a girl – Ella. Skinner and Fish-Face are still in London, at the museum. I need to connect them. Mister Three's going batshit. I can amplify all their signals and help them, but Three's too loud. It hurts. Take me to the roof. I need to hear everything.'

Monstar sighed and blew out his cheeks. He was ridiculously strong and could easily lift the Queen out of her chair, but carrying her up the steep steps to the roof was tough. Which was why she never usually went up there. Monstar would do whatever she asked, though. Gently, he lifted her out of the wheelchair they'd disguised as a movable throne and carried her towards the steps that led

to the roof. TV Boy followed, his legs painfully twisting and buckling as he went.

'What did they tell you this time?' TV Boy asked once they were safely up on the roof. They could see a long way in all directions from here. In the past there had usually been grown-ups hanging around below, trying to get into the warehouse, but since Blue and his friends had left it had been quiet.

'There are so many voices now.' The Queen closed her eyes. 'All shouting at once. It's hard to tune them, to concentrate on just one.'

TV Boy had heard the words, Monstar too, but the Queen hadn't moved her lips; no sound had come out. Hers was the only voice TV Boy could ever hear like this. None of the rest of them knew how to get inside his head.

'I'm trying to find Skinner and Fish-Face,' she went on. 'After Three, Fish-Face was always the loudest. But she's been quiet lately.'

'Not quiet,' said Monstar. 'Drowned out.'

'You're right,' said the Queen. 'There's so much noise. I thought it was white noise at first, but it's not. It's them. The grown-ups. All screaming at once. Three can cut through, when he wakes.'

'He's been waking more and more lately,' Monstar explained. 'Can you feel it, TV? It's all changing out there. The grown-ups are being called away.'

'Hopefully, when they've all gone, I'll be able to hear the others better,' said the Queen. 'And if I can amplify the signal we can all link up properly. It's tiring, though. It's hard work. And the voices, I hate what they talk about. There's one – getting stronger and stronger, from the east, from the city. Calling them in. Everything's changing.'

'What should we do?' Monstar asked. 'Do we stay here?'

'We can't go out there by ourselves,' said the Queen. 'We don't know how to fight.'

'We have our own weapons,' said TV Boy. 'Some skills.'

'We've survived by staying here,' said the Queen. 'We have to wait for Skinner and the others to return. They can set us free.'

'What if they don't return?'

'Then we live out our days here. Skinner was brave to go. They all were. I'm not so brave. I'm not sure I can ever leave. I'm Queen here, but out there what'll I be? A freak. Something to laugh at.'

'You can stop them laughing,' said TV Boy. 'You can get in their heads and mess with their minds.'

'I always thought that what I wanted was to be found, to be rescued by outsiders, but when they came I changed my mind.'

'We might have to do it,' said TV Boy. 'We might have to help.'

'I'm too scared,' said the Queen.

'We're all scared,' said TV Boy. 'But maybe we're like we are for a reason. Maybe it's wrong to stay hidden here.'

The Queen looked at him and then suddenly her eyes rolled up in her head and she zoned out again. TV Boy glanced at Monstar, who looked worried.

And then TV Boy winced. The Queen had done it, amplified a signal, broadcast it . . . and it was Mister Three again. The effect of his voice in TV Boy's head was as unpleasant as he'd feared. What he was shouting about was even worse.

30

Einstein's lab was busy, kids in white coats working everywhere, peering in microscopes, doing complicated experiments that Jackson would never understand, mixing stuff in test tubes and beakers. Leaving slime and smears in little flat dishes. Did *they* even know what they were doing? Or were they just trying to look busy? Trying not to think about what was going on outside. Play-acting. That's what it looked like to her. Doctors and nurses.

And it was a nurse she needed right now. It had been a long day and the kids out in the park had got tired. One of her boys, Cameron, had been injured in a mock battle. He had a knack for getting hurt. A wooden club had smashed his hand. He was standing there now, his bad hand jammed in his armpit. It wasn't too bad, swollen but hopefully no broken bones. He was making a terrible fuss about it, though. There were a few kids here in the labs who acted as doctors. They would check Cameron out and Jackson could leave him with them. She'd brought him here with Achilleus, who thought the whole thing was a big joke. Jackson just wanted to say goodbye and go flop somewhere. If Achilleus joined her that'd be a bonus. Maybe he'd cut her hair like his, with the razor patterns in it. He'd been promising to do it for days. But she was tired enough

not to care too much. Some quiet time by herself would be nearly as good.

She couldn't see any of the medical staff, but she spotted Einstein. He was talking excitedly to a group of kids, waving his arms about. His tangle of dark hair madder than ever, his teeth yellower than ever, his manner snootier than ever.

'Are Alexander and Cass around?' she asked him, not worried about interrupting, even though he looked well hacked off at her.

'Not now, Jackson. I'm busy.'

'Yeah,' said Jackson. 'Me too. I'm busy training to save your arse. And so was Cameron. He needs some help.'

'Show me.'

Cameron explained what had happened while Einstein checked out his hand.

'What is it with you?' he asked, looking at the white-faced boy. 'First you let Paul nearly cut your head off and now you let some kid break your hand.'

'Is it broken?' Cameron asked.

'Might be. Someone find Cass. She's here somewhere.'

'You gonna be able to fight?' asked one of the kids with Einstein. She was a new arrival from the Tower. Jackson didn't know her name.

'Hope so,' said Cameron, forcing a grin. 'Don't want to miss the battle.'

Jackson kept quiet. *Really?* The battle was going to be horrible. She knew that. She'd been out on the streets, had seen massed bunches of sickos first hand. It wasn't fun on any level.

'How's it going, prof?' asked Achilleus. 'You solved the mystery of life yet?'

'Maybe.' Einstein offered Achilleus a mad grin. 'You're fighting sickos — we're fighting germs.'

'Parasites actually.' They all turned to see Skinner coming in with Fish-Face and the Green Man. Jackson was surprised at how quickly she'd grown to accept the Twisted Kids, how quickly she'd forgotten how peculiar they looked. Fish-Face with her distorted fish head, Skinner covered in great folds of skin.

She wasn't sure if she'd ever get used to the Green Man, though. It wasn't just that he was an adult. There was something so creepy about him. Pervy. Not at all helped by the fact that he never wore any clothes. Just went around wrapped in a blanket with a ridiculous green bowler hat stuck on his fuzzy green head. He'd always looked bad, with his covering of green mould and his long hair and fingernails, but he looked worse than ever now. He was sweating and it left nasty green rivulets down the mould that grew on his skin. He was shaking and feverish, his eyes darting about. Jackson had heard that Einstein was experimenting on him, trying out cures and antidotes or whatever.

'It's parasites,' Skinner repeated.

'We're fairly sure there's a parasitical element to it,' said Einstein in his annoyingly superior way. 'But . . .'

'Listen to him,' said the Green Man, glaring at Einstein with his yellow eyes, clicking his fingernails together in a way that made your flesh crawl.

'My lab, my rules, Gollum,' said Einstein. 'You can't just come in here and . . .'

'And tell you the truth?' said the Green Man.

'How can you be so sure?'

'We've received a message,' said Skinner. 'At least Fish-

Face has. She can pick stuff up. Trinity's out there and thoughts are bouncing back to her.'

'OK,' said Einstein, gearing up to be even more annoying than ever. 'Let's examine your last statement. Your fish-faced friend here is receiving spooky telepathic messages from miles away sent by a Siamese triplet.'

'Listen . . .' Skinner sounded upset.

'I haven't finished yet. Let me count the ways that this sucks. One – you lot are a bunch of weirdo, freaky mutants and I'm not sure I trust you for one moment. Two – I can't believe a word any of you say. You could all be nuts for all I know. It certainly appears that way. Three – I know you like to pretend you can communicate telepathically, but I'm going to take some convincing that all the laws of nature can be overturned like this. Four . . .'

'Shut up for one second,' shouted Fish-Face, and everyone was shocked. She was usually so quiet and shy, and now here she was, red-hot and glaring at Einstein. More shark than goldfish.

'There is a law in science,' she went on. 'Everything that *can* happen does happen.'

'I know that,' said Einstein. 'But telepathy falls under the heading of "things that can't happen".'

'It's not telepathy,' said Fish-Face. 'Any more than using the telephone is telepathy. Any more than TV and radio are magic. We hear on a different level, in a different way. We pick up signals you can't detect.'

'Listen to us,' said Skinner. 'You might learn something.'

'Look . . .'

'Do as they say, you stupid jerk,' Achilleus snapped. 'I want to hear this.'

Einstein glared at Achilleus, but kept his mouth shut.

'Go on, Fish-Face,' said Achilleus, and she blushed, looking at the floor, embarrassed, her confidence gone again.

'OK,' she said. 'I couldn't understand everything, but my friends have found out more about the disease. We used to talk about spirits and being possessed, but they're sure now that the disease is caused by tiny parasites that hide by disguising themselves as human cells. And when they get to your brain and start to replace your brain cells their thoughts begin to seep into your thoughts. When they grow larger, they start to communicate with each other. There's a sort of hive-mind thing going on, where the parasites have a shared brain, like an ant colony, all working together, like one single being. They share thoughts and memories.'

'That's unlikely,' said Einstein. 'In fact, it's insane.'

'It's not like any other disease anyone's ever seen before,' said Skinner. 'We told you before that there were spirits in the rainforest. They were parasites, which began infecting insects hundreds of thousands of years ago, and they slowly worked their way up the food chain, adapting to each new host.'

'Oh yes,' Einstein scoffed. 'And I think you tried to tell us they originally came from outer space?'

'Isn't it possible?' said Skinner. 'That tiny microorganisms could survive in space, on a meteor, land here . . .'

'*Theoretically*,' said Einstein with so much edge it sounded like he was saying 'bollocks'.

'Well, whatever you believe about their origins,' said Skinner, 'can't you just accept that parasites have got into the adults and are controlling them?'

'Well . . .' Einstein was looking not so sure of himself. Jackson could see that he was starting to think about this.

'I know there are parasites that can make ants climb to the top of tall plants where their brains explode, sending out spores. And parasites that get into snails, into their eyestalks, and make them sort of glow so that birds spot them and eat them and take the parasites into their own guts.'

'And toxoplasmosis,' said Skinner. 'That makes mice not afraid of cats. This is just bigger and weirder.'

'Maybe . . .' said Einstein and he sat down. 'Talk me through the timeline.'

'OK,' said Skinner. 'About sixteen years ago the parasites get out of the jungle . . .'

'Carried by scientists – like me,' said the Green Man.

'Thanks for that,' said Achilleus. Skinner ignored him and carried on.

'Disguised as human blood cells, the parasites go unnoticed and multiply rapidly in their hosts, for now doing no harm at all. But they're microscopic and can be coughed out, sneezed out, flushed down the toilet into the water supply, and that's how they spread – on the air and in the water – all around the world. Within a year, nearly everyone on the planet is infected. That's the first stage of its life cycle. The spore stage. They get into a body, settle down and start a family. They don't go travelling any more.'

'And that's why you're OK,' Fish-Face said to Einstein. 'Because you weren't around to get infected last time.'

'I suppose that makes sense.' Einstein nodded, thinking hard.

'Us Twisted Kids,' said Fish-Face, 'we're like an experiment. As if the parasites were trying to splice their DNA with human DNA, and it didn't work out too good, but we have some of the parasites' characteristics, like the ultrasound thing.'

'And now the parasites are massing,' said Skinner. 'Or their human hosts are.'

'Why?'

'We think they're getting together for the big bang,' said Fish-Face. 'The next infestation. When their spores will get airborne again. We think it's a sixteen-year cycle.'

'I get it,' said Achilleus. 'I saw this clip one time on YouTube. A friend showed it me cos it was so freaky. There was these bugs in, like, Washington or somewhere. Like chicories, chicklets, sickos, these, like, cricket things.'

'Cicadas?' said Jackson, helping him out.

'Yeah, that's them. Ugly bugs. They scrape their wings together and make, like, the *loudest* noise. And these ones in Washington, they live underground, like worm things, for, like, fifteen, sixteen, seventeen years. And then one day, all of them together, they come out of these holes, all at the same time, and they climb into the trees, millions of them, man, and they turn into flying bugs. They only hang around for, like, a few weeks and then mate and lay they eggs and, when they hatch, the babies go underground and stay there, growing for like seventeen years or whatever, and it happens all over again. *Boom!* Every seventeen years.'

'Is that true?' said Jackson. 'You think the parasites are getting ready to spawn? You telling me they're gonna shoot their germs into the air and try to infect us all?'

'Ain't gonna happen,' said Achilleus. 'Because we gonna massacre them before they get the chance. Simple as that. We won't need no cure, doc. What they say? Kill or cure? This is kill.'

'Oh,' said Einstein with mock innocence. 'But the cure isn't for *them* . . . it's for us.'

Shadowman was at Westminster Abbey. He hadn't slept more than one night in the same place for a long while now. There was so much to do. He had to keep moving. And it was so much easier now that the streets were quiet. Even though Shadowman knew better than anyone why that was. It hadn't been his plan to sleep at the abbey, however, and now it looked like he was going to be stuck here for the night.

Kids were spread out over the pews, talking in little groups. A group of musicians had set up in the choir stalls and were playing a weird drone that rose up and filled the huge, echoing space, not really a tune, but it had started to get under Shadowman's skin. He wondered how long they were going to keep it up and something told him they were settled in for the night. He smiled. He'd slept in stranger places.

He'd delivered Ben and Bernie to Saif, stayed long enough to make sure everyone knew what they were doing, and then left them to get on with their mission at Wembley. Then it was back to his base near Trafalgar Square to spend a night alone and clear his head. Then a night at the Houses of Parliament, talking long into the night with Nicola, seeing if there was anything they could

do about David. Then back to the Natural History Museum to sit in on a meeting with Justin. After the meeting he'd offered to bring some kids over to the abbey. Most of them were greens from St Paul's, like the little girl, Yo-Yo, who had chosen to camp out at the Victoria and Albert rather than here. They were missing their friends – the most religious of Matt's people – who were living here. Right now the hardcore were holding some kind of vigil that seemed to involve lots of kneeling and chanting.

The rest of the kids he'd brought over were a group of Jordan's guys who'd wanted to discuss some things with Matt. They'd gone back some time ago, escorted by Ryan and his hunters. But Yo-Yo and a handful of other greens were still here. Shadowman could see that Yo-Yo wasn't going anywhere. He was responsible for her now. She was young and not at all streetwise. She didn't carry a weapon of any kind. Instead, she'd brought her violin. It was kind of cute, but kind of dumb. Her real name was Charlotte. Apparently The Kid had given her the whacky nickname. More and more kids were giving themselves new names now, becoming new people, forgetting the past and all the hurt. His own nickname was camouflage, something to hide behind. Charlotte seemed happy to be called Yo-Yo. When Ed had rescued Small Sam and The Kid from Matt, Charlotte had gone with them. She stuck close to Sam and The Kid, but he could see how happy she was to be back with her friends again. It was possible she might not want to return to the Victoria and Albert at all.

He looked over to where the little girl was yacking away with her mates, catching up. She was holding her violin. She never put it down.

Shadowman didn't like being responsible for anyone else. Preferred to be a free agent. Could he leave her to it and come back in the morning?

He looked up. The stained-glass windows in the abbey were already growing grey and dim and colourless. It may have felt safe moving in the daylight, but he didn't want to risk travelling at night. Who knew what might come out after dark? Besides, he'd offered to bring Yo-Yo and her friends here mainly because he was interested to find out more about Matt and his God-bothering clan, so he wasn't too sore about staying over. He'd learn more this way.

Matt fascinated him. He was obviously unhinged, but he offered these kids something. Something to believe in. Something outside the bloody misery of their daily lives. It didn't matter really whether Matt was Catholic, Protestant, Jewish, Muslim, Buddhist, Christian Scientist or voodoo. It worked. The kids were happy. Matt had apparently been poisoned by carbon monoxide when he'd tried burning a stack of wood in a brazier inside a chapel at his school . . .

School, what a weird concept that seemed now . . .

Was it the fumes that had affected his mind or something else? Maybe, like a lot of kids, he'd just cracked. And, in a mad world, why not make a madman king? Matt had a bunch of guys who stayed close to him; some seemed quite sensible, holding things together, allowing Matt to go off on whatever mad rants he wanted. Others, like his 'acolytes', as he called them, were as nutty as him. It sounded like it had got well out of hand, though, when Matt had tried to sacrifice The Kid to his pet sicko, the Green Man. Ed had told Shadowman how he'd crashed

that particular party, and it sounded like Jordan Hordern had slapped Matt down when he'd rescued him from a massive sicko attack.

Matt was behaving himself now.

No more dangerous craziness.

Just the old harmless stuff.

Shadowman had spent his time at the abbey getting close to Matt, moving ever deeper into the heart of the organization here. He was good at that. He'd done it so many times in so many different camps. He'd worm his way in, make friends, keep out of trouble, work out who was important, who was powerful, end up at the centre. He'd quickly spotted that a boy called Archie Bishop was second in command to Matt. And Archie was one of the sane ones. Not one of the nutty brigade. Archie was a classic fixer. He didn't have what it took to be in charge, but he was the power behind the throne.

Shadowman was sitting with him now, on a hard wooden pew in the centre of the abbey. This place was massive, like something out of a gothic horror film, made even more so by the flickering candles that were being lit everywhere. Up above the altar was a massive round stained-glass window. When the sun streamed in through it, it must look like God's torch shining directly on you.

Right now Matt was sitting in the centre of an open area with a mosaic floor, talking to some kids who sat in a circle around him.

'So how is he?' Shadowman asked Archie. 'Does he get better or worse?'

'It comes and goes,' said Archie. He was a chubby kid and, like everyone else here, he was dressed all in green. 'After the stuff with The Kid and the siege he calmed

down a lot. I think even *he* realized he'd gone too far, and Jordan Hordern's let him know that if he gets out of hand . . . It wouldn't take much to set him off again, though. You can sense he's sort of waiting for something.'

'Like what?'

'Don't know. A sign. To Matt anything can be a sign. A leaf falling a certain way. A dead pigeon. Someone farting.'

Shadowman laughed.

'You sound like he's – like he's not really your friend,' he said.

'He hasn't got any friends,' said Archie. 'He's above all that, on a different wavelength. You can't really get through to him. I don't think I've had a single normal conversation with him since we left the chapel at Rowhurst.'

'That's gotta be hard work – for both of you.'

'He's his own guy,' said Archie. 'You can't ever get to know what's inside a boy like Matt. You look in his eyes and, man, it's like there's nothing in there. Or like he's talking to someone else. Inside his head. Talking to God. Just not talking to you. It's freaky.'

'Some of the kids at the museum have a theory that the sickos talk to each other with some kind of ultrasound thing,' said Shadowman. 'Almost like telepathy. A different wavelength to the rest of us. A different frequency.'

'Maybe that's what prayer has always been,' said Archie. 'How we talk to God.'

'You really believe in God?'

'Doesn't make any difference really. I believe in Matt.'

Yo-Yo came over, her eyes wide and dark in the low light.

'Can I stay the night?' she asked, like Shadowman was her dad.

'Course you can, darling,' he said. 'I assumed you wanted a sleepover.'

Yo-Yo giggled. 'Sleepovers are something from history.'

'Well, that's what it is,' said Shadowman. 'No other word for it.'

'I can find you both some sleeping stuff,' said Archie.

'Is all right.' Shadowman stretched out his arms and cricked his back. 'I always travel with my own gear. You never know how things are gonna pan out. But maybe you can find something for Yo-Yo.'

'Sure . . . And you'll be able to hear Matt's sermon.'

'Well, that's a bonus,' said Shadowman, and he smiled.

32

'It was all written, scratched into our skin, the words are on us and the words are in us. I am the word. I watched as the Lamb wrote the book with fire. He had a dream and I was in the dream. I saw the fall of the Nephilim. There was a great earthquake. The sun turned black like sackcloth made of goat hair. The whole moon turned blood-red, and the stars in the sky fell to earth. It has fallen: Wormwood, the poison star. And the Nephilim are among us. I have seen it all. It is the truth. It will come to be.'

Shadowman had to admit he was quite enjoying this. It was like a mad play. Made more so by the musicians in the choir stalls keeping up their moody soundtrack. He wasn't alone in his enjoyment. All the green kids were sitting, hypnotised, on the pews, staring up at Matt with wide, shining eyes. Did they understand any of it? Did any of it make sense? What did Matt mean when he said the words were scratched into their skin?

Shadowman studied Matt. His body movement, his eyes as they darted about, now staring up to the heavens, now fixed on his followers. Shadowman was good at reading people and one thing was clear about Matt – he had a secret.

'The kings of the earth, the princes, the generals, the

mighty, they will be saved by the blood of the Lamb. It is coming. The End. There are signs in the sky. An enormous red beast with seven heads and ten horns and seven crowns on his heads, breathing fire across the moon. And there is a war in heaven. The great dragon has been hurled down – that ancient serpent called the devil, or Satan, who leads the whole world astray. He was hurled to the earth, and his angels with him. Some say he is the dragon, and some say he is the dragon slayer . . .'

This hit home with Shadowman. The dragon slayer. St George. He smiled to himself. Matt was clever. If you threw out enough random images you could let people make their own stories out of the parts. Your words could mean anything. Matt began reading from his book now. Archie had told Shadowman all about it. It was made up of scraps of burnt Bible and Matt's own additions.

'Then I heard a loud voice from the temple saying to the seven angels, "Go, pour out the seven bowls of God's wrath on the earth." The first angel went and poured out his bowl on the land, and ugly and painful sores broke out on the people who had the mark of the beast and worshipped his image.'

Shadowman had watched Matt earlier as he changed into his robes for the sermon. His body was pale and skinny, the ribs poking through the skin. And he was slightly stiff. He moved in a twisted sort of way, like he was in pain. His shaved head was small and bony, his eyes deep in dark sockets, the veins showing blue against the stark white of his skin. In the middle of his forehead was a nasty scab. Shadowman had seen several other kids with similar scabs.

'What is that thing?' he'd asked Archie.

'The mark of the Lamb.'

As if Shadowman should know what that meant.

'His blood will save us! Our enemies will drink his blood and it will destroy them. He has a name written on him that no one knows but he himself. He will save us all. His eyes are like blazing fire, and on his head are many crowns. Never again will we hunger. Never again will we thirst. He has the power to turn the waters into blood and to strike the earth with every kind of plague as often as he wants. He has the power of fire, and his blood is our blood and it drowns the heavens!'

A gasp went up from the kids and Shadowman felt the hairs on his skin stand up all over his body. The windows all around the abbey were turning red, or rather the sky outside was, as if the sky was bleeding. That was a hell of a special effect. A hell of a show. A hell of a trick.

A hell of a lucky coincidence?

Matt was trying to carry on, shouting out his nonsense, but he realized he was losing the kids' attention. They were starting to get up, muttering and pointing, staring at the windows. Even the musicians had stopped playing.

Shadowman wanted to see how Matt was going to handle this. He was flustered, his words stumbling. He kept clutching his backside as if he was in pain. He suddenly raised both hands.

'Outside,' he yelled, almost a scream. 'You will see the truth of my words written in the sky.'

There was a mad scramble for the doors, Shadowman following.

The sky above London was glowing red.

'The moon,' someone shouted. 'Look at the moon!'

Shadowman looked.

A hell of a show.

'What did I tell you,' said Matt. '*The whole moon will be turned blood-red*. It is the blood moon. The End is near. The Nephilim are coming.'

Shadowman shook his head. This was some mucked-up shit. He needed to know more. What was Matt's secret?

He needed to get closer.

It was time to go to work.

Matt was kneeling on the cold tiled floor. Half naked, his pale back scarred and scabbed, the backbone pressing through like a buried fossil emerging from the earth. He was alternately clutching his hands in prayer, a leather belt held between them, and beating himself with the belt, which left nasty red welts across his skin.

THWACK.

Shadowman winced. Matt really took this whole God thing seriously.

This was Henry the Seventh's chapel, a separate, more private area up a short flight of steps and through some brass gates at the opposite end of the abbey to the altar and the big rose window. There were candles lit, and Matt was alone, muttering to himself, looking like some medieval martyr in his grey leggings. Shadowman had waited until it was quiet and had crept back here. He stepped softly. He could move unseen and unheard. He'd spent his whole life learning the art. He hung back in the shadows, listening to Matt and wincing each time the leather belt thwacked across his back. Was this why Matt had looked uncomfortable? Like he was hurting? Shadowman waited for his eyes and ears to adjust, until he was able to pick out some of what Matt was saying.

'I have drunk the blood and the blood has drunk me . . .
You cannot harm me . . . You are the Nephilim and I will
destroy you all . . . Be quiet . . . The Lamb will cleanse me
. . . I am stronger than you. I have the blood in me. The
blood of the Lamb and the blood of the dragon. The
Lamb's blood is stronger. The Lamb's blood is pure. I have
seen your moon. You are bleeding. You will all die.'

THWACK.

Shadowman crept closer still. The grey leggings were
all that Matt was wearing. The soles of his feet were black
and calloused. He scrunched up his toes every time the
belt hit his flesh. His whole body was twitching and jerking, and occasionally he would break from prayer and
massage his backside. And then he'd whack himself again.

'This pain will drive out your pain. You cannot hurt
me. I take the pain and forget your wounds. You try to eat
us . . . Not me. Not me . . .'

THWACK.

Eventually Shadowman was right behind Matt who
still hadn't heard him. He was too caught up in his own
world of pain and madness.

'He has written the word on me. I have his mark on my
forehead. He will protect me. You have tried to eat me. But
I am strong because I love the Lamb. Speak to me. Drown
out their voices. Let me hear your voice, strong and clear.
Tell me what to do. Speak to me. Make them shut up.'

'You were bitten,' said Shadowman, and Matt jumped
– as if God really had spoken to him. He threw himself
face down and writhed on the cold floor. And then he
realized it wasn't God, it was Shadowman, and he got his
act together. The whole mad-monk persona was gone,
and in its place was one severely hacked-off boy.

'What are you doing here?' he hissed, fixing his dark, glassy eyes on Shadowman.

'I came to pray with you, brother.'

'No, you didn't. I pray alone.'

'We can all pray. He's not *your* God. He belongs to all of us. I was going to pray to him to give me answers, just like you.'

'You're a liar.'

'Am I? I got my answers.'

'Liar.'

'You were bitten,' said Shadowman. 'Only explanation. You're not communicating with God, you're hearing sickos in your head. You've got some of their bugs in you. I've seen it in others.'

'You've seen nothing. You're not a believer. You will never see or hear.'

'Not like you, no,' said Shadowman. 'I'm not hearing the white noise of parasitic ultrasound. Flies calling to flies. But, you know, seeing and hearing are what I do best.'

Matt got up, stood hunched over, his eyes disappearing into black sockets made deeper by the candlelight, his muscles knotting and unknotting. Shadowman had faced stronger enemies. If Matt wanted a fight, he was ready.

'You've been bitten in the arse by one of them,' he said, and watched as Matt instinctively put a hand to his backside before he could stop himself.

'When did it happen?' Shadowman pressed on. 'A while back, I expect. Right at the beginning. You've got over it and you've learnt to live with it.'

'I am the word of the Lamb. I will order you punished for this.'

'No, you won't. Right now this is a secret between you and me,' said Shadowman. 'I can keep it that way. I don't need to tell anyone. But if you kick up a fuss then I start talking and your secret is out. You're not a holy man – you're just sick. Or maybe that's the same thing. Whatever – I'm guessing you want to keep your secret for a while longer.'

'I can order you silenced before you say anything,' said Matt.

'You can try. But I don't see anyone here's gonna pull it off. I'm the Shadowman. I'm a killer.'

Shadowman moved in on Matt who shrank away from him, looking around for some help. His followers were all up the other end of the abbey. He could cry out, but that might seem a little undignified for this poor man's pope.

'I was not bitten,' said Matt, almost pleading now.

'I can prove it,' said Shadowman. 'One simple way.'

'Keep your hands off me!' Matt had a hint of desperation in his voice, but Shadowman moved in quickly, twisted Matt round and yanked his leggings down just far enough to expose ugly, puckered scarring in the unmistakable shape of teeth marks on one pale buttock.

'That must have hurt,' he said and pulled the leggings back up before shoving Matt away. Matt skittered across the floor and glared at Shadowman, like a trapped animal.

'Don't tell anyone,' he said.

'It's no big deal,' said Shadowman. 'We all have our crosses to bear. I just wanted to make sure. So when was it? Before or after you gassed yourself?'

Matt shook his head. He wasn't going to say anything. Shadowman felt almost sorry for him.

'Listen,' he said. 'I've got nothing against you. Or what

202

you do. Apart from all that weird stuff about sacrificing other kids, but we'll let that go.'

'I help people,' said Matt.

'Yeah. Guess so,' said Shadowman. 'You give these kids something. I don't want to interfere in that. As I say, I can keep this secret, just between you and me. But you're gonna have to talk.'

'It was at school, early on,' said Matt, becoming normal again. Becoming what he was – a frightened and confused boy of fifteen. Not much different to Shadowman.

'A dinner lady did it,' said Matt, slightly ashamed. 'She got to me. I never told anyone. Didn't know what they'd do. I killed her for it and soon afterwards we all ended up in the chapel. A bit like this . . .' He looked around at the carved stone pillars and ornate wooden benches. 'I started to feel . . . hot in the head. Started to hear things. To see things. It's all true, though. What I tell people. I was given visions. They got more intense after I breathed the holy smoke.'

Matt grabbed Shadowman's shirt.

'It doesn't change anything,' he said urgently. 'You mustn't tell people. They have to believe in me.'

'Trust me. I'm not telling anyone,' said Shadowman. 'I can see what you do for these kids. I just like to know the truth.'

'I *am* the truth,' said Matt, letting go of him, and Shadowman could see that he was losing him as he slipped back into his madness. What was he? A holy fool? A mad seer? A fake or a fakir?

Didn't really matter. They were all of them doing whatever it took to get by. Shadowman moved back in on Matt, held his gaze.

'You stay onside now, yeah?'

Matt nodded.

'Be one of us. One of the good guys. If we need you to say things for us you'll go along with it, yeah? We have to win this and we'll use whatever weapons we've got. Including your words. You can claim you saw the blood moon in your dreams. A vision. Whatever. But what it means – that might be for others to decide. You get me?'

'We are all servants of the Lamb,' said Matt.

'I'll take that as a yes.'

Matt nodded.

Shadowman smiled and walked away. There was still a red glow from outside. The blood moon was still up there. So what did it mean? Was it a portent? Or was it just a freak atmospheric condition?

He'd seen it all, but he had to admit that this one was new, and he was more than a little spooked.

Yo-Yo looked around at the hunters. Shadowman could see she was scared of them, with their leathers and their masks and their dogs. She kept close to him. He put a reassuring hand on her shoulder.

'They'll get us safely back home,' he said, and now Yo-Yo looked nervously up at the sky.

'Moon's gone,' he said. 'Sky's a nice clear blue.'

'Let's move out,' Ryan shouted and as they set off Shadowman went over to him.

'You didn't need to come back for us,' he said. 'But thanks.'

'No worries,' said Ryan. 'You see the moon last night? That was well mad.'

'Matt preached a sermon on it,' said Shadowman. 'Was a message from God apparently.'

'Yeah?' Ryan looked up at the sky, his spotty face shining and greasy. 'You know, sometimes I wish God would say things in a way we could understand. He needs to be a lot clearer. So the moon's red – what does it mean, God?'

'Matt could tell you,' said Shadowman. 'But I'm not sure you'd understand that either.'

Ryan laughed. 'The only thing I understand,' he said, holding up his blade, 'is this.'

It wasn't far to the museums from the abbey, but there was no direct route. They could stick to the main roads and go the long way round – straight up through Victoria to Hyde Park Corner then left down the Brompton Road though Knightsbridge – or they could cut off the corner and use the backstreets. That way was shorter, but meant smaller roads and lots of twists and turns.

In the past none of them would have considered the second route for a moment – they'd learnt to stick to wider roads, straight lines with good visibility. Now, though, with the streets empty, Ryan was taking them on the shorter route, cutting between Belgrave Square and Eaton Square and then across Sloane Street and on to Pont Street.

'Don't like to get too close to the palace an' all,' he explained to Shadowman. 'Don't trust David. We've had some bad run-ins with him before now.'

The hunters let the dogs off their leads and they scampered away in all directions, happy to be out and about in the early morning. The boys moved fast, but Shadowman knew that they were keeping alert, their senses tuned. Months of surviving on the streets had taught them deep survival skills.

Shadowman smiled. He only had to drop Yo-Yo off at the V&A and the rest of the day was his. He fell back to where she was struggling to keep up. Her other friends had decided to stay at the abbey, but she was missing Sam and The Kid. She was panting slightly, trying not to look slow or weak. Shadowman was just wondering whether he should ask Ryan to slow down when one of the hunters raised his hand and they all stopped.

'What is it?' Shadowman called out. And then he saw

206

– the dogs were coming back, tails between their legs, fur up. They looked spooked.

'What's the matter with them?' asked Yo-Yo. 'Why are they scared like that?'

Ryan put a finger to his lips. Shadowman listened. The day was quiet. He realized that no birds were singing in the trees. But then, as he concentrated, he heard something, a distant rustling, rushing sound, like something being dragged over gravel. He gave a questioning look to Ryan, who shook his head. He didn't know what it meant either.

'What do we do?' asked one of the hunters.

'I dunno, Zulficker,' said Ryan. 'You got the best ears of any of us. You know what that sound is?'

Zulficker shrugged.

'Is a new one.'

'We should go on,' said Shadowman. 'Safest place will be the museum if there's trouble.'

'Why would there be trouble?' Yo-Yo asked, her eyes very wide. 'You told me it would be safe to go and see my friends.'

'You're safe,' said Shadowman. 'But we always have to be careful.'

Yo-Yo switched her attention to Ryan. 'Are we safe?' she asked.

'Dunno,' said Ryan. 'Probably nothing. Best to start running, though.'

The hunters got their dogs back on their leads and they hurried up the road. At first Shadowman couldn't tell if they were running towards the sound or away from it. As they neared the end of the road and it opened out into a square, however, the sound got noticeably louder. Without saying anything, the hunters formed into a protective

squad round Yo-Yo, who was clutching her violin case as if it was the most precious thing in the world.

'Maybe it's nothing dangerous,' she said to Shadowman, her voice made broken and jerky by the running. 'Maybe it's a good thing?'

'Let's hope. The streets have been empty for days. No reason that should suddenly change now.'

What if St George was on the move, though? That was the thought that was lodged in Shadowman's head. What if he'd brought his army this far already? What if that swishing noise was the sound of a thousand feet scuffling along the road?

'Could it be people?' said Yo-Yo. 'Maybe children, like us?'

Shadowman didn't need to answer her because, as they reached the end of the road, they saw sickos appearing from among the trees in the middle of the square. They were marching relentlessly forward, bringing their terrible stench with them. Yo-Yo screamed. And, as more sickos emerged from all sides, Shadowman understood that the noise was indeed being made by people shuffling along.

Was this St George's army, though, or something different?

'We have to go round them,' he shouted and Ryan didn't need to be told twice. He called to his guys and they ran back the way they'd come. When they came to the next major junction, they turned off to their right, still hoping to move in the general direction of the museum. Shadowman paused briefly to look back. The sickos weren't hurrying to follow them, but they were still coming on. Nothing was going to stop them.

The kids ran hard along the road, but they hadn't gone far when they saw more sickos ahead.

'They're everywhere,' shouted Zulficker, slowing to a halt. Wherever the kids looked there were more sickos filling the streets. Ryan picked the quietest-looking road and raced down it, the others following. Shadowman soon lost his bearings as they pounded up and down the tangle of streets, trying to find a way through.

He could see that Yo-Yo was getting tired. He was tired himself. His lungs and throat were burning. His leg wobbly. It was the sudden short bursts of energy that were draining him. Constantly switching direction, going one way and then the other. Yo-Yo was struggling to keep up and now she tripped and stumbled. Zulficker caught her and scooped her up in his arms, carried her against his chest.

Finally they could run no further. They were trapped. Cut off in a gently curving crescent next to some public gardens. There were sickos everywhere they looked.

'We have to get off the street,' Shadowman shouted, and Ryan agreed. It was always risky breaking into an unknown house – you never knew what you'd find inside. Sickos had a nasty habit of building nests, grouping together in buildings and sleeping through the day, but the kids had no choice. There were too many sickos to stand and fight. They could protect themselves more easily indoors.

The buildings here were tall and white, four storeys high, with iron balconies along the first floors and basement wells protected by spear-topped railings.

Ryan yelled some orders and three of his guys grabbed tools from their belts, picked a front door at random and ran up to force it open. They knew what they were doing and had obviously done this many times before. It only

took them seconds to break in and, as they swung the door open, the rest of the kids bundled in off the street. Shadowman waited on the doorstep until the others were all inside, keeping an eye on the sickos that were streaming towards them. Inside, the dogs were barking furiously.

Shadowman hurried in and slammed the door shut. Ryan's B&E team had already found some furniture to jam up against the door. It wouldn't hold the sickos forever, but it would give the kids an edge, and once again it was expertly and quickly done.

Shadowman was glad that Ryan had come back to escort him and Yo-Yo from the abbey. He usually worked alone and preferred it that way, but right now he was responsible for Yo-Yo, and the sicko threat outside was as bad as he'd ever seen it. He still didn't know if this was St George's army, though. Whoever they were, and wherever they'd come from, they were coordinated, organized, purposeful.

The more he thought about it, the more he reckoned it couldn't be St George's mob. They felt different somehow. And they weren't coming from the north, from Kilburn. They were coming from the west and the south.

In fact, if anything, they were *heading* north – towards Kilburn. As if St George had called in reinforcements.

Was this what he'd been waiting for?

That wasn't a nice thought.

Ryan was issuing orders, and his guys were going through their well-practised routine, some of them securing windows, others staying near the front door to keep it safe. Some were searching the house, making sure there were no sickos already in there. Ryan himself moved Yo-Yo up to the first-floor living room where she would

be out of harm's way. He assigned Zulficker to look after her. Shadowman had come up with them and took the opportunity to look out of the windows at the mob outside. They were milling around, staring up at the house. They reminded Shadowman of the crowds that used to gather outside Buckingham Palace whenever the royal family were due to make an appearance on the balcony. He had a sudden ridiculous urge to open the windows on to the narrow little balcony and wave at them.

They were an ugly bunch. Rotten, diseased, scabby, maimed and mutilated. Shadowman shook his head. How were the kids ever going to get past them?

He scanned the area below. The front door was up a short flight of steps and, with the basement wells on either side protected by railings, it was the only way in.

'Where have they come from?' Yo-Yo joined him, looking anxious and angry. Shadowman led her away from the window.

'I don't know,' he said. 'Best not look at them. Try to ignore them, OK?'

'I don't like this,' said Yo-Yo. 'How many of them are there?'

'We don't know any more than you, darling,' said Zulficker. 'This isn't normal.'

Shadowman took in the living room. This was a posh house, undamaged, unlooted, no signs of any human intrusion, with expensive furniture, paintings on the walls, dusty ornaments, a giant flatscreen TV hanging over the fireplace. The screen was just a black mirror now – it would never show any TV programmes again. A relic of the old world.

Ryan's team returned, their dogs panting, and announced that the place was clean.

'The back's clear,' said one of them. 'There are glass doors from a basement kitchen out to the garden. We could leave that way.'

'The only thing is,' said Shadowman, 'if we go that way we don't have any idea what's past the garden – might just be more of them. We could be surrounded. For the moment, we're safe here.'

'Can't stay here forever,' said Ryan. 'And they don't look like they're going anywhere soon. Dom, take your team and scout it.'

Dom was a big, pudgy-faced guy who seemed to be in charge of a smaller unit. He disappeared off with his guys, but almost immediately Shadowman heard a crash and shouting from downstairs and in a moment one of Dom's guys came running up the stairs.

'They got in the back,' he said, out of breath. 'There's loads of them down there.'

Shadowman turned to Zulficker.

'Stay with her,' he said, pointing to Yo-Yo, and Zulficker nodded.

Shadowman put his hands on Yo-Yo's shoulders. 'It'll be all right. Zulficker will look after you.'

'Mm,' said Yo-Yo, her lips pressed so tightly shut they'd turned white. She had tears in her eyes.

Shadowman grabbed his short spear and ran out, slamming the door shut. Ryan and the rest of his guys were ahead of him. Shadowman took the stairs five at a time, the sounds of a fight getting louder and louder. When he got to the kitchen, it was chaos. The glass doors to the garden were smashed, jagged pieces of glass still hanging in the frame, and the room was already full of sickos – about twenty of them – and more were swarming in.

Shadowman gagged on the reek of massed bodies packed into a small space, sour and fetid and earthy. The smell of decay. Of death.

Their skin was dark with filth and grease, erupting with boils, ravaged by deep sores. Their eyes were mad and yellow, inhuman, their clothes ripped, damp, sticky. Many had body parts missing – fingers, hands, noses, ears, eyes, lips. One mother had lost half her face and, as Shadowman butted her with the shaft of his spear, the other half exploded in a shower of blood and pus and grey jelly.

Ryan and his hunters were jammed against a row of cabinets at the back of the room. Shadowman raised his spear. It was awkward manoeuvring in these cramped conditions, but he managed to shove and kick a knot of sickos back until he had enough room to fight. He jabbed at a mother who was getting too close, striking her in the throat, and she fell back, gurgling. A father immediately took her place and he too went down, his belly pierced. Now Shadowman moved forward – shove and stab, butt and jab.

'Force them out,' he called over to Ryan. 'We need to secure the doors.'

Easier said than done. The sheer weight of numbers gave the sickos an advantage. That, plus the fact that they had no fear of the kids' weapons, meant they were going to be hard to shift. Slowly, though, the kids gained the upper hand, creating a wall of sharp steel and pushing forward, shoulder to shoulder, forcing their way, step by bloody step, towards the garden, stumbling over fallen bodies, avoiding grasping hands and snapping teeth. One of Ryan's guys had got in behind Shadowman and they'd set up a rhythm together. As Shadowman lunged with his spear and then pulled back, the hunter leant in past him

213

with his club and cracked skulls, then Shadowman would lunge again. It worked well, and they were moving ahead of the other kids. Then there was a grunt and a cry off to Shadowman's right and he saw Dom go under, pulled down by several mothers. Shadowman and his teammate stepped in, and while Shadowman cut into the sickos with his spear the hunter managed to get Dom out from the tangle and on his feet again. His face was bleeding, but otherwise he seemed OK.

He thanked Shadowman and then puked on to the floor. Shadowman felt someone grab at his sleeve and turned to drive an elbow into their face. He was back in the fight again, trying to keep his own face away from long nails and grasping hands. He felt like puking himself. Up close, the sickos' hot breath stank like they'd been feasting on the slime from a cesspit.

Ryan gave a great yell and the hunters around him shoved forward together like a rugby scrum, pushing the unprepared sickos on his side of the kitchen almost out of the doors. This opened up space for Shadowman, his partner and Dom to really go to work, cutting, slashing, clubbing. At last he felt something give and the sickos fell back en masse. They were retreating, going out through the broken doors, cutting themselves on the glass as they went. Shadowman shouted, 'Come on!' and all the kids went into a killing frenzy, forcing the last sickos away, leaving a carpet of bodies on the black and white geometric tiles.

A mother turned, in a last act of defiance, snarling at Shadowman, showing broken, blood-reddened teeth. Shadowman had fought enough sickos not to get freaked out, and he raked his spear point down her face. Her nose came away, allowing a torrent of grey jelly to burst out

and pour down her chin. Now a father with an empty eye socket turned on Shadowman and he looked like he had a head full of jelly. It seemed to be moving, squirming inside his skull. Shadowman's partner whacked him with his club and he split like a burster, disintegrating on to the terrace just outside the doors.

And then the room was clear. A squad of hunters came running in, carrying doors they'd torn from their hinges in other rooms. They quickly erected a barricade, blocking the damaged garden doors. Other pieces of furniture were brought in to secure them as Shadowman's partner went round the room finishing off wounded sickos.

'Are they done?' asked Dom, pressing a hand to his face to stop the bleeding.

'Think so,' said Ryan, but they weren't done. Shadowman heard a sound from upstairs – heavy feet on the floor, crashing and banging.

Yo-Yo.

Without thinking, he was out of the kitchen and pounding up the stairs.

And then he was back in the living room. Too late – Zulficker was lying dead on the floor, his eyes gouged out. And there, near the windows, was Yo-Yo, her small body gripped by three sickos. Mouth open in a silent scream, her eyes staring at Shadowman. Still alive.

Had the sickos somehow swarmed up the front of the house and got on to the balcony? No. No. Not possible. This didn't make any sense. They didn't have the intelligence, the skills needed to plan and to climb.

What other explanation was there, though?

Shadowman ran at them, bellowing at the top of his voice.

'No . . . Leave her! No . . .'

But when had it ever made any difference speaking to a sicko? They ignored him and carried Yo-Yo out on to the balcony.

He got close enough to stab one of them, blood spraying into the air; he barged a second one over the balcony. She fell on to the railings below and was skewered. Now Shadowman saw that the sickos had made a sort of human pyramid up the side of the house. They'd climbed over each other to get in and were now passing Yo-Yo down to the massed sickos below.

He speared two mothers at the top of the pile and they tumbled down, but the others were already breaking up the tower and dropping off. He couldn't reach them without climbing out himself. He looked down to see Yo-Yo being swallowed up by the milling horde. He gave a wordless shout of frustration. Hot tears were running down his cheeks. This shouldn't have happened. From out of a clear blue sky. This was supposed to have been a good day.

There was a change in the crowd, a movement. They were parting, like a shoal of fish or a flock of birds, moving as one. And a woman stepped forward. She was very tall and very thin, her arms stiff at her sides. Long, straight grey hair hung down in curtains around her head. She looked up at Shadowman and he felt hypnotised, as if she'd somehow got inside his head. His thoughts were filled with a jumble of terrifying images. He felt sick and giddy. He squeezed his eyes tight shut and swore to himself. He wasn't going to give in to her. He opened his eyes, pulled his arm back, hurled his spear with all his strength, but at the last moment a father stepped in and took the spear in his ribs, falling dead at the mother's feet.

The crowd closed around her and, just like Yo-Yo, she was gone.

Shadowman stood there, gripping the balcony railing, and watched, amazed and appalled, as the sickos started to move away, heading north. In that awful link with the long-haired woman he had grasped some sense of the sickos' purpose. And their power.

Ryan and Dom joined him.

'Where they going?' said Dom.

'I think they're a second army,' said Shadowman. 'With a second leader. And I think they've been called in.'

'You mean they're joining up with St George?' said Ryan.

'If they are then this is way more serious than we thought.'

In a few minutes the road was empty, as if the sickos had never been there.

Shadowman slammed his fists on the metal balcony.

'I was supposed to bring her back safely. This has to end.'

Maxie had a headache. Too much talk. Too much stress. In the past headaches were no big deal. You'd just down a pill without thinking. Take your pick – paracetamol, Neurofen, ibuprofen, aspirin. For Maxie it had usually been paracetamol. Now paracetamol was like gold dust. You could get rich and rule the world if you had a stash of headache pills.

Headaches, cold, fever, random pain, all were magically got rid of by the little white pills. She'd read somewhere that aspirin originally came from the bark of the willow tree – no idea where paracetamol came from. If she could find a willow tree maybe she could strip the bark, chew on that. Ta-dah. No more headaches. Only thing was she had no idea what a willow tree looked like or where to find one. There was so much to relearn, so much that had been forgotten, so much that she'd taken for granted.

OK. Yeah. They could scavenge stuff for now, but eventually it would all run out. Then they'd have to make their own things. Not just headache pills – clothes, weapons, food, tools, tampons . . .

But none of that made any difference, none of that mattered one tiny bit if they couldn't defeat the grown-ups.

Everything came down to that. Every argument ended

up in the same place. Every train of thought stopped at the same station.

Panic Station.

They'd all seen them come through the other morning, after the red moon had turned the sky to blood. Maxie had been alerted by the guards at the museum – 'You have to see this!' The kids had pressed their faces to the windows. Too scared to go outside. Watched, horrified and fascinated, as the horde of grown-ups had dragged themselves past. So many of them coming into London. Could Maxie and her friends really hope to defeat them? That's what everyone had been arguing about here at the Houses of Parliament. Another damned meeting had been hurriedly called once everyone was sure it was safe to walk the streets again.

It was Shadowman who'd done the scouting. Checking it really was as quiet as it looked. He was badly upset by what had happened to Yo-Yo. He looked tired and slightly crazy. He'd spent hours out there. Punishing himself. Desperate to do something. Not that anyone else blamed him for Yo-Yo's death.

Didn't stop him blaming himself, though.

Maxie felt sorry for him. Nobody could have known that the red moon might have been a warning that a new grown-up army was going to come pouring into town, like an unstoppable tide. A flood, an avalanche, a sudden deluge from out of nowhere.

Shadowman had spent ages with Sam and The Kid and the other young ones, talking to them, comforting them, explaining . . . but no matter how hard he talked he wasn't going to bring Yo-Yo back.

Maxie did miss Yo-Yo. Some evenings she used to play her violin down in the main hall, the sound echoing up to

the roof. Sweet and sad. Music was one of the things Maxie missed most. All those tracks on her phone, on her laptop – dead. She'd held on to her things, her electronic devices, for ages, hoping that one day the power would miraculously come back on. But you couldn't carry all that useless stuff around with you forever. Books still worked. Thank God for that. They held all of human history now, all human knowledge. Whatever else happened, they had to protect the books. Protect their memories. If they were to have any hope of rebuilding the world they would have to study the books.

But first they had to defeat the grown-ups.

Defeat the grown-ups. Defeat the grown-ups. Defeat the grown-ups.

'*Panic Station, end of the line, everybody out!*'

The one truly impossible thing they had to do before all the other impossible things could happen.

That's why this argument in the House of Lords was going nowhere. Because deep down, whatever anyone said, they all secretly felt the same thing – they'd been training and drilling and preparing in Hyde Park, but not for this mega army.

David was up and speaking now. Saying what a lot of the other kids thought.

'We can't beat them. How can we? You know it. It's crazy to even try. You all saw how many of them there were. And that's not even counting the ones Jester saw in Kilburn.' He paused and looked over to where Einstein was sitting with Justin a couple of rows in front of Maxie. 'You say you're working on a cure. Brilliant. That's the way to go. It's obvious. We stay safe within our bases. No sicko can break into Buckingham Palace.'

David looked over to where Jordan Hordern's guys were sitting together on the opposite side of the chamber.

'You should go back to the Tower of London,' he said. 'Its walls are three metres thick. No sicko could ever get in there. We've survived this long by staying safe, by protecting ourselves and not taking stupid risks. None of that's changed. We sit it out. The sickos are all diseased, dying. We sit it out and wait for them to drop dead.'

'But they're going to spawn,' said Einstein. 'They're going to throw out a cloud of fresh parasite spores. We could all be infected. We could all be finished.'

'Yes,' said David. 'And I just pointed out that you're working on a cure.'

'It could take us months, years. We don't know.'

'Precisely,' said David, in the manner of someone who was going to slickly switch their argument. 'You don't know, do you?'

'What do you mean?'

'You don't know for certain about this cloud of spores you've been going on about. Where are you getting your information from?'

'From the Twisted Kids. They communicate with each other. They're picking stuff up – like a radio signal.'

David laughed. 'So you're telling us that your facts come from some deformed freaks who claim to be using telepathy to communicate with – with what? The ghost of Wikipedia?'

A laugh rippled round the chamber.

'All I'm saying is that we can't rely on a cure,' said Einstein angrily. 'We might not ever be able to actually make one.'

'So most of what you've been telling us is nonsense, then?' David was enjoying himself. It seemed to Maxie that it was

more important to him to score points here and look clever than it was to actually do anything about the grown-ups.

'Why should I listen to any of you?' he was shouting. 'None of you know anything. You're all in the dark. But I can tell you one truth. If you'd all just listen to me we can survive. We have to cooperate. Not in a pointless, warlike manner, but safe behind our walls. Let me organize things, set up a proper barter system, sharing food and water and weapons. We stay out of danger, we do all we can to stay alive, but the one thing we don't do is fight because that would be suicide.'

'If we let them spawn, that'll be the end of us all,' said Einstein. 'We'll catch the second wave of the disease.'

'But that's just a theory,' said David. 'That's just what you want us to believe.'

Blue stood up now. Maxie could tell he was angry. He had that cold, tense look about him.

'We hit them,' he said. 'We hit them bare hard like we planned it. We destroy them. Can't you see that *now* is the best chance we've ever had? They're all in one place. We can massacre them while they're gathered. We can wipe them out. We're strong, we're armed, we're ready. For the first time since this started we're all united. We make a final battle plan and we kill them all, for all time.'

'But we can't,' said David scornfully and he laughed at Blue. 'They're just too many. Words won't beat them. Our weapons won't beat them. The disease will beat them. If we just sit and wait. It's stronger than all of us. The sickos will all simply burst.'

Now Jordan Hordern spoke out. His face blank and unreadable.

'We *can* defeat them,' he said. 'Nothing's changed. We

have a plan and we stick to it. Just because there's a few more of them it don't make no difference. One final massive hammer blow and it's over.'

'It'd be over all right,' sneered David. 'Over for you, for us. We'd all be dead. They must outnumber us ten to one, a hundred to one, a thousand to one for all I know.'

'I've killed a bare lot of sickos in my time,' said Jordan. 'More'n a hundred. It's no problem. We got warriors. We got roadmen like Blue, like Achilleus, Ollie, Ryan. I seen 'em practising. We got Amazons like Jackson and Maxie and Hayden. We fighters. We killers. Is what we do.'

'Yeah, great speech, big man,' said David. 'And I say let the intelligent kids sort this one out. It's not about fighting. Go home. Look after your own kids, like I'm going to look after mine, and they'll thank you for it.'

'You're weak,' said Jordan. 'You're a coward.'

'No. I'm sensible. Sometimes it takes more courage not to fight.'

The awful thing was Maxie thought maybe he was right. Trying to take down so many grown-ups might be the end of them. Why *not* just wait for them to die? Did Einstein really know that this whole spawning thing was going to happen? For sure?

But she'd stick with Blue. If he wanted to fight then that's what they'd do. He wouldn't take them into a battle he didn't think they could win.

Would he?

Don't think negative thoughts, Maxie. Stay on message . . .

I mean, what if? What if they could kill them all? How good would that be?

Now Nicola stood up.

'I'm not sure any more,' she said. 'I think maybe David's

right. Maybe we've moved too fast on this. We might need to rethink.'

'We can't fall apart now,' said Blue. 'We've worked so hard to build a fighting force. This don't change nothing. I'm with Jordan. A few more sickos. So what?'

'No,' said Nicola. 'I vote for more time to think about this. David's talking sense.'

Maxie felt like everything was slipping away from her. She vividly remembered Jordan marching his army across the bridge. The high hopes, the expectation, the sense that victory was almost theirs. The memory felt so fresh it might have been this morning. And then the moon turned red and a new army marched into town.

How quickly things could fall apart.

'I agree with Nicola,' said Justin, joining the discussion again after a long silence. 'We do need to think about this.'

Maxie groaned, and before she knew what she was doing she found herself standing up next to Blue.

'Not you too!' she yelled. 'You know how serious this is, Justin. Didn't you listen to a word Einstein said?'

'Sit down,' said Justin angrily. 'You're not in charge. I've thought about this and I've changed my mind. That's the whole point of a discussion.'

'What?' said Maxie. 'To just agree with everything that slimeball David says?'

'You're being childish,' said Justin, sounding horribly like a teacher. 'Name calling. You're better than that.'

Maxie muttered a much more obscene name under her breath and sat down.

'We can't risk all our fighters getting killed,' Justin went on. 'We'll need them. I think we should all go back to our camps and discuss this properly among ourselves.'

'What are fighters for?' said Blue. 'Fighting!'

'Defence is always better than attack,' said Justin, sitting down. 'We'll concentrate on helping Einstein find a cure.'

'You are fools!' came a strong, sharp voice from the back.

Maxie sank into her seat. This was all they needed. Mad Matt and one of his nutty religious outbursts.

'The Lamb has sent us a sign. The blood moon. The blood of the Nephilim will flow. The Lamb will give us his strength. We can defeat the old ones. I have seen the kings of the earth and their armies gathered together to make war against the beast and his army.'

'Right,' said David, laughing. 'That kind of wraps it up for me. Are you going to listen to this nutter? Is this the voice of reason? Or are you going to listen to me? A boy who has kept his people safe and well. Come along, we're going back to the palace.'

David got up and walked out. Soon the whole meeting had broken up, leaving Blue yelling at them to come back and calling them all idiots. At last he went over to Justin, filled with a cold, shaking fury.

'How could you do that?' he said. 'How could you ruin all our work?'

'Because I'm scared,' said Justin. And there was no arguing with that. 'Because if we lose the battle then it's the end,' he added.

'And if we win?' said Blue.

'We can't win, Blue,' said Justin sadly. 'It's impossible.'

'OK. It's a type of flatworm. Its scientific name is *Ribeiroia ondatrae*. It's tiny. Microscopic. And it starts out by getting inside snails.'

'Ew. Gross,' said Zohra. 'Is this going to be yucky?'

'Yes,' said Wiki with a big grin. He had a fat scientific book open in front of him on the carpet.

The smaller kids and Wiki were all sitting on the floor of the library, crammed together in a corner. Since Yo-Yo's death they'd been sticking in a tight group.

'It's gross,' said Jibber-jabber, who also had a book open. 'But it's also really interesting. Me and Wiki have been studying all about parasites, yeah, and what they do, yeah, how they control other animals, like how the parasites in the sickos control them, yeah, and you two . . .' He turned to Fish-Face and Skinner, who'd been spending more and more time with the smaller kids lately. 'You might find it really interesting, I think, but we don't mean anything mean by it – it's just stuff we found out. It's like, see, you know, yeah, we found out loads of stuff, like parasitic wasps that turn ladybirds into zombies, horsehair worms that can grow up to thirty centimetres long inside crickets, and, when they're ready, they make the crickets drown themselves in pools of water so that they can

emerge and swim away. That's cool, but the flatworms in the bullfrogs, they're the really cool ones.'

'What bullfrogs?' asked Froggie, obviously wondering if this had something to do with him. 'You said snails.'

'We'll get to the bullfrogs in a minute,' said Jibber-jabber. 'First we got to tell you about the snails. Water snails that live in ponds.'

'Yeah,' said Wiki. 'You see, the flatworms have three different hosts and they control all of them. They start off by getting into the snails' reproductive organs and turning them into parasite-making machines. And then at night, when they're ready, they come out, the flatworm larvae, thousands of them, and swim off to look for their next host.'

'Is that the frogs?' asked Sam. He'd been really depressed lately. Yo-Yo's death had made him think even more about Ella and grow even more scared that he'd never see her again. Whenever he saw Zohra and Froggie, he got jealous. He knew he shouldn't, but all he could think was how unfair it was, that they were together and he'd lost Ella. He hated himself for having these thoughts, even sometimes wishing he could swap Ella for Zohra, but he couldn't stop having them.

He looked around at his friends. They had nothing to worry about. Zohra had Froggie; Fish-Face had Skinner; Wiki had Jibber-jabber and their little dog, Godzilla. What did Sam have?

He had The Kid. That was the one thing that made him happy. He knew The Kid would never let him down. The Kid looked out for him.

The Kid had made him come along to the library today. Sam didn't want to join in anything, but The Kid had

insisted, and now, Sam had to admit, he was interested despite himself, even if he could see what Wiki and Jibber-jabber were doing. They were trying to distract the other children. Stop them from thinking about Yo-Yo. Sam hoped it would work with The Kid, but even *he* had been depressed since that morning when Shadowman came back to the museum with bad news and a violin with no one to play it. Now The Kid, who was usually one of the chattiest boys, was sitting with his knees drawn up to his chin, staring at the carpet. Sam made up his mind that he would work much harder keeping The Kid happy, just as The Kid worked hard to keep him happy.

'Not quite frogs yet, Sam,' said Wiki. 'Just tadpoles. The larvae burrow into them and make their way to where their arms and legs are starting to grow.'

'This is getting worse and worse,' said Zohra, though Sam could see she was really enjoying it.

'Yeah,' said Wiki. 'What they do is create cysts that turn the frogs into mutants.'

'Mutants?' said Skinner, his voice muffled by the folds of skin around his face.

Wiki looked a little embarrassed.

'I didn't mean to be rude,' he said. 'I don't mean to say that you and Fish-Face are mutants.'

'Well, we are,' said Skinner, his skin forming into something like a smile. 'We're proud mutants, like the ones in X-Men.'

Fish-Face giggled, and then put her hand to her mouth to hide it. Shy.

'So what sort of mutants do the frogs turn into?' Skinner asked.

'The cysts affect the growth of their legs,' said Wiki.

'They sprout extra ones, three or four sometimes, grow-ing in all directions, or not enough legs, or deformed legs.'

Wiki showed them a picture of a frog with weird extra sort of half-legs coming out in clusters from its back end.

'That is too much,' said Zohra and she laughed.

'But how does that help the flatworms?' Sam asked.

'The frogs can't move properly,' said Wiki. 'They can't hop away from danger. So, even if they see a bird coming, they can't avoid it.'

'So they get eaten?' asked Froggie, who was taking this personally.

'Yeah,' said Jibber-jabber and he made a pecking motion with his hand at Froggie, who scuttled away from him.

'Big birds like herons come down and gobble up the mutant bullfrogs,' said Wiki, 'and all the parasites inside them. Then the parasites grow again and mate, inside the birds, until the birds poo them out into the water and they can get into more snails, then more frogs, then more birds, round and round and round, yeah, all controlled by these tiny parasites.'

The children all wanted to look at more pictures, even though they found them disgusting. All except The Kid, who got up and walked down to the other end of the library. Sam followed him.

'Hey,' he said, when they were out of earshot. 'Are you OK?'

The Kid turned round. He didn't look OK. Sam had never seen him sad like this. The Kid shrugged.

'I don't want to spoil their joy,' he said. 'Their parasite fun and games.'

'Do you want to talk about it?' Sam asked. 'You usually like to talk. Sometimes talking makes things better.'

The Kid gave a big sigh. Slumped down on to the floor. 'I don't have the words,' he said. 'Not the right ones. Words, words, words. I'm full of words. So many they sometimes poison me. But I don't have the words for this. I can say I'm sad, but that doesn't even half describe how I feel. I can say I'm heartbroken, but that sounds like I'm someone in an old book with people wearing wigs. Distraught, cut up, devastated: they all just sound like what they are, just words. Words, they mean nothing to me now. I'm broken inside. Full of dust. We were going to get married, me and Yo-Yo, and have thirty-seven children. I counted them and we had names for every one. As well as cats. Yo-Yo liked cats. Eighty-three cats. Even though I'm not what you call a cat person. But I'd have done anything for that wee girl. And we were going to live in a house on a hill with a view of the sky. Oh boy. I'm sad, Sam. I'm very sad. But I don't have the words and I don't have any more tears. They were all squeezed out of me. I am made of sorrow, beg steal and borrow, will you still love me tomorrow? I will love her for always and all time, and time beyond time. And I know she's gone to a safe place, a place beyond the stars where no one can hurt you. But still I'm sad. You know about sorrow, Sam. I don't need to tell you. Your sister's gone. We all know sorrow. We've all lost them, the old ones, my granddad. He was the best. Looked after me. Your sister. Everybody's mum and dad. I sometimes wonder how we carry on.'

'But we do carry on,' said Sam. 'She's still alive – Ella – I know she is. I'll see her again, and when I do everything will be all right.'

'Maybe I'll see Yo-Yo again,' said The Kid with a sort of smile. 'Shadowman didn't see her die.'

'You will,' said Sam, although he didn't believe it. In the same way that he didn't really believe he'd see Ella again.

'Oh, the way she plucked her strings,' said The Kid. 'And the way she sawed her bow and made the catgut sing. She was an angel, bringing sweet music to the world. The food of love, play on. She's playing on somewhere, I know it. With a band made of whistles and flutes and toots and banging drums and cymbals, celestas, cellos, cellophane and sell-by dates. I don't know what any of the words mean any more, Sam, not sure I ever did, to be honest. Samwise, Samwich, Sam I am, green eggs and ham . . .'

The Kid fell silent and Sam put his arms round him. Held him tight. The Kid's tears might have dried up, but Sam was crying. For all that they had lost. And then someone else was there, licking and snuffling, and the boys laughed. It was Bright Eyes. And there was Paddy, who'd been out with Achilleus learning his spear skills, running over to fetch her back.

'Leave them, Bright Eyes,' he said, fussing around her. 'Bad girl.'

Paddy got hold of her collar and pulled her away, but Sam and The Kid were still laughing. And Sam wasn't embarrassed now that it looked like he had dog slobber on his cheeks and not childish tears.

He jumped up and rubbed Bright Eyes' ears.

'Yo there.'

Sam looked round to see Jordan Hordern coming in, and the whole atmosphere in the library changed.

Jordan had Blu-Tack Bill with him and a couple of older boys who Sam found slightly scary. Not as scary as Jordan, though. He was the worst. Bill was muttering something. He was probably counting. That's what he did. Sam knew him well enough that whenever he went up or down stairs he always counted the steps, and did weird, complicated mathematical calculations in his head.

Jordan was looking at Paddy. Well, sort of half looking. Jordan hardly ever looked at you directly, and when he did . . .

'We come to ask you something, boy,' he said.

'Yeah?'

Sam could see that Paddy was just as nervous as he was, even though he was trying to hide it. Paddy wasn't as tough as he wanted everyone else to think.

'Whassup?' he said, as casual-sounding as hc could manage, and then held his hand up for one of those complicated handshakes that Sam could never learn properly. Jordan ignored him. Sam had seen how he didn't like to be touched.

'Your dog,' said Jordan.

'What about her?'

'Bright Eyes, yeah? That's her name?'

'Yeah. She's a clever dog. A seeing-eye dog.'

Jordan nodded slowly. 'Thing is – I need a dog.'

'Yeah? There's some around. Ryan and his hunters have loads. They might swap you one.'

'I need *this* dog.'

'But she's my dog.'

'I know. So I'm asking you a favour . . . Paddy. Yeah? That your name?'

'Yeah.'

'Well, Paddy. I'm asking if you'll give me your dog.'

'OK. I get you. But the thing is, she's my dog and I don't want to give her away. She's spoils of war.'

'I know that.' Jordan was staying patient, but there was a coldness in his voice. 'But I'm asking a favour of you. Give me your dog.'

For the first time Jordan looked directly at Paddy, through his thick, broken glasses, and the look was scary as anything. Paddy couldn't hold it for more than a couple of seconds, and then he was staring down at his shoes.

'It's my dog,' he mumbled. 'Bright Eyes.'

Jordan squatted down and held the dog's head, whispered something into her ear. When he stood up, the dog went to his side and sat to heel. Calm and placid. Like it was nothing.

Bill stood back from the others. Nothing to do with him. Leave him out of it. Fiddling with the piece of Blutack he always had with him, shaping it quickly between his fingers – little figures, men and women, animals, numbers, shapes, cubes and pyramids . . . and a dog, which he immediately crushed.

'You can't take her,' said Paddy, his voice shaking, still staring at the floor. 'Not like that. You can't just take her.'

'I'm taking her,' said Jordan. 'OK? That's how it is. I need her. We'll find you another dog. Don't worry.'

'I don't want another dog,' said Paddy. 'I want Bright Eyes. She's a good dog.'

'She's a very good dog.' Jordan snapped a lead on the dog's collar. 'Which is why I want her. You'll get over it.'

Paddy lifted his head. His face was shiny from crying, which made Sam feel not so bad for crying earlier. Paddy tried one last time to argue, but Jordan stared him down and Paddy went quiet. Jordan turned round and walked away with his guys. Taking the dog.

'I won't forget this,' he said as he went out. The kids with Wiki and Jibber-jabber were looking hard at their books, pretending not to notice what was happening. Bill hesitated for a second, looked at his old friends, and then, without saying anything, he followed Jordan out.

'The four-eyed speccy jerk. The cold, dead-staring creep. The bitch!' Achilleus had gone ballistic. He was striding up and down the main hall, past the diplodocus skeleton, waving his spear around, threatening anyone who got close. Maxie was doing her best. She'd tried to calm him down, but that had been an epic fail. Achilleus was just getting worse and worse, and upsetting everyone around him. Paddy was slumped on a bench, looking sad and angry and scared. Scared of what Achilleus might do. And Achilleus's rage had set Paddy off crying again. Maxie knew how much Paddy hated people to see him show any weakness, but the boy was much softer than he acted.

'That was my dog,' Achilleus ranted. 'My dog to do with what I wanted. I gave it to Paddy. It's not Jordan's to take away. He can't march in here like a roadman, thinking he owns the place, and just do what he likes. It's not right. I'm not having it. No way, man.'

'Let's talk about it,' said Maxie, not wanting to give up.

'Nothing to talk about,' said Achilleus. 'Is done. Over. He thinks I'm gonna fight for his poxy army, does he? Well, guess what? I ain't. You get me? You all hear this? I WILL NOT FIGHT FOR THAT JERK!'

'Achilleus.' Maxie was trying not to sound whiny, but that's what she felt like. 'You can't say that.'

'I can. This is me done. Is not my fight any more. Mister Jordan bloody special-needs Hordern can find himself another officer.'

'Come on, Akkie,' said Maxie, avoiding his waving spear. 'This is bigger than one stupid dog.'

'She weren't no stupid dog, though. That's just it. She's clever. That's why this is what it is. Paddy loved that dog. I gave it him. It was mine to give. Not Jordan's to take.'

'Let me try and talk to him.'

'Too late. Jordan hasn't shown me no respect. Nobody appreciates me.'

'We all appreciate you. You know we do.'

'None of you'd be alive if it weren't for me. Well, I'm gonna prove that. Is your fight now. See how you do without me.'

'No, Achilleus. Listen to me. We *do* respect you. We need you now more than ever. We can't do this without you.'

'If Jordan's so good he'll save you all.'

'We'll have a meeting,' said Maxie. 'Call Jordan in. We'll sort it.'

'No more meetings. No more talk. Forget it.'

'At least put the spear down. You're scaring people.'

Achilleus's spear was lethal. God knows how many people he'd killed with it. The point was sharp as a needle.

'This is all I ever was,' said Achilleus, shaking the spear above his head. 'A weapon.'

He broke away and walked quickly to the back of the hall, scattering kids as he went. Then he was bounding up the stairs, three at a time, past the white marble statue of Charles Darwin. Maxie followed hard on his heels, pleading with

him all the way, scared of what he was going to do. She'd never seen him like this before. He'd been arrogant and pigheaded, he'd been full of himself and mean and disruptive, but she'd never really seen him angry.

He switched back on himself at the top of the stairs, heading for the front of the museum. Kids moved out of the way as he bundled past them, ignoring the glass cases with the displays of apes and early humans, going towards the minerals gallery where the kids slept and hung out.

'Akkie!' Maxie shouted, hurrying to catch up with him, terrified that he was going to go into the gallery and do something awful, but he carried straight on past it and up the stairs that led to the top floor.

Right at the top was the cross-section of a giant sequoia four metres wide. As Achilleus neared it, he drew back his arm and let fly with his spear, as if the tree trunk was a giant dartboard. The spear flew straight and clean and hit the sequoia right in the centre, a perfect bull's eye, the point going in several centimetres.

'Done!' shouted Achilleus. 'As long as that spear stays there, I won't fight. If anyone touches it I'll kill them.'

'Please, Akkie.' Maxie was out of breath, choked up. Everything was falling apart. 'Please. Without you . . .'

'Exactly!' Achilleus cut her off. 'Without me. You'll have to get used to it, Maxie, because from now on that's how it is.'

Maxie crushed all her feelings and turned them into anger. She moved in on Achilleus, put her face right in his.

'You can't do this,' she said. 'You can't let your self-love ruin us all. Your petty hurt pride. If other kids find out you're not fighting they might get scared, think it's not worth it. They might all just pull out.'

'I don't care. It's not my problem any more.'

'Would you really risk losing the battle?' said Maxie. 'Watch us all die? Just for this?'

'Yeah,' said Achilleus. 'I would, as it goes. I don't care for no one else. I never did.'

'That's not true,' Maxie snapped. 'What were we just talking about the other day?'

'Dunno. Don't care.'

'"*Arran Lives*". How Freak used to spray it. What it meant.'

'Means nothing. He's dead.'

'No. Back when we left the palace,' said Maxie and she shook him. 'You remember – after Freak had died.'

'What about it?'

'Freak had sprayed "Arran Lives" up on that monument. Tagged it Freaky-Deaky.'

'As I say, Max, what about it?'

'When we all left, you took his spray-can and you wrote your own message – tagged it Akkie Deaky.' Achilleus smiled at her, gave a little laugh. Maxie stared him down.

'You said something to me then,' she said.

'I forget,' said Achilleus with a sneer.

'No, you don't. You told me you'd finally figured out what Freak's message meant.'

'It was just some stupid graffiti,' said Achilleus. 'Didn't mean nothing.'

'You said that Freak was right. That we had to believe what Arran believed. That we had to work together, *be together*, strong – united. You said we had to do the right thing. That everything that happened we had to share, the good and the bad. That we were all in this together.'

'Yeah? Well, I was wrong,' said Achilleus. 'Because it

turned out no one wants to share the good stuff with me, only the bad. I fight for you, I kill for you, I sort out all your problems and I end up like this . . .' He pointed to his ugly, scarred and battered face, his mauled ear. 'When do I get the good stuff?'

'When this is over,' said Maxie. 'When we've won.'

'And until then?' said Achilleus. 'I got to share my dog with Jordan? Well, Akkie don't share his dog, OK? Akkie don't share his dog with no one.'

39

They had come in from all directions. He'd heard them first, buzzing in his skull, chittering and squeaking, getting louder and louder as they got nearer, growing to a roar, until it got so loud he couldn't hear it any more. Silence. His head clear and fresh. New thoughts swimming around inside it like goldfish in a clean bowl.

It was as if he was eating them all, as if they were hamburgers, marching into his guts with big smiles on their faces, and he was cramming them into his gob like a porker at an all-you-can-eat buffet. 'Feed me!' he sang. He had grown huge, fatter and fatter, gorging on them. His army had swelled and he had swelled and his head had swelled. Now he felt like bursting, like something wanted to squeeze its way out of him, a butterfly emerging from a chrysalis.

Let's not get carried away.

Stay focused.

Yes.

How he loved all these old words coming back to him . . .

Focus. Focus. Focus.

Concentrate. That was another one. Hard to do, though. Their voices were all around him, their mind-less, droning drivel threatening to fill his head up again if

he let it. Right now it was as if he had a fence round his head and they were outside, barking and howling and yelping, like foxes trying to get at his sheep. Yammering and yowling. *Yowp, yowp, yowp. Buzz-buzz-buzz* . . . The buzzing of the bees in the lemonade trees. Just a babble. In Babylon.

Except for one voice – pure and cold and sharp. That one could cut through the fence like a knife. Could cut through his skull and poke around inside it, scraping with its needle point. A woman – wouldn't you know it? – nag, nag, nag. He'd felt her as she came into town. She was a leader too, and she had a powerful brain like his. He sometimes wondered if he should kill her. Feed her to the others. But she read his thoughts. Typical woman. They always know what you're thinking. She was standing there now, right in front of him, her long, straight hair hanging down around her face. Not a pretty sight. She stared at him and she stared into him . . .

What you looking at?

And they sort of talked. Thoughts pinged backwards and forwards between them. Good thoughts, bad thoughts, killing thoughts. She knew what he wanted. She knew he hated her for challenging him, but she held him with her strong will. Probing him.

'Leave me alone,' he said. Was it out loud? He couldn't tell. 'This is my army.'

'We are one,' she replied. 'One head, one heart, one soul, one mind.'

Like a soppy love song. Typical woman.

'And you know what we have to do. We have to kill the child – all the children if we must – to stay safe. But him first. He's the most dangerous.'

'You do it,' he said. 'I'll take my chaps and set the world on fire.'

'We have to kill the child.'

'I'll give you help. You can take some of my generals. Take some of my army.'

This was weird. Having a conversation. Like the old days. Chatting up a bird. Ha. Not this one. You wouldn't want nothing to do with this one. She was bad news.

'There are others,' she said. 'Can't you hear them?'

A nightmare. A woman who really *could* read your thoughts.

'Others?'

'Listen . . . Open your mind . . .'

He opened the gate in the fence, just a tiny amount. Suddenly a clamour of voices tried to get in.

Shut up!

Loud as he could. That would rattle their brains. And they quietened down. Yeah, he hadn't lost it.

Who's out there? Who can hear me?

And there they were. Feeble at first, not strong like the woman, but there all right. Other voices. Talking to him.

Where are you from?

From all over. All around. Names and places, north, south, east and west, telling him how they'd come marching in, two by two, four by four, a hundred by a hundred, a thousand upon a thousand . . .

We are many, but we are one. And soon we are going to fly. Fill the skies with our glory.

He heard them all. He understood for a moment what they were. One being. And then another voice. Different. He recognized it. It had been there before. A solo voice in the dark, crying out. And now it was loud and

242

clear and he was confused. Nothing made sense any more. Too many voices. He should never have opened the fence up.

Who are you?

What do you want? What are you doing in my head? Get out. You're not one of us. You are drowning out the babble of my Babylonians. My good soldiers. Ready to blow in like a mighty wind. But here you are and you've cut the signal. You hurt my head. You are doing me in, sunshine. What do you want?

'I want to talk.'

He shook his head, as if the voice was an earwig that could be flung loose. It was frustrating. Just when he was starting to clear his head of the clutter, to see clearly, to get plugged into the horde, to understand his history and mystery and hysteria . . . No, no, no . . . The words were getting muddled. And all because of this new voice. Breaking in like a dirty squatter, finding space where it was quiet and empty.

Who are you? he asked it again.

'Who are *you*?' it replied.

Me? I am the boss, the butcher man. I am St George.

And St George looked at the woman, who looked back at him, head tilted to one side. Could she hear it too?

That voice. Not one of his. Not one of hers. He recognized it all right. He'd heard it before. Now he couldn't shut it up and he couldn't make it go away. It had somehow latched on to him.

Leave me alone . . .

Hadn't made much sense before. Like a foreigner. A bloody immigrant. London was like that now. You never heard an English voice . . . St George and England. He was

that man. In a pub, with a big grin on his face, clutching a pint of beer in his hand. England for the English.

Or was that before?

Concentrate. Focus. The voice was still there. Asking questions. Strong enough to blank out all the other sounds. Stronger even than the woman's voice, which he couldn't hear any more. Well, that was a relief at least. In fact, it had silenced all of them. It was like watching TV with the sound turned down.

But somehow, without the din, without the racket of his racketeers, he felt strangely lonely and abandoned. Cold. These were his people. His tribe. His children. His army. His solar system revolving round the great star. Himself. St George. The biggest star of all. That voice. It was bigger even than him.

It hadn't made much sense before. A weak and squeaking thing it had been. A squirrel in a mighty oak tree, a flea on an elephant's back. *Squeak, squeak, squeak.* He'd tried to talk to it, only he hadn't been able to understand it. Whoever it was, they hadn't known how to use what they had. They'd just made an irritating buzzing noise, like a fly in a milk bottle. And who could ever talk to a fly? I mean, a fly didn't even speak, did it? All that buzzing – that wasn't its voice. That was its wings. Was that all this was? Wings flapping? Fooling him into thinking it was clever, that it had a voice.

If so they had to stop.

They had to SHUT UP!

SHUT UP! SHUT UP! SHUT UP!

He'd said goodbye to all the fleas and flies and the beetles and the bugs and the lemonade trees, back in the big green.

When was that again?

Remind me.

Hundreds. Thousands. Millions of years ago.

In which case . . . How could he remember it?

He turned away from the woman. Walked until he was deep among his people. He had to make sense of all this. Those weren't his memories. So why did he share them? Somebody was playing tricks on him, screwing with his mind, twisting his melons, man.

Somebody deserved a good slapping.

That was the best way to solve problems. Always had been. To do something. To hit someone. To break their neck. But how could you break the neck of someone who was just a fly buzzing in the bottle of your brain?

A bluebottle. He loved it when the words came back to him. So many thoughts and words now − even if they weren't all his own. Thoughts of the universe. The stars in the sky. The big green jungle and the fleas and the flies and the Inmathger . . .

Bloody foreigners.

No, no, no . . . Not his thoughts. That perfect place, all green and fresh. The Garden of Eden. That was it. That's what it was. And the voice?

Telling him what to do.

Was he hearing the voice of God?

Had God given him the sight and the wisdom?

Hello. Are you God?

'Yes.'

What do you want?

'I've been trying to get through to you. I didn't know how.'

I'm listening. You've cracked it. What do you want me to do?

'It's hard − concentrating.'

Don't I know it. Don't force it, son. Just relax and let it go. Don't think about it. Let it flow . . .

'It hurts . . .'

Hard work being God, I'll bet.

'I have to filter out so much other noise.'

They're noisy, aren't they? Your people. Always wanting something. I know what it's like. But I'm glad I'm not the only one. I'm glad there's something out there bigger than me. Makes me not feel so alone. Seems like I've been trying all my life to make sense of the voices in my head. And now I understand. It was you all along, trying to speak to me. Your chosen one. And here you are. And I'm bathed in your light.

'Yes.'

I knew all along really. I could tell you're not like the other ones. My ones. They can't make proper thoughts. They're all just dirty animals. I'm a man. I'm your man. I'm God's chosen man. I'm St George.

'Hello, St George.'

Something I've always wanted to know, God. Do you have another name?

'What?'

You know, I mean, something more than just 'God'.

'Yes. Yes, I do.'

Will you tell me?

'I will. It'll be our secret. If you do what I want you to do.'

I am yours. So what's your name? And what is it you want from me?

'My name is Paul . . . And I want you to kill every one of the children . . .'

40

Jester could see that John wasn't impressed. Basically David should have known that by now – John wasn't impressed by anything. He was a professionally unimpressed person. You could turn into a purple bat with three eyes and a Nerf gun shooting jelly beans out of its arse and John wouldn't be impressed. A shrug. Meh. He was slumped in a chair, staring at Paul with his eyes half closed and his mouth half open. Occasionally he'd let out a little smirking snort of laughter and turn to Carl in the next chair. The two of them would exchange snarky looks and shake their heads.

David was getting sweaty and turning red. Most of the time he behaved like a middle-aged man, but when things got away from him, when he got out of his depth, he'd blush and lose it and turn into a little kid.

'You know,' said John, scratching an armpit. 'One of the things I used to miss about the way things were, was TV. I used to really miss TV. Watching stuff. Not needing to think. But now I don't miss it no more. Is like magic. You've come up with something much better. This is the coolest show I ever seen. What d'you call it? Mug who talks to himself? Muppet with a brain spasm?'

Carl sniggered.

'The Mong Show.'

The focus of their humour was Paul, the messed-up kid from the museum who'd arrived, claiming he could communicate with grown-ups. The Doctor Dolittle of the modern world ... 'I can talk to the strangers.' Or sickos as he called them. Claimed he had some kind of telepathic link. David, as usual, had got carried away, jumped the gun, called people in too early. Like a little kid who gets a magic set for Christmas and wants to show off his new trick before he's properly practised it. 'Look, look, look, the coin will disappear, no wait, oh sorry, I dropped it ...'

Paul was standing there in the middle of the stateroom overlooking the gardens at Buckingham Palace, where the gardeners were hard at work tending to the crops. It was never-ending work.

Paul was concentrating hard, muttering, his lips barely moving.

And that was it.

David really hadn't thought this one through. There was nothing to see. Even if Paul could somehow talk to strangers, how could he prove it? David, as ever, wasn't going to give up, though.

'You don't get it, John,' he snapped at the squatter chief. 'He's communicating with them. He has a telepathic link.'

'Yeah? And so how do I know he hasn't just got a tele-pathic link to my cheesy foot, or a chicken, or a chicken nugget? This is ridiculous, man.'

'It is beyond stupid,' said Carl, dressed, as usual, like a wild kind of pirate – with big boots, a bandanna round his head and baggy trousers cut off just below the knees. John himself was a rare sight. Like he'd been put together from

broken bits and pieces. Ugly and bony, with missing teeth and a nasty, pinched face and small eyes set too close together. He wore an odd selection of clothes – dirty sportswear mostly.

Paul suddenly raised his voice, opened his eyes wide, spoke loud and clear.

'My name is Paul . . .'

And then his lips carried on moving, but Jester couldn't hear any of the words.

John and Carl screamed with laughter, slapping their knees.

'I didn't think it could get any better,' said John. 'But that is the best. We come all this way to find out this amazing piece of information. His name is Paul! Oh great one, chief Jedi, your majesty Pope Paul, what else can you tell us? Please enlighten us. What's your birthday? Can you tell us that?'

But David wasn't giving up.

'Have you made contact?' he said and Paul nodded, staring into the distance, past the palace walls. David looked excited, but John and Carl were just laughing harder.

'Give us another revelation, oh wise one,' said Carl. 'We are waiting for your words, master.'

'He says his name's St George,' said Paul, who was shivering and shaking now, drops of sweat forming on his forehead. Jester had to admit that a tiny shiver passed through his own body as well, and he felt the hairs stand up along his arms.

St George.

That was Shadowman's name for the leader of the strangers' army. But then he too laughed – at himself. It

didn't mean anything. Paul could easily have heard about St George. Hell, Jester might even have talked to Paul about the guy.

Paul was looking really stressed now, like he might become a burster. Well, that'd be a grand finale all right, if he did a full body burst and splattered all over the fancy carpet. Covered John and Carl with gunk.

But he didn't burst. Nothing happened. John got up. 'This is dumb,' he said. 'Me and Carl are going to St James's.'

Paul broke concentration, gasped and fell to his knees. Carl raised his eyebrows at him.

'Nice try, Kermit.'

'Wait,' said David. 'Wait. We can prove it . . .' He threw a look at Jester.

Jester shrugged. 'Prove what exactly?'

'I want to show that Paul can talk to them.'

'Get the royals in,' said Jester and he helped Paul to his feet. 'Can you talk to them again?'

'I think so.'

'Good boy.'

'Not in here!' David squealed in protest. 'They're filthy.'

That was the least of Jester's problems. He really wished David would stop pushing this. Anything could happen with Paul. He was seriously unstable and was in and out of the sick-bay with nosebleeds, fits and fevers. As far as Jester knew, he'd gone nuts after a stranger killed his sister, and now for some reason he blamed other kids for what had happened. Jester had been told by one of the girls who worked in the sick-bay that he had a nasty bite on his neck that wasn't properly healed. He was a tall, thin boy with very pale skin who always wore a greasy black roll-neck jumper – presumably to hide the bite.

250

OK, he'd made some kind of link to the royals before. Could he do it again?

'You sure about this?' Jester asked David.

'We'll carry on the demonstration upstairs.' David gave Jester a sour look and walked out. The others had no choice but to follow, Paul shuffling along behind in a trance.

When they got out into the hallway, John and Carl peeled off.

'We've seen enough,' said Carl.

'For God's sake!' David stopped and turned on them angrily. 'It'll take five minutes. I mean, what else are you going to do? What else *is* there to do? What have you got in your diary that is so important? What is planned for your busy day? Have you got a three-hour session of sitting around scratching your arse booked in? A talk on nose picking? A seminar on dozing off?'

Jester could see that John was about to lose his cool.

'Just think,' he said, stepping in. 'If we *could* communicate with the grown-ups. Tell them what to do.'

'Do what?' said John. 'They're useless.'

'Help us,' said David. 'Ask yourself – what do you want? What do I want? We all want the same thing. We want to deal with those arrogant bastards at the museum, Justin's snotty nerds, the Holloway kids . . . Achilleus.'

'That bastard,' said John.

'You want to be in control of London, yes?' said David. 'Sure.'

Like David, John had been humiliated by the Holloway kids. Jester doubted he'd ever forgive Achilleus for defeating him in single combat.

'Just think,' said David, back in control, selling his gold-plated bullshit. 'Our own army. Isn't that what we've

always wanted? To be strong enough to rule London? To tell everyone else what to do?'

'Right,' said Carl, who was brighter than John. John had mean street smarts, but that was about it. Carl understood the world a lot better than him.

'Let's pretend for a moment your pet monkey actually *can* talk to the walking pus-bags,' said Carl. 'Who's to say they'll do what we want? That don't follow.'

'It does,' said David, beaming at him. 'What do the strangers want?'

'Dunno,' said John. 'Don't care.'

'They want the same as us,' said David. 'To destroy the snotty museum kids and that gimp Jordan Hordern from the Tower of London, strolling over here like he owns the place. We can pull them all down and put them in their place. Because all the strangers have ever wanted to do is kill kids. But if we can make some kind of alliance, some kind of truce with them . . .'

'How d'you make a truce with zombies?' Carl scoffed. 'They don't think. They're nothing.'

'Not all of them,' said David. 'They have a leader – the one Paul's made contact with – St George.'

So we're all going along with that, are we? thought Jester. Contact with the big kahuna. How quickly David could spin things his way.

'He's clever, St George. He controls the strangers. If we can make this link with him stronger then . . .'

'*If* you can,' said John and he spat into an ornamental vase on a stand. 'But there ain't no proof of it.' He at least had seen through David's fog.

'I'm giving you proof,' said David and he grabbed Paul by the shoulders.

'You'll do it, won't you?' he said, but Paul looked dazed and confused.

'I am God,' he said quietly, almost a whisper.

'He'll do it,' said Jester, taking the pressure off Paul before he cracked.

They went up the ornate grand staircase, past the black statue of Perseus holding the severed Medusa's head. John and Carl looked around admiringly.

'When you gonna invite us to come and live here in comfort?' said John.

'I thought you preferred your camp,' said David.

'Yeah, but you got some nice stuff here. Ain't it nice, Carl?'

'It's nice.'

At the top they made their way up a second, less elaborate staircase to the royal apartments, the smell of the royal family getting stronger with every step. Even John and Carl, who, quite frankly, stank, wrinkled their noses and made crude jokes about farting and worse.

As ever, there was a boy guarding the door to the royals' bedroom. He looked bored and sleepy. David said a few words to him while John and Carl pointed at a painting of two nude women and sniggered.

The boy opened the door and the stench hit them like a physical wave. John groaned. The royals were a terrible sight. There were only five of them left, their clothes hanging off them in rags. An older woman, a younger woman and three younger men. They were the healthiest of the ones they'd found hiding here when they'd arrived. Very minor royals. Jester had long ago forgotten who they were exactly. They had so many sores and boils on their faces they didn't even look human. Jester no longer

felt disgusted or disturbed by them, and they certainly couldn't scare him. They were too feeble and degenerate.

They lived like animals in a zoo, crapping on the floor and eating scraps from tin bowls.

The four boys stepped carefully into the room, careful of what they might tread in.

'OK,' said John, sneering at Paul, who looked paler and more feverish than ever. 'It's show time.'

Paul sighed, took a deep breath and fixed his eyes on the royals. 'What do you want them to do?' he asked.

'Anything!' David shouted. 'Do anything! Do something! Show us.'

'He can't do nothing,' said John. 'He's just a nutter. This is a big waste of time.'

But before he'd finished speaking the royals dropped to the floor, like puppets with their strings cut, and John's eyes went wide. Paul's own eyes had rolled back in their sockets and he was shaking and muttering, jerking about like he was possessed.

The royals groaned. One of the younger ones held his head in his hands and rocked from side to side on the carpet. And then they all fell still.

'That wasn't him,' said John. 'A fluke.'

One by one the royals slowly raised their ruined faces to look at John and Carl. And then they started shuffling on their bellies towards the two boys, drooling brown spit over their swollen lower lips on to the carpet.

'OK,' said John. 'You can stop 'em now.'

Jester was impressed because, for the first time ever, John was impressed. More than impressed. He actually looked scared.

'You can call 'em off now, brother.'

The royals kept on coming, wriggling and sliding on their bellies. John and Carl stepped back and now the royals got up on to their knees, bowing down to them, pressing their foreheads to the floor. The older woman, whose lidless eyes were surely blind, raised one hand towards Carl, opened what was left of her mouth and a sound came out, something like speech, something like a sick animal, something horrible. Then she turned one hand round. It was twisted and gnarled, the joints swollen, her little finger missing.

'What's she doing?' said John.

Slowly the woman made a fist and then painfully extended her middle finger.

Jester was laughing. John wasn't. He'd gone white.

'She's saluting you, John,' said Jester, and he clapped Paul on the back. 'She's giving you the finger.'

41

Shadowman was up in the tower at the old cinema again. Watching the sicko army. He felt at home. This was what he did best. Watching. Waiting. Following. Alone. No one else to get hurt. No one else to slow him down and put him in danger.

Always best to be alone.

He had his pack. His food. His water. His weapons. And from here he could see almost the full extent of St George's army. Now maybe twice as big as it had been. More sickos had arrived from all points of the compass, trudging in on that awful morning. Reports had come in from the east, from the Tower of London – Jordan Hordern had a very efficient communication system. And, earlier today, Shadowman had managed to get up to see Saif. Saif had confirmed that more sickos had come in from the north. Shadowman had seen for himself the ones coming over the bridges from the south. Most, though, the largest group, had come from the west. And that had been the group who had taken Yo-Yo. No chance that she might still be alive. He hadn't tried to lie to himself about that.

The best way was just not to think about the girl at all.

Concentrate on the sickos.

So many questions that needed answers.

They were all down there, all the new ones, mixing with St George's original army. What were they doing? What were they waiting for? Why had they gathered? What where they eating? How were they surviving at all? Did they really have a plan of some sort?

What Shadowman wanted more than anything was to get down there, right among them, but it was too dangerous. He'd tried it once and had had to make a quick exit, running as fast as his still weak leg would allow. He'd only just made it. If the sickos hadn't been slow and sleepy and reluctant to leave their nesting ground he'd surely have been caught and swamped. He was being much more careful now.

That had at least answered one question.

He'd thought he might be carrying around a monster death wish, but when he found himself running for his life he knew it had passed. It wasn't his fault what had happened to Yo-Yo. He'd had to tell himself that. Ryan had been just as responsible.

The thing was – nobody could have predicted the arrival of a massive new army when the streets had been so quiet.

You had to tell yourself these stories to stay sane, to stay alive. If you let your mind go soft you were done for. To survive you had to stay strong in the head. Head, heart and hand. If any of them failed you, that was it. There had been a spell after Yo-Yo was killed when Shadowman's heart had been hurt. But he'd slowly built a fresh wall around it. He'd moved away from other kids, and now he was back where he belonged, with his sickos.

He was happy to be here. Happy to watch and wait. Hard of head, hard of heart, hard of hand . . .

He sucked in his breath and held it. There was a change. Black figures were moving out into the main road, heading south. First one or two, then clumps of them, then larger groups, finally a flood filling the whole road, like oil flowing into a channel. Greasy and filthy and rotting.

It reminded Shadowman of match days. Football fans coming down the streets. Slow and purposeful. Massing. Expectant.

St George's army was on the move.

It was starting.

42

'You're looking better. I really think you are.' Fish-Face ran her fingers down the Green Man's arm and then returned to her work. There was a nasty click and then a rattle as one long fingernail dropped to the floor.

Maxie shuddered. Fish-Face was using a pair of heavy-duty kitchen scissors to cut her father's nails. Creepy. Personally she wasn't sure about Fish-Face's judgement. Did Wormwood look less green? Was the evil fungus that covered him going away? He still weirded Maxie out. His pale eyes. The way he always seemed to have some hidden thought brewing in his brain. The way you caught him looking hungrily at you, and if you held his stare he dropped his gaze like a shamed dog.

Fish-Face had done her best to make him normal. She'd managed to cut his hair and now she was getting rid of his horrible long fingernails. She'd also got him to wear clothes, a baggy T-shirt and tracksuit trousers, even though he complained that they hurt his skin. No shoes. He stuck at that. And he still always had his blanket wrapped round his shoulders and his ridiculous green bowler hat jammed on his head. So he was a long way from normal. Was he better physically, though? Was he

healthier at all? Was it just Fish-Face's improvements that had made him look more human?

What a couple they were. Maxie wasn't sure she'd ever get used to the two of them. The way Fish-Face loved the old freak. Maxie knew that Einstein was experimenting on him. Using him as a guinea pig to try out the antidotes he was working on – made from Small Sam's blood. At least Einstein hadn't killed him, like he had the mother on the lorry. He'd made a safer new serum, had tried a tiny, tiny amount at first. Had been building the doses up since. Maxie didn't pretend to understand the mechanics of it, but something must be working.

She'd come to the birds gallery where the Twisted Kids hung out with Wormwood, to try to find Skinner. He was the easiest to talk to and he could translate Fish-Face's more peculiar outbursts. She still seemed to be getting messages from her friend Trinity who had gone out west with Ed.

Maxie needed to know if there was any news from them. Was Ed coming back? She didn't know Ed well, but what she'd seen of him had impressed her. Plus, he'd taken three of their key fighters with him – Kyle, Lewis and Ebenezer. Morale at the museum was disastrously low since Achilleus was refusing to fight. If Ed came back he might help rally the kids. At the moment, apart from a hardcore group here at the museum and most of Maxie's crew, it was only the guys from the east who were prepared to go into battle, and she wasn't really sure how much use the crazy greens from St Paul's were going to be. They were enthusiastic enough – manic, fanatical even – but they weren't exactly fighters. She'd seen them practising in Hyde Park. Their tactics seemed to involve a lot of

prayer and chanting and music and not a lot of combat. Maxie knew grown-ups well enough to know that if the greens went into battle armed only with violins and trumpets they'd be massacred.

There was no God to protect them. Despite what they thought. Maxie had seen enough of the misery in the world to know that. But if Ed came back it would really help.

She had to interrupt this touching scene.

'Is Skinner around?'

'He's up with the smaller kids,' said Fish-Face, without looking up from her work. She was so shy, poor girl.

'Can I help?' she said, twisting her long neck so as not to look at Maxie.

'Maybe.' Maxie explained what she wanted.

'I haven't heard anything for a while,' said Fish-Face when she'd finished. 'At least nothing clear. It's all been too confused, with those new grown-ups going through. And there's so many of them, they block the signals. It's just static out there now, white noise, soup, a thousand voices all shouting at once. You can't make anything out. I'll tell you as soon as I know anything. I will ... but Maxie?' Finally she looked up at Maxie and there was pleading in her huge, wide-set eyes.

'Is everything going to be all right?'

'I don't honestly know,' said Maxie. 'If we can't get everyone back on board and united I don't know what's going to happen. Nobody wants to fight.'

'Is there anything I can do?' said Fish-Face.

'Can you turn back time?'

Fish-Face shook her head.

'No chance of going back and stopping Jordan taking

Paddy's dog then. How about you take us into an alternative universe where the disease never happened?'

Fish-Face smiled shyly and shook her head again.

'Then you're as helpless as me, I'm afraid,' said Maxie. 'Even some of my Holloway kids won't fight without Achilleus – but I don't know what we can do.'

'We could just hope the sickos never attack,' said Fish-Face.

'We'll get the St Paul's crew to pray for it,' said Maxie.

There was shouting from outside and the two girls looked round towards the door.

'What is it?' said Fish-Face anxiously.

'I'll go see.'

Maxie hurried out and went along the wide corridor with the sea monster fossils down either side, towards the main hall. There were kids milling around the diplodocus skeleton, excited, waving their arms, voices raised. As Maxie got closer, she spotted Blue, who seemed to be at the centre of it all. She speeded up and went straight to him. As soon as he spotted her, he broke away from the other kids and took her to one side. He looked serious, trying to keep the stone face on and failing. Something heavy was up.

'They coming,' he said.

'Who? What?'

'The army's moving. We have to get out there. Jordan wants us to make sure the sickos head towards Hyde Park. We have to drive them.'

'Shit.'

This plan had been discussed at length. The kids had spent day after day building barricades and laying down a firewall to try to direct the grown-ups to Jordan's chosen

battleground. But they hadn't nearly finished getting ready. The danger was that the army would simply spread out and advance down all the streets. Or even just go the other way entirely. Nobody really had any idea what their plan might be.

And since Achilleus had thrown his tantrum the kids' army had started to fall apart. They had only half the number of fighters to call on.

'Are we ready?' she asked, looking around at the nervous kids who'd gathered there.

'Course we ain't,' said Blue. 'We never will be.'

Maxie swore to herself. She'd really been hoping that Blue would lie.

'The battle's on and we are gonna show them what we can do!'

Paddy looked at Achilleus's spear, sticking straight out from the slice of tree trunk. God – he must have thrown it really hard. It had gone right in. And that old wood, man, it was like iron. Paddy pulled the end of the spear down and let go. It juddered, like twanging a ruler on the edge of your desk, and Paddy enjoyed the noise it made.

'I'm gonna pull it out,' he said. 'Take it back to Akkie. Show him how strong I am.'

'You're no way strong enough,' said Jibber-jabber. 'You'll never pull it out. Not in a million years – which is about how old that tree is.'

The other kids laughed. His troop. His team. The kids he was going to lead into battle. And now he had the chance to show them what he was. A hero like his hero, Akkie.

'Easy', he said. 'I am Patrick of the Red Branch Knights. The greatest team of superheroes in Irish legend. I am Cúchulainn, back from the dead, reincarnated in this body!'

'And I'm Hercules reincarnated,' said Froggie. 'He's come back to life in my body.' He did a strongman pose,

looking to his sister for approval. Zohra laughed. Zohra always laughed at anything Froggie did.

'I'll show you,' said Paddy and he gripped the spear with both hands. All he'd ever wanted was to be tough. He'd grown up in a big family, two brothers and two sisters. He wasn't the youngest, so he couldn't be the baby and everyone's favourite, like Froggie. And he wasn't the oldest. Couldn't be the leader of the clan, like his big brother, Daragh. He'd been stuck in the middle, ignored, nothing special. He'd been teased at school for his strong Irish accent. Kids would impersonate him. Teachers would tell him to speak more clearly. He'd wished he had superpowers, that he could suddenly grow bulging muscles and leap up and smash people to the ground. He'd worked out in his room in secret using Daragh's weights. They'd hurt his arms, but he knew that if he was tough he could *be* someone.

Not just Akkie's caddie, carrying his spears around. He'd be a hero like his hero.

Except Achilleus wasn't going to fight.

He'd kicked Justin out of his room, an old office at the front of the museum, and taken it over. He hardly ever came out. Sat in the dark with the curtains drawn, swearing at anyone who came close.

So now it was up to Paddy to be the hero of the day.

He pulled on the spear. Achilleus had only thrown it at the slice of trunk. It wasn't like he'd driven it in with a hammer or anything, but it didn't budge. Not even a millimetre. Paddy realized he was looking like a fool.

'Come on, superman,' Froggie shouted. 'Pull out the spear. Pull out the spear.'

Paddy turned and cursed him, shocking the other kids.

'Why don't you pull it out then?' he said. 'If you're so tough. You can't, can you?'

'I never said I could,' Froggie protested.

'Because you can't,' said Paddy.

'I know.'

'None of you can.' Paddy looked around at their faces. 'Nobody except Achilleus can pull this spear out.'

Yeah, that was it. He loved all the old stories that his dad had told him when he was a kid. His dad had been a poet and a storyteller. He'd told Paddy all the Irish tales, and the Scottish tales, and the African ones, the Welsh, the Indian . . . even the English ones. Although, every time he did, he'd say, 'You've got to remember, kiddo, that the Irish tales are best.'

Paddy remembered the story of King Arthur. The sword in the stone. That only the rightful king of England could pull it out.

'Yeah,' he said. 'Only Achilleus can pull this out. Because he's the greatest champion of all. And, when he pulls it out, we'll win. We'll defeat the sickos. And I'll be remembered, and Achilleus will be a hero for all time. Go on!' he shouted. 'Any of you. Try it. See if you can pull it out. I'm telling you, you can't!'

He'd done it now. If any of them did manage to pull the spear out he'd look a right idiot. But he was confident that nobody would. They were all as young as him after all. Jibber-jabber and Wiki tried first. They even both tried pulling on it together. And then Froggie stepped up, for a joke, Zohra clapping and laughing like a mad person.

'Come on,' said Paddy. 'All of you have a go. Maybe one of you is special.'

Next up was The Kid.

'I'm Bernard Pollard!' he said proudly.

'Who's Bernard Pollard?' said Paddy.

'Dunno.' The Kid shrugged. 'It just came to me. Sounded like a proper hero's name.'

'Bernard Pollard?'

'All right then,' said The Kid. 'Sally Abbey.'

'Sally Abbey?'

'Lulu? Twiggy? No! I'm Strongarm MacStrong, the King of Dangerland, brave of heart, and hot of head, and pot of noodles!'

Paddy had no idea what The Kid was on about. He never did. The boy was nuts.

The Kid took hold of the spear and tugged, making an exaggerated straining face, then stepped back.

'It has defeated me,' he said. 'It can't be done. It's an impossibility. An improbability. The spear of destiny. The spearmint of gum.'

That only left Small Sam. Everyone was always talking about how Mad Matt thought Sam was some kind of a god. Well, he could prove it now. He could step up and pull that spear right out of there.

'Go on,' said Paddy. 'You're the chosen one. Grab the spear and lead us all to victory.'

'I'm not the chosen one,' said Sam. 'That's all just stupid stuff. Matt's got it all wrong.'

'But your blood,' said Zohra. 'Isn't there something special in your blood?'

'Yeah,' said Froggie. 'Show us what you can do, Mister Magic Blood. Pull out the spear.'

The others took up a chant – 'Pull out the spear! Pull out the spear!'

Sam looked embarrassed, but, when it became clear

that the only way to get them to shut up was to do what they wanted, he grabbed the spear with both hands and pulled.

Not really making an effort, not expecting it to move . . .

And of course it didn't.

Things had all fallen a bit flat, so Paddy fired them up again. That was his job as their leader. Their captain.

'Nobody can pull it out except the champ,' he shouted.

'And what if he doesn't want to pull it out?' said Wiki. 'What then?'

'He will.'

He had to. Achilleus was Paddy's hero. And what use was a hero if he shut himself away, not speaking to anyone, not wanting to fight?

If he didn't come out and fight then he wouldn't be a hero at all.

She'd been told enough times, been to enough meetings where she'd stood up and shouted about how many grown-ups there were out there; she'd watched the new ones arrive on the morning after the blood-red moon, but it was only now, seeing them in the flesh, massed together, that Maxie believed that they were real. An honest-to-God army.

An army on the move.

And she was so scared she wanted to throw up.

She still couldn't get her head round how many of them there were. It felt like they were going to take over the whole of London.

She couldn't really remember what it had been like when it all started, a little over a year ago now. So much had happened since then, so many awful, terrifying, disgusting, heartbreaking things. The only way to deal with it was to close your mind down, not talk about it, try to pretend it had never happened.

They'd made it through a year. They'd survived this far. And then everything had changed. She still didn't really understand why the sickos had all banded together like this, what they were hoping to do, but it felt like the end. If they couldn't be stopped there was no way the kids in London were going to be able to hang on here. They'd

have to get as far away as they could. But what hope did they have of defeating this horde?

So many. None of the kids had ever had to face an army before.

How could there possibly be enough kids to win this? Even if half of them hadn't stayed behind at the museum, refusing to fight. The dark mood had even affected the Tower of London kids. If Jordan hadn't been so scary, and such an effective leader, Maxie thought that quite a few of them would have avoided the fight as well.

Maxie and Blue and their squad were running around the streets, herding the sickos towards Hyde Park, where Jordan was getting his army ready. At least that was the plan. You might as well try to herd an avalanche. Everywhere they turned, everywhere they looked, there were more of them, a huge, dirty, rotting mass of bodies, giving off that God-awful stench and making a horrible shuffling, hissing, murmuring sound as they walked. One mind. One purpose. They were almost marching in step. An ant colony. A swarm of bees. They were intelligent and had no fear of the light.

The kids made no attempt to fight them, to kill any of them. What was the point? What difference would it make taking out one or two? It would just be a massive waste of time. All they could do was watch them, follow them, chart their progress.

And the sickos were arming themselves. Maxie had never seen that before. They would break away from the main mass in ones or twos and become individuals, broken, diseased, maimed, rotting, falling apart, but still somehow functioning. Some would tear up paving slabs, smash them, keep the broken bits of concrete to use as weapons. Others were ripping out iron railings and fence

posts and road signs, finding anything they could use to attack with. Breaking into shops, coming out with sports equipment and tools and metal clothes rails.

Maxie watched as one father, his face so eaten away it looked like a bare skull, picked up two pieces of broken glass and held them like daggers, ignoring the blood that flowed down them and dripped on to the ground.

She could hear distant bangs and see smoke rising into the sky. Jordan had built firewalls to try to block off some of the side-streets and contain the sickos.

Was it going to be enough?

The only one tiny good thing about all this was that the sickos were at least heading roughly in the right direction, the direction Jordan wanted them to go, so that he could take them on out in the open.

There was no saying that even if they got to Hyde Park they'd stop there, however. There was no saying what they might do.

Maxie thought back to the day when Small Sam had been kidnapped from the car park behind Waitrose. In her mind that was when it all began to change. The start of this new phase. This new intelligent behaviour.

It hadn't sunk in back then. She'd been too worried about other things. Worried about what people would think. She was supposed to have been in charge at their camp that day. It was her fault that Sam had been taken. Why hadn't she been on top of things? Why hadn't she been more worried about the small kids playing in the car park . . . ?

Because grown-ups never came out during the day.

One or two kids had mentioned it at the time. But it didn't seem to be such a big deal. It was a freak thing. There were other more important matters to worry about.

But since that day the sickos had changed completely. They'd become this . . .

This *terror*.

Trudging relentlessly through the streets.

Towards the park? That was surely just wishful thinking.

And then it struck Maxie that there were other things in that direction. Beyond the park. Like the Natural History Museum. Could that be where they were heading?

Maxie was already exhausted. The stress was wearing her down. It gave her some strength to see Blue nearby. The two of them together. That was important. They were a team. He would look after her and she would look after him. It had been unbearable when he'd gone away on his expedition to Heathrow, and now she wasn't going to let him out of her sight. She'd become such a pessimist, convinced that everyone she cared about was going to end up dead.

They stopped running. Maxie had lost sight of what they were supposed to be doing. Her legs ached. Her lungs burned. She wasn't even sure where they were any more. Hoped that somebody in their group knew the way back to the park, to the museum. Blue came over to her, gave her some water.

'We making any difference?' Maxie asked and Blue shrugged.

'We can't control them, that's for sure,' he said. 'Even if there was more of us. This is nuts. They just gonna go where they wanna go.'

'We should get back,' said Maxie, looking around for street names.

'Back where?' said Blue.

'The park, I guess,' said Maxie. 'Sooner or later we have to stop arsing around and fight them.' There was a catch in her voice. Was she tired or did she want to cry?

Blue put his arms round her, and Maxie was reassured by their strength and the warmth of his body. And she realized she was trembling. No — it was him. He leant back and looked her in the eyes.

'We could just run,' he said. 'Turn our backs on all this. You and me, yeah? Get around them and go back up north. What difference are we gonna make? Us two?'

'Are you serious?' said Maxie and Blue shrugged again.

'You must've thought it,' he said.

'I'm trying not to think at all,' said Maxie. 'It's not just the two of us, though, is it? It's everyone else, our friends. Every kid in London.'

'Yeah,' said Blue and he gave her a wide grin. 'But it's a thought, isn't it? A nice thought. Do away with all this, everyone else, all this hassle. Escape . . .'

'Life is hassle,' said Maxie. 'You can't run from it. We go someplace else, we'll just find something else. Maybe something worse.'

'What could be worse than this?' said Blue

'I have absolutely no sodding idea,' said Maxie and the two of them laughed.

'Come on, you lazy slackers!' Blue yelled at the rest of their group. 'We got work to do. Let's get to the park.' And he winked at Maxie.

'For a moment there,' he said quietly, 'everything felt cool.'

'It sure did,' said Maxie. 'For a moment.'

Paddy was marching his troop down the main hall towards the two big doors that led outside. They were formed into two loose ranks and Paddy was shouting orders. Sam wasn't really listening. Lost in his thoughts. Feeling down again. Thinking of his sister, wondering where she was, fearing that he'd never see her again. The Kid looked at him and took his hand and squeezed it. He was weird, The Kid. In his own words he was half crazy. Most of the babble that came out of his mouth made no sense at all. At least no sense that Sam could see. And yet The Kid knew stuff. And he felt things. He knew when Sam was down and did what he could to lift him up. The Kid was what kept him going. They were a team.

The Kid leant over and whispered in Sam's ear.

'I *am* actually Bernard Pollard,' he said.

'I don't know what you mean,' said Sam. 'Is that your real name?'

'I don't think so. But the name keeps popping into my head.'

'OK,' said Sam.

'Listen, microbe,' said The Kid. 'Don't wear such a long face and drawers. The sun will come out again, with his hat on, ten shillings and sixpence. He'll smile at all us

Teletubbies. We'll keep on keeping on. As Gloria Gaylord said, "We will survive."'

'If you say so,' said Sam flatly.

'Hey, I'm just riffing here, trying to put a smile on you. Them sickos out there, we are going to take them all to Wigan and punt them through the goal posts. The landlord in the sky has a plan for us. He didn't get us all this way, alive and all, to let us perish like perishing pilchards. We'll merk them sickos and smirk at the moment. Nice thick gravy. We're all just cavemen now. We will paint our story on the walls.'

'I don't get you,' said Sam.

'Me neither,' said The Kid. 'Sometimes I just have to get the words out or they build up inside me and I think I'll choke on them. I have to say them. Stops me thinking too. Stops me from getting frit.'

'Frit?'

'Afraid, a-scared, a-trembling in fright.'

'Are you scared?' asked Sam.

'Holy moly, guacamole. Of course I'm scared. There's a world of warcraft out there. Old folk on the rampage. By cassocks, revellers and weasels, I'm scared! I hope we can blast them all to kingdom come. And dance a disco dance of triumph.'

'Silence in the ranks,' said Paddy and Sam laughed. Where had he got that one from? *Silence in the ranks*. It was like something from the First World War.

'We're gonna show them that even though we're small we can make a difference,' said Paddy. 'We'll show those sickos.'

'You're showing no one nothing, Paddy!' Everyone stopped. Whitney was blocking the doors, arms folded,

weight on one leg, one eyebrow raised. Sam liked Whitney. She could be really, really scary, but she was also one of the kindest of the big kids. She spent ages with Sam and his friends, making sure they were happy, making sure they were eating, washing, looking after themselves. And now she was going to make sure they didn't fight. Sam had been praying that this would happen. He'd heard the big kids talking. Knew that they'd been letting Paddy play at being a soldier, but there was no way they were going to allow this bunch of squirts to go wandering on to the battlefield to get trampled underfoot.

And Sam was glad Whitney hadn't forgotten. He never wanted to fight again.

'You can't tell us what to do,' said Paddy. 'I'm in charge here. I'm the officer.'

'Yeah, well, I'm your commander-in-chief,' said Whitney. 'You ain't going out there, Paddy. This fight ain't for you.'

'You can't stop me,' said Paddy. And Whitney raised her other eyebrow. This was one of her scariest faces.

'You wanna take me on?' she said and moved in on Paddy. Whitney was big. Whitney was tough. No one argued with Whitney. She went right up to Paddy, looking down at him, towering over him, like the Gruffalo looking at the mouse.

'You disobey me,' she said, 'and it's not sickos you got to worry about. My wrath is mighty. I been given one job – to look after you idiots, to keep you safe.' And she looked square at Sam. Sam knew how everybody was treating him as special, the golden one with the special magic blood. It was no fun being special. He wished he was just plain old Small Sam again.

But he was still really glad they were looking after him.

'So don't get no ideas in your head about going out there to play soldiers, Patrick,' Whitney said and she playfully slapped him round the head, rocking him sideways. If her play slap was like this, Sam wondered what a real slap would be like. Probably would have knocked Paddy's head off.

'You guys got free run of the museum,' she said, walking towards Paddy's troop and forcing them back across the hall towards the stairs. 'You can march around in here. You can do your drills and have mock battles as much as you like, but you DO NOT go outside. You do not go through these doors. You do not even look out the windows. These walls are, like, half a mile thick. With everything locked down tight, there is no way any sickos can get in. And that's how I'm keeping it. This is our castle. I am king of the castle. And you do as I say or I inflict some major pain on you.'

'I'm a warrior,' said Paddy. 'I want to go out and fight. It's my choice. If I want to go out there and die like a hero I can.'

'I'd love nothing more,' said Whitney. 'One less pest about the place. But what about these other kids? Maybe they ain't bustin' to get killed.'

She looked across the ranks and nobody could look back at her. They all stared at their shoes.

'I been given a job and I'm gonna do it,' Whitney said. 'You are pinned down, little man. I suggest you stay pinned.'

'This is all Sam's fault,' said Paddy and he gave Sam a furious dark look.

'What are you talking about?' said Sam.

'It's *you*,' said Paddy. 'It's all about you. Because you're

so special. Because we all have to look after you. If it wasn't for you I could go out there and be a hero. Instead, I'm stuck here with little kids and babies and cowards.'

'I didn't ask for this,' said Sam angrily. 'I never wanted to be special. I don't even know why I am. Why my blood is like it is.'

'You must've been born with it,' said Wiki. 'Like some people have genetic differences, mutations, different immune systems.'

'I still don't know what that means,' said Sam.

'You have natural immunity to the disease. It can't harm you. It's in your blood and the sickos can smell it. It's dumb luck. It's just chance. It could've been any one of us.'

'I wish it was,' said Sam. 'I wish someone else had it instead of me. I don't want to be like this. I don't want to be *special*.'

Paddy was going to say something, but he was distracted by a shout from the back of the hall and two boys came running up to Whitney.

'Whassup?' she asked them as they got near.

'There's been an accident in the kitchen,' said one of the boys. 'Alicia's tipped some boiling water all down her legs.'

Whitney swore. 'She OK?'

'We dunno. Don't know what to do, whether to take her jeans off to look or if that'll make it worse. She's bare screaming.'

Whitney shoved the boys towards the orange zone. 'Go get someone from the medical team and some gear. I'll go see Alicia.'

She gave Paddy's crew all one last dirty look and hurried off.

'It ain't fair,' said Paddy. 'We can fight as good as the rest of them. And the rest aren't even fighting. They need us.'

'Paddy,' Sam shouted. He was getting angry now. 'Whitney's right. This isn't a game. I know you want to be a warrior, a big hero, but you're not. You're a little kid like the rest of us.'

Paddy stared at him. Sam had the awful feeling that he was about to burst into tears. His face had gone red, his eyes shiny.

'And what about *them*?' Paddy shouted, waving his arm at a group of bigger kids who were doing what they always did – sitting around chatting. 'Do they look like grown-ups to you? Do they look like adults? No. We're *all* just kids.'

'Yes, but we're smaller,' said Sam. 'We're younger. We're weaker.'

'I'm not,' said Paddy. 'I've been trained by Achilleus. The best fighter there is. I could take on anyone here.'

'No, you couldn't,' said Sam and immediately wished he'd kept his mouth shut.

'I'll show you,' said Paddy and he stormed off, his face even redder. His muscles all stiff, shoulders hunched over.

'Where's he going then?' said Jibber-jabber.

'Hope he's not going to do something stupid,' said Zohra.

'Of course he is,' said Wiki. 'He's been in a bad mood ever since Achilleus refused to fight.'

'Before that,' said Zohra. 'Ever since Jordan took his dog.'

Sam sat down on a bench with The Kid. Looked over at the group of bigger kids. They were some of the ones who'd chosen not to fight. They all looked tense and worried. There was a horrible atmosphere in the museum. It was making everyone on edge and quick to argue. They

were all wondering just what was going on out there. The fighters had gone charging out, and since then it had been like it always was. Quiet. Boring. Slow. All you could really do was wait. Wait for the fighters to come back and tell you what was happening.

There was a shout from upstairs. Paddy was at the end of the balcony near the minerals gallery, leaning over the stonework, waving a spear in the air.

'You see what this is!' he shouted. 'It's the *Gáe Bolg*. The belly ripper. The greatest spear ever made. Made for a warrior. And I'm taking it into battle.'

The bigger kids looked up and Paddy turned his attention to them.

'Look at you sitting there, doing nothing,' he yelled. 'You should be out there fighting. You're all useless.'

He marched along the balcony, still shouting, but his words were lost, echoing up into the great space of the hall. When he came down the stairs, Sam could see that he'd put on one of Achilleus's tops. A Nike one that was far too big for him. He'd tried to roll the sleeves up, but one of them had come loose and was hanging down over his hand. He was also carrying the iron bucket helmet that Achilleus had brought back from the V&A.

'I'm gonna show you all what to do,' he said, putting the helmet on. 'I'm gonna kill the enemy.'

'You can't,' said Zohra. 'Whitney won't let you.'

'If she tries to stop me I'll kill her,' said Paddy, and Wiki and Jibber-jabber laughed. Paddy turned on them, swinging the spear through the air. It had a wide, leaf-shaped head that was more like a sword blade. It was a really mean weapon, a proper spear, unlike the home-made, sharpened metal spike that Achilleus had embedded in the tree trunk.

Wiki and Jibber-jabber jumped back, swearing at Paddy and shouting at him to be more careful. But Paddy was off on one now. Striding towards the main doors, yelling insults at the bigger kids, who simply looked at him with dull eyes.

'Who's with me?' he said. 'Who wants to be a hero?' A couple of the smaller kids followed him.

'Come on,' Paddy shouted. 'All of you. Let's show them.'

He marched up to the guys guarding the doors. They weren't the regular guards, who'd gone off to Hyde Park, and when Paddy jabbed his spear at them they stood aside to let him out. Most of the Youngbloods went after him, chatting excitedly. They wanted to see what Paddy was going to do. Sam sighed and looked at The Kid. The two of them were still sitting on the bench.

'We can't let him go,' Sam said and The Kid nodded.

When they got outside, they saw Paddy already half-way to the gates. Sam was relieved to see that the guards at the gate were regulars, more serious and better trained than the guys inside. Sam and The Kid arrived to find Paddy in a furious argument with them. It was clear they weren't going to let him out.

Sam looked up as a huge flock of seagulls appeared overhead, as if from nowhere, wheeling and spinning in the air, screaming and swooping. Scavengers. They knew a big meal was coming.

'They're the banshees!' shouted Paddy. 'You know what it means? That someone's gonna die. We're gonna kill the sickos. And look – there.' He pointed to where three crows sat on the railings. There weren't any vultures in Britain, but there were carrion birds, like these, that ate dead things.

'Morrígans,' said Paddy. 'Badb Catha and her sisters — the battle crows. These are good signs.'

Paddy ran at the crows, scattering them, and Sam was glad that he'd been distracted from going out through the gates. But when he got to the railings he didn't stop. He jumped on to a big waste bin and climbed over the fence. When he jumped down, he turned with a wide grin on his face, like a naughty little boy, signalling for the others to follow. And then, despite Sam and The Kid and Zohra arguing with them, one by one, giggling and egging each other on, the other kids joined him.

It was like running away from school. They were being deliberately disobedient. Doing something for themselves. They all climbed over and ran after Paddy who was walking purposefully away along the Cromwell Road. Only Sam and The Kid held back.

'What should we do?' said Sam, his voice cracking. He was nearly crying now. 'We can't let them go out there by themselves.'

The Kid wasn't stupid. He went over to the gatehouse and managed to make himself understood. A boy and a girl set off down the road after Paddy's group, shouting at them to stop, which only made Paddy break into a run. The guy in charge and another girl ran up to the museum to tell Whitney what had happened. Forgetting about Sam and The Kid.

Sam looked at the open gate. He looked at The Kid.

'Come on,' he said. 'We have to help.'

The Kid nodded and they went out into the road.

Maxie and Blue's unit had made it safely to Hyde Park. They'd come in from the east, not knowing exactly what to expect when they arrived.

And then they'd stopped.

Stunned.

They were about halfway down Park Lane, just outside the railings, frozen, trying to take it all in, unable to put a proper sentence together. Just grunts and swear words and sentences started and abandoned.

They couldn't have imagined this.

The whole park seemed to be filled with grown-ups. A great dark mass of them, greasy and stinking. So many it was appalling.

In the end Blue broke the spell. He yelled at the kids, forcing them on, south down Park Lane, past the fenced-off area that had been used for concerts, until they found a relatively safe place to enter the park. They got a better sense of what was going on from inside. The grown-ups had come in at the top and apparently stopped. So far they didn't seem to have made it past the halfway point where Jordan had set up his defensive lines. He'd fortified a roughly rectangular position next to the Serpentine with sharpened stakes in the ground and barricades made from

metal fencing and bits of scavenged wood. He'd even cut down some trees and hauled them into place. The barricade began at the eastern corner of the lake and ran in a straight line northwards to the LookOut. The LookOut was one of two clusters of Royal Parks buildings that Jordan had used like forts in his wall, securing the top east and west corners. The defences ran between them and then cut back south again to meet up with the Serpentine near the bridge. The wide expanse of water protected their rear.

Jordan had made the LookOut building his headquarters. It was a modern building protected by metal fencing. Jordan had cut down most of the surrounding trees to reinforce the fence and give better lines of sight. He'd also erected a viewing platform on its roof so that he could see out across the battlefield. Maxie was just glad that the sickos had obliged him by coming here. Almost as if it had been planned and agreed on, like a pitched battle from the past. Otherwise this would have been a lot of work for nothing.

She spotted Jordan up on his platform, sitting in a plastic chair. Blu-Tack Bill was at his side and Paddy's dog, Bright Eyes, was waiting patiently at the bottom of the big ladder Jordan was using to get up on to the roof.

That bloody dog. It had caused all the trouble with Achilleus. So petty. Such a stupid little thing to get upset about.

Although Maxie knew that wasn't really why Achilleus was pissed off.

It was all about pride. Respect. The macho code that caused so many problems among boys.

And Achilleus being pissed off meant that now almost half the kids wouldn't fight.

Great.

Maxie rolled her shoulder, trying to get rid of a knot of tension. She sighed. Maybe those kids wouldn't have fought anyway. Maybe they'd just been looking for an excuse. Even so, Maxie could have killed Jordan and Achilleus for acting like a couple of dickheads.

It was ironic. They needed macho dickheads to fight this battle. But it was Achilleus's pumping testosterone that was keeping him away, sulking in his room.

Maxie looked around. Those kids who had turned up were silent, just staring out at the sicko army that faced them from the other side of the barricades across the long grass. They were probably all thinking the same thing as Maxie – was it too late to turn and run? Jordan didn't seem to be giving any orders. He just sat there. Even he seemed stunned by what they had to deal with.

For their part, the grown-ups also seemed to be waiting. Standing still and staring back.

Over to Maxie's left, formed up in neat rows, all dressed in green, were the St Paul's kids, carrying banners and musical instruments, Matt standing at their centre, unreadable.

'We will destroy the Nephilim!' he shouted.

'Yeah, right,' Blue muttered, but Matt wasn't finished.

'I saw an angel standing in the sun. Who cried in a loud voice to all the birds – "Come, gather together for the great supper of God, so that you may eat the flesh of kings, generals and mighty men, of horses and their riders, and the flesh of all people, small and great." I saw the beast and the demons of the earth and their armies gathered together to make war against the King and his army. The beast was hurled to the earth, and his angels with him, but he will be slain. The rest of them will be

killed, and all the birds will gorge themselves on their flesh . . .'

Blue pushed his way into the compound where the LookOut was. Maxie followed him in. Blue went right over to the ladder and started climbing up to the roof, Maxie hard behind him.

'This is crazy,' Blue shouted out to Jordan.

'You telling me, soldier,' said Jordan as Blue reached his platform. 'We need ten times the numbers we got. But we don't got 'em. So we just have to do what we can with what we are.'

'We can't attack.'

'Is probably right. We might just have to stay behind our defences and see what happens.'

'Why aren't they moving?' Maxie called up to Jordan. 'What are they waiting for? Why don't they attack?'

'Dunno,' said Jordan.

'It is really freaking me out.'

'I hope you got a good plan?' Blue said.

Maxie looked at Jordan. He nodded and chuckled. 'As Mike Tyson once said – "Everybody has a plan until they get punched in the mouth."'

'That's reassuring,' said Blue and Maxie noticed that little Bill was whispering and muttering something into Jordan's ear. Jordan turned and muttered something back to him.

Maxie had no idea exactly how many grown-ups were out there, but if anyone knew, if anyone could count them, it was Bill.

The calculating part of Maxie's own mind had shut down. She couldn't take in the big picture, could only concentrate on details. A single white cloud in the sky. A

boy down below picking his nose. A girl literally wetting herself. The sun glinting on a spearhead. A bird singing in a nearby tree – almost the only sound in the whole park, despite the vast number of people here. And Bright Eyes, lying peacefully at the bottom of the ladder, eyebrows twitching, her ears occasionally swivelling. Details.

Jordan climbed down from his platform and walked to the edge of the roof. It was flat but gently sloping, and he could see all his troops from here.

'When I give the signal,' he shouted, 'I want all the officers to take your troops to where we planned. We start with missiles. We fire at them and we keep firing. We throw everything we got at them till there ain't nothing left to throw. We don't go to them and fight unless we absolutely got to. For now, we defend.' He looked around. 'Where's my musicians?' he shouted.

Four kids came hustling over from the St Paul's contingent. Two trumpeters and two drummers. They climbed up with some difficulty and joined Jordan and the others on the roof. Maxie remembered the long, boring hours spent learning the various signals. She supposed now, though, that they'd be useful. They had to work together as one efficient unit if they were to stand any hope of defeating the sickos.

Jordan raised his hand to give the agreed signal. And then lowered it slowly, shaking his head at the musicians.

The front rank of the sicko army had parted and two grown-ups were walking out through the gap.

One was a big and grossly fat father, with wire-framed glasses that had lost their glass. He was wearing a tattered vest with a red cross of St George on it and a pair of baggy cargo shorts.

This must be St George. Couldn't be anyone else.

The other was a tall, thin mother with long grey hair that hung over her face and down to her waist. Her arms dangled straight and unmoving at her sides. Maxie had a horrible image. That these two were the parents of the whole army. It wouldn't have surprised her if they'd reached out and held hands.

'That's their general,' said Blue. 'Could we take him down? Shoot the bastard now and maybe they'll fall apart.'

'Maybe,' said Jordan. 'But I think they too far away. Out of range.'

'Worth a try,' said Blue.

'Wait!'

Everyone was startled. It wasn't that the voice was particularly loud, or particularly forceful, but everything had been so quiet before, so tense, that the shout was totally unexpected.

Everyone turned to look where it had come from and there was David, walking along the front of the grown-up army, with Jester, Pod and his personal guard in their red blazers. Behind them came Just John and Carl the pirate from the squatter camp – both grinning – and Paul Channing.

A moan came from those fighters who knew Paul. He'd gone on a killing spree in the museum before disappearing. They'd all hoped he was dead. He evidently wasn't. That was where he'd gone – to David.

'It's not too late,' said David, standing next to the two grown-ups. 'We can stop this now. You don't have to fight. If you accept me as your leader I'll send these grown-ups away. It'll be over.'

'What's he talking about?' Blue muttered to Maxie.

288

'God knows,' said Maxie.

'Let's shoot him down while we got the chance,' said Blue, and Maxie gave a nervous little laugh.

'Wasn't joking.'

'You don't control nothing, David,' Jordan shouted at him.

'Oh yes?' said David. 'Then watch this.'

He said something to Paul who nodded and closed his eyes. Seemed to be concentrating on something. David looked at St George and the mother, and, as he did so, St George bowed his head and a moment later the entire army of grown-ups, as one, in perfect synchronization, bowed their heads too.

Maxie knew then that it was all over. They couldn't possibly fight this.

From his position on Park Lane Ryan saw the sickos bow their heads. He and his hunters were supposed to be patrolling the perimeter, making sure all of the sickos stayed together, but they'd seen the army come in and couldn't help themselves; they had to watch the spectacle, the mind-blowing number of them.

And now this. Like something from *Lord of the Rings*. An army with one mind.

'This is off the scale,' said Dom.

'We need to keep moving,' said Ryan, rallying his guys. 'We do our job.'

And they ran off, heading north, working their way round the army anticlockwise.

Sam and The Kid were just behind the two older gate-keepers, who were running after Paddy, shouting at him to stop, to go back to the museum. The rest of the Youngbloods were strung out down the road, Froggie lagging at the rear, Zohra holding back to be with him. They'd gone some way down the Cromwell Road before Paddy had turned off to the right, heading towards the park. At least that's where Sam assumed he was going. He wasn't sure Paddy really knew his way around here. If Sam had been going to the park he would have gone left out of the museum gates, not right like Paddy had done. They were some way to the west of the museum now.

'Paddy,' he called out. 'You're being an idiot.' And now Paddy stopped, turned round, his face red with anger, made worse by running. He held up his spear, as if he was going to attack Sam and the two older kids.

'Shut up, you little fart,' he snarled.

'I'm not that much smaller than you actually,' said Sam as he got closer.

'You are.'

One of the older kids swore and pointed ahead. An old mother with wobbly legs was staggering down the road

towards them. And then two ancient fathers came out from behind an abandoned lorry.

The two older kids ran off up the road towards them, weapons at the ready. The Youngbloods watched, Paddy's shoulders heaving up and down as he got his breath back.

'OK,' said Sam. 'I am smaller than you, but that's not the point. We shouldn't be out here. We don't know what we're doing. It's too dangerous. You can get yourself into trouble if you want, that's up to you, but the others are following you.'

'That's because I'm their leader.'

'And if you were a good leader you'd take them straight back to the museum.'

The two older kids were approaching the three grown-ups carefully. Getting ready to attack. The mother had raised her fingers like claws and was baring her gums at the kids.

'You really want to fight things like that?' said Sam.

'Why not?' said Paddy.

'Look at us!' Sam shouted.

'Yeah,' said Paddy. 'Look at us! Form up into ranks. We march up there in formation and show them what we are.'

There was a ragged, not too enthusiastic cheer from the others, who still had their eyes fixed on the three grown-ups. Paddy grinned.

'They're with me all the way.'

'Listen,' said Sam. 'We need to go back. We don't know what's out here. We've even come the wrong way. I'm going back now – you should all come with me.'

'Don't listen to him,' said Paddy as the Youngbloods formed into a ragged bunch around him. 'He's a coward.'

'I am not a coward,' said Sam angrily.

'He's not, he's not,' said The Kid, who sounded like he might start crying. 'I been with him in many fights. There's no yellow streak in the boy. No shark-infested custard. No yellowskin bellyskin. He's more of a warrior than any of the rest of you.'

'And you can shut it an' all, you loony,' said Paddy.

'I'll trust you to keep a civil tongue in your head,' said The Kid, and he made a mock snooty expression that made a couple of the other kids laugh. Paddy cut them off.

'You're messed up,' he said.

'No,' said Sam. 'You're messed up. We joined in the training for fun, for something to do, to stop getting bored. We never thought you'd actually take us into a battle. We can't really do that!'

He pointed. The two older kids were fighting the grown-ups now; they'd cut down one of the fathers and were now hacking at the mother.

'I'm a killer,' said Paddy. 'Ripped open a nasty father's belly just the other day. We'll go without you.' He checked his troop. 'Where's Zohra and Froggie?'

'They're catching up,' said Sam. 'Froggie can't go so fast. What good's he going to be in a fight?'

But Paddy didn't reply. He just stood there, staring, his face suddenly bone-white.

Sam turned to see what he was looking at.

The road behind them was full of grown-ups. They had already surrounded Froggie and Zohra.

'Oh my God!' said Paddy. 'What are we going to do?'

'We have to save them,' said Sam.

'Yeah, yeah, I know, right, yeah . . . we need to save them.'

'Then lead us,' said Sam angrily. 'Lead us into battle. We can't let Froggie and Zohra get killed.'

'Will they?' said Paddy, panicked. 'Will they kill them? Truly?'

'Yes.'

'We need the big kids,' said Paddy, but, when they turned to look the other way, they saw that grown-ups had filled the road that way as well and there was no sign of the gatekeepers.

'Move,' said Sam. 'Do something.' He shoved Paddy, who raised his spear but didn't budge. Sam could see just how scared he was, pale and sweating and wide-eyed. Weirdly, Sam didn't feel any fear himself, just a horrible numbness, a feeling that he'd always known this was going to happen and there was nothing he could do about it.

Wiki and Jibber-jabber pushed in behind Paddy who was still frozen with fear.

'Go on,' said Wiki. 'We have to save Zohra and Froggie and get back to the museum.'

'Yeah,' said Paddy, psyching himself up. 'Come on. Let's go.'

And finally he started to walk, his spear held out in front of him.

He broke into a run, and the others ran too, their feet slapping on the hard road surface.

The grown-ups got closer.

And closer.

Sam could see them more clearly now. He wasn't very good at judging, but he thought there were maybe twenty or thirty of them, a mix of fathers and mothers. All ages. Their clothes were tattered, their skin smeared, crusty with dirt, covered in huge wet sores. Some were missing

hands, even whole arms; most were bald, and now Sam saw that some of them carried weapons. He wanted to stop running – he was at the front with The Kid and Paddy, caught up in the charge. Scared at last. So scared his head was throbbing. He had a short spear of his own that a girl at the museum had made for him. The Kid was armed with his two long knives. The other Youngbloods had a mix of spears and swords, but none of them was very good at using them.

Paddy let out a war cry – '*Raaaaaaaargh!* Cúchulainn!'

His bucket helmet was wobbling on his head. Too big. He tried to straighten it and it fell off, clattered into the road, useless.

Sam saw a sicko turn. He was dressed in a Manchester United shirt and had a face that seemed more intelligent than the others. It looked almost like he was smiling. He twisted his head in a weird way and the other grown-ups stopped what they were doing and came round to face Paddy's charge.

Paddy couldn't stop now even if he'd wanted to. He smashed into the sickos, wildly slashing with his spear. It was called the belly ripper and – whether it was skill or luck – it did what it was supposed to do. It tore through the stomach of a thin father, spinning him round and knocking him down, spilling his innards on to the ground.

And then Sam came in, looking up at the grown-ups who towered over him, and he knew that he was never going to get out of this.

Sam couldn't see what anyone else was doing; he was having to concentrate too hard on not getting hurt. He was surrounded by grown-ups, ducking under swinging arms, backing away from clumsy swipes with various weapons. He had two things on his side, his size and his speed. Most of the grown-ups were hardly aware that he was down there, dodging about among their legs. They moved slowly, barging into each other, like a herd of cows bunched up in the corner of a field. Only the father in the Manchester United shirt seemed to have any intelligence. He was obviously the one in charge. The rest of them were simply doing what he wanted them to. He had two short steel rods with sharp ends, one in each hand. He was waving them about and clashing them together, like a toddler going nuts in a playgroup.

Sam didn't bother trying to attack. He was only using his spear to defend himself, poking it at anyone who came close. What more could he do? He didn't have the strength to do much damage. He was just trying to find out what had happened to Froggie and Zohra. He'd become separated from The Kid, but he didn't worry too much about him. The Kid was a survivor. He'd lived out on the streets by himself. He knew what to do in a fight.

Sam pushed forward, between two mothers, one of whom appeared to be wearing an old wedding dress, and found himself in a more open piece of road. And there was Zohra, crouching over her brother, who was lying on his back. Not moving. She was using her back as a shield, protecting Froggie from three scrawny and ragged mothers who were clawing at him.

Sam went in. Anger had taken over now, no time for fear, no worrying about his size. He jabbed his spear at a mother, got her in the neck, and then The Kid was at his side.

'Shish kebab, Cisco Kid, Sister Ray!' he shouted, killing a second mother. The two of them then took on the third one, who had worked out what was happening and reared up at them, ready to attack, belching a foul blast of hot breath at them. She stuck her tongue out; it was huge and bulging with growths.

'Snickersnee, that's a pointless answer and a pointed stick!' shouted The Kid, rushing at her, and without thinking Sam was with him and the mother went down under their attack, Sam stabbing again and again with his spear.

'We got them,' said The Kid. 'They going down like kettles. Keep close, I'll watch your back, you wash my socks . . .'

Next moment Wiki and Jibber-jabber were there, as inseparable as Sam and The Kid. Sam went over to Froggie. He was badly wounded, but still alive, thank God. Blood was coming from beneath his small body and forming a puddle in the road. His face was very pale and he was shaking; his mouth moved, but no sound came out. Zohra was crying and trying to comfort him, totally unaware of the battle going on around her.

'It's all right, Froggie,' she was saying. 'It's all right, baby. I'm here. I won't leave you. I'll never leave you.'

And then the grown-ups were surging towards them, the guy in the football shirt at their head. But Paddy and the others came in from the side and formed up with Sam and The Kid, making a circle round Froggie, facing outwards. They weren't able to do much more than keep back those sickos who tried to get close.

'We're trapped,' said Jibber-jabber. 'There's too many of them.'

'Like I can't see that,' said Paddy angrily.

'I'm just saying.'

'Kill the guy in the Man U shirt,' said Wiki. 'Kill him and the others won't know what to do. He's their leader.'

'How do we do that?' said Paddy, trying to turn his fear into anger.

Sam checked who was with them. At least three other Youngbloods were missing, and there was still no sign of the two gatekeepers. Another movement among the grown-ups; a gap opened up, and Sam caught a glimpse of a small body lying in the road, a group of sickos clustered round it. He couldn't tell who it was.

He felt like cursing Paddy, turning his own fear to anger. This was all Paddy's fault, but what difference would it make? Getting cross. How would it help? If they were all going to die, best die as friends.

And then something changed. There was shouting, the sound of fighting, and the grown-ups broke apart enough for Sam to see that Whitney had arrived with some other kids from the museum, including the other two guards from the gates. They were better armed than Paddy's group, bigger, more experienced fighters. They cut

through the grown-ups towards the Youngbloods who were all shouting and screaming for help.

'We're getting you out of here,' said Whitney. Sam could see she was furious. Paddy had put everyone at risk. And then Whitney saw Zohra kneeling over Froggie.

'Get up,' she said. 'We gotta go.'

'I'm not leaving Froggie,' said Zohra. 'He's hurt.'

'Out of my way.' Whitney squatted down and picked Froggie up in her big arms. Sam saw that his back was soaked with blood.

'Move it,' Whitney screamed and they were off, trying to get clear of the grown-ups. Sam went after her. Praying that it was over. That they were safe. More and more grown-ups were arriving, though, streaming in from the side-streets. And they were all heading for Sam. At least that was how it felt to him. It freaked him out, and the next moment he found his way ahead blocked.

Blocked by Man U, his eyes fixed on Sam, as if he recognized him. The father's head jerked from side to side really quickly, spraying spit everywhere, like he was having a fit.

The other grown-ups were ignoring Whitney and the others, who had gone on ahead. Only The Kid was with Sam. Sam tried to swallow, but it hurt too much. His mouth was horribly dry. He jerked his spear point around, trying to protect himself, and The Kid was in and out, moving fast, cutting and stabbing and jumping clear.

'Help Sam!' he called. 'Help us!' But nobody could hear.

'We're stuck,' said Sam.

'Duck!' The Kid shouted and Sam looked round just in time to see that Man U had thrown one of his steel rods. It turned end over end in the air and Sam hurled himself

to one side. The rod went past him and got a mother in the eye, embedding itself in her head.

'Remember what Wiki-dicky said,' The Kid shouted. 'Get the leader.'

Yes, thought Sam. If it was the last thing he was ever going to do, he was going to kill the bastard in the Man U shirt.

Sam had always been an Arsenal fan.

He roared and screamed and charged, somehow got under the guy's flailing arms, and rammed his spear into his chest and let go. Man U fell backwards with a grunt and a hiss of air and the others stopped what they were doing, as if confused, suddenly dull-eyed and purposeless. The Kid cut a path clear and dragged Sam away.

'Run,' he shouted. 'Run like the wind in the willows!'

And Sam was running, The Kid by his side, and there was Whitney, lagging behind, slowed down by the weight of Froggie. Zohra was with them, one hand on Froggie's lolling head. Sam and The Kid caught up.

'We're nearly there,' said Sam and Whitney turned to grin at him.

'I'm gonna kill the lot of you when we get back,' she said and then she gasped, stumbled, fell down on her knees, dropped Froggie and crashed on to her face. One of Man U's rods was sticking out of her back.

Sam stopped, his breath frozen in his chest. Looked round. Man U was still alive, standing there, covered in blood, Sam's spear still in him. He took two steps towards Sam and then collapsed.

'Froggie, no!' Zohra screamed, and she ran to where her brother lay still and lifeless. There was no more blood to come out of him. Sam went to Whitney. She was dead

too. He swore, but The Kid was already tugging at his arm. There was nothing Sam could do. Even without their leader, the grown-ups were steadily advancing, not fast, but fast enough to be on them soon.

'What do they want?' said Sam. 'Why don't they stop?'

'They want you, small fry,' said The Kid. 'They're drawn to you like moths to a flaming light bulb.'

Sam knew he was right. This had all been about him. He should have stayed inside. They should all have stayed inside.

He looked at Zohra. She was holding Froggie.

'Leave him,' he said. 'We have to go.'

'I won't,' she said, her face wet with tears and smudged with blood. 'He's my brother. He needs me.'

Sam fought back tears of his own, remembering Ella, who he'd promised to look after. She was probably dead too. Her small body lying broken and forgotten in a field somewhere. He went to Whitney, took hold of the steel rod, closed his eyes and pulled it out. When he opened his eyes again, Paddy was with him.

'I'm the leader,' he said. 'I'm the warrior. I'll fight them. I'll protect you, Zohra.'

'They're too many,' said Sam. 'We have to get Zohra back. We have to run.'

Paddy wasn't listening. He gave his war cry and ran at the advancing grown-ups, slashing with his belly ripper. One went down, two, three. Paddy was winning . . .

And then Paddy was down. Hit from behind by a sicko with a rock. Sam wondered if this was how legends were born, from ugly, scrappy, horrible fights like this. Talked up into tales of heroic acts and deeds. Creating a lie of bravery and glory.

In a moment Paddy had disappeared under a pile of grown-ups, who were tearing at him with their teeth and nails.

The Kid was tugging at Sam's sleeve again.

'We can't do anything, sport,' he said. 'Except run.'

'Zohra.'

But Zohra wasn't listening. She was lying with Froggie on the tarmac, her arms wrapped round him.

Sam let The Kid pull him away. And they stumbled and staggered down the road towards the museum gates. Sam risked glancing back once. Zohra hadn't moved. And then he couldn't see her any more. She was swallowed up by the horde, which now filled the road from side to side.

And still the rest came on, eyes fixed on Sam.

Sam ran.

They made it back to the museum where the bigger kids were waiting for them, shouting at them to hurry. They dragged Sam and The Kid through the gates and slammed them shut. Locked them. A lot of museum kids were lined up along the fence. Sam saw that they had bows and missiles, javelins, crossbows, slings.

As soon as the grown-ups came close enough, the kids started to fire at them. Many went down, but still they kept on coming, until they were pressing against the fence from the other side, and the kids were stabbing at them through the bars. One or two grown-ups had enough intelligence to climb the fence, but they were easily cut down or knocked back. Sam looked along the row of hideous, distorted faces squeezing between the iron bars.

And he went cold.

Man U was still alive. Pushing against the railings as if he could somehow force himself through. Grey jelly was

oozing from his nose, his mouth, his eyes, his ears, the wound in his chest. Sam went over to him.

'Bastard,' he said. 'Dirty bastard.' Still the worst insult he knew, the name he'd always been told he must never call anyone. He realized he was still holding Man U's metal rod. He shoved it up through the father's open mouth and into his skull, releasing a fresh shower of grey slime. Man U smiled at him. Could he not be killed? Had the grown-up turned into the thing they had been called but never were: the living dead – zombies?

And then the smile died and Man U died. The light went out and he was slipping down and the other grown-ups were once again confused and dull. The only thing keeping them going now was the scent of Sam.

It wasn't enough. The museum kids hacked at them and slowly, slowly, they started to move away, defeated. The road cleared. Sam moved along the fence until he could see bodies lying in the road. The larger ones were the few grown-ups who'd been killed, and the smaller ones were Paddy and Zohra and Froggie.

Whitney was lying near to them, and further on were three more bodies – the rest of Paddy's friends who'd been killed in a stupid, pointless fight.

'We have to bring the bodies in,' he said to no one in particular. He looked around. No one was listening. No one was with him.

49

Maxie was still up on the roof of the LookOut, wishing something would happen. Anything. But the grown-ups just stood there, and David stood with them, waiting. Just John and Carl leering, mucking about, parading up and down in front of the rotting, diseased army, taunting the kids. At one point John even turned round and bared his arse at them. Funniest thing Carl had ever seen.

Maxie didn't laugh. She was remembering something.

A memory had come back to her. Very strong. Something she'd forgotten about altogether. When was it? She was still at primary school. Must have been Year Two or Three. She'd been crossing the road with her mum. At the top of the Camden Road. Yeah, of course. It was getting clearer. Coming back to her in a rush. It had been right opposite Waitrose, where she'd ended up living years later. There was a wide junction there, a big crossroads, the Holloway Road going one way, Camden Road going the other. And on the far side – what was it called? – Tollington Road. Yeah. Four lanes of traffic there. All facing her. Waiting. Her mum had risked the crossing. The green man was flashing and beeping even before they'd started across.

'Come on, Maxie, hurry up . . .'

God, it was coming back to her as clearly as if it was happening right now.

They were nearly over to the other side when Maxie realized she'd dropped her dolly-bug.

Dolly-bug. Maxie smiled. She'd forgotten all about dolly-bug too. It had been a big, stupid, plastic ladybird. God knows where it had first come from. And for a while she couldn't bear to be parted from it. She slept with it. She took it to school in her bag. Just some crappy piece of plastic, with half its legs missing. But it had been the world to her. And now she'd forgotten it had ever existed; that little girl crossing the road had been a different person. How could you ever get from there to here? Impossible.

She could recall the feel of it, the smooth, shiny plastic, the smell of it. The way she used to trace the black dots with one finger, counting them.

And she'd dropped it, halfway across the road. Without thinking, she'd pulled away from her mum's hand and run back. Saw it lying there. Picked it up. Her mum was shouting, running back to get her. And Maxie had looked round at the row of cars – and it was as if they were watching her, wanted to harm her, were planning to come charging and roaring at her. All they wanted was to run her down and nothing would stop them. All four lanes. Held back by the lights, but ready, straining, to be set loose.

And then they'd started to move, coming towards her, faster and faster . . .

And her mum had dragged her to the side and yelled at her and Maxie had cried.

She had been so scared. It was the sight of the cars before they moved, the knowledge that they were about to come for her, that had been most frightening.

That was exactly how it felt now. Looking at the grown-ups. They were ready – ready to come roaring at her – and from this distance they were as faceless and evil as that waiting line of cars.

The memory triggered a load of others. Flitting past. Nothing to hold on to. Memories of Waitrose, the months spent there, fighting off the grown-ups, learning to survive from day to day. Memories of Arran . . .

Arran who had died.

Arran and all the others.

Another life. Another time.

The only reality now was that mob of grown-ups, waiting to attack. Was there going to be anything on the other side? Was a giant hand going to pull her across to safety? Or was this it? Did it all end here today?

She looked around. Jordan was sitting up on his platform, talking quietly and urgently with Blu-Tack Bill. He still hadn't given the order for his troops to take their proper places. Maybe he didn't want the enemy to know his plans. Or maybe he just didn't know what to do now that David was involved. David had punched him in the mouth before the battle had even started.

Well, Maxie wouldn't wait any longer. She climbed the crude steps to the top of Jordan's platform. Jordan gave her a dirty look. She didn't have the authority to be up here.

'We have to do something,' she said.

'Is *my* decision,' said Jordan.

'Then make it.'

'Things have changed.'

'Really? What's changed? They're still as many as they were. They may be more organized, but they're organized

305

by David somehow. Does that scare you? What does *he* know about fighting battles? Come on, Jordan, that's why we put you in charge and not him. He doesn't have a clue. Once this thing kicks off it's gonna be chaos. How's he gonna know what's happening? He'll just tell them to attack and that's it. So how is that any different to how it was before?'

Jordan said nothing for a few seconds and then nodded. Didn't look at Maxie.

'Good point,' he said.

'So do we get into position?'

'We got no choice. We got to kill those things before they spawn. Or whatever it is they planning to do.'

'Yeah,' said Maxie. 'It's pretty straightforward. We kill them all and go home.'

Jordan smiled, nodded again, had a few quiet words with Bill. And then someone was running over from the west, shouting up to Jordan. Maxie saw that it was Hayden, one of the Tower girls. She climbed up the ladder on to the roof.

'There's been an attack,' she said.

'Where? What do you mean?' Maxie saw that Jordan wouldn't look at her either.

'At the museum,' said Hayden. 'A breakaway group of sickos went round and attacked from the west.'

'Why they do that? They never gonna get in there.'

'Some smaller kids were out on the streets. It looked like maybe they weren't trying to get into the museum as such.'

'Was Sam with them?' Maxie asked, suddenly anxious. This whole thing was about protecting Sam. Whitney had orders not to let him out of the museum.

'Yeah.'

Maxie could hardly bear to ask it. 'Is he . . . all right?'

'I think so. Some kids were killed, though.'

'Do you know who?'

'Whitney . . .'

'Not Whitney.' Maxie cut her off. Whitney was one of her girls. Please not Whitney.

'Yeah. Afraid so,' said Hayden. 'And Paddy. Only two names I remember . . . oh yeah, Froggie and his sister?'

'Oh Jesus. Paddy. Was Achilleus not there to protect them?'

'He's still hiding out in his room apparently.'

'He liked that boy,' said Jordan flatly. 'What happened to the sickos?'

'Quite a few were killed. The rest just sort of wandered off. Probably making their way back here.'

Now Jackson climbed up on to the roof. What with the musicians who were sitting there, patiently waiting for orders, it was becoming a popular spot.

'I'm going back,' she said.

'What you mean?' Jordan asked.

'I'm going back to make sure everything's all right at the museum,' said Jackson. 'What if the grown-ups attack again? What if they get to Sam?'

'No way they can get inside the museum,' said Jordan.

'But what if they do?' said Jackson. 'This is all so different. We don't know what they might be able to do.'

'I need you here,' said Jordan. 'Without Achilleus, you in charge of his unit.'

'Will can take command till I get back,' said Jackson. 'But I have to see that they're all right back there. Cameron's in charge, but he can be dozy. We didn't think we needed someone good at the museum.'

'Well, you needed *here*,' said Jordan. 'Half your fighters are still back there. They never come to the battle.'

'I still need to make sure the museum's all right,' said Jackson. 'What's the point of winning a war if when you go home your country's been blitzed? Everyone killed? What is it exactly we're fighting for here?'

'Jackson, wait,' said Jordan. But Jackson was already climbing down. She got to the bottom and Maxie watched her walk quickly away to the south.

Before Jordan could say anything they heard David calling over from the front line of grown-ups.

'Well?' he shouted. 'Have you made your decision? Fight or live?'

Maxie swore. Right now she hated David more than she thought she could ever hate anyone.

'Fight or live?' Jordan repeated. 'I choose live.'

'You're surrendering?' said Maxie.

'Not the way I style it,' said Jordan. 'I'm fighting and I'm winning and I'm living. The full package.'

He stood up and finally gave the order to his musicians. The trumpeters blared out the signal. The drummers beat out a rhythm. Off to the left, the rest of Matt's musicians joined in and the green kids raised their banners.

'We will defeat the Nephilim!' Matt shouted, his hoarse voice rising above the din. 'They are locusts. In number they are like the sand on the seashore. They have one purpose. They will make war against the Lamb, but the Lamb will overcome them because he is Lord of lords and King of kings — and with him will be his chosen and faithful followers.'

Maxie's heart was thumping. She looked over at David who was furious. Red-faced. Quickly getting out of the way so that he wasn't trapped between the two armies.

'You're a fool!' he screamed. 'You're all fools. You can't possibly win.'

'Ollie,' Jordan called. 'Shut him up. Take him out.'

Ollie was waiting with his missile unit behind the barricade that connected the LookOut building with the parks buildings over to the west.

Ollie looked confused, came closer.

'You mean?'

'Shoot him,' shouted Jordan. 'Shoot all the front rank.'

'Too far away,' said Ollie, and Maxie wondered if they were, or whether Ollie was just saying that because he didn't want to hurt another kid, even one as rotten as David.

'Well, when they near enough. You go to it, soldier.'

'We will.'

Bill whispered something into Jordan's ear. Jordan nodded.

'On my command,' Jordan shouted. 'Bill knows the distances.'

The missile kids were all taking their positions, climbing up on to platforms built into the barricade.

Maxie slid down the ladder and went to find Blue, who was waiting with their unit. She hugged him quickly, broke away. There would be no more of that until this was over. Right now it was time to fight.

But God, she was scared. She bent down and threw up into the grass. She wasn't alone; all around her kids were puking, crying, holding each other.

'You know why you did that?' said Blue, an amused expression on his face

'Because I'm terrified.'

'No. Is because your body doesn't want to waste blood

on digesting food. It needs to save it in case it's needed somewhere else. That guy Shadowman told me.'

'In case I need to bleed,' said Maxie. 'I'm glad you shared that with me.'

'We the same blood,' he said. 'If you bleed I bleed.'

'I don't want you to bleed for me, you idiot,' said Maxie. 'I want you to make *them* bleed.'

'Is what I intend to do.'

'They're coming!' someone shouted and Maxie looked round.

Sure enough, the grown-ups were moving, shuffling forward as one, heading straight towards the defences. St George and the long-haired woman held back, letting their troops pass them, so that they wouldn't come in range of the missiles. And instead another group came to the front to lead the army in.

Maxie recognized them. She'd seen them before somewhere.

'Where are they from?' she asked Blue. 'I know them.'

'The palace,' said Blue. 'That's the royal family.'

Maxie couldn't believe it. She started to laugh. This was too much. The most surreal day she had ever lived.

A stupid day to die.

'You've got to come! Before it's too late, it's too late! You've got to come fast. You've got to help us. We're in terrible danger. You have to get here as soon as you can. They're being killed. Sam! They're after Sam. Help him. Help the boy. They've killed the boy. You have to help us! They've killed the boy. Come now! Please come now! We need you . . . Mister Three? You've got to hear me. Mister Three, wake up! Anybody! Can you hear me? They've killed the boy!'

Skinner was in a panic. And it was Fish-Face who'd done it to him when she'd gone into meltdown – twittering, flapping her arms, filling his head with her noise. He knew that she was attempting to communicate with the others. With the Warehouse Queen, and with Trinity who'd gone west with Ed. He knew she was only trying to help, but he could feel her panic in his mind, and her message was getting distorted, tangled, garbled, swirling and whirling and painful. He wanted to keep her out. To shut her up. Even though he knew that it was important she tried to contact the others. There was a danger, though, that her tangled broadcast would just confuse them. It was so strong and insistent. No avoiding the main point of the message. That was coming through loud and clear . . .

HELP!

It was the details that were in danger of getting muddled.

It was like a repeated SOS from a downed aeroplane or something, sending out its distress signal over and over again.

Skinner felt awful. Twisted up inside. He and Fish-Face had been in the main hall when Whitney had gone charging past, shouting, 'Help him! Help the boy! They're after Sam – we have to help him.'

They'd followed her outside and witnessed the fight in the street. It was then that Fish-Face had started broadcasting her manic message, channelling what Whitney had shouted and adding stuff of her own. Doing it automatically, without even thinking. The words had smashed into Skinner's consciousness, making it hard to think, and they were still there, like moths batting at a bright window.

Skinner had gone over to the fence and seen the last of the smaller kids come stumbling back to safety. Watched as the sickos crowded along the railings and the museum kids stabbed at them and pushed them back. Watched in panic as some of the sickos tried to climb the railings and were killed. And all the while Fish-Face was broadcasting her SOS – 'They're after Sam. Help him. They're being massacred.' Panicked thoughts and confused words, round and round.

And they'd seen the bodies lying in the street.

Skinner had been desperately sad. He'd liked Whitney. She was funny and tough. And, when he found out that Paddy was among the dead, he was even sadder. Paddy had been so full of life. And of course that had set Fish-Face off worse, adding Paddy into her distress signal.

'They've killed the boy. They've killed the boy.'

A new message, round and round. Fish-Face wasn't thinking about what she was saying. It was straight from her heart, her raw emotions spilling out on to the wind, like seed pollen. In the end Skinner had taken hold of her and brought her back inside. Taken her to the birds gallery where they lived. Tried to calm her down. Hoping she wasn't going to crack up. She'd always been quite delicate, hysterical sometimes, and it hurt – having her pain jammed into his head.

She was like a frightened bird and here in the gallery, surrounded by the crazy forms of all those real stuffed birds, it felt like madness.

'Fish-Face,' he said, holding her. 'Come on. Calm down. You need to do this properly, to concentrate. Please. It's all right, Sam's safe. It's all right . . .'

Her father came in. Wormwood the Green Man. He'd have heard her as well, felt her inside his mind. He put his long arms round her.

'You have to stop,' he said. 'You have to stop this now. If you send out these crazy messages they won't know what you mean.'

'They have to come,' said Fish-Face. 'They have to come and help. We need all the help we can get.'

'I know that,' said Wormwood. 'But you must be calm.'

Skinner studied him. He was looking more and more like an ordinary man every day. Whatever drug, whatever cure, whatever antidote Einstein was giving him, it was working. If they just had more time they might be able to beat the disease. It all depended now on what was happening with Jordan's army, so close and yet so far away in Hyde Park. Did they have any hope of holding back the sickos? Of killing enough of them to win the day?

313

Fish-Face was right. The kids needed all the help they could get. Skinner wondered if he should go and join the fight. Pick up a sword or a spear and help. Would he actually *be* any help, though? He'd never really been in a fight, let alone a full-scale battle.

He didn't need a sword or a spear, though, did he? Skinner's best weapon was his ability to give the shout – the shout inside. The shout that silenced all thought. The shout that could short-circuit someone's brainwaves enough to paralyse them for a moment.

What good was that, though? Really? It was like a freeze-attack, a magic upgrade in one of the tower defence games he used to love playing on his laptop before the electricity went off.

It was useful in a tower defence game, but was it useful in real life?

Strange how the Twisted Kids had developed different strengths. Like the way Fish-Face and the Warehouse Queen could communicate over huge distances, Mister Three as well, when he was awake, like a human telephone. And there was Monstar, stronger than any man . . .

Skinner felt a stab of longing. He missed his friends.

Fish-Face had calmed down now, her signal just a soft murmur instead of a shriek. She was nodding as Wormwood whispered comforting words into her ear.

'We should go and see how they are,' said Skinner. 'We should make sure Sam's all right. If he gets hurt, if he gets killed, then this will have all been for nothing.'

As soon as he said it, he wished he hadn't because it set Fish-Face off into another panic, yelling out her crazy SOS.

'They're after Sam. They're after Sam. You have to help

314

us. They've killed the boy. They've killed the boy. They've killed the boy . . .'

'Please,' said Skinner. 'Try to stay calm. I'm going to see Sam. Send a more controlled message.'

He left the birds gallery and walked down to the main hall. There was a cluster of kids by the diplodocus. Skinner could see Sam and The Kid. They looked OK. They were talking quickly, trying to explain to the small crowd what had happened. Some of the kids were crying, hugging each other. Whitney had been really popular, and Paddy and the five other smaller kids who'd been killed had many friends here. The two older kids as well.

Now the big front doors opened and Jackson came striding in. Everyone turned to her. She looked angry at first, and then relieved when she too saw that Sam was unhurt. Sam repeated what he had just told everyone else. Explaining what had happened in the fight, who'd got hurt, who'd been killed, who wasn't coming back.

'Has anyone told Achilleus yet?' Jackson asked. No one said anything. They stared at the floor. Some shook their heads. Nobody had dared.

'I'll do it,' said Jackson.

'I'm coming with you,' said Skinner. Skinner liked Achilleus. Achilleus had been part of the team that had made its way out to Heathrow and found the Twisted Kids at the warehouse. Achilleus had fought bravely and brought Skinner and Fish-Face and Trinity safely into town. He teased Skinner, but in a funny way they had a bond. Skinner felt that Achilleus was an outsider as well.

'I'm coming too,' said Sam. 'He'll be upset.'

And of course where Sam went The Kid went. So the four of them walked upstairs and round to the front of

the building where Achilleus was holed up. With every step, Skinner grew more nervous and unsure. How was Achilleus going to react? Should he have left Jackson to it?

Well, there was no turning back now. He'd look bad.

He swallowed.

Jackson knocked. There was no response.

Skinner hoped someone would say – 'OK, let's come back later . . .'

But Jackson knocked again.

Skinner stood back as Jackson gave a third knock. Harder this time. And she carried on knocking until there was a grunt from the other side.

'I need to talk to you,' said Jackson loudly, putting her face close to the door.

'Go away,' said Achilleus. 'I'm not in the talking mood.'

'Something's happened,' said Jackson. 'I seriously need to talk to you about it.'

'I said go away,' said Achilleus.

'Something's happened to Paddy,' said Jackson.

For a moment there was silence from the other side, and then a rattle and Achilleus pulled the door open. Skinner saw his ugly, scarred and battered face. And, for the first time ever, he saw worry in the boy's eyes.

'What you mean?' he said. 'Where is he?'

'Can we come in?' asked Jackson. Achilleus stared at the four of them. What must they look like? Jackson, big and tough, with a razor-cut pattern in her cropped hair just like Achilleus. She'd done it herself in the end and it was a bit rubbish. Then there was Skinner with his folds of skin. Finally the two little boys, Sam serious and worried-looking, The Kid wearing his usual dress over his trousers, his wild hair sticking up in all directions.

Was this really the best way to tell someone their friend had died?

Well, there wasn't any other way.

Achilleus retreated into the darkness of the room and the four of them went in. This used to be an office and then it had been Justin's room. Achilleus had kicked Justin out and made it his own. But it was still bare and cold.

Achilleus stared at Jackson, waiting for her to speak.

'I'm sorry. It's not good,' said Jackson. 'Paddy went out. He left the museum. He wanted to join the fight. He wanted to be you. A hero. He took your Nike top, and your spear, the one he gave that weird Irish name to . . .'

'The Gay Bulge,' said Achilleus flatly.

'Yeah. That.' Jackson dried up. Didn't know how to carry on.

'He had your helmet as well,' said Sam. 'It fell off . . .'

'What happened to him?' said Achilleus. 'Tell me.'

'They killed him,' said Sam. 'Grown-ups. They ambushed us. I tried to stop him. I tried to get him to go back. He wanted to show everyone what he was made of. Whitney got killed. And Froggie. Paddy went back to try and save him. He *was* a hero. He died a hero.'

'A hero?' Achilleus was staring at Sam, like he didn't know who Sam was, like he couldn't understand the language, like Sam was a foreigner or something. You could see that Achilleus couldn't take it in. And then he did something that Skinner never expected. Had never seen him do before. Never imagined he ever would see. Achilleus started to cry.

'He was just a little boy,' he said. 'He wasn't a soldier. He would never have been a warrior. I would never have let him. He was just a little boy.'

318

Jackson went and put her arms round him and he collapsed against her, his whole body shaking with sobs. And she helped him on to a pile of cushions and he slumped into them, boneless and shaking. Jackson cradled his head in her strong arms.

'He was a good kid,' said Achilleus, his voice muffled and thick. 'I used to tease him. Never told him what I really thought. There was always time. Thought we'd have plenty of time. Thought we'd have years. He was my friend. I never told him. Never will.'

Skinner was embarrassed. He didn't know where to look, what to say or what to do. Sam and The Kid went over and they put their arms round Achilleus too. Skinner joined them. And they stayed like that for a long time. There was nothing more to say. There was nothing anyone could do. You couldn't bring a dead person back to life.

At last Skinner felt Achilleus stop shaking. He sniffed, stood up and moved away from the others towards the windows. He wiped his face and smashed his fist against the wall, letting out a harsh bark of anger and a string of swear words.

And then suddenly there was a commotion at the door and people burst into the room.

It was Einstein, with a couple of his science kids from the pod. Einstein looked furious. He yelled at Achilleus.

'See what you've done! See what's happened now. They went out there because of you. The sickos could've killed Sam. They might kill all of us. And what do you do? How do you help by sulking in here like a baby girl?'

Achilleus stared at him with his hurt eyes, and again he had that look of incomprehension. Like he didn't know what Einstein was saying.

'What are you going to do about it?' said Einstein.

'Go away,' said Achilleus, his voice dull and cold. 'I don't wanna talk to you.'

'Yeah,' said Jackson. 'Not now, Einstein.'

Einstein ignored her. He strode over to Achilleus and stuck a finger in his face.

'You're supposed to be a great fighter,' he said, spraying Achilleus with spit. 'I can't see any evidence of that right now. You let that little boy go out there and do your fighting for you. You let him get killed. And they could've killed Sam. What if that had happened? I mean, God, we're lucky it was only Paddy . . .'

'Go away,' said Achilleus again.

'No,' said Einstein. 'I'm not going. Look at you, *crying*. What is that? Self-pity?'

'Leave him alone,' said Jackson. 'Can't you see he's really upset?'

'I loved that boy,' said Achilleus.

'That's a bit *gay*, isn't it?' said Einstein and he gave a dismissive snort.

In one quick movement Achilleus took Einstein by the throat and slammed him against the wall. When he spoke, there was no anger in his voice, just a horrible coldness.

'What do you mean by *gay*?' he said. 'You mean gay as in homosexual? Or gay as in a bit crap?'

'I suppose I mean both,' said Einstein, refusing to be intimidated.

'So it's gay to have feelings, is it?' said Achilleus. 'It's crap to have feelings?'

'Hit a nerve, have I?' said Einstein. 'Worried about your sexuality, are you, big man?'

'No,' said Achilleus. 'I'm not worried at all. I *am* gay.

For as long as I've understood what the word meant I've known what I am. It's no big deal. And I loved Paddy.'

'Bit young for you,' sneered Einstein.

Achilleus slapped him hard with his free hand. Leaving a nasty red mark on Einstein's cheek.

'I didn't love Paddy in that way,' he said. 'He was just a boy. But I did love him as a friend. Just as I love Jackson, and Sam, and Skinner, and all the decent people in the world. And just as I do not love you, Einstein, because you have no feelings. The only reason I'm not gonna kill you is because I'm not stupid. I realize how valuable you are. Maybe you can stop the disease. But I'm warning you – if you can't stop it, if your experiments are a waste of time, then I will seek you out and I will twist your neck until there's no life left in you.'

He let Einstein go and Einstein stood there, coughing and spluttering, rubbing his bruised neck. Then he gave a sideways look to Achilleus and went out, trying to look as dignified as he could.

Jackson touched Achilleus gently on the shoulder.

'I didn't know,' she said. 'I guess I should've done. I just never thought that a mashed-up thug like you could be gay at all.'

'Anyone can be,' said Achilleus. 'And I meant what I said about you. I like you. You're good. In another world, if I wasn't gay, who knows? But I am and I'm cool with it.'

'I need to go back,' said Jackson. 'Will you be all right? The battle must've started by now. Will you come?'

Achilleus shrugged. 'I don't know if I'd be much use right now,' he said. 'Not sure I could even pick up a spear.'

'Well, if you change your mind,' said Jackson, 'it's still there.'

'What is?' said Achilleus.

'Your spear. Sticking out of that tree upstairs.'

'Paddy said that whoever pulled the spear out would be the greatest champion of all,' said Sam. 'And they'd win the day for us all. He tried, we all tried, but none of us could pull it out.'

'Right now,' said Achilleus, 'I'm not sure I could either.' Tears came back into his eyes and he angrily swiped them away. 'He was just a little boy. He never deserved that.'

He sniffed again. Dragged his sleeve across his eyes to dry them.

'I'm not gonna cry any more,' he said. 'Einstein was right. I should've been looking after Paddy. Then this wouldn't have happened.'

They left him alone, and Skinner went off by himself. Climbed up to the next level and stood looking at Achilleus's spear embedded in the wood. He put his hands to it, hands that were nearly obscured by great folds of skin.

He held tight and he pulled.

The spear stayed where it was.

For a few minutes the sky was full of missiles. Ollie had never seen anything like it. He'd shouted the order – 'Now! Shoot them down now!' – and his missile unit, spread out along the barricades, had let loose.

First the bows.

The sounds of the bowstrings twanging, the arrows flying, their feathered flights hissing and fluttering, had all mixed together into a single great sigh, as if the kids had been holding their breath and now they were releasing it in one mighty exhalation.

There had been enough arrows to darken the sky. They'd curved up, seemed to hang there for a moment and then fallen down, smacking into the front ranks of the sickos – arrow after arrow after arrow.

David's captive royals had been at the head of the army, as if leading them into battle. A row of them, decrepit, falling apart, their tattered dresses and fancy uniforms flapping on their scrawny bodies. One wore a tiara and it had glinted in the sun.

Ollie remembered how David had talked of using them to take over London. To be the figureheads of his new era.

His own royal family.

They'd been the first to fall. One moment they were

there, some even looked like they might be smiling, proud
. . . and the next moment total annihilation. They were
gone. The arrows had slammed into them and cut them
down to nothing. And the sickos behind marched over
their bodies and trampled them into the dirt.

Still the missiles flew. Ollie couldn't see how anything
could survive that attack. But on they came.

And in a scarily short amount of time the archers had
run out of arrows.

Then came the javelins.

The breathy flutter of bows was replaced by the grunts
of the kids hurling spears, the thud and thwack as the
weapons hit their targets.

And on they came. Closer and closer. Until you could
clearly see their faces. And now it was the turn of the
slingers, Ollie among them. They fitted their missiles,
stretched back their slings and let fly. Slingshot rained
down on the sickos.

All around him, kids were now throwing whatever
they had at the advancing army. Stones and rocks, sticks,
bits of scrap metal and concrete, anything hard and sharp
or heavy enough to do damage.

Until there was nothing left to throw.

Had it made any difference? Ollie had seen a lot of
sickos go down. But the ones behind had simply walked
over them and kept on advancing. They had no fear.
That's what made them such a deadly enemy. They just
kept on walking into the storm that the kids were sending
at them. A normal army might have broken, fallen back,
run away from that hail of death. But grown-ups – you
could do what you liked to them and they would just keep
on coming. Ollie knew that it would be very different

when kids started to get killed, which they would soon enough – they might easily panic and run. Fear was a mighty weapon, but only one side was able to use it today.

Now the sickos were at the barricades, pushing at them, trying to climb over, expressionless and single-minded. Like a herd of cattle who would keep pushing and pushing. Some were being impaled on the sharpened wooden stakes Jordan had driven into the ground, the sickos behind ramming them further on to the spikes.

Ollie gave the order for his troops to fall back. Some of them had weapons for close-up fighting, but not all. Until they found more missiles they weren't going to engage with the enemy.

Jordan had another task for them. It was their job to take any killed or wounded away.

They left the fighting to the other units, who were armed with long spears and pikes. They were thrusting them at the sickos and for now the barricades were holding, but it would only be a matter of time before the piles of fallen sickos on the other side got higher. They were slowly creating a sort of ramp so that the sickos who filled the gaps from behind would be able to get closer and closer to the top.

Jordan had expected this and had prepared for it. He gave a signal to his trumpeters who sounded a prearranged blast. A group of kids opened up a section of the barricade in the centre, releasing the pressure and allowing a mob of sickos to spill through. Another blast and the barricades were forced shut, but not before the press of sickos along the front had thinned as they tried to get to the opening, and in the chaotic tangle they were crushing each other.

Jordan had a division of troops waiting inside the

perimeter to deal with the sickos who had come through. These were kids who were skilled at close-up fighting, mostly from the Tower of London. They dealt ruthlessly with the incomers, using short spears, clubs, axes and swords. In a surprisingly short while the sickos who had made it through were either dead or so severely wounded that they were out of action.

Ollie started shouting orders again.

It was his unit's job to clear away the bodies.

They fixed surgical masks over their mouths and noses, pulled on thick gloves and got to work. They went racing over with carts and trolleys and loaded the bodies on to them. It was disgusting work, and many of the kids went green and were too sick to help. Ollie yelled and shoved and made the others keep going. If you just did it, got on with it without thinking, it could be done. The sickos had been bad enough to start with, their bodies bloated and twisted, oozing pus and covered in boils and sores, but in the vicious fighting they'd been cut to pieces and many were splitting at the seams. Some fell apart as you tried to lift them. It wasn't just blood that came out of them, it was other bodily fluids: the contents of their guts and a strange grey jelly that looked almost alive.

Ollie followed Jordan's plan. They took the bodies down to the extreme left of the barricades, where they butted up to the Serpentine. The fighting was less intense here, as it was basically the side of the kids' encampment. The biggest press of sickos was along the front.

Ollie's guys started to pile the bodies along the bottom of the barricade, building a wall of flesh out of them. Other kids waited with sprays and buckets, ready to pour acid and disinfectant and various flammable chemicals on

to the corpses. If it came to it this section would be set on fire to create an extra defence to keep the enemy out.

It took a long while to shift all the bodies, and once the operation was complete there was no rest because Jordan repeated the tactic, opening the barricades and letting more sickos through.

Ollie watched as the fresh intake of grown-ups was chopped down. So far no kids appeared to have been harmed. Certainly Ollie hadn't been asked to deal with any. About a third of the sickos were armed, but only with makeshift weapons, sticks and stones, broken glass, jagged bits of metal, anything they'd been able to get their hands on. If any kid went down and was attacked by the mob they wouldn't last long, but these kids were used to fighting and looking out for each other.

By the end of the second influx, however, Ollie saw that the defenders were getting tired. They couldn't keep this tactic up all day without something going wrong. Sooner or later mistakes were going to be made. Too many sickos coming through at one time. The barricades not being closed fast enough. The sickos forcing a wider gap . . .

And there was always the danger that the attackers would breach the wall somewhere else or start to get over the top.

It was even possible that the sheer weight of the sickos, the numbers of them pushing relentlessly forward, would simply flatten the barricades and roll over the kids like a tsunami.

Don't think about that. Just do what has to be done.

Ollie and his team went to the fallen bodies, piled them on to their carts. Shifted them to the side wall. Came back.

Looked out at the sicko army on the other side of the barricades.

They looked no different. As many of them as when they'd started. This was going to be a long day. Ollie closed his eyes. Rubbed the back of his neck. It would be so easy now to find a hidden spot and go to sleep.

He thought of Lettis back at the museum. He had somehow persuaded her to stay. She clung to him all the time. He'd had to pull her fingers from his sleeve. She was still completely freaked out. Unable to cope. He'd promised her he'd be back. He'd survive this. Return and look after her again. Could he keep that promise?

He had to. Because if he didn't . . . if they lost . . . it would mean that all these fighters would be dead. No one to defend the museum. No one to protect Lettis and Einstein and Small Sam. The antidote would never be finished. The disease would have won.

There was a shout. A trumpet blast. The barricades were opening for a third time.

Ollie opened his eyes.

There was work to do.

'We're going to help.' Wormwood was standing in the doorway to the birds gallery, holding some equipment and dressed in leather armour. If it hadn't been for his stupid green bowler hat he would have looked like a proper warrior from ancient history, ready to do battle with the Romans, his face streaked with fearsome green warpaint. The gear he was carrying looked like more bits of armour and an assortment of weapons. He must have been over to the Victoria and Albert Museum next door to collect it all.

'You mean . . . ?' Skinner felt a stab of panic.

'I mean we're going to the battle,' said Wormwood. 'So you'll need some protection. I've persuaded a group of kids to take us up there. Don't look so gawpy – it was your idea.'

Wormwood put the gear down on a display cabinet and Skinner rummaged through it. With his extreme skin condition, it was hard to find clothes that fitted, but there was an ornate filigreed breastplate that wasn't too uncomfortable, and a helmet that looked like a wide-brimmed steel hat.

'I'm not sure what difference we're going to make,' he said, aware that he must look completely ridiculous. Like something from a Hieronymus Bosch painting.

'We're taking our own special skills to the fight,' said Wormwood.

'Fish-Face too?' said Skinner

'Fish-Face especially,' said Wormwood. 'We're going to get inside their heads. They're being controlled, directed; there are strong voices calling to them. If we can interfere with all that then we can help these kids.'

'Really?' said Skinner. What if this was just madness? What if Skinner had been fooled by the apparently normal way Wormwood was behaving? What if he was being taken in by a lunatic?

'I know one of the voices,' said Wormwood. 'I've felt him out there for a long time, calling to his flock. I've heard his whispers in my head like curling smoke. Didn't know who it was before. There was just this huge dark presence. I know him now, though. They call him St George. He's strong. We've got to go out there and mess him up.'

Skinner looked at Fish-Face. She'd been standing there, not speaking, rubbing her thin hands together anxiously. Moving her head from side to side with jerky little movements. Skinner had always thought that she looked more like a baby bird than a fish. She was so delicate. So frail. You felt that if you jumped out on her and shouted boo she'd break like a Christmas bauble. He'd seen her startled into gibbering hysteria by a daddy-long-legs. How was she going to react to a full-scale battle?

'Are you really sure about this?' he asked Wormwood. And Wormwood looked at him with his pale, watery eyes, his head tilted to one side.

'I'm coming out of a fog,' he said. 'I'm coming down to earth. Like Beauty's Beast or the Frog Prince. Einstein's medicine kiss has turned me back into . . .'

'Into what?' said Skinner, grinning. 'A prince?'

'I wouldn't go that far,' said Wormwood. 'But these kids here, they're extraordinary. What they're doing could be the only hope of a future. Look at me . . .'

He grabbed Skinner, putting his face close. There were still patches of green mould on his skin, but they were clearing up, leaving behind rawness, spots and deep sores. Despite the damage done, however, he looked healthier than when he'd been totally covered in green fuzz.

'It's working,' said Wormwood. 'The disease is beaten. Us three here, we don't really matter that much. This cure is more important. So we have to go out there and do what we can.' He let Skinner go and tapped his head.

'I can feel him in my brain, scraping at the insides of my skull – St George. But we can shut him up. We can help direct Fiona.'

'Fiona?' said Skinner.

'Don't you know?' said Wormwood. 'That's her name.' And he put an arm round Fish-Face's narrow shoulders. 'With my insight and her power, with your shout, we can make a difference.'

Boggle was waiting out on the front steps of the museum with four of his friends and a big-nosed kid called Andy, who'd arrived at the museum with the Holloway kids. Andy was telling them about how he wanted to join up with Matt's believers.

'They know the truth,' he was saying. 'They know that if we pray then the Lamb will protect us.'

'Sure,' said Boggle.

'Matt predicted this whole thing. *Everything*. And he'll protect me. I used to think a gun was all you needed, but the Lamb is stronger. His blood will save us.'

'Whatever,' said Boggle. 'But I guess it's brave of you to go to the battle.'

'I'm not being brave,' said Andy. 'I just know I'll be safer with Matt. You're the one who's brave, going out there with no protection. No Lamb to watch over you. Nothing to help you except the weapon you carry in your hand. That's brave. Not to believe in anything. I wish I was brave like you, but I'm not.'

'You've lost me, soldier.'

Boggle had never thought of himself as brave. As soon as he'd heard that there was an option not to fight, he'd taken it. But now his guilt had got the better of him. His

guilt and the weird green guy. And there he was now, coming out of the big main doors with the girl who looked like a reflection in the back of a spoon and the boy who looked like a Shar Pei dog, his hands and face covered by overlapping folds of skin.

'You sure you know the way?' said Wormwood as he got close.

'It won't be hard to find a battle,' said Boggle.

And they were off. Moving fast. Only way to do it. Move fast and don't stop to think. Go straight there and take it as it comes. He had friends there. Offering their lives. He couldn't hide at the museum any longer, knowing they might be dying. Oh crap, though. Oh crap. What was it going to be like?

He'd seen a programme once about the First World War. He'd known about the trenches and how terrible they were. How it felt like being in hell. A world of mud and death and horror. He'd done all that at school. But, in the programme, they'd shown that just a little way behind the trenches life went on as normal. Locals were living in their villages and farming the fields. They could see the flashes and flares of the artillery, hear the booms, but they ignored them.

Now Boggle was leaving the safety of the village and moving up to the frontline.

Soon they were hurrying along Exhibition Road, with its weird zigzag of coloured paving stones. There was a sound in the distance, growing louder with every step. Not quite the big guns of the trenches, more like what you used to hear when there was a football match on – a distant sort of roaring. Boggle had grown up near the Chelsea ground and that sound had been a familiar part of his childhood.

They ran across Kensington Gore and went in through the park gates. So far they'd seen nothing. Boggle hadn't known quite what to expect. He knew there was a huge army of sickos here somewhere, but had no idea whether they'd have taken over the whole park, or whether Jordan's army was holding them in one place. They saw some figures up ahead, but they were children. They'd created a sentry point and Boggle asked them the best way to go.

'The bridge is blocked off,' said the girl who seemed to be in charge. 'If you want to get to the fighting you need to take a boat over the Serpentine.'

Boggle's group hurried on and turned right, past the sad, crappy circle of the Princess Diana Memorial Fountain, into Rotten Row. This was where people used to ride horses up and down, a wide, straight, tree-lined walkway. A little way along there was a café on the edge of the lake where more armed kids were waiting. They were in charge of the rowing boats that were ferrying people and supplies across to the camp. A boat was just coming in and Boggle saw that it contained several wounded kids, one of whom was wailing and crying. Boggle looked just long enough to be sure he didn't know any of them and then turned away.

They were still too far from the battlefield to clearly see what was going on, but the football-crowd roar was louder, a mix of kids shouting and that strange hissing, swishing noise that large groups of sickos made.

Boggle's group clambered into two different boats and they were rowed across the water, the oars splashing rhythmically.

When they landed on the other side, Boggle found himself desperately short of breath, even though he hadn't

been one of the ones rowing. He realized he was having a panic attack.

'Hang on a moment,' he said and then leant over with his hands on his knees, waiting for the panic to pass. Waiting for the fizzing and bubbling in his head to die down and his knees to stop trembling. One of his mates patted him on the back.

'It's OK, Boggle,' he said. 'It's OK.'

That's what this was all about. *Friends*. Looking out for each other. He should have been here earlier.

He straightened up. The others were all staring to the north where the fighting was. Past a stretch of open ground were the kids at the barricades, and, beyond them, what looked like a living black wall, or a single disgusting creature, like a giant slug. What exactly was happening he had no idea. It was all just chaos and confusion. He could see kids running. Weapons rising and falling.

He looked around the faces of his little group. His four mates were pale and glassy-eyed. The weird girl, Fish-Face, looked like she'd gone into some kind of trance. The Green Man was muttering into her ear. Skinner was just standing there, staring. Amazing how expressive that face could be when all you could really see were the eyes.

But there was no doubting the expression.

It was pure terror.

He turned to Boggle.

'I should've stayed in bed this morning,' he said. 'It was very warm.'

Boggle gave him a quick hug.

'If we win this we can have as many lie-ins as we want.'

'Then let's go fight for our lie-ins!' said Skinner. 'For warm beds and nothing more to fear!'

Jordan Hordern closed his eyes. He could tell much more clearly what was going on if he wasn't distracted by the blurred shapes he saw when he looked out through his cracked glasses. With his eyes shut, he could picture the battlefield as if it was a chessboard, or a gaming board, with all the troops like well-ordered little figures. Bill's running commentary told him exactly what was going on. Bill had a genius for reading the world. For counting everything in it.

The sounds also helped. Nearby were the grunts and yells and screams of the kids. The clash and scrape of steel. Beyond that, falling away into the distance, was the hiss and drone of the sickos. So many of them.

It was as if he was looking down on the battle from above. Like when you looked at a satellite map on Google Earth. He could clearly see the kids in a small area, hemmed in by the stretch of water at their rear, the barricaded road by the bridge to their left, and the longer barricade to their right, where most of the fighting was, joining up with the north-east corner of the lake. That was a weak spot. The sickos couldn't outflank them and get round to their rear because the Serpentine created a huge barrier there. But if they could get in at the corner,

between the barricades and the lake, they might be able to flood into the enclosure.

Jordan knew that. He had to hope that the enemy didn't.

He could clearly see the barricades, like three sides of a long rectangle. And outside the rectangle – sickos. Bill couldn't count them all because he couldn't see them all, but at least Jordan knew how many were in the front ranks. There was no fog of war here. Just absolute crystal mathematical clarity.

But the numbers were scary. He was letting through a few sickos at a time to reduce them. Bill was feeding those numbers into his head and Jordan was constructing a world out of them. Like a computer. In the end that's what the universe was. Just numbers. You could make anything out of numbers.

But numbers couldn't lie. Two and two could only ever make four. That's why Jordan liked them so much – numbers. You didn't need to think about it, to read clues, to interpret what you could see. Not like people. People were complicated. You couldn't always tell what they were thinking or why.

Today, though, was about trying to save people. Could he use mathematics? Could he somehow make the small number of kids greater than the large number of adults? That was the trick he had to pull off.

What mathematical formula could he use?

None that he knew of.

Right now it was just a slow, steady slog and a basic process of subtraction.

Tiny numbers being taken off a huge number.

David was frustrated. As soon as the battle had started, it had turned into a huge, shapeless mess. He'd discussed various plans with Jester and Pod and Paul – as much as you could discuss anything with Paul. He was what David's father would have described as 'away with the fairies'. He seemed to understand, though, what was required. He had his link with St George and had ensured some sort of cooperation.

David had even let John and Carl have their say. They'd made a clear plan. The kids from the palace and the squatter camp weren't going to join in any actual fighting; that would be going too far. They were going to hold back in the concert area and, when the battle was decided, they would march in and take over.

So here they all were, camped out with David's red-blazered guards and John's unruly scum. Well. In times like this you made an alliance with whoever you could. And right now David was allied with an army of diseased adults and this manky bunch of plebs. None of them were to be trusted. If any of St George's army came near they had to be threatened away. Using Paul seemed to be the most effective way. He could get inside their brains.

And that was what he was doing now. Directing St

George, holding that awful chaotic mass vaguely together. At least that's what David hoped was happening. It was very frustrating. He couldn't really see what was going on and he realized with bitterness that he hadn't properly thought this through.

The thing was he hadn't thought this far ahead because he hadn't planned for it to happen this way. His whole idea had been that Jordan Hordern would see that he didn't have a chance, and simply surrender and hand over power to David. Then David would join his army with Jordan's and use Paul to defeat St George.

That had been the plan.

Trashed.

Because Jordan bloody Hordern hadn't bloody surrendered, had he? And now David was stuck here with St George's army, with no idea what he was going to do next. Already Paul was looking knackered. This was draining all his energy. If he lost the link who knew what would happen? Would St George's army turn on David? He was ready to make a quick getaway if needed, run back to the museum, leave John and Carl's mob to fight a rearguard action.

He hoped it wouldn't come to that. He felt reasonably safe here for now. He had his boys and their rifles to protect him.

It was just . . .

It wasn't supposed to have ended up like this.

He wasn't supposed to actually be fighting other kids.

'I think it's just about safe.' Jester was crossing the open area past some concession stands to where David was waiting. Jester had been checking out an old PA tower.

'We can get up there, I reckon, and have a better idea of what's going on.'

'How far up did you go?' David asked.

'High enough to make sure it's safe.'

'Who's winning?'

Jester looked at David. 'Who do you want to win?'

'Well, I don't want St George to win obviously,' said David. 'Actually what I mean is we *can't* let him win. In the end. I want him to do just well enough so that Jordan Hordern has no choice but to make a deal with me. If both sides take enough damage we can go in and clean up. Take over.'

'Just like that,' said Jester. David knew he was being sarcastic. He didn't want to go into this now because it was too complicated.

'Come along,' he said. 'Help me get up there.'

David wasn't the best climber in the world and Jester was no help. Jester managed to clamber up to a sort of small platform near the top before David was even half-way up. David went huffing and puffing and struggling up behind him, scared that he would slip. How ironic would that be? To get this close to victory only to lose it all by falling off a stupid speaker tower. Once he was up, though, he had a pretty good view of the battlefield. Not that it encouraged him particularly. It was stalemate. St George's lot were pressed uselessly up against Jordan's barricades. What kind of a tactic was that?

'Do you really want to kill all those kids?' said Jester. 'Not much point being king of the world if there's no people in it.'

'I don't know what I want,' said David, somehow finding it easier to talk freely up here, away from everything, floating above the ground. Not part of things any more.

'Except for them to surrender,' he went on. 'And accept

my offer. Accept *me*. But if they don't then yes, they will all die. That's their choice.'

'I don't believe you,' said Jester. 'You're not serious. Come on. It's not too late to stop this.'

David said nothing. He looked out over the fighting down below. He realized he was shaking. There was a tightness in his throat and he felt tears biting to get out. He knew why he felt like this. Because for the first time in his life he wasn't sure of things any more. He wasn't sure he was doing the right thing. Until he knew what to do he couldn't risk speaking and betraying his emotions to Jester.

He studied the battle. Trying to make sense of it. And slowly it became clear what he needed to do. He had to break the stalemate. They had to create a breach. St George should concentrate his forces on the weakest point of the barricades and push his way through, pour in and overwhelm the kids. Yes. A plan. Control. Forget everything else.

'Where's the weakest point?' he said.

'On which side?' said Jester.

'Jordan's weakest point,' David snapped. 'Where is it?'

Jester said nothing for a while as he scanned the defences with a small pair of binoculars.

'Really?' he said.

'Really.'

'I'd say over there.' Jester was pointing to the eastern corner of the Serpentine, where a pile of twisted scrap metal and branches, mixed together with bits of corrugated iron sheeting and doors, made a hefty but slightly ramshackle section of the barricade.

'If St George concentrated his troops down there,' said

Jester, 'I reckon they could get round the end of the barricade, by the water.'

'Go and tell him,' said David. 'I'm staying up here.'

'Tell who what?'

'Tell Paul, of course,' said David. 'Tell him our plan.'

'*Your* plan,' said Jester.

'Don't pretend you're not part of this,' said David. 'We're in this together.'

Jester looked at him and David read something in his eyes. Jester was thinking of pushing him off the tower.

David smiled.

'You don't have the guts,' he said.

Jester shook his head, looked away, started to climb down.

David was still smiling. Take control. That was the way to do it. Concentrate on your plan and don't worry about anything else.

That was the way to be a winner.

And winning was all that ever mattered.

He was a thousand-feet tall. He was St George, the mighty leader of a great army. His own army. The British army. The greatest army in the world. They'd conquered half the globe. Beaten Napoleon and Hitler and the other one . . . the other man . . . Someone else. What was his name? Sauron? Wasn't important. But he was St George. A crusader. God had talked to him and given him a holy mission.

That's what had happened.

Yes.

That's what had happened.

The voice from outer space. It had told him to go to war. Helped him marshal his troops, line them up and send them in to fight. His brain had woken. Everything was so clear and bright. The world was his. All the ragged threads were pulling into shape, coming into place, his whole army like a single giant arrow, aimed at the enemy.

Now God was telling him where to send his troops. The weak point. And he would send them. Send them to glory. He was Churchill and Wellington and King Arthur and all the other great leaders. He looked around for a lieutenant. There was one, the broken shaft of an arrow sticking out of his chest.

St George focused on him and sent him over to the left,

to the corner of the lake, taking his veterans with him. Hardened fighters with strong minds. They could push their way through the barricades and slaughter the enemy. The forces of evil. The devil's horde. The army of demons, disguised as children.

St George grinned. His brain was working well. He could win this. He'd been saving his best troops and now was the time to send them in to fight. You could forget the other ones. Rubbish. They were weak and stupid. Cannon fodder.

Now! He sent out the call. His lieutenant was roaring, with the taste of triumph in his gob.

Now!

Go to it . . .

58

Maxie was at the front, thrusting her spear over and over into the shapeless mass of sickos. Occasionally one of them grabbed the shaft and held fast, but Blue was working alongside her, ready with his own spear, and he'd stab at them until they let go. It was exhausting work and Maxie was relieved when she heard the trumpet blast that meant it was time for her unit to drop back and let another unit have a go.

She moved away, legs like concrete, watching the fresh bunch of kids move in to take her place on the frontline. She looked along the barricades. The kids manning them seemed pitifully few, spread out thinly along the fighting platforms. For a few blessed minutes it wasn't her problem, though. She and Blue wandered down to the Serpentine where some youngers were waiting with bottles of water. Jordan had thought of everything – except how to win this thing. Nothing seemed to have changed. It felt like there were as many of St George's army out there as when they'd started. They were just going to keep on pushing until they forced their way through the barricades or were able to climb over the top.

She and Blue flopped on to the grass. Looked at each

other. Too tired to say anything. Too scared to admit that this was hopeless. Wishing the day would end.

Maxie closed her eyes. So tired she instantly fell asleep.

A second? Half a second? A microsecond? However long it was, it wasn't enough, because the next thing she knew she was jolting awake, her neck hurting with the spasm. And then there was screaming off to the right. Kids running in fear and panic across the encampment.

'What is it?' she said, struggling to her feet.

Jordan's trumpeters were blaring out new commands. What did they mean? Her brain had slowed. She couldn't remember the signals. And then she heard someone shouting the one thing she'd been dreading.

'They've breached the wall!'

'Come on,' Blue yelled.

Maxie left her spear where it was, sticking in the ground, and drew out her katana. Better for hand-to-hand. And she ran after Blue, suddenly flooded with energy. They raced over to where the action was. A whole section of the barricades had been pushed in at the corner of the lake and sickos were flooding through the gap. Many, many more of them than those that came through in Jordan's controlled releases.

She and Blue started roaring commands, pulling kids off other parts of the defences, getting those that were resting back on to their feet. They formed their own unit into the tight fighting formation they'd practised so often. Pressing together and protecting the fighter to their left, moving forward slowly but steadily. They had to contain the sickos where they were and not let them spread out, and they had to close the breach.

Grown-ups were pouring in, though, like water

through a burst dam. Maxie's unit pushed into them and soon there was a desperate bloody fight on. It started well, the unit was holding, pressing the sickos back to the waterside, but the more they pressed in one section, the more the sickos burst out in another. There were just too many of them. Maxie was aware of Ollie's unit off to her left, moving in with spare crowd-control barriers. Using them like bulldozers to force the sickos back. And then she wasn't aware of anything except the mass of bodies in front of her.

It was dirty, close-up fighting. The kids hacked and cut and pummelled and stabbed and shoved. The sickos in return fought savagely, clawing at the kids. Those that were armed steamed in, arms pumping, their crude weapons rising and falling. Maxie saw kids going down all around her.

This could break their defence – and the more kids that were drawn here, the more vulnerable the barricades were becoming. She dropped back and glanced over. In several places she could already see sickos getting over the top of the barricades.

She screamed her anger, ran back in and lashed out at the knot of sickos directly in front of her, ramming her katana into a mother's mouth, pulling it back, aiming at a father's gut. Slashing across the neck of another. She formed up with Blue and one of Jordan's kids. A big guy who was working hard with a heavy sword. Heavy enough to split a father's skull and spill his brains on to the blood-wet grass.

He grunted as he swung again, cutting into another father's upper arm. And then a mother rushed at them and Maxie thrust her katana into her chest.

'There!' Blue was pointing to where a father seemed to be leading the attack. He had an arrow in his chest, but it didn't seem to be affecting him at all. In fact, it looked old and grubby, like it had been there for some time. He was better armed than the sickos around him, with a machete in each hand. He was whirling them around, cutting any kids who got near.

Maxie wondered if she could get close to him and take him out, whether it would make a difference, but she had to forget about that for the moment as a surge of new arrivals came through the gap and he was hidden from her.

The day darkened and she looked up to see the sun obscured by a cloud, and she was surprised to see how low it was in the sky. Had they really been at this all day? It would be dark before long. And what then? Would the sickos just keep on coming?

Jordan's troops had to rest. Without sleep, they'd be useless.

'Get on it, Maxie!' Blue was laying into a group of sickos.

'Sorry.' Maxie raised her sword and slashed it down diagonally across the chest of a particularly ugly father with growths the size of tennis balls on his naked skin. The sickos were pressing harder and the kids were having to fight back with all their strength. Maxie's leather jacket was splashed and greasy with blood. She wondered if she'd ever get it clean. Wondered if she'd live long enough to try.

'Push them back,' she yelled and her section barged forward, and then everything changed. It was like a ripple passed through the ranks of the grown-ups. They'd been

fighting as a single beast, purposeful and organized, and now suddenly all order fell away.

She saw the father with the twin machetes looking confused, alone, the horrible arrow in his chest rising and falling with his breathing.

'With me!' she yelled. Blue joined her and Jordan's guy with the heavy sword. Breaking ranks, but desperate to do something. Something that counted. Something that hurt the sicko army.

'That one!' she screamed. 'Get that one. Ignore the rest.'

The father was aware of them coming. He focused on them, the machetes slicing through the air. Blue made a feint to distract him, while Maxie lunged, but a lucky swing from one of the machetes – the guy wasn't even looking at her – knocked the katana from her hand and sent it flying away. She was unarmed. Now Jordan's guy went in. Maxie didn't know his name. Wanted to thank him. But, as the boy charged, the father slipped and dodged the blade and the boy was off balance, trying to bring his heavy sword back round.

Too late. The father cut him once, twice, both blades thwacking into the boy's neck. He gasped and fell. Breathed out one last time and was still.

Maxie never would know his name.

Blue was in now, trying to stab the father with his spear. With fierce luck, though, the father was still unhurt. His lips were shrivelled, his yellow teeth exposed so that it looked like he was smiling.

Maxie grabbed the boy's sword. It was closer than hers. It seemed to weigh a ton, but she saw that Blue was in trouble. The father whirling at him and unstoppable.

Unstoppable?

349

No. Maxie brought the sword crashing down. It cut through the father's right shoulder, his arm spinning off with a machete still clutched in its hand. He turned, that death's-head grin still on his face, and again Maxie brought the sword down on to him, severing his other arm. Blue stepped in from behind and skewered him. It was over. The father fell face first into the churned-up mud, driving the rest of the arrow right through his body. He gurgled in a puddle of blood. Bubbles burst the surface, swelled and popped. And then there were no more bubbles.

Maxie felt a tiny stab of hope. Like light coming through the crack under a door. All around her the sickos were fighting each other now, ignoring the kids, and she saw that it wasn't just the ones who'd broken through. The whole army had collapsed into a seething mass of violence.

The sickos were tearing each other apart.

Fresh energy filled the kids; they swept over the disorganized sickos, driving them back, striking them down, closing the gap. Making the barricades safe.

What had happened?

Maxie saw a knot of kids close to the LookOut compound, Ollie with them, his red hair standing out like a beacon. She went over.

At the centre of the knot were Fish-Face, the Green Man and Skinner, eyes closed, arms linked. Skinner's mouth wide as if he was silently shouting.

'What's going on?' she asked Ollie.

'They're messing with their minds,' said Ollie, and he smiled.

It was as if a shockwave had passed through St George's army, and David's head was suddenly filled with a screaming white noise, all his thoughts obliterated. He clung on to the strut of the speaker tower. Saw that the grown-ups below had lost all sense of order and purpose. They'd broken into mad, scrabbling groups, fighting amongst themselves, clawing and biting and thrashing each other with their crude weapons.

This was a disaster. As soon as the pain had passed, he started to climb down. Somehow he made it safely, his head still throbbing and ringing, and he struggled over to where Paul was clutching his head. Jester was with him, looking worried.

'What's happening?'

Paul said nothing. David shook Jester.

'Jester? What's happening?'

Jester shook his head. He couldn't speak. Now David shook Paul.

'What have you done?'

'It's not me – it's not me,' said Paul. He looked in pain. 'Something happened. Voices in my head. Like a jamming signal . . .'

'We need to think,' said David. 'We need a plan.'

'I can't think,' Jester growled, his hands furiously rubbing his temples.

'We must!' David shouted. 'We need a new plan. We need to stop this fight and get the children to do what we want. Help me, Jester.'

St George roared his frustration. It had all been going so well and now it was falling apart. He'd been in charge. Lifted up by the voice of God. He'd felt proud. His chest swelling. He was a holy warrior doing God's will. But now he had doubts. Something told him you couldn't always trust the voices in your head.

Was it God? Or was it the devil? Had he been tricked? Good men were always tempted. Bad people tried to lead them away from the righteous path.

The only person he could trust was himself.

His army had lost its shape, had lost its common aim. Order had turned into confusion because the gods were arguing among themselves. The other voices had come in and they were screaming at him, screaming at his troops, causing fear and violence. He tried to scream back, but he didn't have the skills.

There was someone who did. Where was she? The tall woman who had come in with the new troops. He pushed through his mob, pulling men and women aside, flinging them to the ground, snarling and grunting and biting until he saw the woman's head, taller than the ones around her.

He went up to her, grabbed her. She turned and looked at him. He tried to speak, forgetting that he couldn't. What came out of his mouth weren't proper words. He just hoped that she could read his mind.

God! A nightmare. A woman who can read your mind.

But this one could. And, what's more, he could read hers. He felt her worry. She turned and walked away, pulling him with her as if she had a fish hook in his brain. She dragged him nearer to the front, where a rise in the land allowed them to see the child demons more clearly. St George could make out the building with the platform on the roof, where the demon general sat.

The woman was pointing to something. Three figures. He couldn't make sense of them. A man with green skin, two children who looked like freaks – true demons. It was them. They were the false gods. They were the ones disrupting his army. He howled. They had to be stopped.

Now he felt the tall woman's voice inside him, loud and strong. And for a time St George was blind. A blankness filled his head. He was among the stars, in the emptiness of the universe, and all there was were the voices, arguing, the woman and the demons. She was sending her shout back at them. He forced his eyes to see. Looked at her, her long hair hiding her face.

He should never have listened to her. To God. To anyone. He didn't need the voices. He was his own general. She was taking his glory away from him. Bloody women. Nag, nag, nag.

He was a butcher.

His world was simple.

He turned to the tall woman, struck her down with the back of his hand. She lay here, looking up at him like a frightened animal. That was how it should be.

And she had shut up as well.

Good.

Blessed silence.

Everything was as it should be.

It had stopped. The sickos were falling back. Leaving the barricades.

'I don't believe it,' said Blue. 'They're retreating.'

Maxie didn't allow too much hope to creep in under the door. In her experience hope usually led to disappointment.

Indeed, a space opened up and David appeared with his gang. He was brave enough to come closer now that he knew that Jordan's troops had used all their missiles.

'You giving up?' Jordan called over to him.

'We haven't even started,' David shouted back. 'You haven't seen anything yet. But you've seen enough to know that you can't win this. Seriously, I don't want you all to die. And you don't have to. Simply surrender. I'm giving you till the morning. Think about my offer. Think about it all night as you try to sleep. Think about what will happen tomorrow now that you've seen what happened today. How many we are. When I come back in the morning, I want an answer. Do you let me take full command or do you let Jordan carry on leading your army into defeat?'

The guy was good, Maxie had to admit. He was using psychological tactics. He knew how terrified the kids would get in the night and how their terror would grow towards the morning. They'd suffered quite a few casualties, mostly from when the sickos had broken through. Maxie had seen many dead bodies of children being taken away with the injured. Jordan was quick to make sure they weren't left for others to see. But the kids would talk. Talk about their losses, and talk about the losses they would

suffer tomorrow. Talk about the fact that, despite killing a lot of the sickos, they really hadn't made any difference at all.

How many of the other kids would desert in the night? How many would go and plead with him, try to get him to change his mind? What would Jordan do? Somehow he had to inspire his army. Give them fresh bravery and morale.

Maxie sat down. Blue came and sat next to her, his arm round her shoulders.

'That guy David is a jerk,' he said.

'He's just trying to freak us out,' said Maxie. 'Get us to give up.'

'Yeah, but why did he stop?' Blue asked. 'He could've just gone on fighting all night. Them sickos don't give up. They prefer to do their killing at night. They can smell us; they don't need to see us. So why did he stop?'

Maxie shrugged.

'Because he needs to rethink,' said Blue. 'With the Green Man and the Twisted Kids in the fight, things have changed. He wants it to look like he's on top, but he ain't. Or he wouldn't have stopped.'

'I hope you're right,' said Maxie. 'But the more I think about it, the more I think I should've gone with you earlier.' She smiled at him. 'We should've run. We should've gone to a tropical island and sat on the beach.'

'One day we will,' said Blue. 'Trust me. One day that beach will be ours.'

'I don't want to see you, Jordan. I don't want to speak to you. I don't want to even acknowledge your existence.' Achilleus was slumped on a pile of cushions in the corner of the room.

Justin sighed. It smelt stale and sweaty in here. This had been his room, but Achilleus had kicked him out and Justin wasn't about to argue with him. The window was closed, the curtains were drawn and the room was dark. Achilleus was playing with Skinner's cat. Dragging a piece of string across the floor that the cat clumsily tried to catch.

'Well, I exist,' said Jordan. 'Get over it.'

'If I had my way you wouldn't exist.'

Jordan had come to Justin and Justin had set up this meeting. He was staying out of it. Nothing he could contribute. This was macho talk and Justin had never been any good at that. He just had to try to make sure the two of them didn't kill each other.

'D'you think you could take me?' said Jordan. Not looking at Achilleus. Not looking at anything.

'I never seen you fight.' Achilleus sized Jordan up.

'I know you're good,' said Jordan. 'I know your rep. But I ain't come here to fight. I come to apologize.'

Achilleus gave a snort of laughter. 'You? Say you're sorry? Am I about to be pranked?'

'No. I'm saying sorry for real. And I am – sorry.'

'For real?'

'Yeah. What I said.'

Achilleus was still staring at Jordan. Jordan was turned the other way. But still he had them both pinned. Justin didn't know how he did it. How he stared you down without actually looking at you. It was a skill. He looked at the floor or the wall or into infinity, and somehow that was stronger than looking right at you.

'What I did,' said Jordan. 'The way I did it. Wasn't right.'

'You're telling me, four eyes.'

Jordan sighed. 'If only I had that.'

'What?'

'Four eyes. But I ain't. I only got two and they don't work so well.'

'What else is new?' said Achilleus. 'We can all see your specs, roadman.'

Jordan sucked his teeth. The cat went over to him and he moved away from it. Didn't like cats.

'Is worse than that,' he said. 'That's why I did what I did. I'm gonna tell you something I ain't never told no one else before, not properly. To show you that I mean it, when I say I'm sorry. I'm gonna take off my armour and show myself to you.'

'You gonna justify yourself?'

'Nope. I accept it was wrong. But I'm gonna explain. Explain why I went about things in the wrong way and caused offence. I didn't mean to disrespect you. Wasn't the idea. Didn't realize that dog meant so much to you. Didn't know how proud you was.'

'Is that an insult?'

'Is a fact. You gonna argue it?'

'Nope.'

'OK,' said Jordan. 'So what I'm saying, I didn't realize how much it was gonna hurt the boy.'

'You made Paddy cry,' said Achilleus. 'So how come you didn't realize what you was doing when it went down?'

'Crying?' Jordan shrugged. 'Is a big, bad world, soldier. I made a small boy cry. Small boys is always crying. They get over it. Didn't seem so bad to me. All that crying stuff – I don't get it. That's the problem. I get it now that I was acting in a heartless fashion. Acting like a jerk. Like I owned this place and everyone in it. I don't.'

'Is right,' said Achilleus.

'Is why I'm saying sorry. I upset him, I hurt him, I upset you, I hurt your pride. Was never my intention. I was blind.'

'So what is it you wanna tell me, roadman?' said Achilleus. 'What's the big revelation?'

'What I said.'

'You lost me now. Rewind. Did I miss the explanation?'

'I was blind.' Jordan paused. Swallowed. Looked at Achilleus now, his eyes big and fishlike behind his scratched specs. 'What I did, I did for one reason and one reason alone . . . I was scared.'

'Seriously? Don't shit me, man.'

'Every day I get scared. What scares you, soldier?'

'Nothing,' said Achilleus. 'Nothing scares me.'

'I don't believe you.'

'Is the truth. Nothing scares me any more. Because the worst thing in the world has already happened – the thing I was most scared of. You know what it was? That some-

body I loved would get hurt. Would die. And now that's happened, so there's nothing to be scared of any more. I'm just a machine. I got no heart.'

'Nobody is a machine.'

'I am. Whatever last bit was human inside me is gone.'

'Then I need you to be a *killing* machine, Achilleus. I need you out on the battlefield. I need you to take your revenge.'

Achilleus didn't say anything for a long while. Justin could see that he was thinking. They'd both got Jordan wrong. He was more complicated than they'd imagined. More intelligent.

'You still ain't told me this big thing, roadman,' said Achilleus eventually.

'What I'm scared of?'

'Yeah. What is General Jordan almighty Hordern so scared of that he would act like a dick and screw everything up?'

Now Jordan did something Justin wasn't expecting. He took off his glasses and stared at Achilleus with naked eyes. Eyes that looked suddenly small and weak and vulnerable. He was a different person.

'I'm scared of this,' Jordan said, pointing to his eyes. 'What's happening to me. I'm scared of going blind.'

'You're going blind?' Achilleus frowned.

'Only two, three other people know it. My helpers and the little guy, the one they call Blu-Tack Bill. I'm losing my eyesight, Achilleus, that's why I need the dog. To be my eyes.'

'Why didn't you say?'

'Because I'm like you. Scared of showing weakness. That's the big one, ain't it? The real killer. That we're

nothing. And, without my eyes, that's what I am. As I say
– is why I need the dog. Is why I need Blu-Tack Bill. Boy
can see the world. Count it. My brain and his brain don't
work like other people's. My brain is complicated and
without my eyes it gets shut in.' He tapped his skull.
'Trapped in there, spinning around, nothing to fix on.
I'm scared I'll go proper crazy. That's scary, man. But
with the dog and with Bill I can stay in touch with the
world. I can read the numbers. I can stop myself from
going mad. I can not be weak.'

Achilleus nodded. Smiled. Clicked his tongue.

'I can answer your question now, roadman,' he said.
'The answer is yes.'

'What's the question?'

'Could I take you? Yeah. I could kill you easy. Because
you're blind.'

Jordan gave a sort of smile now.

'Not quite yet,' he said. 'But if not now then soon
enough. Then you will be stronger than me, Achilleus.
You'll be the big man, no dispute. I can't say more sorry
than that. Can't do no more than show you my naked heart.'

'Tell me about your heart,' said Achilleus. 'It ever been
broken?'

'Like in a girl's book?'

'Suppose.'

'I don't really know what it means.'

'But you know what it's like to lose someone you love?'

'No,' said Jordan. 'I never loved anyone. Not like that.
My brain don't work that way. My heart. Can't do it.
Can't make it happen. All I got is my complicated brain.
That's why I do things the way I do. Don't understand all
that stuff – *emotions*. I don't know about what you felt for

the boy. I just know that some things have gotta be done. And I do them.'

'Paddy,' said Achilleus.

'Huh?'

'He had a name. He wasn't "*the boy*". He was called Paddy. Paddy the Caddie. Patrick.'

'Paddy.' Jordan said the world like he was trying something out for the first time. 'OK.'

'You done?'

'I guess,' said Jordan. 'I'm just saying I can't feel for people the way you do, Achilleus, and I was scared, so I did the wrong thing. The wrong way. I'm sorry for that. And I'm sorry for what happened to Paddy. But if I want to make sure that don't happen to every one of us I need you back in the battle. We need you to fight, Achilleus. If you fight, others will join us.'

'Can we win?'

'We can win. If we fight. But the kids are losing the will. With me as general, and Bill as my eyes, and you as a hero, and all the other kids behind you, we can run them down and end this thing. Without you . . . we all die.'

'Wrong place, wrong time.'

Nicola looked at Ryan. His horrible mask was pushed up on top of his head; his ugly, acne-scarred face was shining and greasy. Amazing how quickly you got used to these things. How normal it seemed. To be talking to a boy dressed in leather and studs, with a huge dog on a lead, and a string of human ears hanging off his belt.

Nicola had spent the day sitting in the House of Lords with all her other kids. They'd been gloomy and tense and more than a bit numb, aware that over in Hyde Park a battle was being fought for them, ashamed that they hadn't sent anyone to fight – and also relieved.

They'd waited for news. Obviously hoping that it would be good news. If St George beat Jordan then they'd have to turn the Houses of Parliament into a fortress and defend themselves from the oncoming army. Surely that was better, though, than risking everything out on a battlefield? These buildings were secure. They could hold off an attack for a long time. Nicola had a certain amount of food stored up. They were organized. They had a routine. They could hold out for . . .

Who was she kidding? They wouldn't be able to survive a siege for more than a few days before supplies started to run

out. But nobody wanted to think that far ahead. Nobody wanted to think about the future at all. They talked about anything other than the battle, and sickos, and St George's army. If they ignored it maybe it wasn't really happening?

So they'd sat there in small groups. No energy. Occasionally one or two of them would wander outside, listening, watching for any signs.

They heard nothing. They saw nothing. Another grey day.

Until Ryan came.

Nicola had been most restless of all. She'd had an arrangement with Ryan. To come here at the end of the day and tell her what was happening. It had been his job, him and his hunters, to patrol the edges of the park, to keep a lookout for any signs of sickos trying to get round the sides. He would know what was going on better than anyone.

And he'd come as promised. And given her the news.

Right now he was telling her how they'd missed the attack on Paddy and the smaller kids.

'Sicko raiding party come in from the west. We was, like, twenty minutes too late to help them. Should've been there. It burns me up that we weren't. Hated today. Wanted to fight. Properly fight. It was frustrating, you know?'

'Did you see any sickos at all?' asked Nicola. 'I mean, outside the park?'

'We killed a few of them, yeah,' said Ryan. 'There was a couple of small groups broke away and came wandering round the side-streets. We hunted down as many as we could find. But we wanted to be there in the thick of it, you know? Jordan's told us not to worry. If things go wrong we'll be more than busy.'

Nicola was trying to forget how nervous she was. If she

363

didn't fixate on it maybe it would go away? Hearing about the kids being killed near the museum had brought home to her how dangerous this whole thing was.

They were on one of the riverside terraces at the back of the buildings. Nicola looked out over the great Thames. Flowing by, oblivious. In the moonlight it was a magical, shimmering, sliding, silvery living thing. She swallowed. Psyching herself up. The two of them had been dancing round the main issue. Ryan had told her how David had sided with St George. How the battle had gone. She had to know the rest.

'So . . . Ryan?' She heard herself talking, as if it was someone else. 'Will they fight tomorrow? Or will Jordan surrender?'

'Jordan? You joking me. You've met the guy – that is one pig-headed dude. They both of them are. Too proud.'

'What's David playing at?' said Nicola, shaking her head, watching a dead body float past, swollen and pale. 'What the hell is he doing? Helping St George. Has he gone insane?'

'Happened a long time ago. You really only just noticed?'

Nicola smiled. 'I've tried to work with him,' she said. 'I thought I could stop him from doing some of the madder stuff. Thought I could balance him out. But he's gone too far this time.'

'I always knew that guy was bad news,' said Ryan. 'He's been nothing but trouble for my guys. Never expected him to pull down something like this, though.'

'I need to talk to him,' said Nicola.

'The only way you could do that,' said Ryan, 'is to go up there. He's camped out in the park with all of John's crew. Doesn't want to get too far from St George's army, I guess.'

Nicola thought about this. Horrified by the thought of getting so close to that mass of diseased oppoes. But if it was the only way . . .

She wasn't a fighter. Very few of the kids at the Houses of Parliament were. They paid people like Ryan to do that sort of thing for them. She'd told herself that it really wouldn't make much difference if they joined in the fight. They'd just get in the way. But there was something she could do. She could talk to David. She knew how to do that. Maybe she could talk some sense into him, make him see how crazy he was acting. Stop him from actually fighting against other kids. Helping St George kill children.

Yes. That would be her contribution. She could go to sleep tonight without feeling a crushing weight of guilt on her chest, knowing that she'd done something. That she'd tried.

'Take me there,' she said.

'For sure?' said Ryan. 'You want me to take you up to David's camp?'

Nicola nodded. Stood up. 'I'll get my things.'

Ten minutes later they were tramping along Birdcage Walk towards the palace, John's deserted squatter camp off to their right in St James's Park. Nicola felt secure with Ryan's hunters all around her, their dogs pulling on their short, thick leads. The streets were completely empty. Ryan had explained that all the sickos were clustered in the park now so the walk there shouldn't be too dangerous. When they arrived, however – that would be a different story.

'How many sickos are there?' Nicola asked.

'Too many to count,' said Ryan and Nicola felt a flush of acid in her stomach. Wanted to puke. With each step closer, she fought harder and harder to stop herself from

turning and running back home. She had to push herself on, though, for the sake of everyone else.

'Supposed to be a truce,' said Ryan as they turned north at the palace, heading up towards Green Park. There were lights in some of the palace windows. Candles burning. David had left most of his people here, only taking his personal guard and his best fighters to the battle.

Ryan looked across the parade ground and spat.

'Don't know how you make a truce with animals,' he said. 'But David seems to have some kind of control over them. Whatever the case, we can't take you all the way.'

'What?' Nicola was suddenly made useless by panic. Hardly able to walk. 'Why not?'

'There's too many of them sickos in there,' said Ryan. 'The dogs'll go nuts. Give us away. And if the sickos got a smell of us, decided to attack, no way we'd get out of there alive.'

'And what about me?' said Nicola.

'That's your worry,' said Ryan. 'Your decision, girl. You go in there, you're on your own. But we'll wait for you.'

'Where?'

'Is a big old hotel on Park Lane – the Dorchester. Is a mess in there, but we use it sometimes to sleep and that. We can defend it if necessary. We'll wait for you there and when you come back out you can either sleep there with us or we'll get you home safely. Depends how late it gets.'

Nicola looked up at the sky. So many stars out tonight.

'I won't be long,' she said. 'And I want to sleep in my own bed.'

They approached the Dorchester from the tangle of streets at its rear, so that they didn't have to go up Park Lane where they would have been too exposed. Ryan led

them in through a service area. The hunters all had torches and switched them on once they were inside. The hotel had been ransacked and looted, smashed to pieces like many buildings when everything started to fall apart. Ryan led them up some stairs to the sixth floor where they'd secured a suite of rooms. There was a good view over Hyde Park from here.

Ryan took Nicola to the window. She could see the moon glinting on the Serpentine, silver and bright like the Thames. Along its north shore was Jordan's camp, small fires dotted around. She could make out the barricades that Ryan had described and then – a huge dark mass spreading out across the park.

'Is that them?' she asked.

'What else?' said Ryan.

'They're so many.'

'More'n I've ever seen in one place. See that fire there?' Ryan was pointing downwards, closer to the hotel. Nicola looked to where a bright blaze was flickering red and orange and yellow, sparks rising up into the night.

'That's where David is,' said Ryan. 'They built themselves a big bonfire. He's in there with his guards and most of the kids from the squatter camp . . . You reckon you can find your way back here all right?'

'I think so.'

'You got a torch?'

Nicola shook her head, feeling foolish, and Ryan gave her his.

'You want us, we'll be here.'

'I won't be long,' said Nicola, praying that this was the truth.

62

Nicola closed her eyes and took a deep breath, her chest juddering. She couldn't get enough oxygen inside her. Her lungs didn't seem to be working properly. Her heart didn't seem to be working properly. Nothing seemed to be working properly. Her legs wouldn't move. She was stuck halfway across Park Lane. The only thing that seemed to be working was her bladder. She needed to pee so badly.

I can do this, she told herself. *I can make a difference. Move . . .*

And, miracle of miracles, she *was* moving, across the road, heading towards David's fire like a moth towards a candle, praying she didn't meet any sickos on the way. Because she knew that if she even saw one sicko in the distance you'd find her tearing back to the Dorchester, screaming like a baby.

She couldn't see very much down here at street level. She'd turned her torch off so as not to attract attention and there were trees all around the edge of the park, but she made her way carefully along the railings until she saw a gate up ahead. And people.

Dear God, make them be children . . .

As she got closer, she saw pale faces staring back at her. They *were* children, though not any of David's lot from

the palace. These must be John's kids. The ones who lived in filth and squalor over in St James's Park. They watched her, not saying anything. Eyes dead. Giving her nothing.

Well, there was one thing Nicola wasn't fazed by – *kids*. She could always hold her own with kids. Even grubby, hard-faced ones like these.

'Choowant?' One of them jerked his chin at her as she drew near.

'I want to talk to David,' she said.

'We not supposed to let no one in. We not letting no one in,' said the boy.

Nicola laughed at him. 'Do I look like a sicko to you?' she said. 'My name's Nicola, I'm a friend of David's. I want to talk to him.'

'We not supposed to let no one in,' the boy repeated, enjoying his power.

'Nah, let her in,' said another boy. He had thick arms and thick legs and a thick neck. 'She's stush. We'll have a party.'

Nicola stared him down.

'Let her in,' said a girl. 'She ain't dangerous.'

'Thanks,' said Nicola and the girl ignored her. The boys stepped aside to let her through, the one with the thick neck making a couple of sexual comments that Nicola barely registered.

This was the part of the park where they used to have concerts. Nicola had been here one time with some friends to see Kasabian. Couldn't remember much about the gig, just how crowded it had been and how hard it was to see anything.

David had made himself a safe area here. His own little barricaded settlement, protected by rickety wooden

fencing that looked like it wouldn't stop a primary-school outing, let alone an army of sickos. She guessed it was more a psychological barrier than a physical one.

There seemed to be a hierarchy in the camp, with John and his squatters around the outside, then a ring of palace kids and finally, nearer to the fire, in a tight circle, a ring of boys wearing red blazers and holding rifles. David's personal guard.

What a creep. Who needed their own personal guard?

She pushed on through the sprawled kids. Comments from all around her. The boys making sexual remarks, the girls commenting on the way she looked. Several of them made fun of her red hair. Didn't bother her. She'd heard it all before.

There was a stink here, partly masked by the smoke from the fire, and looking out past the kids and the fence she could see the huge dark mass of grown-ups beyond. She really wanted to throw up. It seemed insane that she could be this close to so many sickos and they weren't trying to kill her.

Not yet anyway.

She saw David, sitting with Jester and a very pale-skinned boy wearing a black roll-neck jumper. That was Paul. The weird kid from the museum.

Nicola stopped a while, studying the three of them while they were unaware of her presence. Paul was sitting upright, staring straight into the fire as if reading something in its shifting shapes. Jester was lost in thought, wrapped in his patchwork coat. She knew that each patch was taken from the clothing of a friend of his who'd died. If the sickos won tomorrow he'd have enough to make a hundred coats.

David himself looked very tired; worried, in a way she'd never seen before. And that gave her hope. If he had doubts about all this she could play him more easily. She noticed that there was a space around the three of them. The other kids not wanting to get too close. She went over and stood in the gap, right in front of David, and he slowly looked up. Not expecting to see her here. It was a few moments before his mind adjusted and he figured out who she was, and then he smiled, which made him look five years younger, like a little boy.

It was a real smile. Warm. He was genuinely happy to see her. He struggled up on stiff legs. It was damp out here and Nicola could already feel that her back was hot where it was facing the fire, whereas her front was freezing.

'Hello,' she said.

'Nicola,' he said, and shook her hand like a boring uncle at a family do rather than a fifteen-year-old boy.

'I want to talk to you,' said Nicola.

'Yuh,' said David. 'Of course, yeah.'

'In private,' said Nicola.

David smiled even more widely.

'In private, yes . . . Yes.'

They walked away towards a cluster of concession stands and found somewhere to sit on a couple of old plastic chairs.

'So what are you doing here?' said David. 'What d'you want to talk about?'

'What do you think?' said Nicola.

'You've thought about what I said?' said David, babbling slightly, the words tumbling out. 'About us being a proper partnership.'

'I've thought about that, yes, but . . .'

'And we *can* win this thing, you know,' David interrupted. 'And then you and I can be the joint rulers of London. Of everywhere actually. And I can do it with you. I mean, you'll be, like, my queen. We'll do it together. Rule together I mean. And also . . .' He tailed off into silence.

'That's not what I came to say,' said Nicola.

'What then?' said David

'My God,' said Nicola, her voice shaking with emotion. 'I mean, *David*, what are you *doing*? What is all this? What are you doing here with grown-ups?'

David looked hurt, and then he tilted his head back and looked down his nose at her.

'I'm winning is what I'm doing,' he said. 'Beating snotty Jordan Hordern and his snotty army.'

'But they're *children*,' said Nicola. 'Like us! They're not the enemy. It's the grown-ups we're supposed to be fighting.'

'I made Jordan an offer,' said David as if he was being completely rational, saying the most normal and obvious thing in the world. 'They could easily have surrendered if they wanted. All they had to do was let me be in charge. It was their choice.'

'No, it wasn't,' said Nicola. 'How can you say such a thing? It was your choice. You chose to side with the wrong army.'

David stared at her for a long time and then suddenly he lunged, grabbing her with his hands, crushing her against his body and putting one hand behind her head and forcing his mouth on to hers. She kept rigid, her mouth closed, giving nothing. He slobbered over her face for a few seconds, then let go. Looked away. Ashamed. Nicola wiped her mouth.

'You promised me,' said David.

'I never promised you anything,' said Nicola.

'You said you'd be my girlfriend,' said David.

'No. I would never have said that.'

'You implied that you might,' said David. 'Were you just leading me on?'

Nicola laughed slightly hysterically.

'I wasn't doing anything,' she said. But deep down she knew that she *had* tried to manipulate him. She *had* given hints that he might be in with a chance. But only tiny hints, nothing definite.

'If you'll be my girlfriend,' said David quietly, still not daring to look at her, 'I'll stop this. I'll take my troops away. I'll go back to the palace. I'll stop Paul from communicating with St George. If you'll only be my girlfriend.'

'Is that what you need?' said Nicola. 'An excuse to stop doing this? To save face?'

'I didn't mean it to go this far,' he said. 'I'm not a bad person. Am I?'

Nicola touched him gently on the shoulder. Could she stop this? With just one word? Say yes to him . . . Was that all it would take . . . ?

David looked round eagerly, Nicola's hand still gently resting on his shoulder, but he could tell by the look on her face that she wasn't offering him anything more than this. She couldn't disguise it. She couldn't outright lie to him.

'David,' she said. 'It doesn't work like that. You can't *make* me be your girlfriend. I like you. I just don't like you in that way. I'm sure you can find someone else. There's plenty of girls at the palace who worship you. Just not me. I could never fake it. Can't you see that?'

'It's you I want.'

'Forget it, OK? You've got to stop what you're doing here. You've got to because that's the right thing to do. Not because I tell you to. Not because if you do I'll kiss you and everything will be like a fairy tale.'

David suddenly jumped up and pushed Nicola over. She tumbled out of her chair and sprawled on to the damp grass. He stood over her, staring down, his finger pointing, struggling to speak.

He said nothing. Simply turned and marched back towards the fire. Nicola got up and went after him, pulling at his jacket.

'Stop,' she said. 'Come back. Let's talk about this.'

He walked on. 'There's nothing to talk about,' he said. 'You've made it really clear that you despise me. I'm just a bit of crap on your shoe.'

'No,' said Nicola. 'I didn't say that. I never said anything like that. Don't be stupid. I said I like you. Just not in that way . . .'

David went over to one of his boys, grabbed the rifle from his hands and waved it at Nicola.

'You see this?' he said. 'I have this. I have power. I can get what I want.'

Nicola giggled, not quite believing this, getting more hysterical. David's guys had got those rifles at the Imperial War Museum and she didn't even know if they worked, whether they knew how to fire them. She'd always assumed that they were just for show. Now here was David coming over all macho. She knew she shouldn't laugh. It was only making him worse. But he looked silly waving the gun about. It wasn't his style, and she hoped that others might join in, make him see how foolish he was being.

'Come on. Is that it?' she said. 'You're going to shoot me if I don't kiss you?'

That got the attention of some of the kids nearby. It was getting interesting now.

'Shut up,' David hissed.

'Are you going to lunge at me again?' said Nicola.

'Shut up. I didn't.'

'He did,' said Nicola, looking round at all the faces goggling at her. 'He did. Over there. Just now. He said that if I agreed to be his girlfriend he'd stop fighting the other children.'

There was some laughter, a low hum of excitement.

Nicola had her audience. If David wasn't going to fix this mess, she was. She could make a difference.

'Listen to me. All of you. Listen to what I'm saying. See sense. Don't listen to David. I seriously think he's nuts. Yeah? You're all on the wrong side. You've got to see that. Those are your friends over there. They're children like you. And David, just because he can't get a snog, is going to take his gun and go marching around shooting people to show what a big man he is. You don't have to follow him. Go home.'

But nobody stood up. Nobody said anything. Nobody shouted out 'She's right!' and came over to stand by her side like they would have done in a Hollywood film. They just stared at her, enjoying the show. This tripped a switch in Nicola. She was an itchy tangle of anger and fear and embarrassment and too many other too complicated emotions to make sense of. She watched herself. Knew that she was only going to make things worse. Knew she should stop. But couldn't.

She went over to David and gave him a shove.

'You're a dick,' she said. 'You're an idiot. I take it all back. I hope you never get a girlfriend. I don't think you've ever had one. Who the hell would ever want to kiss you? You're revolting. You make my skin crawl.'

A couple of kids clapped. Nicola was blushing. Knew she had to leave before she said anything else.

This wasn't like her. She wanted to say sorry, but was worried that the words would stick in her throat. She turned and walked away and, as she walked, she felt a thump in her back. Thought that David must have punched her, pushed her, because the next thing she knew she was lying on the ground.

She couldn't believe it. He'd knocked her over. The bastard. Typical male way to win an argument – with violence. Then Nicola realized that there was a noise ringing in her ears. There had been a sharp crack. A bang. And she couldn't move her legs. A terrible cold pain was spreading across her back and deep into her chest. She managed to twist round far enough to see David standing there, white-faced, utterly shocked, his mouth hanging open. The rifle in his hands pointed at her.

No. Not that. She couldn't believe it. Had he shot her? Had he really shot her? There was blood in her mouth and in her throat. She was struggling to breathe. She wanted to say something, but felt a clamp round her head, crushing it tighter and tighter, her sight blurring and fizzing.

She couldn't believe it. It made no sense at all.

Of all the things she thought might happen when she came here, this wasn't one. To be shot like this. Tears came into her eyes. She closed them, laid her head down on the grass and in a few moments her tears were the only part of her moving.

Her heart had stopped.

'We have to surrender,' said Justin, dusty morning light shining down on him from the high windows in the museum. 'We can't beat them. I've spoken to everyone who was there. All that will happen is our best fighters will get killed. We have to change our tactics. Let David take control. What difference does it make? We pull back into our buildings if we have to, make the museum secure. If the sickos try to get in we kill them. But it's crazy to be trying to fight a battle up there in the park. I'm going to get Nicola. We'll go up there together and see Jordan, talk to him. Talk to David. They've both got to stop this before it's too late.'

'Is already too late.' Achilleus's voice rang down from the upper gallery. Sam looked up to see him leaning over the balcony.

Sam and all the other kids in the museum were gathered round the diplodocus. Justin hadn't had time to call an official meeting in the Hall of Gods, so he was talking to them from halfway up the steps by the statue of Charles Darwin.

'We have to fight.' Achilleus came striding along the gallery and everyone watched in silence as he got to the end, came down and stood next to Justin. He was wearing his battle gear.

'We have *not* run out of time,' said Justin. 'Most of our fighters are still alive.'

'Can they fight airborne spores?'

'What?'

'Can they fight viruses? Bacteria? Parasites? With swords and spears and clubs?'

'What's that got to do with anything?' said Justin. 'We're talking about an army of sickos.'

'You don't get it, do you?' said Achilleus. 'It's not about fighting people, it's about fighting disease. The sickos are carriers. We gotta stop them before they infect us. Before they turn us into them.' He scanned the faces in the crowd until he saw who he was looking for.

'Yo, Einstein,' he shouted. 'Get up here.'

Einstein came out of the crowd and sauntered up the steps to Achilleus, trying to look casual, but you could tell he was scared, wondering what Achilleus was going to do to him. Sam remembered their horrible argument yesterday.

'I don't like you one bit,' said Achilleus. 'Never have. Never will. But I guess you're smart and you know what you're doing. So tell it like it is, from what you know – tell these people what'll happen if we don't stop that army out there. Right now. If we don't kill every last one of them.'

'OK,' said Einstein. 'Basically Achilleus is right. They're gathered here together because they want to spawn. Disperse. Broadcast. Whatever you want to call it. They want to send their spores out. They want to spread the disease.'

'So why are they fighting us?' called out Wiki. 'Why are they killing us, if we're supposed to be the new hosts?'

'I don't know. Something's gone wrong. Maybe because we attacked them they've gone into automatic fight mode.

Maybe it's St George. Maybe he's strong enough to beat the disease's programming. His human will is overriding his genetic impulse to multiply. That and David's influence. Getting Paul up there to communicate with them. Or maybe we're a threat. Us. Specifically. I mean, we know they want to kill Small Sam because they're aware that he carries the antidote. His blood is the one thing that can destroy the disease.'

'So we *got* to kill them,' said Achilleus. 'And we gotta kill them fast. No two ways about it. We gotta stop them before they're ready to pass the parasites on and create a whole new generation of sickos.'

'Yeah? And where were you yesterday?'

Sam was amazed. It was Jibber-jabber. Calling Achilleus out. His voice full of hurt and hate. How was he brave enough to stand up to him? Was it just that he'd been a good friend of Paddy?

Achilleus looked at him and nodded slowly.

'You're right, younger,' he said. 'Where was I yesterday? Not where I should of been.'

'Yes,' said Jibber-jabber. 'Paddy wanted to do your fighting for you – he was ashamed of you. If you'd been out fighting it wouldn't have happened; and they wouldn't be dead, Paddy and the others, they wouldn't all be dead.'

Achilleus was still staring at Jibber-jabber.

'Come with me,' he said. 'All you lot – what did Paddy call you? The Youngbloods – you come with me, yeah? The rest of you. Wait here.'

Sam looked at The Kid who was sitting cross-legged on the floor next to him. The Kid shrugged.

'Where he goes my rosemary grows,' said The Kid and he stood up.

Two minutes later Sam and the smaller kids were all clustered round the sequoia at the top of the museum. Achilleus's spear was still sticking out of the centre.

'I can't undo what I did,' said Achilleus. 'Can't put things right. But I will fight today. And I will beat the enemy – for Paddy. And for you guys. His death will mean something – it'll mean victory for us kids. And you guys will keep his name alive. He'll be a hero. You'll talk him up. A bigger hero even than me. Paddy's gonna win this battle for all of us. OK?'

The Youngbloods nodded. Achilleus gripped the spear.

'What did Paddy say?' he asked. 'About this spear?'

'Whoever pulls it out is, like, king of the world,' said Jibber-jabber.

'For Paddy,' said Achilleus, and he pulled the spear out as easily as if it had been stuck in a cushion.

'I'm sorry,' said Jibber-jabber. 'For what I said.'

'Don't be sorry,' said Achilleus. 'You were right. I was wrong. Remember this – heroes are usually dicks.'

Jibber-jabber laughed and Achilleus cuffed him round the head.

'Come on,' he said. 'Let's get all those other dicks up and doing some good.'

Achilleus walked fast down the stairs, shouting all the way.

'Anyone who can fight!' he yelled. 'Not the little ones, not the scientists, but any of you wasters that trained in the park and are supposed to be up there now. Any of you who, like me, spent yesterday sitting on your arses, you're coming with me. We're going to the fight.'

'All right,' someone shouted back. There was a rumble of chatter around the hall as Achilleus marched down the

final run of steps and headed towards the doors. Kids started to cheer and clap, slapping him on the back. He pulled the doors wide and waited there as the other kids streamed out past him.

Sam went over to him.

'I wish I was big enough to fight,' he said.

'You fighting them in your own way, cuz,' said Achilleus, squatting down to Sam's level. 'We doing this for you. We giving you a future.'

'And for Paddy,' said Sam. 'Like you said. Make it so that his death wasn't just a pointless thing.'

'I can't do that,' said Achilleus. 'Not really. See, death is always pointless. And death is the *only* point. We all end up there sooner or later. I know about death. It don't scare me. I'm taking it to the enemy.'

He pushed his way through the rest of the crowd and went out into the white morning light.

Skinner had slept badly. Too many voices in his head creeping into his dreams. Fish-Face broadcasting her endless, mind-blowing SOS call, not even aware she was doing it. Some part of her brain sending it out even as she slept. And behind it, sneaking through the shadows, the whispers from the sicko army, squeaking and chattering to each other like a swarm of insects. And the louder voice of St George. Not words from him as such, just feelings coming through, bad feelings of blood and violence. Occasionally another voice probing. Skinner thought that one must be Paul, the boy from the museum who'd gone mad.

Skinner wished he'd gone back to the museum to sleep in the relative peace of the birds gallery. But Wormwood had insisted they stay here in Jordan's camp in case anything happened in the night. In case the sickos tried to attack. In case David's overnight truce had been a bluff. In case Fish-Face started to hear anything coming back.

Wormwood's voice stayed out of his head. But whenever Skinner had woken up, which was often, the Green Man had been sitting there, his face catching the moonlight in a way that made it seem to glow. Just sitting and staring, tapping his fingertips together. Fish-Face had cut off his hideous nails, but he hadn't got out of the habit.

Jordan's troops had been mostly sleeping on the ground, huddled together for warmth, but some had brought tents with them, and some had bedded down inside the parks buildings that formed the buttresses along the barricade.

The stink of the grown-ups had filled the night. The smell of rotting meat and sewage. Jordan had lit a series of fires along the centre of the camp; some kids had had the job of throwing stuff on them to keep them going, keep them smoking in the hope that the smoke and heat would drive the smell away. It didn't seem to make much difference. There were just too many sickos out there.

Jordan had been back to the museum in the night. Skinner had watched him being rowed across the lake, and he'd watched him return some time later.

It had been a restless night. A horrible night.

He'd woken with the morning light. All around, the kids stirring, cold and tired and damp. Terrified no doubt. As terrified as he was. But he was here. He was among them. One of them. Sleeping out in the open. Sharing the experience. Like at a music festival. The sort of thing he'd read about and watched on TV and dreamt about when he was growing up, shut away from the world in the Promithios laboratories.

He was alive.

Wasn't there a saying? That you were most alive when you faced death. He had seen something of the world. He was here for the final battle.

Fish-Face was still asleep, her face twitching. He left her alone. Wishing he could have slept longer.

He stretched, all his joints clicking. He shook himself, went to a fire to try to soak up the last of its warmth. The

folds of his skin had trapped moisture from the hazy morning air and he was itchy all over.

There was a thin mist across the ground, though the sky above looked fairly clear. It was going to be a beautiful day. Sunny and warm. If this had been a film, the director would have made the day match the feelings of the kids. A sense of doom and dread and disaster. A cloudy, stormy sky, the rain lashing down and the ground turned to mud as the two armies desperately fought to the death . . .

But nature didn't care, did it? Nature just happened. Like the disease. It was just a part of nature. You couldn't really say it was any more evil than the cold virus or the flu virus. In fact, you couldn't call it evil at all. The disease just did what it did. Nature just did what it did. Some creatures survived and some didn't. The ones who survived weren't any better than the ones that died. There was no good and evil in nature. No right and wrong.

It would be nice to survive, though, Skinner had to admit. It would be nice to see a bit more of the world.

He went down to the Serpentine and along the bank to the corner where the sickos had got in yesterday. It had been repaired and strengthened and Jordan had stationed one of his strongest units there to defend this potential weak spot. Some of them were on the other side, driving in more stakes, facing outwards.

Skinner turned and walked back the other way. Kids were getting the boats ready to take the dead and dying and the injured across the water. Some were scrubbing the blood off from yesterday.

Further along, Ollie was up and about, organizing his troops. In the night Skinner had seen the bravest of these guys sneaking out in small groups to try to retrieve as

many arrows, spears and javelins as they could. They had nowhere near as many as yesterday when they'd started, but at least they'd have enough for one last volley. Other kids were returning from forays around the surrounding area, where they'd been pulling up more railings, tearing into the buildings along Kensington Gore, grabbing anything they could use in the battle today.

And there was Jordan, climbing up on to his platform with Blu-Tack Bill, Bright Eyes sitting patiently at the bottom of the ladder, waiting for him. Poor Paddy. He'd had his dog taken away from him and then his life. Jordan might as well keep the animal now.

Just past the LookOut was the group of kids all wearing green. Matt's gang from St Paul's. They were sitting neatly in a semicircle facing Matt, who appeared to be giving a sermon. Or was it a pep talk? A rallying call.

'Blessed are you who stay awake and worship the Lamb. We have kept our vigil, and we will plough the blood of the Nephilim into the fields of the Lord. They are the spawn of Gog and Magog. In number they are like the sand on the seashore. They have marched across the breadth of the earth and surrounded the camp of God's people. But fire will come down from heaven and devour them. And their leader, Satan himself, will be thrown into a lake of burning sulphur, where he will be tormented day and night forever and ever. They are the spirits of demons, and word has gone out to the kings of the whole world, to gather them here to do battle in the place that is called Armageddon . . .'

Skinner moved quickly on, hearing Matt shouting after him, glad he'd got away. Matt seemed to be ranting about him now.

'His voice is like the sound of rushing waters, and out

of his mouth comes a sharp sword with which to strike down the nations . . .'

This was madness. These kids had made their own crazy mind-castle and were happy within its walls. They felt safe there. It had been the same with the Twisted Kids. They'd lived their lives away from all this, in their own little hothouse world, playing their games. They'd constructed their own universe inside the warehouse. They'd been the normal ones. The rest of the world was weird. Skinner guessed that everyone probably felt the same way.

He heard a snatch of song in the distance and a movement caught his eye. He looked across the lake.

And froze.

Surely not? He must be imagining it.

No – they were unmistakable. It couldn't be anyone else. One moment he'd been thinking about the Twisted Kids, back at the warehouse, and the next moment – there they were.

He could see the Warehouse Queen in her wheelchair throne, being pushed along by Monstar. And there were the others – TV Boy, Flubberguts, Betty Bubble . . . all of them. And they were singing their song . . .

> 'We are the Twisted Kids. Twisted gits, the gifted twits!
> We are the screwed-up, twisted kids,
> Our life's a joke, our legs are crap,
> We try to walk but slip and slap.
> You wouldn't want to ask us round for tea . . .'

Skinner ran back to where the boats were.

'Can someone row me across?' he shouted. A girl shrugged and nodded that he should jump into her boat.

Two other kids pushed them out into the deeper water and the girl began to pull steadily and surely across the lake, Skinner sitting in the back. Halfway across he couldn't hold back his excitement and he stood up and started to wave.

'Sit down,' said the girl. 'You'll tip us over. We're nearly there.'

Skinner apologized, and when they reached the other side the Twisted Kids were waiting for him. There was a crazy round of hugs and greetings and laughter. A crowd of local kids had formed round them, pointing and staring, amazed.

'What are you doing here?' said Skinner.

'We got Fish-Face's message,' said the Warehouse Queen. Or, at least, she put the words into Skinner's head.

'We couldn't sit there in the warehouse and wait for things to be decided without us,' said TV Boy. 'We've come to do all we can.'

'We'll get your throne up on to the roof of the Look-Out,' Skinner said to the Warehouse Queen. 'Near the general. Because you can shout the loudest of us all.' He laughed, his tiredness and gloom forgotten.

'Between us we can completely block the sickos' signals,' he babbled on. 'They won't be able to get even halfway organized. They'll be just a mob. Paul won't have any effect on them. They'll be ploughed into the earth!' He laughed again.

'You've come,' he said. 'We're all together again.'

Ryan's dog was restless this morning. Being this close to so many sickos was freaking her out. Sickos stank bad enough to Ryan's nostrils. And he didn't have much of a sense of smell – thank God. One small advantage in this stinking, rotten world. So what must it be like for the dogs? Being so close to the awful stench and the bad vibes that the sickos gave off.

Ryan rolled his shoulders and swung his arms. It had been cold in the night and the day hadn't warmed up yet. He'd have liked to be standing out in the sunlight, but was holding back here in the shadows with Dom, so as not to be seen.

Where the hell was Nicola?

They needed to be moving on soon and she'd still not come back. She'd told him that she wasn't going to be long, but she'd been out all night. He liked Nicola. She'd always been good to him – straight and fair – and they'd had a strong relationship based on helping each other. In quiet moments he thought about her in other ways, but knew she was out of his league.

'We waiting much longer?' asked Dom.

'Two minutes. We just need to speak to someone from David's camp.'

'What about them?'

Dom nodded and Ryan looked over to where two of John's squatters were wandering across Park Lane towards them. Going home. Ryan wondered how many others were leaving the battle and drifting away. He stayed hidden and, as soon as the boys had come close, he and Dom stepped out.

'Hold up.'

The two squatters were clearly terrified of Ryan's dog and didn't put up any kind of fight. Not that that was what Ryan was looking for.

'It's all right, cuz,' he said. 'Just want some intel.'

'Yeah?' said one of the squatters, not taking her eyes off the dog. The dog, in turn, wasn't taking her eyes off the boy. She hadn't been fed yet this morning.

'You were with David and the others last night?' Ryan asked.

'Yeah,' said the squatter.

'Did you see a girl?'

'Yeah.' The squatter giggled. 'A few.'

Ryan looked at him long enough to make the smile fade away.

'One girl in particular,' he said. 'Nicola. Tall. Red hair. In charge at the Houses of Parliament. Went to talk to David.'

The boy nodded. 'Yeah,' he said. 'She dead.'

'What you mean?' said Ryan, wondering if this was a joke.

'I mean what I say,' said the boy. 'She dead. She had some kinda argument with David, I think. Ain't that right, bro?'

The other boy nodded.

'David shot her in the back,' he said. '*Bang*. Had some

of his boys take the body away. Gave it to the sickos. Get rid of the evidence, I guess.'

Ryan was hearing but not hearing. Understanding but not understanding. There but not there.

This didn't make any sense to him. He'd brought the girl here. He was responsible for her.

'You saying she really dead?' he said. 'For real?'

'For real,' said the first boy. 'No two ways about it. She gone.'

Ryan had a sudden urge to lash out and punish these two kids for Nicola's death, but that would be as senseless as what David had done. Instead, he just swore at them and they hurried away.

'You believe that?' he said to Dom.

'Unbelievable, man.' Dom was shaking his head.

'Get the others,' said Ryan. 'We gotta take the news to her people.'

They ran all the way to the Palace of Westminster, Ryan turning the facts over and over in his head, trying to make sense of them. When they got there, they brought fear and confusion with them. If he had been stunned by what had happened, unable to believe it, Nicola's kids fell apart. The place became filled with wails and angry shouts.

Ryan couldn't take it. He went and sat out front with his hunters, wondering what they should do next.

And then, one by one, kids started to come out and join him. They were using their anger, turning it into action.

'We want to fight,' said a kid called Bozo, who always wore a policeman's helmet. 'We want to fight against David.'

Soon Ryan was marching past the big arch in the middle of the roundabout at Hyde Park Corner with a small army of Nicola's kids at his back, armed and ready to get in the

fight. Ryan looked up at the statue on top of the arch. He'd never been sure what it was supposed to be. It was made out of black metal and was of a woman with wings, maybe an angel, standing in the back of a chariot, being pulled by four horses. She had a wreath in her hand.

'Victory,' said Bozo, who had caught him looking.

'You're kidding me.'

'I'm pretty sure.'

'Let's hope so, eh?' said Ryan. 'Is a good sign.'

Some of the other kids were shouting and pointing now, getting overexcited. Ryan saw what had stirred them up – a group of people coming along the road from the west, making for the gateway into the park.

'Chill out, soldiers,' he said, shaking his head. 'They ain't no enemy. I know those guys.'

He'd recognized the boy who was leading the group. Muscular and powerful-looking, with a distinctive pattern of razor cuts in his short hair. It was Achilleus.

'Yo! Fam!' he called out, and Achilleus stopped.

Ryan jogged over and they gripped forearms. Achilleus was the best fighter Ryan had ever seen. He'd been pissed off that Achilleus hadn't come to the fight on the first day, but he had his reasons. And now he had his reasons to fight.

Ryan's mood was lifting. He could forget what David had done to Nicola and concentrate on the here and now. No more sneaking around the edges. Forget what Jordan wanted, he was going into battle. With Achilleus at his side.

'Is early still,' said Ryan as they started to walk. 'Can't hear no sounds of fighting. Jordan gonna be well pleased to see you.'

'We ain't going to his camp,' said Achilleus. 'We gonna hit the sickos from the side while they still sleeping. They

won't be expecting us. Nobody will be. We go in hard and roll them back. Don't stop until every last one is dead.'

They pushed into the park, Achilleus and Ryan out in front, then Ryan's hunters, then the mob of other kids who had merged into a single unit. Achilleus was leading them round the Serpentine to the east.

'This ain't Jordan's tactics,' said Ryan.

'You don't need tactics when you fighting dumb animals like sickos.'

'This lot ain't so dumb.'

'They dumb enough,' said Achilleus.

'You seen how many they are?'

'Don't care,' said Achilleus. 'I'll kill them all myself if I got to.'

'Jordan won't like it,' said Ryan.

'Doesn't have to. He can command the defence. I'm commanding the attack.'

They could hear music now, the strange, ragged mish-mash played by Matt's musicians from St Paul's, banging and clashing and the harsh rasp of horns. They rounded the lake and there were the barricades, kids on the other side. Some of them had spotted Achilleus and were running to the barricades, cheering and shouting. Achilleus raised his spear above his head, holding it like a banner, and he forged ahead, not slowing, in fact walking faster, eager to get to the sickos.

And there they were. They'd been sleeping in piles, half on top of each other, and were coming awake, standing up, looking around, as if all the graves in a cemetery had emptied and the dead were coming back to life.

'You were right,' said Achilleus, and he whistled. 'That is a bare lot of pus-bags.'

'You still don't want to sign in with Jordan?'

'I got the smell of blood in my nose,' said Achilleus. 'I need to kill something.'

Ryan had been swept along with him this far. He was used to fighting, but only in small groups. This was way different. Apart from his hunters, the kids with him weren't the most experienced fighters. They were the ones from the Houses of Parliament and the museum who had avoided the fight on the first day. He didn't want to imagine how they must be feeling right now. Being pulled straight into a battle. This can't have been what they were expecting when they woke up this morning. But there was no time to think about any of that because Achilleus had started to run, and Ryan ran, and they all ran, and the hunters let the dogs loose and they were in among the enemy.

The dogs were snarling and biting at the sickos, who were milling in confusion, not ready for an attack. Ryan lashed out to left and right, bringing two sickos down. Achilleus was already working hard. His spear swiftly and expertly hammering and hammering at the sickos, stabbing them in their faces, their chests, their sides, their backs, their bellies. Ryan was aware of other kids all around him, driving into the sickos and pushing them back.

The rest of St George's army had come alive now and were surging in all directions, some coming towards Ryan, some crashing into the barricades. Ryan saw arrows and spears in the air, sticks and stones, a hail of death flying over the barricades and raining down on the sickos.

There was no turning back now.

'What's going on, Bill? You have to tell me what's happening. Give me the numbers, Bill.'

'New fighters,' said Bill. 'Coming in from the east. Attacking the enemy in his left flank.'

'The numbers, Bill, give me the numbers.'

Bill started to rattle off the sicko numbers in that section, and the numbers of the new arrivals.

'This wasn't the plan,' said Jordan, keeping his eyes shut.

'It's working, though,' said Bill. 'The kids are pushing forward. And the ones here in the camp are excited. They're ready to fight now. Wait a minute. Now something's happening over to our left.'

'What is it?' said Jordan. 'What's happening? I haven't given any orders yet.'

'The green kids are going out,' said Bill.

'What you mean?' said Jordan and he opened his eyes, tried to see what Matt was doing, but it was nothing but a blur. Too far away. 'Are they running away?'

'No, they've opened the barriers, but they're not letting sickos in, they're going out.'

'The numbers,' said Jordan. 'I need the numbers.'

And again Bill rattled them off. Jordan made quick

calculations in his head. Studied the map he kept in there. Quickly adjusted his tactics.

Realized that it might work.

'OK,' he said. 'We got a pincer movement going on. Two smaller forces coming in on the flanks. We won't make a frontal assault yet, though, not till I know more.'

He shouted a series of commands to his trumpeters who started blasting out the signals – getting his best troops together. When he knew the shape of the battle, when he knew which flank attack was most effective, he'd send troops out to reinforce them.

Everything was back on track.

Jackson was standing with her troops. She couldn't wait to get out there. Yesterday had been a long, grinding slog of defending the barricades, letting in small forces of sickos, dealing with them, then going back to the barricades. The rhythm and the tactics had changed today. It was no longer just a matter of waiting. Defending. There was going to be a proper attack, she could feel it. She'd watched Achilleus go past with his troops. Watched them plough into the sickos. She wanted to be out there with him. She wanted to be fighting. Anything was better than this waiting.

She had her eyes fixed on Jordan, up on his platform. Desperate for his signal. Willing him to give the command. To go out either right or left. To help Achilleus or to help Matt. A good general always reinforced his stronger units. Surely that would be Achilleus. The weaker units had to be abandoned. That was just how it was. Matt had gone out there trusting that the Lamb would protect him. His troops seemed to be mostly armed with banners. They

were chanting. What hope did they have? If Jordan sent her out to back up Achilleus they could power through there, cut St George's army in half.

Come on. Come on.

And then Jordan said something to Bill, the trumpeters blasted out their signal and Jackson was shouting.

'Go right! Go right!'

She was running. Ollie's squad was opening the barriers. Jackson's troops were out of the camp, into open ground.

'Keep up! Keep together. Don't forget your training!'

Soon they were pushing through the rear ranks of Achilleus's unit, the stragglers, the ones who were too reluctant or too scared to properly get into the fight. She charged forward, smashing stray sickos out of her way as she passed, flattening them with single, well-aimed blows from her heavy sword. It didn't take her long to get right to the front, where she found Achilleus surrounded by dead sickos.

'Glad you could join us,' she said as she fell in beside him.

'And I'm glad *you* could join *us*,' said Achilleus.

He was painted red with blood. His hands, his face, his arms, his chest, his legs. And he was stepping over the bodies of the sickos he'd cut down, moving steadily forward. Leaving the wounded ones for the troops behind him to finish off.

Jackson joined him, cutting, chopping, slicing . . . This wasn't easy, though. It was the hardest thing she'd ever done. There were just so many of them to kill. Too many. After the first brief burst of exhilaration, the charge to battle, the shouts and whoops of her kids, she'd got bogged down. Clogged in the thick of it. This was grim work,

grim and bloody and exhausting. She was sweating, gasping for breath, her sword arm burning, as she cut into the bodies that swarmed around them.

And now they weren't moving forward any more. They were being forced back by the sheer weight of sickos. She was hit by doubt. What chance did they have? These few kids against so many? She felt like she was fighting in slow motion. Even Achilleus was tiring. She could read his body language. You couldn't keep up that level of energy all day. She saw her friends starting to go down, swamped by adults. Tried not to think about their clawing fingers and tearing teeth.

'To me!' she bellowed, the effort hurting her throat. 'Stay close! Group together! Protect each other!'

She was desperate. For the first time she was scared. They were all going to be killed. Achilleus had got it wrong, Jordan had got it wrong, she'd got it wrong . . . And then she felt a mighty punch in the chest. Her head rattled. She was rocked back. Fell down, winded, stretched out on the grass, deaf. Found herself looking up at the sky, trying to make sense of what she was seeing. A ball of flame rising into the air.

As her senses returned, she struggled to sit up. All around her kids and adults alike were sprawled on the ground, stunned. She recalled a brightness just before the thump. And as she looked further she saw at the rear of the sicko army another blinding white flash followed by a red flare and an orange flash. Next moment a belch of filthy black smoke exploded into the sky, which was suddenly filled with what looked like a pink mist. At the same time there came a bang that deafened her again and left her head throbbing.

Her hearing came back in a shrieking whine and she saw Achilleus stand up nearby.

'What was that?' she said, struggling to her feet. All around her were fallen bodies. For the moment the fighting had stopped.

'I dunno,' said Achilleus, shaking his head. 'Fire and brimstone?'

There was a third mighty bang. Then another. And another. Jackson clamped her hands over her ears. In all she counted nine explosions. Ripping into the sicko army. She could hardly think straight. Her brain was spinning in her skull.

'Looks to me,' said Ryan, grinning at the two of them as he came over, 'like someone's blowing the crap out of the sickos. That pink mist in the sky? That used to be people.'

'Let's finish this thing,' said Jackson, and she and Achilleus and Ryan and the rest of their kids charged forward with a great shout.

There was a long moment of silence, as if the whole world had been shocked into numbness, and then bits started to fall from the sky. Soot and blasted metal, burnt pieces of flesh, a thin drizzle of blood.

Hideous screaming then filled the park. Ben looked up, seagulls, hundreds and hundreds of them, circling and then beginning to swoop down in a feeding frenzy.

'Man, that was peak,' said Bernie.

Ben couldn't believe it. Nine out of the ten car bombs had gone off. Everything they'd rigged up had worked. The explosives, the self-driving cars, the makeshift triggers. Everything.

They'd lifted the explosives from the hell of Wembley. The stadium had been filled with a disgusting pile of human bones, the flesh mostly either rotted away or eaten by rats. The cars had been fitted with a simple combination of crook locks and wooden wedges jammed over the pedals to keep them on track. The triggers were simple clock timers attached to the detonators they'd found at Wembley.

It had been a rush to get them ready on time, working for days and nights up at Saif's camp in IKEA. Like one of those cable shows where men with beards made things from scrap. They wished they'd been ready yesterday, but hadn't wanted to risk going off half-cocked. It had to work.

And my God, did it work! They must've blasted half St George's army into dust. They looked round to where Saif and Shadowman were watching the carnage from behind some safety barriers. The two boys high-fived each other and then came over and hugged Ben and Bernie.

'They weren't expecting that,' said Saif.

'I'm just pissed off that the last one didn't explode,' said Bernie. 'Ten out of ten I was hoping for.'

'Nine is plenty good enough,' said Saif. 'You two don't need to come and fight,' he added. 'Take yourself somewhere safe and stay out of it. You done your part.'

'Don't worry,' said Bernie. 'We're not intending to fight.'

'Takes all sorts to win a war,' said Shadowman. 'Stay alive.'

'Now it's our turn to fight,' said Saif, turning to face his troops who were lined up on North Carriage Drive and the Bayswater Road. They were ready to march against St George's army from the rear once all the chemicals had burned themselves out.

'You with us, Shadowman?'

'Something I have to do first,' said Shadowman.

'Always the same with you,' said Saif. 'Always got your own plans.' And he slapped Shadowman's palm again. 'You know I never liked you at first, fam. Didn't trust you. Thought I knew best.'

'No problem,' said Shadowman. 'We all make mistakes. Main thing is – we gotta win this. That's all that matters.'

Shadowman hurried away. Skirting along the top of the park towards Park Lane, moving fast, his grey cloak flapping behind him, his pack strapped tightly to his chest, his crossbow slung across his back. He then headed south down Park Lane towards where David and Jester had their HQ. He was confident he could get close without being seen. This was what he did best. He was always happiest working alone. Watching without being seen. He could hide three metres from someone and they'd never know he was there.

As he got closer to David's camp, he slowed down and moved more cautiously. Lots of kids were leaving the park and crossing the road. Like rats escaping a burning building. They looked mostly like John's squatters, though Shadowman spotted a couple of red blazers in among them.

Shadowman strolled over and merged in with them, walking casually. He knew that if you acted like you were supposed to be there people didn't question you. He was checking their faces, looking for one in particular. No good – he needed a better view. He spotted a tree with some accessible lower branches near the edge of the park. He drifted over and pulled himself quickly up into it,

keeping the trunk between him and the deserting kids. He climbed higher. The tree was just tall enough to give him a reasonable view of the battlefield.

The explosions had made a massive difference. Where once the sickos had seemed to fill the park, the rear half of them had gone – reduced to smoking debris. And most of the rest had broken up into small clumps, ragged and disorganized. To the south, kids were streaming out of Jordan's encampment and tearing into them.

The battle was far from over, though. The sickos still massively outnumbered the children, and in the centre was St George – like a queen bee in the middle of a swarm – his sickos grouping up round him in a big circle. Slowly more were joining, getting organized again. And there, closer, another organized group, centred round a second powerful sicko.

No – definitely not over yet.

Shadowman switched his attention back to the road. He took out his binoculars and focused them on the deserting kids. Scanning them for a familiar coat. You couldn't miss it. And only one person wore one like it.

A coat made of different coloured patches.

Shadowman had unfinished business.

It was only by pure chance that Jester had seen him. He'd sneaked to the edge of the camp to hide his coat under a hut. He stood out too much in it. He didn't want to risk David or any of his guards spotting him as he made his getaway. He'd been super sensitive, looking around in all directions, *and there he was*, climbing up into a tree – Shadowman. Dylan Peake. Jester's oldest surviving friend and the person who most wanted him dead in the world.

Jester sucked in his breath and then let it out with a curse. He knew in his bones that Shadowman was looking for him. He was up in the tree, perched there, scanning the road with his binoculars. He was good. Shadowman had always been good. If Jester hadn't been alert to even the smallest movement he'd never have seen him up there, still now, blending in, the same colour as the tree trunk.

Jester had had it all planned. He was doing what he did best. Saving his own skin. He was going to go back to the palace while David wasn't there and make it his own. Lock David out. It was the only sensible thing to do. Jester could do deals with everybody. Make friends. Get all this crap sorted out. David had been a good leader, but he'd lost it. When leaders wig out, you had to get rid of them.

Killing Nicola. That was wrong. However you looked at it. David had gone too far. Someone really needed to stop him.

Jester would leave that to a soldier. He was a thinker not a fighter.

Jester knew what Shadowman would say if he found him. Shadowman was one of those irritating people who always tried to do the right thing. Tried to be good.

He'd lay into Jester. Attack him for what David had done. Say that Jester was part of it. Say that Jester couldn't just run . . .

The thing was, Shadowman was right.

Jester swore. Sat down behind the hut where Shadowman couldn't see him. Fought back tears. He reached under the hut for his rolled-up coat.

He couldn't leave the battle like this. He had to try to stop David. If Jester was ever going to look Shadowman in the eye again . . . No, not just Shadowman. If Jester was

ever going to be able to look at his own reflection in the mirror again he had to do the right thing.

For once in his life he had to think about someone else.

He put his coat on.

He was going back.

'It's all right. It's all right. Hold on.' Archie Bishop was with one of the guys who'd joined them recently. The boy had a big nose and Archie was pretty sure he was called Andy. Didn't know anything else about him. Never would now. In the last few days a lot of other kids had joined up with Matt. Drawn by the promise of heavenly protection. Of something else to believe in outside this world of pain and death and filth.

And most of them were dead.

Andy had a piece of fencing stuck through his body. A long, jagged bit of wood. Archie had watched helplessly as a mother had rammed it into him and then moved on.

Archie had his arms round Andy and was covered in his blood. He wasn't sure how much longer he could keep going. At least half of his friends from St Paul's had been killed. They'd tried to protect themselves from the surging mass of sickos around them, but they hadn't been strong enough. Religious chants and banners were no protection against teeth and fingernails, twisted bits of metal, rocks and spikes. Only the best fighters were left standing, or maybe just the luckiest ones, those that had better weapons. But they'd become cut off from the main body of Jordan's army and now, in the confusion and

chaos of the battle. Archie had no idea what was happening anywhere else. Were the kids winning? Or were the sickos massacring them all?

'Attack me! I am the one! I am the Nemesis! Attack me!' Matt was pushing past, holding up the first banner they'd ever made, the one that showed the Lamb and the Goat – the shining boy and the shadowy boy. With the legend 'Angus Day'. Funny if it wasn't so tragic. Like this whole day really.

Matt marched into the surrounding sickos and they fell aside, moved away from him like water when you dropped oil in it. Opposing magnets. They wouldn't touch Matt. It was as if he had an invisible force field around him, which in turn made *him* invisible. Like dark matter. Archie grabbed him and pulled him back.

'You stay with us,' he said. 'Protect us.'

'Why won't they attack me?' said Matt, looking desperate.

'How am I supposed to know?' Archie shouted. 'But if you can protect us then please do.'

Matt grabbed Archie's arm so tightly it hurt, a mad look in his eye.

'Help is coming,' he said. 'The Lamb is sending his angels. I see heaven standing open and there before me are two white horses, and their riders are dressed in shining gold. And they follow a king, dressed in a robe dipped in blood. The armies of heaven are following him, riding locusts that look like horses prepared for battle, and their teeth are like lions' teeth. They are strong, they have breastplates of iron, and the sound of their wings is like the thundering of many horses and chariots rushing into battle.'

Archie wanted to hit him. They had to fight, not wait for heavenly superheroes.

'Can you hear them!' Matt cried out. 'They are coming! They have heard us calling to them. The Nephilim have killed the boy, but the Lamb lives! They're coming. Can't you hear them?'

Archie could hear nothing, except the relentless, dreary drone of the fighting, the hiss of the sickos, the gasps and grunts and wheezing breath of the exhausted kids, the screams of the dying. Was Matt really expecting a swarm of locusts to come to their rescue? Locusts, or angels, or golden figures on horses . . .

'Listen! Can't you hear them?'

Archie was listening, but he felt a fool for doing it. There was no buzz, no hum, no beating of wings.

'Don't give up!' Matt shouted. 'I hear the voice of many angels, numbering thousands upon thousands, and ten thousand times ten thousand. They are coming. He has not abandoned us. The Nephilim will be defeated.'

Archie had to believe him. He had no choice. The alternative was to accept defeat. To accept oblivion. Hope was all they had left. Hope and belief.

The Lamb would protect them.

Paul looked up at the sky. Boney-M was there, and he had his friends with him. They were black shapes circling, their leathery wings tattered and ripped, their broken limbs held together with scraps of skin and sinew, their dark faces twisted, beady black eyes staring down at the battlefield. And every now and then one of them would come screaming down, take up a soul and carry it off to hell. They were cleaning the battlefield. Taking their harvest.

Now Boney-M himself swooped straight down at Paul. Paul shielded his face, yelled in fear, but Boney settled on the ground, clattered about, his long beak clacking. Staring at Paul, swearing at Paul, laughing at him.

'You terrible streak of shite,' he said. 'You think you're God? You're not even fit to lick my toenails. Been talking to them, have you? The stinking sickbags? Giving them the word of God? Really? Earth to Sonny Jim – *you're not God. I am.* The great God of War. Me and my Valkyries will strip the battlefield and make an army of the dead. You never were anything. You never amounted to anything. What was all this for? Your sister? Those children didn't kill your sister and you know it. The Collector. Remember him? The greasy fat blob of guts. You know

full well it was him that killed your Olivia. This whole thing has been a waste of time. They've beaten you, the sickos. They put their poison in you, their parasites. That's all you are, a carrier for their germs. A dupe. And you see him, there, coming towards you . . . ?'

Paul turned quickly as Boney collapsed into harsh laughter. Jester was pushing his way through David's kids towards him. Paul turned back to Boney-M.

'What does he want?' he said, but Boney-M had gone, and when Paul looked up at the sky there were only seagulls there.

Jester looked at Paul. He didn't know the boy at all. Had no idea what his story was. Why he was so unhinged. How he could communicate with the sickos. He'd run away from the Natural History Museum and joined David at the palace only a couple of weeks ago. He'd been crazy when he turned up and he was crazy now.

All Jester knew at that moment was that Paul was helping David, and David was helping St George. And Jester had to stop it. He should have done this before. He should never have let it get this far. He looked past Paul, past their flimsy wooden barricades, to where the vile horde of adults was trudging slowly towards Jordan's kids. Ignoring David's camp.

It wasn't David's wooden wall that was keeping the sickos from attacking them. It was Paul, using whatever weird skill he had. It was all down to his link with the sickos. However it worked, it had to be shut off, and there was a chance now, a tiny chance, that Jordan could swing the battle. Obliterate St George and his army, stop them from being any kind of threat. Surely every sicko for miles

around was gathered here today. What if the kids could wipe them out?

Jester was going to do it. He was going to do the right thing. He was going to stop Paul from helping.

'Paul!' he shouted. 'Stop this. Switch it off. That signal in your head. The voice you use to talk to them. Silence it.'

Paul shook his head. He was dripping with sweat, bone-white, the veins showing beneath his skin, his eyes red and feverish. He was trembling. But he was shutting Jester out.

'I said stop,' Jester yelled. 'Stop now. Stop what you're doing.'

'I can't stop it,' said Paul, his voice not much more than a whisper. 'It's too late. It's done. Let them all die. Let this be the end. The end of everything. Armageddon. Let it all finish now. No more pain. No more fear. Why struggle? Why fight against it? Let it all come down . . .'

'*You* might not have anything to live for,' said Jester angrily, tears in his eyes, 'but *I* do. All those other kids out there do. You can't allow them to die. You're not more important than them.'

'We're none of us important,' said Paul. 'We're all just parasites. What difference does it make if we live or die?'

'All right then,' said Jester. 'If that's how you want it then that's how it's gonna be.'

He threw himself at Paul, grabbed him by the throat and toppled him to the ground. He could hear kids behind him shouting. Ignored them. Kept up the pressure on Paul's neck.

He didn't know if he could do it. If he could take Paul's life. Even knowing that if he did he could be saving

hundreds more. In the end Paul was a boy like him, and he had a look of such deep sadness in his eyes it was making Jester weak. He was just about to let go when something appalling happened. The side of Paul's neck gave way like wet paper, as if there was nothing under the skin, the flesh all rotted away to nothing. Jester's fingers sank inside Paul's neck and his head flopped to one side as a gout of green and yellow pus squelched out from under his roll-neck collar. Jester yelled in fright and jerked his hand away. It was dripping with grey jelly. More of the jelly was oozing out of Paul. It seemed to be alive, writhing and bubbling and crawling. Paul pulled down his collar. There was a huge dark hole in his neck, packed with living jelly.

'Thank you,' he said, smiled and his eyes rolled up in their sockets and closed.

Jester doubled over and was sick into the grass.

Someone was pulling at his coat. Jester felt it rip. He looked round. It was David. He pulled Jester to his feet and away from Paul. Jester couldn't look back, but David's eyes were fixed on Paul's dead body.

'What have we done?' said David. 'What were we thinking . . . ?'

Jester could feel a change. The link with the sickos had been broken. The magic circle was no more.

They had no protection.

Franny was working in the palace garden. She had a small team with her, heads down, kneeling by a vegetable bed. As long as they worked, they didn't have to think about what was going on in Hyde Park. All the kitchen staff were still here, the garden workers, the nursing and household staff. All going about their business as if nothing was any different. Occasionally the wind would change direction and they'd hear sounds from the park – music, the cries of birds, shouting. Screams. Not enough to tell them exactly what was going on, but enough to remind them that something was. Something huge and momentous. And then there had been a series of explosions.

She was pleased that David was out there fighting the adults. Ridding the world of them. He would come back in triumph as their saviour. He'd be pleased that Franny had kept things together here at the palace. Maybe he'd even . . . ?

No. He never thought of her that way. She was just good old Franny. Franny who looked after the garden. Franny who kept everything in order, who made sure they always had food.

She straightened up. Her back was stiff. She arched her

spine, pulling her shoulders back, hands behind her head, and glanced up at the palace.

She frowned.

Pod was back. She set off running towards him, dodging between the beds, up to where he stood by the main doors that led from the palace to the garden.

Was it over? Had he come back to tell them the good news? Victory? No . . . As Franny got nearer, she could see that he was troubled. Frowning and fidgety, running his fingers through his thick helmet of hair.

'What's up?' she said. 'Is everything all right?'

Pod shook his head.

She hadn't seen him like this before. Pod never worried about things. He just got on with stuff.

'What is it?' Franny asked, desperate for news. 'Why are you back? Is David back?'

'No,' said Pod. 'He is *not*. David is not back.'

'What's he doing?' said Franny. 'Are we beating the strangers?'

'We're not even fighting them,' said Pod.

'What do you mean? Why aren't we fighting them?'

'Because we're on their side,' said Pod and he laughed the worst, most horrible laugh Franny had ever heard.

Most of the other gardeners had come up to see what was going on. They were crowding round Pod, all asking for answers.

'You've got to tell us,' said Franny. 'We don't know anything here.'

And then Pod looked at her, with horror in his eyes, and he told her. And as he talked Franny put her hand in her mouth, biting the soft flesh between her thumb and forefinger. So hard it started to bleed. She felt like she was

going to be sick. When Pod told her how David had shot Nicola, she actually screamed.

'I had to come back,' said Pod. 'I couldn't stay there. It's wrong what David's doing. If he comes back here we mustn't let him in.'

Franny was trembling. *Not let David back in?* The world was shifting all around her. Everything she believed in was being turned upside down. What were they going to do without David? But what had David done? It couldn't be true. It made no sense.

And then three of Pod's guys came running out of the doors and into the garden.

'You gotta come quick,' one shouted and Pod hurried inside.

Franny followed. Desperate to keep up with what was going on. They got to the central courtyard. People had gathered here and there was a babble of voices. A group of palace kids were arguing with a group of squatters from St James's Park.

'Oi! What are you doing?' Pod shouted when he saw what was going on. 'You shouldn't be here.'

'No, what are you doing here?' said a squatter. Franny recognized him as their leader, John. 'Shouldn't you be in the park with King David? Partying with your zombie brothers?'

'No,' said Pod. 'We're not supporting David any more.'

'Neither are we,' said John. 'We've come to defend the palace for when David comes back against you.'

Pod smiled. Franny didn't. Pod wasn't the brightest bulb on the Christmas tree. She wanted to shout out – *you shouldn't trust these people.*

One of Pod's guys came over.

'This lot got in before we could close the doors,' he said. 'There's bare more out on the parade ground. Do we let them in?'

'I'm not sure they should come in,' said Pod.

'Nice way to make us welcome,' said John. 'We thought you was our friends. We supposed to be allies. We have an agreement.'

'Your agreement was with David,' said Franny.

'No matter,' said John. 'We can make a new agreement with you. I'm just gonna go open the doors first.'

'No, you're not,' said Pod.

'Could you even stop us?'

Franny saw that the squatters were all armed and a couple turned to threaten the palace kids. The squatters were outnumbered, but they were a vicious-looking bunch.

'Get out of here,' said Pod, red with anger.

John looked round the courtyard. Franny wondered if he was remembering his humiliation here, when Achilleus had beaten him in single combat.

Then he slapped Pod round the face, stunning him into silence.

'We taking over,' he said. 'See? David had his chance and he blew it. This is our place now.'

The other squatters sniggered.

'No,' said Pod. 'No, no, no. This isn't right. We need to talk about this.'

'Talk about this,' said John, and he shoved his spear through Pod's chest. Pod choked and grunted. He gave a low growl in his throat and slowly sank down until he was sitting on the ground, his jumper already soaked with blood. Franny ran to him and he held tight to her. He was shivering, his face white.

'I'm really disappointed,' he said, and then went limp in Franny's arms.

'Let the others in,' said John. 'We're in charge here. Let's raise our flag and celebrate.'

'Yeah,' said Carl, John's second in command. 'It's party time!'

The sickos were slowly closing in from all sides. Like an overflow of thick brown sludge. Jester watched as a group of them reached down and took hold of Paul's body and pulled it into the mob, as if they were one huge organism and their hands were feelers, sucking him into their gut. Jester didn't want to picture what they would be doing to Paul. Other fallen bodies around them were being dragged away in the same manner.

David and Jester were now surrounded by a circle of the palace guard, wearing their red blazers, their guns facing out. It was like a scene from history – the Battle of Waterloo or Custer's last stand. A tiny force holding out against an unimaginably large one. David's boys had started by firing volleys, but now all they managed were ragged, weary shots as they reloaded, working their way through the few bullets they had left in their magazines. The air was filled with the smell of cordite and they were surrounded by a thin haze of smoke. With each bang, a sicko jerked back or fell, but the ones behind just kept on coming, trampling over the dead and wounded, coming closer and closer, ever closer.

There was no way to stop them.

Jester had a sword in his hand. He'd never been the greatest fighter in the world. He was better than David,

though. He'd never seen David even try to fight. He didn't even have a weapon. Jester was ready. He would fight hard, though he knew he was going to lose in the end. He could already picture those filthy hands grasping for him, those mouths slobbering at his face.

He looked to David. He was trying to be brave. Standing tall, a leader to the last . . . but his face was pale, the muscles rigid and frozen.

'We nearly did it,' he said.

'Was it so important?' said Jester. 'Was it worth losing our lives, just to be at the top of the heap?'

'I don't know.'

'Did we do anything right?' said Jester.

'I don't know, I don't know, I don't know.'

Jester turned to David. He was crying.

'All I want now is my mum,' he said. He looked about ten years old. 'All I want is to be with her. I want her to hold me and say she loves me. I want her to tell me that everything's all right. That's how the world used to be. It was simple. And then we grew up. I just want my mum.'

David broke down completely, shaking with sobs. Jester put his arms round him and held on to him. Maybe he wouldn't fight at all. Maybe he'd just let them roll over him and be done with it. The guns were silent, emptied of their bullets. They were being pulled out of the boys' hands. Jester could hear the screams as the sickos came in. He felt the great crush of them around him – rotten, decaying, falling apart, clawing at the boys.

'We're just kids,' said David. 'How could we be expected to make the right decisions?'

Jester closed his eyes and held David tight.

'It's all right,' he whispered in his ear. 'It's over now.'

For a while there it had looked like they were going to win. Ollie had watched Achilleus's group attacking from the right and Matt's group going in from the left. He'd watched Jordan send Jackson out to reinforce Achilleus, pushing hard on the right and forcing the sickos back. And then there had been the explosions, cutting into the rear of St George's army. This had encouraged Jordan enough to open the barricades on the left to let more troops out. These new reinforcements hadn't made it to where Matt's group was surrounded in the middle of the battlefield, though. They'd got bogged down in the sheer press of sickos and now both groups were marooned and the mob of sickos – stung from the right, blasted from the rear, held down in the centre – had gone into a sort of stampede and come pushing and crashing and charging right over the reinforcements and into the encampment. Jordan had ordered fires to be lit, burning some of the sickos on the left, but it wasn't enough. They had got in and were now filling the camp. Even Jordan had been forced to come down off his platform to rally his troops. Stand tall at their centre.

Ollie needed to see what was happening. He climbed on to the roof of the LookOut and scanned the battlefield.

Blu-Tack Bill was up here by himself, absorbed with the lump of Blu-tack he spent all his time moulding into different shapes, ignoring the battle.

Ollie could see that the sickos were crammed into the area inside the barricades. Most of the kids had formed up around Jordan, but there was a second group of fighters down by the water's edge, trying to protect the Twisted Kids. Maxie and Blue were with them.

Some of the Twisted Kids were fighting back. Ollie could see Monstar picking sickos up and hurling them away, trying to protect the Warehouse Queen, who was concentrating on sending out her signal to disrupt the attackers. The signal was still working. Most of the sickos who got too close seemed to get possessed by demons, as if stung by a swarm of bees. They would go berserk, lashing out at anyone or anything around them. The organized attack of yesterday had long ago fallen apart. Sickos were just as likely to be fighting each other as the outnumbered kids who were so desperately clinging on here.

This wasn't a clear, ordered battle that you could draw a plan of afterwards, with neat blocks of infantry and cavalry and artillery moving around on the battlefield in the direction of nice bold arrows. It was a chaotic, milling riot. Sickos wandering around, lashing out at whoever was nearest to them, occasionally getting hold of a kid and tearing them to bits. The whole camp was filled. The kids by the water couldn't run. The lake was at their backs. The kids who had been ferrying the wounded across the water had taken their boats to the other side and were cowering over there.

Ollie saw Skinner, his mouth open in his silent shout. He seemed to be able to direct the noise at the sickos. But

occasionally it would break through and Ollie would feel as if a power drill was spinning inside his brain. Luckily this only ever seemed to last for a few moments before Skinner refocused the signal on the sickos. The Twisted Kids were being steadily beaten down, though. They'd made a sort of force field around themselves, but some sickos were still breaking through and tearing at them. And then Skinner was hit by something. A sicko with an iron spike had got in close. Ollie saw Skinner flinch and felt his cry of pain. It filled every brain in the area, scraping at their nervous system. It was as if Ollie himself had been stabbed. He even had to look to make sure he wasn't.

He jumped down off the platform, started pulling kids together, creating a small fighting unit. Jordan's defence was stronger and better organized than the smaller force of kids by the Serpentine. Jordan could spare the numbers.

'Come on,' said Ollie. 'We're going to help.'

He picked up a sword that someone had dropped and pushed his way through the scrum of sickos in front of him, hacking to left and right, dodging between bodies. He and his group were fast and determined. They managed to make it down to the lakeside unhurt and cut their way through the sickos surrounding the Twisted Kids. Maxie saw them arrive and came over.

'Are you the cavalry?' she said.

'I wish,' said Ollie. 'You need to come over to the other side and join up with Jordan.'

'Do you reckon we can make it?'

'We just did.'

'OK.'

Maxie and Blue started shouting commands, drawing their kids into a protective semicircle, holding the sickos

back. Ollie went to the Twisted Kids. As well as Skinner, at least two more of them were down. Ollie could see a kid who looked like Legs being mauled under the feet of a knot of snapping sickos. A determined group of fathers was coming in at Monstar, seemingly aware that if they could get to the Warehouse Queen and silence her their lives would be easier. Ollie and his team were just able to push back their attack. He could see that Skinner was hurt, bleeding badly, but still alive. TV Boy was holding him in his lap. It was hard to see just how bad Skinner's wound was as it had got round the side of his breastplate and was hidden by the armour.

'You all right, Skinny?' Ollie asked him and Skinner gave a small, tight nod. He was obviously more hurt than he wanted to let on.

'We need to get you to safety,' said Ollie. 'We gotta move. Can you make it?'

Skinner nodded again. Monstar had heard their conversation and he started to organize the Twisted Kids.

Ollie became aware of a deep bass rumble, a roaring and whining, as if the combined mass of the sickos were growling in their throats. He wondered what fresh horror this might be.

'All of you!' he yelled. 'We have to join up with Jordan's group and form a defence around the LookOut. We need to get together, stay together and fight together. Follow me and Maxie and Blue. Protect your friends. Don't think about it, just go.'

He moved forward, pleased to see that all the others came with him. They reformed into a wedge, weapons bristling on either side, pushing through the sickos. Maxie encouraging them, Blue yelling at them, more terrifying

than the enemy, Ollie bringing up the rear, moving backwards, the way he preferred to fight. The Twisted Kids were being kept safe in the centre, the stronger ones carrying the less able, all the while sending out their mental disruption field.

Step after step. Cut after cut. Blow after blow.

Ollie became aware of that ominous rumble again and tried to shut it out of his mind. All he needed to do now was concentrate on the sickos in front of him. Try not to get killed. Join up with Jordan. Create a much stronger unit. Shut out the fear. Keep moving. Keep fighting. Stay alive. Even if it was for only one more precious minute . . .

John's squatters were running wild in the palace, beating up Franny's friends, pushing over statues, slashing paintings, smashing ornate plates, breaking windows and mirrors.

The palace kids could do nothing but try to keep out of the way, run and hide. Franny had gone out into the garden. She was horrified to find a group of boys pulling up plants, kicking the beds.

'No,' she screamed at them. 'What are you doing? That's our food, our only way of surviving. Do anything, but leave the food, leave our crops.'

The squatters had just turned and laughed at her. She'd fallen to her knees, seen that her dress was spattered with Pod's blood.

She was filled with a cold fury. This was so senseless. She wasn't going to let them destroy everything she'd spent a year building up. She strode round towards the shed where they kept the tools, pushing squatters out of the way. Some of her gardeners saw where she was going and came with her. They got into the shed and grabbed tools – axes, spades, tree saws . . .

Franny had a big garden fork. She came striding out. Back round the side of the buildings. Saw John standing

by the doors, looking out over the garden, laughing and cheering his people on. She walked towards him, broke into a run. Faster and faster. At the last moment he turned, but it was too late. She rammed the fork into his chest, just as he had rammed his spear into Pod. He made no noise. Said nothing. He was killed instantly. He fell down, Franny's fork still sticking out of him. Franny stood there, looking around, unable to believe what she had just done. Everyone had frozen. Her friends, the squatters, all staring at her . . .

What would happen now? There was no going back. What would they do to her?

And then she heard a sound. One she didn't expect to hear. Nothing about this day made any sense. She didn't believe any of it.

It was the sound of laughter.

The squatters were laughing.

Shadowman had watched from the tree as David's small force was overwhelmed by sickos. Nothing left of them now. David gone. Jester gone. Shadowman didn't know what to think. Jester had been his friend once.

And now he was dead. Like so many others.

Jester hadn't run. He'd died bravely. Shadowman felt tears running down his face. He wiped them away.

For now, he had to shut down his emotions. There was work to be done. The sickos hadn't been defeated.

The rage of the battle had sucked the sickos out of the entertainments area and back into the open ground around Jordan's encampment. Shadowman climbed down out of his tree and moved in closer, crossing the patch where he'd seen Jester die. Nothing was left of David and his kids except for scraps of red blazer and shredded pieces of unidentifiable flesh and bone. Shadowman worked his way across and climbed a speaker tower that gave him a good view of the wider battlefield.

Could one person really make a difference? Ben and Bernie. There were only two of them, but they'd taken out half of St George's troops. What could Shadowman do to match that?

He had a bolt already fitted in his crossbow and wanted

to make sure he used it well. He couldn't get to St George, who was protected right at the heart of his army. But there was clearly more than one mind at work here, directing the sicko army.

While the order of the attack had been disrupted, there were still parts of the army that functioned better than others. From down below it had looked like chaos, but from high up here Shadowman could make out an underlying shape to the battle. A purpose.

He had seen over and over how St George used his more intelligent lieutenants to organize his troops. Man U and Bluetooth, the One-Armed Bandit and Spike. He was pretty sure they were all dead now, but someone was still down there, getting inside the sickos' minds.

What could Shadowman do, though? From here the army was just a solid mass. He remembered how he'd once shot a bolt blindly into a group of St George's sickos who'd been killing some children. Where had that been? Somewhere up near Hampstead Heath? Later on he'd discovered that, against all the odds, he'd hit a sicko in the chest. And that had been Spike.

What were the chances of hitting anyone important from up here?

He got out his binoculars and scanned the battlefield.

And then he saw the tall woman. With the long, straight hair. The one who had organized the attack on Yo-Yo. There she was, her head towering above the crouched and slouching sickos around her. She was leading a large group of them, round the back of the main army and down the side. Shadowman could see that her plan was to attack the rear of the kids who were engaged in a hard-fought stand on this side of the battlefield.

Shadowman swung his binoculars round, trained them on the kids. He could just make out Ryan, Achilleus and Jackson, battling hard among the swarming sickos.

He aimed his crossbow carefully at the Tall Woman. Loosed off a shot. Missed. Was she too far away?

Calmly he fitted another bolt. Aimed again and missed again. He had hit Spike when he hadn't been aiming for him, but that had been pure luck. Up here like this, from this distance . . .

He thought of all the kids he'd known who'd died in the last year. Too many to count. And then there were all the kids he hadn't known, the nameless kids he'd watched die at the hands of sickos.

He thought of the boy in Waitrose – his head carried out on a stick by St George. He thought of all the kids across north London, pulled out of their hiding places, torn apart and eaten. He thought of Yo-Yo, disappearing through the window. Thought about how he hadn't been able to save her . . .

The third bolt hit home firmly between the Tall Woman's shoulder blades and she fell down. Instantly her group broke up, all sense of purpose gone. Like a pulled thread from a woven pattern, the sicko army lost its shape.

Could one person make a difference?

Shadowman climbed down from the scaffold tower and started to work his way round towards where Achilleus was fighting for his life.

It was time to join the battle.

75

Ollie was so wiped out he wondered if he was going nuts. Losing it big time. Hearing things that couldn't be there. Things from the past. From television and films. The *old* world. Gunshots, car horns, engines, horses . . .

He was packed into a tight corner, his sword rising and falling, rising and falling . . . One by one the children around him were going down. He'd lost track of Maxie and Blue and the Twisted Kids. His focus had narrowed down to the small area in front of him, killing any sickos that came into it, his arm ready to drop off, his lungs on fire, his guts in a tight, painful knot.

And then he felt something, a subtle release of pressure, as if a taut wire holding the sickos together had snapped. They fell back and Ollie could take a deep breath. He heard distant cheers and shouts of encouragement. What was happening? One way to find out. He smashed his way over to the ladder, managed to haul himself up to the roof of the LookOut. Jordan was back up there, Blu-Tack Bill whispering in his ear.

'What is it?' said Ollie. 'What's changed?'

Bill pointed and Ollie looked out over the park to the west, not trusting his eyes. He rubbed his aching temples, looked again.

He wasn't going nuts. He wasn't imagining things. There was a line of cars advancing across the park, pickup trucks with troops in the back, other kids riding horses. He saw a boy and a girl dressed in gold on big white chargers.

At the front was a blue people carrier. Could it be the one that Ed had left in? Ollie watched as it stopped and the doors slid open.

Yes. It *was* Ed. With Kyle and Lewis and Brooke and Ebenezer. Trinity as well. And Ella with a boy who had a horribly scarred face. Ed was already shouting commands. Kids were leaping down from the trucks. Others were firing arrows, rifles.

Ollie laughed.

'It's Ed,' he shouted. 'The cavalry's arrived. It's Ed! We're gonna do this, Jordan. We're gonna beat St George.'

He looked around wildly, trying to see if any of Jordan's trumpeters were alive. Saw a huddle of them hiding among some wheelie bins at the rear of the LookOut.

'Up here!' he screamed. 'Get up here and bring your trumpets.'

He turned to Jordan. 'We need to break out of this camp,' he said. 'Lead us out of here so we can join up with Ed.'

Jordan nodded, started giving orders to the trumpeters who were scrambling up to join them. Soon their horns were blaring, giving hope to all the kids who were fighting in small knots across the park. Ollie could see Matt's banners and a clump of green kids in the middle. Further away, Will and Hayden with a group of Tower kids, trapped among some trees; in another circle, to the right, were Jackson, Achilleus and Ryan.

Ollie was waving his arms and yelling, though there was no way they could hear him.

'Don't give up! Ed's back. Join together.'

He shook Jordan.

'Tell the trumpeters,' he said. 'Tell them that we all need to join together.'

'I've told 'em, soldier,' said Jordan. 'It's happening. I've given the signals. So let's go.'

Ollie glanced at Ed's troops who were slowly advancing. Archers firing flat and low, javelin and spear throwers hurling their weapons into the retreating sickos; those with guns taking careful aim, experienced fighters charging in.

Ollie jumped down from the platform, flushed with a new energy and hope. Jordan's ragged troops were starting to form a line. Jordan came down and forced some sense of order and discipline into the weary mob.

And then they were moving, across the camp, cutting down any sickos who tried to stop them, out through the gap between the barricades, out into the main body of St George's army.

Jackson had sensed the change as well. Two changes. First a loosening of discipline among the already wild sickos and now a loss of fight. As if they knew they were beaten. For the first time they were retreating.

'This is new,' she said and Achilleus grunted.

They heard the trumpets sounding and Jackson tried to remember what all the different commands meant.

'I think we need to try and join up with the rest of the army,' she said as something clicked into place in her exhausted brain. 'A last rally.'

'Come on then,' said Achilleus. He was a fierce sight, caked with blood, some dark and drying, some fresh and bright. She looked down at herself. Knew she must look

the same. Ryan's leather was black with gore, ripped in patches, the bits of fur he wore matted and dripping.

'Let's move it,' he said and the three of them were shouting commands, forming their kids into a tighter unit. There were maybe a third of them left from when they'd started. Nearly all of Nicola's kids were dead. The last to die had been Bozo, still wearing his policeman's helmet. But the new arrivals from the museum hadn't done much better. Jackson had seen Boggle stabbed through the heart as he'd tried to save a friend from a group of young mothers.

Maybe if they could link up with other fighters the rest of them had a chance of surviving this.

They started to push their way across the slippery grass, keeping the barricades on their left as protection, their strongest fighters on the right to keep the sickos back, aiming towards the few remaining green banners of Matt's group in the middle of the park. On the way they picked up smaller, isolated groups of fighting kids, swelling their numbers as they trudged on. It wasn't a question of fighting. All they could do was push and shove and smash sickos out of their way.

They *were* advancing, though, slowly and agonizingly. Protecting each other. Jackson found herself crushed up against Achilleus, struggling to breathe as her chest and lungs were squeezed by the crush of bodies.

'Don't give up, girl,' he said.

'Not planning to, boy,' she replied.

Achilleus rammed his spear point into a father's mouth and he dropped out of their way.

But they were stuck now, too many bodies in front of them.

'This way!' It was Shadowman, off to their right. He had taken charge of a smaller group and they'd cut a path towards Matt's kids.

'Push right!' Jackson yelled. 'Go right!'

Their unit wheeled, pulling round the dense knot of sickos who'd been blocking their path. Moved quicker, Shadowman falling in beside her and Achilleus. And then Jackson looked up. She could see a banner fluttering in the breeze above their heads.

They'd made it to Matt. The pressure was relieved as the two groups joined together and filled out into a circle. There was Matt, surrounded by the last shattered survivors from St Paul's. They were singing and Matt was yelling something incoherent about angels that Jackson couldn't understand at all.

'Together,' Jackson ordered them. 'Stay together. We're moving on. We have to link up with the main army.'

With the St Paul's kids joining their force, they were able to push on faster, the sickos moving away from them. Jackson had even joined in the singing, wordlessly, just bellowing out a noise, bellowing out the joy of still being alive.

They walked, side by side, they speeded up, they broke into a run, they charged past sickos, swatting at them as they went, and at last they met Jordan's forces who were erupting from the encampment. Now they were one army. And Jordan was taking charge. Leading them on westwards.

They formed into a massive fighting unit with Jordan, Achilleus, Ryan, Jackson, Maxie, Blue and Ollie at the front. Jackson had no idea where exactly they were heading or why. She was just happy to follow Jordan. He seemed to have a plan.

The sickos had lost all discipline now. They even appeared to have lost the will to fight. They were hurrying away from Jordan's force. But there was more fighting up ahead. The sickos were running on to the weapons of another unit.

And then Jackson saw what was happening. Reinforcements had arrived. Ed had returned. Jordan was linking his forces up with his.

And what forces! Jordan could see cars and vans, trucks, kids on horses with lances, archers, kids with guns . . .

'Halle-bloody-lujah!' Jackson shouted, and lunged at a mother who came close, smashing her spear into the sicko's face, destroying her nose and upper jaw.

Hallelujah. Lord knows where Ed had found his own army, but thank God he had.

Jordan's troops surged in and linked up with them, and they turned as one and attacked. Now was the time to kill. To take their revenge. There was no stopping the kids now. Jackson knew they would be merciless, utterly merciless, in flattening the disorderly remains of St George's army.

A war cry of triumph erupted along the lines, as steadily they drove forward, cutting, slicing, stabbing, pushing, crushing skulls with clubs, splitting bones with sword and axe.

Destroying the threat that had terrified them for the last year. Preyed on them. Ruined their lives.

Jackson spotted Ed, his scarred face cold and terrifying, moving like a machine, Kyle at his side with a look of intense joy on his face.

They were going to win.

It had been one of the tensest few hours that Ed could remember. Ironic, really, as nothing had actually happened – there had been no threat, no sign of any sickos, no danger on the road until they'd come rumbling into Hyde Park.

But the journey had still seemed to take forever. Made almost unbearable by the fact that he'd had no idea what to expect when he got here. Trinity had picked up the message from the Twisted Kids, blurted it out – 'The boy was dead, the kids need your help, hurry before it's too late . . .'

Too late for what? Ed had some of the toughest fighters he'd ever met with him. The toughest and best equipped. They had vehicles, which meant they could travel fast. But not fast enough. What if they were too late? Would the day end in blood and disappointment?

And then when they'd got here, seeing the park full of so many sickos, living and dead, for a moment Ed had been afraid, wondering what they could do. But then the battle fury had come on him.

He had known what he could do.

This was his chance to crush them all. To take the battle to the sickos for a change. To tip the balance. He didn't

care about himself. Didn't care whether he lived or died. He'd become an animal. Killing without thinking. How could he ever go back to being a normal boy? He had taken death into his heart. It would never leave. He was a weapon.

And he would kill. For all those who still lived. Who deserved a future.

He was pressing forward, his mortuary sword doing its deadly work, for Sam and Ella. For DogNut and Macca and Adele. For Jack and Bam and all his friends from Rowhurst. This was going to be their day.

His sword came crashing down, cutting through a father's neck, and on down through his shoulder and out at his armpit, cutting his body in two. And Kyle was with him, his axe crushing a mother's skull. Now Ed drove his sword forward into a father's belly, twisted, pulled it out, kicked him to the ground. Trampled over the body and moved on.

And on. He would go on until every last sicko was killed.

His people were dying. They were going down all around him. The voices in his head falling silent. His great swarm, this army that he'd put together, was dying. He howled with rage. This was not how it was meant to end. He was supposed to win. He was St George. He was the hero. He was supposed to kill the dragon. He wouldn't give up. Not yet. He would tear the heart out of the living. Even if he was the only one left, he would eat the children. He would devour them. The children that had caused all this trouble.

He punched his way to the front, shoving his people out of the way, and came to a small group of children who were cut off under some trees, tore into them, battering them with his bare hands, and picked up an axe.

Yes. A cleaver. He was a butcher. And he would butcher these bastards. He tried it, swinging at a girl, cutting her head half off. He smiled. The voices in his head had properly gone now. All of them. The children who'd been screaming at him had shut up too.

Everything was clear and bright. He thundered on, his great legs stamping at the ground.

I will kill them, he thought. *This isn't over.*

*

Ed looked along the line. They were marching in step – Ebenezer, Kyle, Malik, Maxie, Blue, Jackson, Achilleus, Ryan, Lewis, Ollie, Jordan . . . and there was Shadowman, joining on the end, his grey cloak flapping behind him.

Nothing could stop them. Nothing could defeat them. They were a team. Working together. Time seemed to slow. Ed was acutely aware of everything around him – the birds circling in the sky, the trees, the sickos crumbling before them.

The birds circling. The earth turning. Circling the sun. The planets and stars turning in the sky.

Such a long year it had been. Leaving Rowhurst on the coach. Greg driving. Greg the butcher. Greg who had killed Jack and Bam . . . Driving into London, joining up with Jordan and his guys at the Imperial War Museum. Helping Jack get home. Watching him and Bam die. And then the fire. It had swept through south London, forcing them all northwards. The battle at the bridge, the mad scramble to get on the boat, drifting down the Thames to the Tower of London. The months there, learning how to get from one day to the next. Turning, turning, turning. Raiding, scavenging, growing food, purifying water. The daily fight for survival. Turning, turning, turning.

Such a long year.

He tried to look ahead.

After this battle would there be anything left? Nothing he could see. Blackness. No, not even blackness. Whatever the world had been like before he was born and after he was dead. Nothing. Not existing.

All that mattered now was this moment. Making it count.

And then Ed saw him.

Breaking out of the mass of sickos. A red cross on a white vest. Splattered with gore. A bloody cleaver in his hand.

There was no mistaking that huge head. That face. Greg.

Greg the butcher. Greg who had thought the disease couldn't get him. Greg who had killed Ed's best friends. Greg who had given him his scar. Greg who had ruined him.

Could it really be him?

Could Greg really be St George?

Ed pushed his way over to Shadowman, smashing his sword sideways at a father without even registering he'd done it.

'Is that *him*?' he said.

'That's St George,' said Shadowman, and Ed gave a harsh bark of anger.

He'd thought he'd never see Greg again. Thought he must have died months ago. It had never occurred to him for one moment that the leader of this army could be his own enemy.

'This one's mine,' he said, pushing ahead of the others. 'Leave him.'

And, as the rest of the line of heroes hammered into Greg's army, Ed strode towards their leader.

He was alone with St George who was wearing Liam's glasses. His own son, who he'd suffocated to death on the coach, trying to protect him. Ed had forgotten what a brute of a creature he was. His thick legs sticking out of baggy shorts. His head bald and covered in boils. His arms like joints of meat.

Ed went to him, lifted his sword, swung it. Greg twisted and caught the blade on his cleaver, deflecting it. Luck? Or skill? Didn't make any difference, Ed had to try again.

This time he swung low, but a mother came in from the side and got in the way of the blow, taking it herself. The blade struck her deep and embedded itself in her hip bone. Ed could feel it stuck fast. He jerked it and tugged at it, but it wouldn't come loose. The mother went down, taking the sword with her. Ed glanced round just in time to see Greg coming at him, his cleaver swinging down from above his head. Ed threw himself forward over the mother's body, letting go of his sword and flattening himself on the ground which had been churned up into a foul, sticky mixture of blood and mud and spilt guts. He rolled to the side as Greg swung again.

He was just able to get up and he stumbled head first into a group of sickos. He realized now that he was cut off from the others. Sickos had come in from all around and formed a protective circle round their leader. Ed felt hands clawing at him. He bit a rotten finger that probed his mouth. Something struck him hard on the side of the head and, with ears ringing, he powered up, straightening his legs and crashing the top of his skull into a father's jaw. He then turned and barged his way through the ever-thickening crowd of sickos, trying to find open ground, slipping and sliding in the mud.

He had to get his sword. It was his only hope.

Greg was snarling and hissing, trying to get to Ed, cutting down any sickos that got between them. Ed saw the mother lying face down, his sword handle pointing up at the sky, the point stuck in the ground, the side of the blade jammed in her hip. He ducked under another wild swing from Greg and, as Greg was turned away, off balance, Ed spun round at him and smashed an elbow into his face, knocking him back. Greg staggered on stiff legs, trying to

stay upright, and then shook his head. He glared at Ed. The sickos fell back, clearing a path between the two of them. Ed was bleeding from where he'd been hit in the head. The blood was getting into his eye, blinding him. He wiped it away, but only succeeded in smearing mud across both eyes. He spat and swore, blinking away gritty tears.

Greg rolled his great fat head on his neck, closed his eyes and squeezed his lips together, like someone enjoying a delicious mouthful of food. A juicy, bloody steak . . .

And then he opened his eyes and locked them on Ed, started advancing, the cleaver swishing from side to side.

Ed put his hand to the sword hilt and gripped as tight as he could, simultaneously pulling it and kicking at the mother's body, trying to break the bones and loosen their grip on the steel.

His eyes stayed fixed on Greg.

And Greg was running.

He came at Ed, roaring, swinging his cleaver, his powerful legs working like pistons. A mad bull.

Ed stood there. Facing him. His chest exposed. Kicking, tugging, kicking.

He felt something give. A bone snap.

Greg was on him, cleaver raised in triumph, ready to bring it crashing down.

Ed stepped aside to the left, twisted his whole upper body round with a burst of power, transferring the energy to his arm, and the sword came loose, and up, and the blade sliced clean through Greg's fat neck, sending his head flying.

It was done.

'Yes!' Shadowman had broken through the ring of sickos moments before Ed killed St George, and watching his

great head spring loose from his body made Shadowman shout with joy.

The other kids came in behind Shadowman, but already it was clear that the battle was over. In cutting off St George's head, Ed had cut off the head of the army. The sickos fell into utter disorder and confusion and the army of children swept over them.

'Don't leave a single one alive,' Jordan shouted. 'We kill them now. And we stop the disease.'

Shadowman held back. He wasn't needed any more. He watched Ed sit on the grass and put down his sword. The huge, heavy mortuary sword he'd found at the Tower of London. Very few kids would have been able to use that weapon.

Kyle went over to Ed and sat next to him, draped an arm across his shoulders. Ed was lost in his own thoughts and memories and Shadowman left them to it.

He looked over at St George's headless body, lying behind Ed and Kyle. Blood was oozing from the neck, and that vile grey living jelly. It looked like his whole body was filled with it. And, as Shadowman watched, the body twitched, shuddered, pushed up on its elbows, up on to its knees, stood up, still clutching the axe in its hand, raised the axe above Ed's head.

Shadowman froze.

They'd never called the adults zombies. Not properly. They weren't the living dead from horror films. At least they hadn't been up until now. Shadowman had never seen anything like this before.

St George's body moved to swing the cleaver and Shadowman moved too. His crossbow came up, he pulled the trigger and a bolt slammed into Greg's chest. It was like

bursting a balloon. Greg's body exploded, showering grey gunk all around. The jelly formed into clumps, wriggling and writhing. There seemed to be half-formed insect parts in it, claws and feelers and eyes, wing casings.

'Peak!' said Kyle, who had turned to see what Shadowman was firing at. He waggled a hand in appreciation. 'That would've gone mental on YouTube.'

'We have to burn them,' said Ed, standing up and coming back to life. 'We build a pyre of the dead and burn them all.'

'Sounds good to me,' said Kyle, but Shadowman wasn't really listening. He was looking at St George's head.

The eyes were bulging out of it, further and further, the mouth moving into a smile, the tongue wagging. And then the eyes burst from their sockets and insect legs protruded. Others poked out from the nose, the ears, the severed neck. They tried to get a grip, but were weak and deformed, not ready to emerge. Kyle walked over with his great battleaxe and split the skull in two and then crushed the pieces.

'That's enough for one day,' he said.

Chris Marker was sitting at the big table in the library with his team around him, his writers, the boys and girls whose job it was to record everything in the history books they were writing – *The Chronicles of Survival*. They all had big books open in front of them, old ledgers they'd found in a storeroom at the museum. The pages were blank. Their pens and pencils sat on the table ready to be used, but for now they waited in silence.

Lettis was with them. She'd always been one of the more enthusiastic writers. But ever since she'd nearly died in a sicko attack out near Heathrow she'd fallen silent and not been able to write. She carried her own journal with her all the time, like a precious doll, never letting anyone else see it.

She sat there now. Still and quiet. Chris had given her a ledger to write in, but all the while she just stared into the distance at horrors only she could see, out of the library, out of the museum, out of London, west towards Heathrow . . .

Chris looked around the room. What he saw was also invisible to the others and he never talked about it. The room was full of ghosts. The Grey Lady who'd travelled with him here from the Imperial War Museum and others that he'd met when he arrived. They were always with

him. Waiting there. Not frightening – comforting, really, to know that he was never alone.

He wondered about these ghosts. Wondered what they might be thinking. If anything. They couldn't talk to him. People thought ghosts were the spirits of dead people. People who had died long ago and couldn't bear to leave a place or had unfinished business there.

Chris thought this was wrong. He thought ghosts were from the future. He thought ghosts were the spirits of characters from books yet to be written. One day someone would properly write their stories and they would go into the pages of a book and live there until someone read that book. Then they would travel into the minds of the readers and live on safely there forever. For now they were just waiting. Waiting for their stories to be written.

He heard a rattling noise and looked over to Lettis. She'd picked up a pencil and a sharpener. She put the pencil in the sharpener and started to turn it. She gave Chris a small smile.

'Are you back with us?' Chris asked and Lettis nodded. 'Are you going to write with us?'

Lettis nodded again. She put her pencil to the paper and began to write . . .

My name is Lettis Slingsbury and this is my journal. I am writing these words and I will tell what happened at the Battle of Hyde Park . . .

Jordan found Hayden and Partha's bodies under some trees. Told Bill to add them to the list of the fallen. Nobody would be forgotten.

The battle had carried on for the rest of the day. It had

been a grinding slog of slowly and methodically hacking at the sickos, cutting them down, herding them together, rounding up the strays, slaughtering them. And when, later in the afternoon, the rest of Ed's army had arrived on foot from the west, the process had speeded up. Now the light was failing and Jordan could hardly see anything.

The kids had won, but Jordan felt no sense of triumph. He'd lost so many people. He'd told Achilleus that he didn't feel anything, that his brain didn't work that way, but he felt something now. For the first time ever – a sense of loss. A sense of not being able to go back.

These weren't toy soldiers, chess pieces to move around a board. They'd been living, breathing children and now they were no more.

He had a duty to them. To make the world a better place. To rebuild. To make a future for the living.

He saluted the dead and moved on.

Archie found Matt standing by the lake. Staring at the water. All around kids were tending to the wounded.

'You OK?' said Archie. 'We won.'

'I can't hear him any more,' said Matt.

'Hear who?'

'God,' said Matt. 'He's abandoned me.'

'He's set you free,' said Archie. 'You live your life your way now.'

'It's so quiet. Empty.'

'Silence at last,' said Archie. 'Isn't that heaven?'

'Look at that,' said Ryan. 'Would you look at that? I can't believe it.' And he swore.

He was holding up his left arm and his hand was

missing. A kid from the museum was binding a strap tightly round it to stop the bleeding. The weird thing was it didn't hurt. He guessed his body had gone into massive shock and was flooded with so much adrenalin he was still upright and dealing with it.

'Bastard cut my hand off. *Bastard . . . !*'

It had happened near the end. Ed had gone after St George and been surrounded by sickos. Ryan had been trying to fight his way through. He liked Ed. First thing that went wrong, a sicko killed his dog. A fat father with a spear he must have taken off a dead kid had stuck the poor bitch. Ryan had killed the father, had gone to pull the spear free, and out of nowhere another father had come at him with a sword. Swung it at Ryan. Cut his hand clean off at the wrist.

'Bastard.' He looked at the museum kid. She was pale and shaking, but she'd managed to stop the bleeding.

'Am I gonna live?' he asked.

'I don't know. I think so. I hope so. I don't know.'

'You know what they do in movies?' said Dom, who actually seemed to be enjoying this.

'What?' said Ryan, not sure he wanted to hear.

'They, like, burn the stump.'

'You ain't burning me,' said Ryan. 'If I ain't bled to death yet then I'm gonna live. Maybe I'll get a hook?'

'That's good,' said Dom. 'Think practically. Look on the bright side.'

They nodded. Ryan still couldn't believe it, though. The bastard had cut his hand off.

Brooke found Ed sitting by the remains of St George. His sword across his knees. She helped him to his feet. He looked numb.

'It's over,' she said.

'This part is, yes,' he said. 'The rest is going to be hard.'

'But you don't have to do it by yourself.'

Ed smiled, the scarred half of his face twisting into a painful-looking shape. He touched Brooke's scar.

'Will you help me?' he said.

'We'll help each other,' said Brooke.

Malik came over. His chewed-up face the worst of them all. With him were Trinity and another Twisted Kid, limping and wriggling on disjointed limbs.

'He's alive,' said Malik.

Brooke felt a wash of acid in her stomach. She'd seen what had happened with St George and for moment she thought Malik was talking about him.

'Sam,' he explained. 'As far as they know, he's safe back at the museum. They kept him out of the fight. It was another kid in Trinity's message. Another kid that died . . .'

'Oh thank God,' said Brooke, and instantly felt ashamed that she'd been pleased by the death of another boy.

'You coming with me?' Malik asked, and Ed looked blank.

'Coming where?'

'What's this all been about?' said Malik. 'Reuniting a little boy with his sister. Those two, they've shown us how to be. As long as there's people like them in the world, we're gonna be OK.'

'You're not so bad yourself, man.' Ed's face twisted into a horrible smile.

'We've all done bad things,' said Malik. 'Terrible things. You think we'll ever forget?'

Ed shook his head. 'We'll take our memories with us when we die. But we did what we did, and we fought here

today so that those that come after us will have a good world, and no nightmares at night, and no terrible thoughts to haunt them.'

'You know before?' said Malik. 'Before all this, the disease and everything, I used to think that life was boring. Boring and hard. Everything seemed like such hard work. I was weary. But, you know, my only worry was getting a good score on Call of Duty, yet everyone was moaning and saying what an awful place the world was, what awful things we were doing to it. Everyone was saying we were all going to hell. But, like, we had *peace* and we had no real worries, no real enemies. We just didn't know what we had. We didn't know that hell was coming – but not the hell everyone thought. The bad things that happen are never the bad things we're all warned about, so there's no use worrying about them. I wish I could go back and say to people – look at what you got! You got life, you got freedom – make the most of it.'

He stopped and looked out across the battlefield. 'And if I could show them *this*. *This* is hell.' And then he pointed to his ravaged face. 'And *this*. Yeah . . . Enjoy what you got while you got it. Now – let's find that little boy. Make it right.'

Maxie and Blue were lying on the ground, looking up at the sky. They'd walked as far away from the battle as they could, to the other end of the park. It was quiet here. Apart from a faint smell of smoke in the air you'd never have known what had just gone down.

'We won't get up until at least the afternoon,' Blue was saying. 'And we'll just, like, *stroll* down to the beach and these, like, waiters will bring us cocktails.'

'Cocktails?' said Maxie. 'For breakfast?'

'Why not? And we go swimming, and the water will be bright blue and sparkling, and we'll dive under, like scuba-diving, yeah? And see sharks . . . But nice sharks, yeah? Cool ones. And in the evening there'll be, like, a barbecue. *Ribs.* You like ribs?'

'I like ribs,' said Maxie. 'Maybe some fish as well, though, yeah?'

'Fish?' said Blue. 'Whoever had a fantasy about eating fish?'

'Me,' Maxie protested. 'I love fish.'

'So much to learn about you, girl.'

'Nothing to learn about you,' said Maxie. 'I could have guessed you'd liked barbecued ribs. All boys do.'

'And at night we'll dance,' Blue went on. 'There'll be some banging beats. Like the old days. We'll dance until we can't dance no more and the sun will come up and then we'll go back to bed. And nothing will ever hurt us again.'

Wormwood was up on the roof with his daughter, his Fish-Face, his Fiona. They were just sitting there, arms round each other. Not speaking. At peace. *I am Worm-wood*, he thought. *Mark Wormold. And I am probably the last adult left in London.*

Jackson stood there, tears on her cheeks, not knowing what to say. Sometimes it was best to say nothing.

Skinner was dying. Achilleus knelt by his side, holding his hand.

'I'm sorry,' said Achilleus. 'If you'd stayed at home. If you'd stayed back at your warehouse this wouldn't have happened.'

'If I'd stayed at the warehouse you'd all have been killed,' said Skinner. 'We made a difference, didn't we?'

Achilleus squeezed his hand. 'You made a difference, cuz.'

'And I *lived*,' said Skinner. 'For a while I lived. I saw the world. I lived among normal children, and I was normal.'

'You've always been normal,' said Achilleus. 'And I'm glad to have known you.'

'You'll look after my cat for me, won't you?' said Skinner. 'You'll look after Mrs Jones . . .'

'Course,' said Achilleus. 'Even if she is riddled with toxoplasmosis.'

Skinner laughed painfully. 'I wouldn't have changed anything,' he said. 'I'll be in the book, won't I? In Chris Marker's history?'

'Yeah,' said Achilleus. 'You sure will. You'll have your own chapter. We won here today. We stopped the sickos. We stopped their disease – at least here. And now we can work on the cure in peace. We saved the museum, we saved Sam. And we couldn't never of done it without you. You a hero . . .'

Achilleus let Skinner's hand go. Jackson didn't know how much Skinner had heard of the last bit, because the light had gone out in him. Achilleus stood up. Saw Jackson. Hugged her. Broke away.

'Let's get to work,' he said. 'We got to start clearing up this mess. There is gonna be one big bonfire tonight.'

And he walked away. Alone.

Jackson watched him go. Walking with his head held high. His spear in his hand. And as she watched she saw a boy join him. It was Will from the Tower. Achilleus stopped to say something to him and then the two of

them walked on, and Will put his hand lightly on Achilleus's shoulder.

Ella was sitting in the back of the people carrier. A small group of fighters had stayed with her to make sure she was all right, but no sicko had come near the car. She had hidden on the floor, squashed down between the seats, her hands pressed to her ears. Too small to fight, but big enough to be terrified. She'd done so much, had such an adventure, survived so many awful things, that to come back to this battle was not how she wanted her story to end. She hated that all the good people might die. But the good people hadn't died. Sometimes stories really did have happy endings. She was watching her friends walk across the grass towards her. Ed and Brooke and Lewis and Kyle and Ebenezer, and with them her best friend in all the world.

Scarface. Malik. He was handsome to her. Like someone from a fairy story. The Beast.

She sobbed. Happy and sad and still frightened all at the same time.

What about Sam?

What about her brother? What had happened to him?

Small Sam was standing on the steps at the front of the museum when he saw his sister. He'd been with some of the little kids – Wiki and Jibber-jabber and The Kid and a couple more, just sitting there, talking quietly, wondering about the future, playing with Godzilla – when he'd spotted her walking along the road past the railings, with Ed and Brooke and a boy with a horribly scarred face.

Sam hadn't recognized her at first. It was only a few weeks since they'd been separated, but so much had happened that it felt like years. Felt like they were both different people.

Ella looked older, taller than he remembered. Thinner definitely. More grown-up. For a little while he could look at her without her seeing him. She was staring down at her feet as she walked. And then she glanced over through the railings at him and his group. There was no sign on her face that she'd recognized him. Maybe, like her, Sam had changed too much. Or maybe she just hadn't picked him out from the crowd.

He didn't know what to do. All he'd thought about since the mother snatched him from the Waitrose car park was seeing Ella again, being together again. He'd pictured the two of them laughing and happy, and people slapping

them on the back. A party. Introducing her to all his friends, to The Kid and Wiki and Jibber-jabber. And now he felt awkward and embarrassed. He couldn't move.

The Kid poked him in the ribs with his elbow.

'Is that her? Is that your sister swinging out there? Is that your Ella guru? Is this the happy-ever-after ending?'

'Yes,' said Sam. 'It is.'

And The Kid shoved him, pushing him up off the steps and on to his feet.

'Go to her, you idiot child. Go on.'

Sam started walking. Ella had come through the gates now and she'd definitely seen him. She'd stopped and was just standing there, staring. And Sam walked faster, and faster, and then he was running, and he ran into her arms.

She was Ella. Just as she'd always been. His sister. Ella, Ella, Ella. And now they were together and nothing was ever going to separate them again.

THE ENEMY
SERIES TIMELINE

The disease first appears. Scared Kid video posted.

Ed, Jack and Bam leave Rowurst school and meet Greg/St George.

Coach arrives at Imperial War Museum.

St George kills Bam and Jack.

The Great Fire/Battle of Lambeth Bridge.

DogNut, Ed, Kyle and Jordan arrive at the Tower of London.

A year passes.

DogNut leaves the Tower.

DogNut arrives at Buckingham Palace.

Shadowman and Jester leave the palace.

Jester and Shadowman attacked at King's Cross station.

Jester arrives at Waitrose.

Holloway crew set off for the palace.

Sam escapes the fire at the Emirates.

Shadowman witnesses death of Callum.

DogNut, Courtney and Brooke ambushed at Green Park.

Holloway crew arrives at the palace.

Sam arrives at the Tower.

Achilleus fights Just John at the palace.

Holloway crew leaves the palace. Paul frees the sickos.

Holloway crew arrives at the Natural History Museum with Brooke.

Blue and Einstein leave the Natural History Museum to find medicines.

Blue and Einstein meet the Twisted Kids.

Blue returns to the Natural History Museum.

Tish sets off from St Paul's.

Sam leaves the Tower.

Maeve, Robbie and Ella leave the Natural History Museum.

The Kid meets the Green Man.

Shadowman witnesses the massacre in Kilburn.

Ed rescues Shadowman.

Ed and Sam arrive at the Natural History Museum.

Ed sets off to find Ella.

The crews gather at the Houses of Parliament.

Battle of Hyde Park.

DEAD

ENEMY FEAR

FALLEN SACRIFICE

HUNTED THE END

Go back to the begining with
THE ENEMY,
the first mind-blowing book in
this KILLER series.

1

Small Sam was playing in the car park behind Waitrose when the grown-ups took him. He'd been with some of the little kids, having a battle with an odd assortment of action figures, when it happened. They weren't supposed to play outside without a guard, but it was a lovely sunny day and the little kids got bored indoors. Sam wasn't the youngest of the group, but he was the smallest. That's why they called him Small Sam. There had originally been two other Sams, Big Sam and Curly Sam, who had curly hair. Big Sam had been killed a few months ago, but Small Sam was stuck with the name.

It was probably because of his size that the grown-ups went for him. They were like that – they picked out the youngsters, the weaklings, the little ones. In the panic of the attack the rest of Sam's gang got back safely inside, but Sam was cut off and the roving pack of grown-ups trapped him in a corner.

They had come over the side wall, led by a big mother in a tracksuit that might once have been pink but was now so filthy and greasy it looked like grey plastic. She had a fat, egg-like body on top of long skinny legs. Her back was bent and she ran stooped over, but surprisingly fast, her arms held wide like a scorpion's claws, her dirty blonde hair

hanging straight down. Her face blank and stupid. Breathing through her mouth.

Small Sam was too scared even to scream or call for help, and the grown-ups made no noise, so the whole scene was played out in horrible silence. The mother blocked off the route back towards the building while two lanky fathers ran at him from either side. Sam dodged them for a few seconds, but he knew they'd get hold of him in the end. By the time help came from inside, the grown-ups were gone back over the wall, with Sam stuffed inside a sack.

Maxie led a group of bigger kids out into the car park. Even though they were armed with spears and clubs and good throwing rocks they moved cautiously, not knowing exactly what to expect.

'We're too late,' said Callum, scanning the empty car park. 'They've got him.'

'Shame,' said a stocky, dark-haired kid called Josh. 'I liked him. He was funny.'

'That's the second attack this week,' said Maxie angrily. 'What's going on? Either the grown-ups are closing in on us or they're getting braver.'

'They ain't brave,' said Josh, spitting on the ground. 'If they was still here I'd show them brave. I'd mash their ugly faces. Nothing scares me.'

'So why were they here?' asked Maxie.

'They're just hungry,' said Josh.

'We're all hungry,' said Callum.

'We should have been here,' said Maxie. 'We should have been watching over them.'

'We can't be everywhere at once,' Callum pointed out. 'There's not enough of us, not with Arran out with the scavs. Our job's to keep a look-out from the roof. The little

kids knew they weren't supposed to be out here. Nobody should be out here. We should all stay inside.'

'We can't stay inside all day,' scoffed Josh. 'We'd go crazy.'

'It's good inside,' said Callum.

'You're just scared to come outside,' said Josh with a smirk.

'No I ain't,' said Callum. 'No more scared than you.'

'Nothing scares me,' said Josh.

'Then you're just stupid,' said Callum.

'Nah,' said Josh. 'The thing about grown-ups is, some of them are strong, some of them can run fast and some of them are clever, but the strong ones are slow, the fast ones are stupid and the smart ones are weak.'

'Tell that to Small Sam,' said Maxie angrily, 'and to Big Sam and Johnno, and Eve and Mohammed and all the other kids we've lost.'

'Grown-ups won't get me,' said Josh.

'What?' said Callum. 'So it was their fault they got taken? Is that what you're saying?'

'Yeah, I am,' said Josh.

'Shut up,' Maxie snapped at the two of them. Then she said the thing that nobody wanted to admit. 'We can't go on like this.' Her voice was heavy with bitterness. 'Soon we're all going to be dead. I can't stand it any more.'

She threw down the spear she had been carrying and sat on the ground, resting her head in her hands.

It was her fault. That was all she could think. *It was all her fault.*

When Arran was away she was supposed to be in charge. She couldn't remember when it had been decided – *Arran was the leader, she was second in command* – it must have happened early on, when most of the kids had been too

frightened and confused to do anything for themselves. Arran and Maxie had just got on with it, organizing everyone, keeping their spirits up. Arran was clever and likeable. Right from the start he'd kept his head and not panicked. He'd been captain of the football team at William Ellis School and nothing ever seemed to freak him out.

The two of them had worked together. A team. Maxie had always been good at getting other children to help out. There were better fighters than her, true, but they were happy for her to tell them what to do. They didn't want the responsibility. And when Arran wasn't there, she was the leader.

So, it was all her fault. Another kid gone. She shut down part of her mind. She didn't want to think about what the grown-ups would do to Small Sam.

She started to cry. She didn't care who saw it.

Callum looked at Josh. They both felt awkward. In the end it was Josh who squatted down next to her and put an arm round her shoulders.

'It's all right, Max,' he said quietly. 'We'll be all right. Something'll happen, someone will come. Something's gonna change. When Arran and the others get back we'll talk about it maybe, yeah? Make a plan?'

'What's the point?' said Maxie.

'When Arran gets back, yeah?'

Maxie looked up into Josh's concerned, grubby face.

'Sorry,' she said.

'Come on,' said Callum. 'Let's try and find out how they got over the wall. Then we should get back inside.'

'Yeah.' Maxie jumped up. It was OK as long as you were doing something, as long as you didn't stop and think.

She wished Arran were here, though. She always felt safer when he was around.

It was just . . . What was he going to think?

Another kid gone.

All her fault.

HAVE YOU READ THEM ALL?

THEY'LL CHASE YOU.

THEY'LL RIP YOU OPEN.

THEY'LL FEED ON YOU...

ZOMBIE

**MORE
BLOOD.**

**MORE
ZOMBIES.**

**MORE
TERROR.**

THE STORY
CONTINUES ...

ALERT

THE ENEMY

HOME BOOKS EVENTS **AUTHOR** EXTRAS COMPETITION

THE AUTHOR

Charlie Higson is the author of the phenomenally successful Young Bond series which has now sold over a million copies in the UK and has been translated into 24 different languages.

Charlie is a man of many talents. He is a successful actor, comedian and writer for television and radio, but has been writing books for children since 2005. The Young Bond series started with SilverFin and was followed by Blood Fever, Double or Die, Hurricane Gold and By Royal Command.

Charlie has always been a fan of '70s and '80s horror. While at university he studied gothic literature, a film course on horror and wrote a dissertation on David Cronenberg, as well as putting on all night horror movie showings.

After studying at the University of East Anglia, Charlie formed a band, The Higsons. He then became a decorator before turning to the world of television and going into partnership with his friend Paul Whitehouse. His successes include Saturday Live, the Harry Enfield Television Programme, The Smell of Reeves and Mortimer, Shooting Stars, Randall and Hopkirk Deceased, the film Suite 16, Swiss Toni and of course, the Fast Show.

In 2006 he joined up again with Paul Whitehouse to co-create the hit radio series DOWN THE LINE for BBC

Tweets   Follow

DavidGArnold
@DavidGArnold
Retweeting all there nice things about last nights concert in order to tempt you to those
davidarnoldmovies.co.uk.wordpress.com
Retweeted by charlie higson

BBC Press Office
@bbcpress
Final thoughts on Daily Mail's "BBC spends less than half its cash on programmes" story - here's a summary. pic.twitter.com/krppV0U2nD
Retweeted by charlie higson

- ## ZOMBIE GALLERY
- ## EDGE-OF-YOUR-SEAT VIDEOS
- ## DEADLY DOWNLOADS

www.the-enemy.co.uk

PLATFORM

For loads more about the
books and authors you love,
make sure you follow
Penguin Platform.

SHARE, CREATE, DISCOVER AND DEBATE.

He just wanted a decent book to read ...

Not too much to ask, is it? It was in 1935 when Allen Lane, Managing Director of Bodley Head Publishers, stood on a platform at Exeter railway station looking for something good to read on his journey back to London. His choice was limited to popular magazines and poor-quality paperbacks – . the same choice faced every day by the vast majority of readers, few of whom could afford hardbacks. Lane's disappointment and subsequent anger at the range of books generally available led him to found a company – and change the world.

'We believed in the existence in this country of a vast reading public for intelligent books at a low price, and staked everything on it'
Sir Allen Lane, 1902–1970, founder of Penguin Books

The quality paperback had arrived – and not just in bookshops. Lane was adamant that his Penguins should appear in chain stores and tobacconists, and should cost no more than a packet of cigarettes.

Reading habits (and cigarette prices) have changed since 1935, but Penguin still believes in publishing the best books for everybody to enjoy. We still believe that good design costs no more than bad design, and we still believe that quality books published passionately and responsibly make the world a better place.

So wherever you see the little bird – whether it's on a piece of prize-winning literary fiction or a celebrity autobiography, political tour de force or historical masterpiece, a serial-killer thriller, reference book, world classic or a piece of pure escapism – you can bet that it represents the very best that the genre has to offer.

Whatever you like to read – trust Penguin.